Nora Roberts

Summer Pleasures

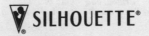

D0996199

SILHOUETTE®

*Silhouette and Colophon are registered trademarks of
Harlequin Books S.A., used under licence.
Silhouette Books, Eton House, 18-24 Paradise Road,
Richmond, Surrey TW9 1SR*

*First published in 2004 by Harlequin Mills & Boon Ltd.
This edition published 2008.*

SUMMER PLEASURES © Harlequin Books S.A. 2002

*The publisher acknowledges the copyright holder of the
individual works as follows:*

*Second Nature © Nora Roberts 1986
One Summer © Nora Roberts 1986*

ISBN: 978 0 263 86733 6

078-0808

*Printed and bound in Spain
by Litografia Rosés S.A., Barcelona*

CONTENTS

Second Nature

To Deb Horm, for the mutual memories

Prologue

...with the moon full and white and cold. He saw the shadows shift and shiver like living things over the ice-crusted snow. Black on white. Black sky, white moon, black shadows, white snow. As far as he could see there was nothing else. There was such emptiness, an absence of color, the only sound the whistling moan of wind through naked trees. But he knew he wasn't alone, that there was no safety in the black or the white. Through his frozen heart moved a trickle of hot fear. His breath, labored, almost spent, puffed out in small white clouds. Over the frosted ground fell a black shadow. There was no place left to run.

Hunter drew on his cigarette, then stared at the words on the terminal through a haze of smoke. Michael Trent was dead. Hunter had created him, molded him exclusively for that cold, pitiful death under a full moon. He felt a sense of accomplishment rather than remorse for destroying the man he knew more intimately than he knew himself.

He'd end the chapter there, however, leaving the details of Michael's murder to the readers' imagination. The mood was set, secrets hinted at, doom tangible but unexplained. He knew his habit of doing just that both frustrated and fascinated his following. Since that was precisely his purpose, he was pleased. He often wasn't.

He created the terrifying, the breathtaking, the unspeakable. Hunter explored the darkest nightmares of the human mind and, with cool precision, made them tangible. He made the impossible plausible and the uncanny commonplace. The commonplace he would often turn into something chilling. He used words the way an artist used a palette and he fabricated stories of such color and simplicity a reader was drawn in from the first page.

His business was horror, and he was phenomenally successful.

For five years he'd been considered the master of his particular game. He'd had six runaway best-sellers, four of which he'd transposed into screenplays for feature films. The critics raved, sales soared, letters poured in from fans all over the world. Hunter couldn't have cared less. He wrote for himself first, because the telling of a story was what he did best. If he entertained with his writing, he was satisfied. But whatever reaction the critics and the readers had, he'd still have written. He had his work; he had his privacy. These were the two vital things in his life.

He didn't consider himself a recluse; he didn't consider himself unsociable. He simply lived his life exactly as he chose. He'd done the same thing six years before...before the fame, success and large advances.

If someone had asked him if having a string of bestsellers had changed his life, he'd have answered, why should it? He'd been a writer before *The Devil's Due* had shot to number one on the *New York Times* list. He was a writer now. If he'd wanted his life to change, he'd have become a plumber.

Some said his life-style was calculated—that he created the image of an eccentric for effect. Good promotion. Some said he raised wolves. Some said he didn't exist at all but was a clever product of a publisher's imagination. But Hunter Brown had a fine disregard for what anyone said. Invariably, he listened only to what he wanted to hear, saw only what he chose to see and remembered everything.

After pressing a series of buttons on his word processor, he set up for the next chapter. The next chapter, the next word, the next book, was of much more importance to him than any speculative article he might read.

He'd worked for six hours that day, and he thought he was good for at least two more. The story was flowing out of him like ice water: cold and clear.

The hands that played the keys of the machine were beautiful—tanned, lean, long-fingered and wide-palmed. One might have looked at them and thought they would compose concertos or epic poems. What they composed were dark dreams and monsters—not the dripping-fanged, scaly-skinned variety, but monsters real enough to make the flesh crawl. He always included enough realism, enough of the everyday, in his stories to make the horror commonplace and all too plausible. There was a creature lurking in the dark closet of his work, and that creature was the private fear of every man. He found it, always. Then, inch by inch, he opened the closet door.

Half forgotten, the cigarette smoldered in the overflowing ashtray at his elbow. He smoked too much. It was perhaps the only outward sign of the pressure he put on himself, a pressure he'd have tolerated from no one else. He wanted this book finished by the end of the month, his self-imposed deadline. In one of his rare impulses, he'd agreed to speak at a writers' conference in Flagstaff the first week of June.

It wasn't often he agreed to public appearances, and when he did it was never at a large, publicized event. This particular conference would boast no more than two hundred published and aspiring writers. He'd give his workshop, answer questions, then go home. There would be no speaker's fee.

That year alone, Hunter had summarily turned down offers from some of the most prestigious organizations in the publishing business. Prestige didn't interest him, but he considered, in his odd way, the contribution to the Central Arizona Writers' Guild a matter of paying his dues. Hunter had always understood that nothing was free.

It was late afternoon when the dog lying at his feet lifted his head. The dog was lean, with a shining gray coat and the narrow, intelligent look of a wolf.

"Is it time, Santanas?" With a gentleness the hand appeared made for, Hunter reached down to stroke the dog's head. Satisfied, but already deciding that he'd work late that evening, he turned off his word processor.

Hunter stepped out of the chaos of his office into the tidy living room with its tall, many-paned windows and lofted ceiling. It smelled of vanilla and daisies. Large and sleek, the dog padded alongside him.

After pushing open the doors that led to a terracotta patio, he looked into the thick surrounding woods. They shut him in, shut others out. Hunter had never considered which, only knew that he needed them. He needed the peace, the mystery and the beauty, just as he needed the rich red walls of the canyon that rose up around him. Through the quiet he could hear the trickle of water from the creek and smell the heady freshness of the air. These he never took for granted; he hadn't had them forever.

Then he saw her, walking leisurely down the winding path toward the house. The dog's tail began to swish back and forth.

Sometimes, when he watched her like this, Hunter would think it impossible that anything so lovely belonged to him. She was dark and delicately formed, moving with a careless confidence that made him grin even as it made him ache. She was Sarah. His work and his privacy were the two vital things in his life. Sarah was his life. She'd been worth the struggles, the frustration, the fears and the pain. She was worth everything.

Looking over, she broke into a smile that flashed with braces. *"Hi, Dad!"*

Chapter 1

The week a magazine like *Celebrity* went to bed was utter chaos. Every department head was in a frenzy. Desks were littered, phones were tied up and lunches were skipped. The air was tinged with a sense of panic that built with every hour. Tempers grew short, demands outrageous. In most offices the lights burned late into the night. The rich scent of coffee and the sting of tobacco smoke were never absent. Rolls of antacids were consumed and bottles of eye drops constantly changed hands. After five years on staff, Lee took the monthly panic as a matter of course.

Celebrity was a slick, respected publication whose sales generated millions of dollars a year. In addition to stories on the rich and famous, it ran articles by eminent psychologists and journalists, interviews with both statesmen and rock stars. Its photography was first-class, just as its text was thoroughly researched and concisely written. Some of its detractors might have termed it quality gossip, but the word *quality* wasn't forgotten.

An ad in *Celebrity* was a sure bet for generating sales and interest and was priced accordingly. *Celebrity* was, in a tough competitive business, one of the leading monthly publications in the country. Lee Radcliffe wouldn't have settled for less.

"How'd the piece on the sculptures turn out?"

Lee glanced up at Bryan Mitchell, one of the top photographers on the West Coast. Grateful, she accepted the cup of coffee Bryan passed her. In the past four days, she'd had a total of twenty hours sleep. "Good," she said simply.

"I've seen better art scrawled in alleys."

Though she privately agreed, Lee only shrugged. "Some people like the clunky and obscure."

With a laugh, Bryan shook her head. "When they told me to photograph that red and black tangle of wire to its best advantage, I nearly asked them to shut off the lights."

"You made it look almost mystical."

"I can make a junkyard look mystical with the right lighting." She shot Lee a grin. "The same way you can make it sound fascinating."

A smile touched Lee's mouth but her mind was veering off in a dozen other directions. "All in a day's work, right?"

"Speaking of which—" Bryan rested one slim jean-clad hip on Lee's organized desk, drinking her own coffee black. "Still trying to dig something up on Hunter Brown?"

A frown drew Lee's elegant brows together. Hunter Brown was becoming her personal quest and almost an obsession. Perhaps because he was so completely inaccessible, she'd become determined to be the first to break through the cloud of mystery. It had taken her nearly five years to earn her title as staff reporter, and she had a reputation for being tenacious, thorough and cool. Lee knew she'd earned those adjectives. Three months of hitting blank walls in researching Hunter Brown didn't deter her. One way or the other, she was going to get the story.

"So far I haven't gotten beyond his agent's name and his editor's phone number." There might've been a hint of frustration in her tone, but her expression was determined. "I've never known people so close-mouthed."

"His latest book hit the stands last week." Absently, Bryan picked up the top sheet from one of the tidy piles of papers Lee was systematically dealing with. "Have you read it?"

"I picked it up, but I haven't had a chance to start it yet."

Bryan tossed back the long honey-colored braid that fell over her shoulder. "Don't start it on a dark night." She sipped at her coffee, then gave a laugh. "God, I ended up sleeping with every light in the apartment burning. I don't know how he does it."

Lee glanced up again, her eyes calm and confident. "That's one of the things I'm going to find out."

Bryan nodded. She'd known Lee for three years, and she didn't doubt Lee would. "Why?" Her frank, almond-shaped eyes rested on Lee's.

"Because—" Lee finished off her coffee and tossed the empty cup into her overflowing wastebasket "—no one else has."

"The Mount Everest syndrome," Bryan commented, and earned a rare, spontaneous grin.

A quick glance would have shown two attractive women in casual conversation in a modern, attractively decorated office. A closer look would have uncovered the contrasts. Bryan, in jeans and a snug T-shirt, was completely relaxed. Everything about her was casual and not quite tidy, from her smudged sneakers to the loose braid. Her sharp-featured, arresting face was touched only with a hasty dab of mascara. She'd probably meant to add lipstick or blusher and then forgotten.

Lee, on the other hand, wore a very elegant ice-blue suit, and the nerves that gave her her drive were evident in the hands that were never quite still. Her hair was expertly cut in a short swinging style that took very little care—which was every bit as important to her as having it look good. Its shade fell somewhere between copper and gold. Her skin was the delicate, milky white some redheads bless and others curse. Her makeup had been meticulously applied that morning, down to the dusky blue shadow that matched her eyes. She had delicate, elegant features offset by a full and obviously stubborn mouth.

The two women had entirely different styles and

entirely different tastes but oddly enough, their friendship had begun the moment they'd met. Though Bryan didn't always like Lee's aggressive tactics and Lee didn't always approve of Bryan's laid-back approach, their closeness hadn't wavered in three years.

"So." Bryan found the candy bar she'd stuck in her jeans pocket and proceeded to unwrap it. "What's your master plan?"

"To keep digging," Lee returned almost grimly. "I do have a couple of connections at Horizon, his publishing house. Maybe one of them'll come through with something." Without being fully aware of it, she drummed her fingers on the desk. "Damn it, Bryan, he's like the man who wasn't there. I can't even find out what state he lives in."

"I'm half inclined to believe some of the rumors," Bryan said thoughtfully. Outside Lee's office someone was having hysterics over the final editing of an article. "I'd say the guy lives in a cave somewhere, full of bats with a couple of stray wolves thrown in. He probably writes the original manuscript in sheep's blood."

"And sacrifices virgins every new moon."

"I wouldn't be surprised." Bryan swung her feet lazily while she munched on her chocolate bar. "I tell you the man's weird."

"*Silent Scream*'s already on the best-seller list."

"I didn't say he wasn't brilliant," Bryan countered, "I said he was weird. What kind of a mind does he have?" She shook her head with a half-sheepish smile. "I can tell you I wished I'd never heard of

Hunter Brown last night while I was trying to sleep with my eyes open.''

"That's just it." Impatient, Lee rose and paced to the tiny window on the east wall. She wasn't looking out; the view of Los Angeles didn't interest her. She just had to move around. "What kind of mind *does* he have? What kind of life does he live? Is he married? Is he sixty-five or twenty-five? Why does he write novels about the supernatural?" She turned, her impatience and her annoyance showing beneath the surface of the sophisticated grooming. "Why did you read his book?"

"Because it was fascinating," Bryan answered immediately. "Because by the time I was on page 3, I was so into it you couldn't have gotten the book away from me with a crowbar."

"And you're an intelligent woman."

"Damn right," Bryan agreed and grinned. "So?"

"Why do intelligent people buy and read something that's going to terrify them?" Lee demanded. "When you pick up a Hunter Brown, you know what it's going to do to you, yet his books consistently spring to the top of the best-seller list and stay there. Why does an obviously intelligent man write books like that?" She began, in a habit Bryan recognized, to fiddle with whatever was at hand—the leaves of a philodendron, the stub of a pencil, the left earring she'd removed during a phone conversation.

"Do I hear a hint of disapproval?"

"Yeah, maybe." Frowning, Lee looked up again. "The man is probably the best colorist in the country.

If he's describing a room in an old house, you can smell the dust. His characterizations are so real you'd swear you'd met the people in his books. And he uses that talent to write about things that go bump in the night. I want to find out why.''

Bryan crumpled her candy wrapper into a ball. ''I know a woman who has one of the sharpest, most analytical minds I've ever come across. She has a talent for digging up obscure facts, some of them impossibly dry, and turning them into intriguing stories. She's ambitious, has a remarkable talent for words, but works on a magazine and lets a half-finished novel sit abandoned in a drawer. She's lovely, but she rarely dates for any purpose other than business. And she has a habit of twisting paper clips into ungodly shapes while she's talking.''

Lee glanced down at the small mangled piece of metal in her hands, then met Bryan's eyes coolly. ''Do you know why?''

There was a hint of humor in Bryan's eyes, but her tone was serious enough. ''I've tried to figure it out for three years, but I can't precisely put my finger on it.''

With a smile, Lee tossed the bent paper clip into the trash. ''But then, you're not a reporter.''

Because she wasn't very good at taking advice, Lee switched on her bedside lamp, stretched out and opened Hunter Brown's latest novel. She would read a chapter or two, she decided, then make it an early night. An early night was an almost sinful luxury after the week she'd put in at *Celebrity*.

Her bedroom was done in creamy ivories and shades of blue from the palest aqua to indigo. She'd indulged herself here, with dozens of plump throw pillows, a huge Turkish rug and a Queen Anne stand that held an urn filled with peacock feathers and eucalyptus. Her latest acquisition, a large ficus tree, sat by the window and thrived.

She considered this room the only truly private spot in her life. As a reporter, Lee accepted that she was public property as much as the people she sought out. Privacy wasn't something she could cling to when she constantly dug into other people's lives. But in this little corner of the world, she could relax completely, forget there was work to do, ladders to climb. She could pretend L.A. wasn't bustling outside, as long as she had this oasis of peace. Without it, without the hours she spent sleeping and unwinding there, she knew she'd overload.

Knowing herself well, Lee understood that she had a tendency to push too hard, run too fast. In the quiet of her bedroom she could recharge herself each night so that she'd be ready for the race again the following day.

Relaxed, she opened Hunter Brown's latest effort.

Within a half hour, Lee was disturbed, uncomfortable and completely engrossed. She'd have been angry with the author for drawing her in if she hadn't been so busy turning pages. He'd put an ordinary man in an extraordinary situation and done it with such skill that Lee was already relating to the teacher who'd found himself caught up in a small town with a dark secret.

The prose flowed and the dialogue was so natural she could hear the voices. He filled the town with so many recognizable things, she could have sworn she'd been there herself. She knew the story was going to give her more than one bad moment in the dark, but she had to go on. That was the magic of a major storyteller. Cursing him, she read on, so tense that when the phone rang beside her, the book flew out of her hands. Lee swore again, at herself, and lifted the receiver.

Her annoyance at being disturbed didn't last. Grabbing a pencil, she began to scrawl on the pad beside the phone. With her tongue caught between her teeth, she set down the pencil and smiled. She owed the contact in New York an enormous favor, but she'd pay off when the time came, as she always did. For now, Lee thought, running her hand over Hunter's book, she had to make arrangements to attend a small writers' conference in Flagstaff, Arizona.

She had to admit the country was impressive. As was her habit, Lee had spent the time during the flight from L.A. to Phoenix working, but once she'd changed to the small commuter plane for the trip to Flagstaff, her work had been forgotten. She'd flown through thin clouds over a vastness almost impossible to conceive after the skyscrapers and traffic of Los Angeles. She'd looked down on the peaks and dips and castlelike rocks of Oak Creek Canyon, feeling a drumming excitement that was rare in a woman who wasn't easily impressed. If she'd had more time...

Lee sighed as she stepped off the plane. There was never time enough.

The tiny airport boasted a one-room lobby with a choice of concession stand or soda and candy machines. No loudspeaker announced incoming and outgoing flights. No skycap bustled up to her to relieve her of her bags. There wasn't a line of cabs waiting outside to compete for the handful of people who'd disembarked. With her garment bag slung over her shoulder, she frowned at the inconvenience. Patience wasn't one of her virtues.

Tired, hungry and inwardly a little frazzled by the shaky commuter flight, she stepped up to one of the counters. "I need to arrange for a car to take me to town."

The man in shirtsleeves and loosened tie stopped pushing buttons on his computer. His first polite glance sharpened when he saw her face. She reminded him of a cameo his grandmother had worn at her neck on special occasions. Automatically he straightened his shoulders. "Did you want to rent a car?"

Lee considered that a moment, then rejected it. She hadn't come to do any sight-seeing, so a car would hardly be worthwhile. "No, just transportation into Flagstaff." Shifting her bag, she gave him the name of her hotel. "Do they have a courtesy car?"

"Sure do. You go on over to that phone by the wall

there. Number's listed. Just give 'em a call and they'll send someone out.''

''Thank you.''

He watched her walk to the phone and thought he was the one who should have said thank-you.

Lee caught the scent of grilling hot dogs as she crossed the room. Since she'd turned down the dubious tray offered on the flight, the scent had her stomach juices swimming. Quickly and efficiently, she dialed the hotel, gave her name and was assured a car would be there within twenty minutes. Satisfied, she bought a hot dog and settled in one of the black plastic chairs to wait.

She was going to get what she'd come for, Lee told herself almost fiercely as she looked out at the distant mountains. The time wasn't going to be wasted. After three months of frustration, she was finally going to get a firsthand look at Hunter Brown.

It had taken skill and determination to persuade her editor-in-chief to spring for the trip, but it would pay off. It had to. Leaning back, she reviewed the questions she'd ask Hunter Brown once she'd cornered him.

All she needed, Lee decided, was an hour with him. Sixty minutes. In that time, she could pull out enough information for a concise, and very exclusive, article. She'd done precisely that with this year's Oscar winner, though he'd been reluctant, and a presidential candidate, though he'd been hostile. Hunter Brown would probably be both, she decided with a half smile. It would only add spice. If she'd wanted a bland, simple life, she'd have bent under the pressure and married Jonathan. Right now she'd be planning her next garden party rather than calculating how to ambush an award-winning writer.

Lee nearly laughed aloud. Garden parties, bridge parties and the yacht club. That might have been perfect for her family, but she'd wanted more. More what? her mother had demanded, and Lee could only reply, Just more.

Checking her watch, she left her luggage neatly stacked by the chair and went into the ladies' room. The door had hardly closed behind her when the object of all her planning strolled into the lobby.

He didn't often do good deeds, and then only for people he had a genuine affection for. Because he'd gotten into town with time to spare, Hunter had driven to the airport with the intention of picking up his editor. With barely a glance around, he walked over to the same counter Lee had approached ten minutes before.

"Flight 471 on time?"

"Yes, sir, got in ten minutes ago."

"Did a woman get off?" Hunter glanced at the nearly empty lobby again. "Attractive, mid-twenties—"

"Yes, sir," the clerk interrupted. "She just stepped into the rest room. That's her luggage over there."

"Thanks." Satisfied, Hunter walked over to Lee's neat stack of luggage. Doesn't believe in traveling light, he noticed, scanning the garment bag, small Pullman and briefcase. Then, what woman did? Hadn't his Sarah taken two suitcases for the brief three-day stay with his sister in Phoenix? Strange that his little girl should be two parts woman already. Perhaps not so strange, Hunter reflected. Females were born two parts woman, while males took years to grow out of boyhood—if they ever did. Perhaps that's why he trusted men a great deal more.

Lee saw him when she came back into the lobby. His back was to her, so that she had only the impression of a tall, leanly built man with black hair curling carelessly down to the neck of his T-shirt. Right on time, she thought with satisfaction, and approached him.

"I'm Lee Radcliffe."

When he turned, she went stone-still, the impersonal smile freezing on her face. In the first instant, she couldn't have said why. He was attractive—perhaps too attractive. His face was narrow but not scholarly, raw-boned but not rugged. It was too much a combination of both to be either. His nose was straight and aristocratic, while his mouth was sculpted like a poet's. His hair was dark and full and unruly, as though he'd been driving fast for hours with the wind blowing free. But it wasn't these things that caused her to lose her voice. It was his eyes.

She'd never seen eyes darker than his, more direct, more...disturbing. It was as though they looked through her. No, not through, Lee corrected numbly. Into. In ten seconds, they had looked into her and seen everything.

He saw a stunning, milk-pale face with dusky eyes gone wide in astonishment. He saw a soft, feminine mouth, lightly tinted. He saw nerves. He saw a stubborn chin and molten copper hair that would feel like silk between the fingers. What he saw was an outwardly poised, inwardly tense woman who smelled like spring evenings and looked like a *Vogue* cover. If it hadn't been for that inner tension, he might have dismissed her, but what lay beneath people's surfaces always intrigued him.

He skimmed her neat traveling suit so quickly his eyes might never have left hers. "Yes?"

"Well, I..." Forced to swallow, she trailed off. That alone infuriated her. She wasn't about to be set off into stammers by a driver for the hotel. "If you've come to pick me up," Lee said curtly, "you'll need to get my bags."

Lifting a brow, he said nothing. Her mistake was simple and obvious. It would have taken only a sentence from him to correct it. Then again, it was her mistake, not his. Hunter had always believed more in impulses than explanations. Bending down, he picked up the Pullman, then slung the strap of the garment bag over his shoulder. "The car's out here."

She felt a great deal more secure with the briefcase in her hand and his back to her. The oddness, Lee told herself, had come from excitement and a long flight. Men never surprised her; they certainly never made her stare and stammer. What she needed was a bath and something a bit more substantial to eat than that hot dog.

The car he'd referred to wasn't a car, she noted, but

a Jeep. Supposing this made sense, with the steep roads and hard winters, Lee climbed in.

Moves well, he thought, and dresses flawlessly. He noted too that she bit her nails. "Are you from the area?" Hunter asked conversationally when he'd stowed her bags in the back.

"No. I'm here for the writers' conference."

Hunter climbed in beside her and shut the door. Now he knew where to take her. "You're a writer?"

She thought of the two chapters of her manuscript she'd brought along in case she needed a cover. "Yes."

Hunter swung through the parking lot, taking the back road that led to the highway. "What do you write?"

Settling back, Lee decided she might as well try her routine out on him before she was in the middle of two hundred published and aspiring writers. "I've done articles and some short stories," she told him truthfully enough. Then she added what she'd rarely told anyone. "I've started a novel."

With a speed that surprised but didn't unsettle her, he burst onto the highway. "Are you going to finish it?" he asked, showing an insight that disturbed her.

"I suppose that depends on a lot of things."

He took another careful look at her profile. "Such as?"

She wanted to shift in her seat but forced herself to be still. This was just the sort of question she might have to answer over the weekend. "Such as if what I've done so far is any good."

He found both her answer and her discomfort reasonable. "Do you go to many of these conferences?"

"No, this is my first."

Which might account for the nerves, Hunter mused, but he didn't think he'd found the entire answer.

"I'm hoping to learn something," Lee said with a small smile. "I registered at the last minute, but when I learned Hunter Brown would be here, I couldn't resist."

The frown in his eyes came and went too quickly to be noticed. He'd agreed to do the workshop only because it wouldn't be publicized. Even the registrants wouldn't know he'd be there, until the following morning. Just how, he wondered, had the little redhead with the Italian shoes and midnight eyes found out? He passed a truck. "Who?"

"Hunter Brown," Lee repeated. "The novelist."

Impulse took over again. "Is he any good?"

Surprised, Lee turned to study his profile. It was infinitely easier to look at him, she discovered, when those eyes weren't focused on her. "You've never read any of his work?"

"Should I have?"

"I suppose that depends on whether you like to read with all the lights on and the doors locked. He writes horror fiction."

If she'd looked more closely, she wouldn't have missed the quick humor in his eyes. "Ghouls and fangs?"

"Not exactly," she said after a moment. "Not that

simple. If there's something you're afraid of, he'll put it into words and make you wish him to the devil.''

Hunter laughed, greatly pleased. ''So, you like to be scared?''

''No,'' Lee said definitely.

''Then why do you read him?''

''I've asked myself that when I'm up at 3:00 A.M. finishing one of his books.'' Lee shrugged as the Jeep slowed for the turn off. ''It's irresistible. I think he must be a very odd man,'' she murmured, half to herself. ''Not quite, well, not quite like the rest of us.''

''Do you?'' After a quick, sharp turn, he pulled up in front of the hotel, more interested in her than he'd planned to be. ''But isn't writing just words and imagination?''

''And sweat and blood,'' she added, moving her shoulders again. ''I just don't see how it could be very comfortable to live with an imagination like Brown's. I'd like to know how he feels about it.''

Amused, Hunter jumped out of the Jeep to retrieve her bags. ''You're going to ask him.''

''Yes.'' Lee stepped down. ''I am.''

For a moment, they stood on the sidewalk, silently. He looked at her with what might have been mild interest, but she sensed something more—something she shouldn't have felt from a hotel driver after a ten-minute acquaintance. For the second time she wanted to shift and made herself stand still. Wasting no more words, Hunter turned toward the hotel, her bags in hand.

It didn't occur to Lee until she was following him

inside that she'd had a nonstop conversation with a hotel driver, a conversation that hadn't dwelt on the usual pleasantries or tourist plugs. As she watched him walk to the desk, she felt an aura of cool confidence from him and traces, very subtle traces, of arrogance. Why was a man like this driving back and forth and getting nowhere? she wondered. Stepping up to the desk, she told herself it wasn't her concern. She had bigger fish to fry.

"Lenore Radcliffe," she told the clerk.

"Yes, Ms. Radcliffe." He handed her a form and imprinted her credit card before he passed her a key. Before she could take it, Hunter slipped it into his own hand. It was then she noticed the odd ring on his pinky, four thin bands of gold and silver twisted into one.

"I'll take you around," he said simply, then crossed through the lobby with her again in his wake. He wound through a corridor, turned left, then stopped. Lee waited while he unlocked the door and gestured her inside.

The room was on the garden level with its own patio, she was pleased to note. As she scanned the room, Hunter carelessly switched on the TV and flipped through the channels before he checked the air conditioner. "Just call the desk if you need anything else," he advised, stowing her garment bag in the closet.

"Yes, I will." Lee hunted through her purse and came up with a five. "Thank you," she said, holding it out.

His eyes met hers again, giving her that same frozen
jolt they had in the airport. She felt something stir
deep within but wasn't sure if it was trying to reach
out to him or struggling to hide. The fingers holding
the bill nearly trembled. Then he smiled, so quickly,
so charmingly, she was speechless.

"Thank you, Ms. Radcliffe." Without a blink,
Hunter pocketed the five dollars and strolled out.

Chapter 2

If writers were often considered odd, writers' conferences, Lee was to discover, were oddities in themselves. They certainly couldn't be considered quiet or organized or stuffy.

Like nearly every other of the two hundred or so participants, she stood in one of the dozen lines at 8:00 A.M. for registration. From the laughing and calling and embracing, it was obvious that many of the writers and would-be writers knew one another. There was an air of congeniality, shared knowledge and camaraderie. Overlaying it all was excitement.

Still, more than one member stood in the noisy lobby like a child lost in a shipwreck, clinging to a folder or briefcase as though it were a life preserver and staring about with awe or simple confusion. Lee could appreciate the feeling, though she looked calm and poised as she accepted her packet and pinned her badge to the mint-green lapel of her blazer.

Concentrating on the business at hand, she found a chair in a corner and skimmed the schedule for Hunter Brown's workshop. With a dawning smile, she took out a pen and underlined.

CREATING HORROR THROUGH
ATMOSPHERE AND EMOTION
Speaker to be announced.

Bingo, Lee thought, capping her pen. She'd make certain she had a front-row seat. A glance at her watch showed her that she had three hours before Brown began to speak. Never one to take chances, she took out her notebook to skim over the questions she'd listed, while people filed by her or merely loitered, chatting.

"If I get rejected again, I'm going to put my head in the oven."

"Your oven's electric, Judy."

"It's the thought that counts."

Amused, Lee began to listen to the passing comments with half an ear while she added a few more questions.

"And when they brought in my breakfast this morning, there was a five-hundred-page manuscript under my plate. I completely lost my appetite."

"That's nothing. I got one in my office last week written in calligraphy. One hundred and fifty thousand words of flowing script."

Editors, she mused. She could tell them a few stories about some of the submissions that found their way to *Celebrity*.

"He said his editor hacked his first chapter to pieces so he's going into mourning before the rewrites."

"I always go into mourning before rewrites. It's after a rejection that I seriously consider taking up basket weaving as a profession."

"Did you hear Jeffries is here again trying to peddle that manuscript about the virgin with acrophobia and telekinesis? I can't believe he won't let it die a quiet death. When's your next murder coming out?"

"In August. It's poison."

"Darling, that's no way to talk about your work."

As they passed by her, Lee caught the variety of tones, some muted, some sophisticated, some flamboyant. Gestures and conversations followed the same wide range. Amazed, she watched one man swoop by in a long, dramatic black cape.

Definitely an odd group, Lee thought, but she warmed to them. It was true she confined her skill to articles and profiles, but at heart she was a storyteller. Her position on the magazine had been hard-earned, and she'd built her world around it. For all her ambition, she had a firm fear of rejection that kept her own manuscript unfinished, buried in a drawer for weeks and sometimes months at a time. At the magazine, she had prestige, security and room for advancement. The weekly paycheck put the roof over her head, the clothes on her back and the food on her table.

If it hadn't been so important that she prove she could do all this for herself, she might have taken the chance of sending those first hundred pages to a publishing house. But then... Shaking her head, Lee watched the people mill through the registration area, all types, all sizes, all ages. Clothes varied from trim professional suits to jeans to flamboyant caftans and smocks. Apparently style was a matter of taste and taste a matter of individuality. She wondered if she'd see quite the same variety anywhere else. Absently, she glanced at the partial manuscript she'd tucked into her briefcase. Just for cover, she reminded herself. That was all.

No, she didn't believe she had it in her to be a great writer, but she knew she had the skill for great reporting. She'd never, never settle for being second-rate at anything.

Still, while she was here, it wouldn't hurt to sit in on one or two of the seminars. She might pick up some pointers. More importantly, she told herself as she rose, she might be able to stretch this trip into another story on the ins and outs of a writers' conference. Who attended, why, what they did, what they hoped for. Yes, it could make quite an interesting little piece. The job, after all, came first.

An hour later, a bit more enthusiastic than she wanted to be after her first workshop, she wandered into the coffee shop. She'd take a short break, assimilate the notes she'd written, then go back and make certain she had the best seat in the house for Hunter Brown's lecture.

Hunter glanced up from his paper and watched her enter the coffee shop. Lee Radcliffe, he mused, finding her of more interest than the local news he'd been scanning. He'd enjoyed his conversation with her the day before, and as often as not, he found conversations tedious. She had a quality about her—an innate frankness glossed with sophistication—that he found intriguing enough to hold his interest. An obsessive writer who believed that the characters themselves were the plot of any book, Hunter always looked for the unique and the individual. Instinct told him Lee Radcliffe was quite an individual.

Unobserved, he watched her. From the way she looked absently around the room it was obvious she was preoccupied. The suit she wore was very simple but showed both style and taste in the color and cut. She was a woman who could wear the simple, he decided, because she was a woman who'd been born with style. If he wasn't very much mistaken, she'd been born into wealth as well. There was always a subtle difference between those who were accustomed to money and those who'd spent years earning it.

So where did the nerves come from? he wondered. Curious, he decided it would be worth an hour of his time to try to find out.

Setting his paper aside, Hunter lit a cigarette and continued to stare at her, knowing there was no quicker way to catch someone's eye.

Lee, thinking more about the story she was going to write than the coffee she'd come for, felt an odd tingle run up her spine. It was real enough to give her an urge to turn around and walk out again when she glanced over and found herself staring back at the man she'd met at the airport.

It was his eyes, she decided, at first not thinking of him as a man or the hotel driver from the previous day. It was his eyes. Dark, almost the color of jet, they'd draw you in and draw you in until you were caught, and every secret you'd ever had would be secret no longer. It was frightening. It was...irresistible.

Amazed that such a fanciful thought had crept into her own practical, organized mind, Lee approached him. He was just a man, she told herself, a man who worked for his living like any other man. There was certainly nothing to be frightened of.

"Ms. Radcliffe." With the same unsmiling stare, he gestured to the chair across from him. "Buy you a cup of coffee?"

Normally she would've refused, politely enough. But now, for some intangible reason, Lee felt as though she had a point to prove. For the same intangible reason, she felt she had to prove it to him as much as to herself. "Thank you." The moment she sat down, a waitress was there, pouring coffee.

"Enjoying the conference?"

"Yes." Lee poured cream into the cup, stirring it around and around until a tiny whirlpool formed in the center. "As disorganized as everything seems to be, there was an amazing amount of information generated at the workshop I went to this morning."

A smile touched his lips, so lightly that it was barely there at all. "You prefer organization?"

"It's more productive." Though he was dressed more formally than he'd been the day before, the pleated slacks and open-necked shirt were still casual. She wondered why he wasn't required to wear a uniform. But then, she thought, you could put him in one of those nifty white jackets and neat ties and his eyes would simply defy them.

"A lot of fascinating things can come out of chaos, don't you think?"

"Perhaps." She frowned down at the whirlpool in her cup. Why did she feel as though she was being sucked in, in just that way? And why, she thought with a sudden flash of impatience, was she sitting here having a philosophical discussion with a stranger when she should be outlining the two stories she planned to write?

"Did you find Hunter Brown?" he asked her as he studied her over the rim of his cup. Annoyed with herself, he guessed accurately, and anxious to be off doing.

"What?" Distracted, Lee looked back up to find those strange eyes still on her.

"I asked if you'd run into Hunter Brown." The whisper of a smile was on his lips again, and this time it touched his eyes as well. It didn't make them any less intense.

"No." Defensive without knowing why, Lee sipped at her cooling coffee. "Why?"

"After the things you said yesterday, I was curious what you'd think of him once you met him." He took a drag from his cigarette and blew smoke out in a haze. "People usually have a preconceived image of someone but it rarely holds up in the flesh."

"It's difficult to have any kind of an image of someone who hides away from the world."

His brow went up, but his voice remained mild. "Hides?"

"It's the word that comes to my mind," Lee returned, again finding that she was speaking her thoughts aloud to him. "There's no picture of him on the back of any of his books, no bio. He never grants interviews, never denies or substantiates anything written about him. Any awards he's received have been accepted by his agent or his editor." She ran her fingers up and down the handle of her spoon. "I've heard he occasionally attends affairs like this, but only if it's a very small conference and there's no publicity about his appearance."

All during her speech, Hunter kept his eyes on her, watching every nuance of expression. There were traces of frustration, he was certain, and of eagerness. The lovely cameo face was calm while her fingers moved restlessly. She'd be in his next book, he decided on the spot. He'd never met anyone with more potential for being a central character.

Because his direct, unblinking stare made her want to stammer, Lee gave him back the hard, uncompromising look. "Why do you stare at me like that?"

He continued to do so without any show of discomfort. "Because you're an interesting woman."

Another man might have said beautiful, still another might have said fascinating. Lee could have tossed off either one with light scorn. She picked up her spoon again, then set it down. "Why?"

"You have a tidy mind, innate style, and you're a bundle of nerves." He liked the way the faint line appeared between her brows when she frowned. It meant stubbornness to him, and tenacity. He respected both. "I've always been intrigued by pockets," Hunter went on. "The deeper the better. I find myself wondering just what's in your pockets, Ms. Radcliffe."

She felt the tremor again, up her spine, then down. It wasn't comfortable to sit near a man who could do that. She had a moment's sympathy for every person she'd ever interviewed. "You have an odd way of putting things," she muttered.

"So I've been told."

She instructed herself to get up and leave. It didn't make sense to sit there being disturbed by a man she could dismiss with a five-dollar tip. "What are you doing in Flagstaff?" she demanded. "You don't strike me as someone who'd be content to drive back and forth to an airport day after day, shuttling passengers and hauling luggage."

"Impressions make fascinating little paintings, don't they?" He smiled at her fully, as he had the day before when she'd tipped him. Lee wasn't sure why she'd felt he'd been laughing at her then, any more than why she felt he was laughing at her now. Despite herself, her lips curved in response. He found the smile a pleasant and very alluring surprise.

"You're a very odd man."

"I've been told that, too." His smile faded and his eyes became intense again. "Have dinner with me tonight."

The question didn't surprise her as much as the fact that she wanted to accept, and nearly had. "No," she said, cautiously retreating. "I don't think so."

"Let me know if you change your mind."

She was surprised again. Most men would've pressed a bit. It was, well, expected, Lee reflected, wishing she could figure him out. "I have to get back." She reached for her briefcase. "Do you know where the Canyon Room is?"

With an inward chuckle, he dropped bills on the table. "Yes, I'll show you."

"That's not necessary," Lee began, rising.

"I've got time." He walked with her out of the coffee shop and into the wide, carpeted lobby. "Do you plan to do any sight-seeing while you're here?"

"There won't be time." She glanced out one of the wide windows at the towering peak of Humphrey Peak. "As soon as the conference is over I have to get back."

"To where?"

"Los Angeles."

"Too many people," Hunter said automatically. "Don't you ever feel as though they're using up your air?"

She wouldn't have put it that way, would never have thought of it, but there were times she felt a twinge of what might be called claustrophobia. Still, her home was there, and more importantly, her work. "No. There's enough air, such as it is, for everyone."

"You've never stood at the south rim of the canyon and looked out, and breathed in."

Again, Lee shot him a look. He had a way of saying things that gave you an immediate picture. For the second time, she regretted that she wouldn't be able to take a day or two to explore some of the vastness of Arizona. "Maybe some other time." Shrugging, she turned with him as he headed down a corridor to the right.

"Time's fickle," he commented. "When you need it, there's too little of it. Then you wake up at three o'clock in the morning, and there's too much of it. It's usually better to take it than to anticipate it. You might try that," he said, looking down at her again. "It might help your nerves."

Her brows drew together. "There's nothing wrong with my nerves."

"Some people can thrive on nervous energy for weeks at a time, then they have to find that little valve that lets the steam escape." For the first time, he touched her, just fingertips to the ends of her hair. But she felt it, experienced it, as hard and strong as if his hand had closed firmly over hers. "What do you do to let the steam escape, Lenore?"

She didn't stiffen, or casually nudge his hand away as she would have done at any other time. Instead, she stood still, toying with a sensation she couldn't remember ever experiencing before. Thunder and lightning, she thought. There was thunder and lightning in this man, deep under the strangely aloof, oddly open exterior. She wasn't about to be caught in the storm.

"I work," she said easily, but her fingers had tightened on the handle of her briefcase. "I don't need any other escape valve." She didn't step back, but let the haughtiness that had always protected her enter her tone. "No one calls me Lenore."

"No?" He nearly smiled. It was this look, she realized, the secret amusement the onlooker could only guess at rather than see, that most intrigued. She thought he probably knew that. "But it suits you. Feminine, elegant, a little distant. *And the only word there spoken was the whispered word, 'Lenore'!* Yes." He let his fingertips linger a moment longer on her hair. "I think Poe would've found you very apt."

Before she could prevent it, before she could anticipate it, her knees were weak. She'd felt the sound of her own name feather over her skin. "Who are you?" Lee found herself demanding. Was it possible to be so deeply affected by someone without even knowing his name? She stepped forward in what seemed to be a challenge. "Just who are you?"

He smiled again, with the oddly gentle charm that shouldn't have suited his eyes yet somehow did. "Strange, you never asked before. You'd better go in," he told her as people began to gravitate toward the open doors of the Canyon Room. "You'll want a good seat."

"Yes." She drew back, a bit shaken by the ferocity of the desire she felt to learn more about him. With a last look over her shoulder, Lee walked in and settled in the front row. It was time to get her mind back on the business she'd come for, and the business was Hunter Brown. Distractions like incomprehensible men who drove Jeeps for a living would have to be put aside.

From her briefcase, Lee took a fresh notebook and two pencils, slipping one behind her ear. Within a few moments, she'd be able to see and study the mysterious Hunter Brown. She'd be able to listen and take notes with perfect freedom. After his lecture, she'd be able to question him, and if she had her way, she'd arrange some kind of one-on-one for later.

Lee had given the ethics of the situation careful thought. She didn't feel it would be necessary to tell Brown she was a reporter. She was there as an aspiring writer and had the fledgling manuscript to prove it. Anyone there was free to try to write and sell an article on the conference and its participants. Only if Brown used the words *off the record* would she be bound to silence. Without that, anything he said was public property.

This story could be her next step up the ladder. Would be, Lee corrected. The first documented, authentically researched story on Hunter Brown could push her beyond *Celebrity*'s scope. It would be controversial, colorful and, most importantly, exclusive. With this under her belt, even her quietly critical family would be impressed. With this under her belt, Lee thought, she'd be that much closer to the top rung, where her sights were always set.

Once she was there, all the hard work, the long

hours, the obsessive dedication, would be worth it. Because once she was there, she was there to stay. At the top, Lee thought almost fiercely. As high as she could reach.

On the other side of the doors, on the other side of the corridor, Hunter stood with his editor, half listening to her comments on an interview she'd had with an aspiring writer. He caught the gist, that she was excited about the writer's potential. It was a talent of his to be able to conduct a perfectly lucid conversation when his mind was on something entirely different. It was something he roused himself to do only when the mood was on him. So he spoke to his editor and thought of Lee Radcliffe.

Yes, he was definitely going to use her in his next book. True, the plot was only a vague notion in his head, but he already knew she'd be the core of it. He needed to dig a bit deeper before he'd be satisfied, but he didn't foresee any problem there. If he'd gauged her correctly, she'd be confused when he walked to the podium, then stunned, then furious. If she wanted to talk to him as badly as she'd indicated, she'd swallow her temper.

A strong woman, Hunter decided. A will of iron and skin like cream. Vulnerable eyes and a damn-the-devil chin. A character was nothing without contrasts, strengths and weaknesses. And secrets, he thought, already certain he'd discover hers. He had another day and a half to explore Lenore Radcliffe. Hunter figured that was enough.

The corridor was full of laughter and complaints

and enthusiasm as people loitered or filed through into
the adjoining room. He knew what it was to feel enthusiastic about being a writer. If the pleasure went
out of it, he'd still write. He was compelled to. But it
would show in his work. Emotions always showed.
He never *allowed* his feeling and thoughts to pour into
his work—they would have done so regardless of his
permission.

Hunter considered it a fair trade-off. His emotions,
his thoughts, were there for anyone who cared to read
them. His life was completely and without exception
his own.

The woman beside him had his affection and his
respect. He'd argued with her over motivation and
sentence structure, losing as often as winning. He'd
shouted at her, laughed with her and given her emotional support through her recent divorce. He knew
her age, her favorite drink and her weakness for cash-
ews. She'd been his editor for three years, which is as
close to a marriage as many people come. Yet she had
no idea he had a ten-year-old daughter named Sarah
who liked to bake cookies and play soccer.

Hunter took a last drag on his cigarette as the president of the small writers' group approached. The man
was a slick, imaginative science fiction writer whom
Hunter had read and enjoyed. Otherwise, he wouldn't
be there, about to make one of his rare appearances
in the writing community.

"Mr. Brown, I don't need to tell you again how
honored we are to have you here."

"No—" Hunter gave him the easy half smile "—you don't."

"There's liable to be quite a commotion when I announce you. After your lecture, I'll do everything I can to keep the thundering horde back."

"Don't worry about it. I'll manage."

The man nodded, never doubting it. "I'm having a small reception in my suite this evening, if you'd like to join us."

"I appreciate it, but I have a dinner engagement."

Though he didn't know quite what to make of the smile, the organization's president was too intelligent to press his luck when he was about to pull off a coup. "If you're ready then, I'll announce you."

"Any time."

Hunter followed him into the Canyon Room, then loitered just inside the doors. The room was already buzzing with anticipation and curiosity. The podium was set on a small stage in front of two hundred chairs that were nearly all filled. Talk died down when the president approached the stage, but continued in pockets of murmurs even after he'd begun to speak. Hunter heard one of the men nearest him whisper to a companion that he had three publishing houses competing for his manuscript. Hunter skimmed over the crowd, barely listening to the beginning of his introduction. Then his gaze rested again on Lee.

She was watching the speaker with a small, polite smile on her lips, but her eyes gave her away. They were dark and eager. Hunter let his gaze roam down until it rested in her lap. There, her hand opened and closed on the pencil. A bundle of nerves and energy wrapped in a very thin layer of confidence, he thought.

For the second time Lee felt his eyes on her, and for the second time she turned so that their gazes locked. The faint line marred her brow again as she wondered what he was doing inside the conference room. Unperturbed, leaning easily against the wall, Hunter stared back at her.

"His career's risen steadily since the publication of his first book, only five years ago. Since the first, *The Devil's Due*, he's given us the pleasure of being scared out of our socks every time we pick up his work." At the mention of the title, the murmurs increased and heads began to swivel. Hunter continued to stare at Lee, and she back at him, frowning. "His latest, *Silent Scream*, is already solid in the number-one spot on the best-seller list. We're honored and privileged to welcome to Flagstaff—Hunter Brown."

The effusive applause competed with the growing murmurs of two hundred people in a closed room. Casually, Hunter straightened from the wall and walked to the stage. He saw the pencil fall out of Lee's hand and roll to the floor. Without breaking rhythm, he stooped and picked it up.

"Better hold on to this," he advised, looking into her astonished eyes. As he handed it back, he watched astonishment flare into fury.

"You're a—"

"Yes, but you'd better tell me later." Walking the rest of the way to the stage, Hunter stepped behind the podium and waited for the applause to fade. Again he skimmed the crowd, but this time with such a quiet intensity that all sound died. For ten seconds there wasn't even the sound of breathing. "Terror," Hunter said into the microphone.

From the first word he had them spellbound, and held them captive for forty minutes. No one moved, no one yawned, no one slipped out for a cigarette. With her teeth clenched tight, Lee knew she despised him.

Simmering, struggling against the urge to spring up and stalk out, Lee sat stiffly and took meticulous notes. In the margin of the book she drew a perfectly recognizable caricature of Hunter with a dagger through his heart. It gave her enormous satisfaction.

When he agreed to field questions for ten minutes, Lee's was the first hand up. Hunter looked directly at her, smiled and called on someone three rows back.

He answered professional questions professionally and evaded any personal references. She had to admire his skill, particularly since she was well aware he so seldom spoke in public. He showed no nerves, no hesitation and absolutely no inclination to call on her, though her hand was up and her eyes shot fiery little darts at him. But she was a reporter, Lee reminded herself. Reporters got nowhere if they stood on ceremony.

"Mr. Brown," Lee began, and rose.

"Sorry." With his slow smile, he held up a hand. "I'm afraid we're already overtime. Best of luck to all of you." He left the podium and the room, under a hail of applause. By the time Lee could work her way to the doors, she'd heard enough praise of Hunter Brown to turn her simmering temper to boil.

The nerve, she thought as she finally made it into the corridor. The unspeakable nerve. She didn't mind being bested in a game of chess; she could handle having her work criticized and her opinion questioned. All in all, Lee considered herself a reasonable, low-key person with no more than her fair share of conceit. The one thing she couldn't, wouldn't, tolerate was being made a fool of.

Revenge sprang into her mind, nasty, petty revenge. Oh, yes, she thought as she tried to work her way through the thick crowd of Hunter Brown fans, she'd have her revenge, somehow, some way. And when she did, it would be perfect.

She turned off at the elevators, knowing she was too full of fury to deal successfully with Hunter at that moment. She needed an hour to cool off and to plan. The pencil she still held snapped between her fingers. If it was the last thing she did, she was going to make Hunter Brown squirm.

Just as she started to push the button for her floor, Hunter slipped inside the elevator. "Going up?" he asked easily, and pushed the number himself.

Lee felt the fury rise to her throat and burn. With an effort, she clamped her lips tight on the venom and stared straight ahead.

"Broke your pencil," Hunter observed, finding himself more amused than he'd been in days. He glanced at her open notebook, spotting the meticulously drawn caricature. An appreciative grin appeared. "Well done," he told her. "How'd you enjoy the workshop?"

Lee gave him one scathing look as the elevator doors opened. "You're a fount of trivial information, Mr. Brown."

"You've got murder in your eyes, Lenore." He stepped into the hall with her. "It suits your hair. Your drawing makes it clear enough what you'd like to do. Why don't you stab me while you have the chance?"

As she continued to walk, Lee told herself she wouldn't give him the satisfaction of speaking to him. She wouldn't speak to him at all. Her head jerked up. "You've had a good laugh at my expense," she grated, and dug in her briefcase for her room key.

"A quiet chuckle or two," he corrected while she continued to simmer and search. "Lose your key?"

"No, I haven't lost my key." Frustrated, Lee looked up until fury met amusement. "Why don't you go away and sit on your laurels?"

"I've always found that uncomfortable. Why don't you vent your spleen, Lenore; you'd feel better."

"Don't call me Lenore!" she exploded as her control slipped. "You had no right to use me as the brunt of a joke. You had no right to pretend you worked for the hotel."

"You assumed," he corrected. "As I recall, I never pretended anything. You asked for a ride yesterday; I simply gave you one."

"You knew I thought you were the hotel driver. You were standing there beside my luggage—"

"A classic case of mistaken identity." He noted

that her skin tinted with pale rose when she was angry. An attractive side effect, Hunter decided. "I'd come to pick up my editor, who'd missed her Phoenix connection, as it turned out, I thought the luggage was hers."

"All you had to do was say that at the time."

"You never asked," he pointed out. "And you did tell me to get the luggage."

"Oh, you're infuriating." Clamping her teeth shut, she began to fumble in her briefcase again.

"But brilliant. You mentioned that yourself."

"Being able to string words together is an admirable talent, Mr. Brown." Hauteur was one of her most practiced skills. Lee used it to the fullest. "It doesn't make you an admirable person."

"No, I wouldn't say I was, particularly." While he waited for her to find her key, Hunter leaned comfortably against the wall.

"You carried my luggage to my room," she continued, infuriated. "I gave you a five-dollar tip."

"Very generous."

She let out a huff of breath, grateful that her hands were busy. She didn't know how else she could have prevented herself from slapping his calm, self-satisfied face. "You've had your joke," she said, finding her key at last. "Now I'd like you to do me the courtesy of never speaking to me again."

"I don't know where you got the impression I was courteous." Before she could unlock the door, he'd put his hand over hers on the key. She felt the little tingle of power and cursed him for it even as she met his calmly amused look. "You did mention, however, that you'd like to speak to me. We can talk over dinner tonight."

She stared at him. Why should she have thought he wouldn't be able to surprise her again? "You have the most incredible nerve."

"You mentioned that already. Seven o'clock?"

She wanted to tell him she wouldn't have dinner with him even if he groveled. She wanted to tell him that and all manner of other unpleasant things. Temper fought with practicality. There was a job she'd come to do, one she'd been working on unsuccessfully for three months. Success was more important than pride. He was offering her the perfect way to do what she'd come to do, and to do it more extensively than she could've hoped for. And perhaps, just perhaps, he was opening the door himself for her revenge. It would make it all the sweeter.

Though it was a large lump, Lee swallowed her pride.

"That's fine," she agreed, but he noticed she didn't look too pleased. "Where should I meet you?"

He never trusted easy agreement. But then Hunter trusted very little. She was going to be a challenge, he felt. "I'll pick you up here." His fingers ran casually up to her wrist before he released her. "You might bring your manuscript along. I'm curious to see your work."

She smiled and thought of the article she was going to write. "I very much want you to see my work." Lee stepped into her room and gave herself the small satisfaction of slamming the door in his face.

Chapter 3

Midnight-blue silk. Lee took a great deal of time and gave a great deal of thought to choosing the right dress for her evening with Hunter. It was business.

The deep-blue silk shot through with thin silver threads appealed to her because of its clean, elegant lines and lack of ornamentation. Lee would, on the occasions when she shopped, spend as much time choosing the right scarf as she would researching a subject. It was all business.

Now, after a thorough debate, she slipped into the silk. It coolly skimmed her skin; it draped subtly over curves. Her own reflection satisfied her. The unsmiling woman who looked back at her presented precisely the sort of image she wanted to project—elegant, sophisticated and a bit remote. If nothing else, this soothed her bruised ego.

As Lee looked back over her life, concentrating on her career, she could remember no incident where she'd found herself bested. Her mouth became grim as she ran a brush through her hair. It wasn't going to happen now.

Hunter Brown was going to get back some of his own, if for no other reason than that half-amused smile of his. No one laughed at her and got away with it, Lee told herself as she slapped the brush back on the dresser smartly enough to make the bottles jump. Whatever game she had to play to get what she wanted, she'd play. When the article on Hunter Brown hit the stands, she'd have won. She'd have the satisfaction of knowing he'd helped her. In the final analysis, Lee mused, there was no substitute for winning.

When the knock sounded at her door, she glanced at her watch. Prompt. She'd have to make a note of it. Her mood was smug as, after picking up her slim evening bag, she went to answer.

Inherently casual in dress, but not sloppy, she noted, filing the information away as she glanced at the open-collared shirt under his dark jacket. Some men could wear black tie and not look as elegant as Hunter Brown looked in jeans. That was something that might interest her readers. By the end of the evening, Lee reminded herself, she'd know all she possibly could about him.

"Good evening." She started to step across the threshold, but he took her hand, holding her motionless as he studied her.

"Very lovely," Hunter declared. Her hand was

very soft and very cool, though her eyes were still hot with annoyance. He liked the contrast. "You wear silk and a very alluring scent but manage to maintain that aura of untouchability. It's quite a talent."

"I'm not interested in being analyzed."

"The curse or blessing of the writer," he countered. "Depending on your viewpoint. Being one yourself, you should understand. Where's your manuscript?"

She'd thought he'd forget—she'd hoped he would. Now, she was back to the disadvantage of stammering. "It, ah, it isn't..."

"Bring it along," Hunter ordered. "I want to take a look at it."

"I don't see why."

"Every writer wants his words read."

She didn't. It wasn't polished. It wasn't perfect. Without a doubt, the last person she wanted to allow a glimpse of her inner thoughts was Hunter. But he was standing, watching, with those dark eyes already seeing beyond the outer layers. Trapped, Lee turned back into the room and slipped the folder from her briefcase. If she could keep him busy enough, she thought, there wouldn't be time for him to look at it anyway.

"It'll be difficult for you to read anything in a restaurant," she pointed out as she closed the door behind her.

"That's why we're having dinner in my suite."

When she stopped, he simply took her hand and continued on to the elevators as if he hadn't noticed.

"Perhaps I've given you the wrong impression," she began coldly.

"I don't think so." He turned, still holding her hand. His palm wasn't as smooth as she'd expected a writer's to be. The palm was as wide as a concert pianist's, but it was ridged with calluses. It made, Lee discovered, a very intriguing and uncomfortable combination. "My imagination hasn't gone very deeply into the prospect of seducing you, Lenore." Though he felt her stiffen in outrage, he drew her into the elevator. "The point is, I don't care for restaurants and I care less for crowds and interruptions." The elevator hummed quietly on the short ascent. "Have you found the conference worthwhile?"

"I'm going to get what I came for." She stepped through the doors as they slid open.

"And what's that?"

"What did you come for?" she countered. "You don't exactly make it a habit to attend conferences, and this one is certainly small and off the beaten path."

"Occasionally I enjoy the contact with other writers." Unlocking the door, he gestured her inside.

"This conference certainly isn't bulging with authors who've attained your degree of success."

"Success has nothing to do with writing."

She set her purse and folder aside and faced him straight on. "Easy to say when you have it."

"Is it?" As if amused, he shrugged, then gestured toward the window. "You should drink in as much of

the view as you can. You won't see anything like this
through any window in Los Angeles."

"You don't care for L.A." If she was careful and
clever, she should be able to pin him down on where
he lived and why he lived there.

"L.A. has its points. Would you like some wine?"

"Yes." She wandered over to the window. The
vastness still had the power to stun her and almost...almost frighten. Once you were beyond the city
limits, you might wander for miles without seeing another face, hearing another voice. The isolation, she
thought, or perhaps just the space itself, would overwhelm. "Have you been there often?" she asked, deliberately turning her back to the window.

"Hmm?"

"To Los Angeles?"

"No." He crossed to her and offered a glass of
pale-gold wine.

"You prefer the East to the West?"

He smiled and lifted his glass. "I make it a point
to prefer where I am."

He was very adept at evasions, she thought, and
turned away to wander the room. It seemed he was
also very adept at making her uneasy. Unless she
missed her guess, he did both on purpose. "Do you
travel often?"

"Only when it's necessary."

Tipping back her glass, Lee decided to try a more
direct approach. "Why are you so secretive about
yourself? Most people in your position would make

the most of the promotion and publicity that's available.''

''I don't consider myself secretive, nor do I consider myself most people.''

''You don't even have a bio or a photo on your book covers.''

''My face and my background have nothing to do with the stories I tell. Does the wine suit you?''

''It's very good.'' Though she'd barely tasted it. ''Don't you feel it's part of your profession to satisfy the readers' curiosity when it comes to the person who creates a story that interests them?''

''No. My profession is words—putting words together so that someone who reads them is entertained, intrigued and satisfied with a tale. And tales spring from imagination rather than hard fact.'' He sipped wine himself and approved it. ''The teller of the tale is nothing compared to the tale itself.''

''Modesty?'' Lee asked with a trace of scorn she couldn't prevent.

The scorn seemed to amuse him. ''Not at all. It's a matter of priorities, not humility. If you knew me better, you'd understand I have very few virtues.'' He smiled, but Lee told herself she'd imagined that brief predatory flash in his eyes. Imagined, she told herself again and shuddered. Annoyed at her own reaction, she held out her wineglass for a refill.

''Have you any virtues?''

He like the fact that she struck back even when her nerves were racing. ''Some say vices are more interesting and certainly more entertaining than virtues.''

He filled her glass to just under the rim. "Would you agree?"

"More interesting, perhaps more entertaining." She refused to let her eyes falter from his as she drank. "Certainly more demanding."

He mulled this over, enjoying her quick response and her clean, direct thought-patterns. "You have an interesting mind, Lenore; you keep it exercised."

"A woman who doesn't finds herself watching other people climb to the top while she fills water glasses and makes the coffee." She could have cursed in frustration the moment she'd spoken. It wasn't her habit to speak that freely. The point was, she was here to interview him, Lee reminded herself, not the other way around.

"An interesting analogy," Hunter murmured. Ambition. Yes, he'd sensed that about her from the beginning. But what was it she wanted to achieve? Whatever it was, he mused, she wouldn't be above stepping over a few people to get it. He found he could respect that, could almost admire it. "Tell me, do you ever relax?"

"I beg your pardon?"

"Your hands are rarely still, though you appear to have a great deal of control otherwise." He noted that at his words her fingers stopped toying with the stem of her glass. "Since you've come into this room, you haven't stayed in one spot more than a few seconds. Do I make you nervous?"

Sending him a cool look, she sat on the plush sofa

and crossed her legs. "No." But her pulse thudded a bit when he sat down beside her.

"What does?"

"Small loud dogs."

He laughed, pleased with the moment and with her. "You're a very entertaining woman." He took her hand lightly in his. "I should tell you that's my highest compliment."

"You set a great store by entertainment."

"The world's a grim place—worse, often tedious." Her hand was delicate, and delicacy drew him. Her eyes held secrets, and there was little that intrigued him more. "If we can't be entertained, there're only two places to go. Back to the cave, or on to oblivion."

"So you entertain with terror." She wanted to shift farther away from him, but his fingers had tightened almost imperceptibly on her hand. And his eyes were searching for her thoughts.

"If you're worried about the unspeakable terror lurking outside your bedroom window, would you worry about your next dentist appointment or the fact that your washer overflowed?"

"Escape?"

He reached up to touch her hair. It seemed a very casual, very natural gesture to him. Lee's eyes flew open as if she'd been pinched. "I don't care for the word *escape*."

She was a difficult combination to resist, Hunter thought, as he let his fingertips skim down the side of her throat. The fiery hair, the vulnerable eyes, the cool gloss of breeding, the bubbling nerves. She'd make a fascinating character and, he realized, a fascinating lover. He'd already decided to have her for the first; now, as he toyed with the ends of her hair, he decided to have her for the second.

She sensed something when his gaze locked on hers again. Decision, determination, desire. Her mouth went dry. It wasn't often that she felt she could be outmatched by another. It was rarer still when anyone or anything truly frightened her. Though he said nothing, though he moved no closer, she found herself fighting back fear—and the knowledge that whatever game she challenged him to, she would lose because he would look into her eyes and know each move before she made it.

A knock sounded at the door, but he continued to look at her for long silent seconds before he rose. "I took the liberty of ordering dinner," he said, so calmly that Lee wondered if she'd imagined the flare of passion she'd seen in his eyes. While he went to the door, she sat where she was, struggling to sort her own thoughts. She was imagining things, Lee told herself. He couldn't see into her and read her thoughts. He was just a man. Since the game was hers, and only she knew the rules, she wouldn't lose. Settled again, she rose to walk to the table.

The salmon was tender and pink. Pleased with the choice, Lee sat down at the table as the waiter closed the door behind him. So far, Lee reflected, she'd answered more questions than Hunter. It was time to change that.

"The advice you gave earlier to struggling writers

about blocking out time to write every day no matter how discouraged they get—did that come from personal experience?"

Hunter sampled the salmon. "All writers face discouragement from time to time. Just as they face criticism and rejection."

"Did you face many rejections before the sale of *The Devil's Due*?"

"I suspect anything that comes too easily." He lifted the wine bottle to fill her glass again. She had a face made for candlelight, he mused as he watched the shadow and light flicker over the cream-soft skin and delicate features. He was determined to find out what lay beneath, before the evening ended.

He never considered he was using her, though he fully intended to pick her brain for everything he could learn about her. It was a writer's privilege.

"What made you become a writer?"

He lifted a brow as he continued to eat. "I was born a writer."

Lee ate slowly, planning her next line of questions. She had to move carefully, avoid putting him on the defensive, maneuver around any suspicions. She never considered she was using him, though she fully intended to pick his brain for everything she could learn about him. It was a reporter's privilege.

"Born a writer," she repeated, flaking off another bite of salmon. "Do you think it's that simple? Weren't there elements in your background, circumstances, early experiences, that led you toward your career?"

''I didn't say it was simple,'' Hunter corrected. ''We're all born with a certain set of choices to make. The matter of making the right ones is anything but simple. Every novel written has to do with choices. Writing novels is what I was meant to do.''

He interested her enough that she forgot the unofficial interview and asked for herself, ''So you always wanted to be a writer?''

''You're very literal-minded,'' Hunter observed. Comfortable, he leaned back and swirled the wine in his glass. ''No, I didn't. I wanted to play professional soccer.''

''Soccer?''

Her astonished disbelief made him smile. ''Soccer,'' he repeated. ''I wanted to make a career of it and might have been successful at it, but I had to write.''

Lee was silent a moment, then decided he was telling her precisely the truth. ''So you became a writer without really wanting to.''

''I made a choice,'' Hunter corrected, intrigued by the orderly logic of her mind. ''I believe a great many people are born writer or artist, and die without ever realizing it. Books go unwritten, paintings unpainted. The fortunate ones are those who discover what they were meant to do. I might have been an excellent soccer player; I might have been an excellent writer. If I'd tried to do both, I'd have been no more than mediocre. I chose not to be mediocre.''

''There're several million readers who'd agree you made the right choice.'' Forgetting the cool facade, she propped her elbows on the table and leaned forward. "Why horror fiction, Hunter? Someone with your skill and your imagination could write anything. Why did you turn your talents toward that particular genre?"

He lit a cigarette so that the scent of tobacco stung the air. "Why do you read it?"

She frowned; he hadn't turned one of her questions back on her for some time. "I don't as a rule, except yours."

"I'm flattered. Why mine?"

"Your first was recommended to me, and then..." She hesitated, not wanting to say she'd been hooked from the first page. Instead, she ran her fingertip around the rim of her glass and sorted through her answer. "You have a way of creating atmosphere and drawing characters that make the impossibility of your stories perfectly believable."

He blew out a stream of smoke. "Do you think they're impossible?"

She gave a quick laugh, a laugh he recognized as genuine from the humor that lit her eyes. It did something very special to her beauty. It made it accessible. "I hardly believe in people being possessed by demons or a house being inherently evil."

"No?" He smiled. "No superstitions, Lenore?"

She met his gaze levelly. "None."

"Strange, most of us have a few."

"Do you?"

"Of course, and even the ones I don't have fascinate me." He took her hand, linking fingers firmly.

"It's said some people are able to sense another's aura, or personality if the word suits you better, by a simple clasp of hands." His palm was warm and hard as he kept his eyes fixed on hers. She could feel, cool against her hand, the twisted metal of his ring.

"I don't believe that." But she wasn't so sure, not with him.

"You believe only in what you see or feel. Only in what can be touched with one of the five senses that you understand." He rose, drawing her to her feet. "Everything that is can't be understood. Everything that's understood can't be explained."

"Everything has an explanation." But she found the words, like her pulse, a bit unsteady.

She might have drawn her hand away, and he might have let her, but her statement seemed to be a direct challenge. "Can you explain why your heart beats faster when I step closer?" His face looked mysterious, his eyes like jet in the candlelight. "You said you weren't afraid of me."

"I'm not."

"But your pulse throbs." His fingertip lightly touched the hollow of her throat. "Can you explain why when we've yet to spend even one full day together, I want to touch you, like this?" Gently, incredibly gently, he ran the back of his hand up the side of her face.

"Don't." It was only a whisper.

"Can you explain this kind of attraction between two strangers?" He traced a finger over her lips, felt them tremble, wondered about their taste.

Something soft, something flowing, moved through her. "Physical attraction's no more than chemistry."

"Science?" He brought her hand up, pressing his lips to the center of her palm. She felt the muscles in her thighs turn to liquid. "Is there an equation for this?" Still watching her, he brushed his lips over her wrist. Her skin chilled, then heated. Her pulse jolted and scrambled. He smiled. "Does this—" he whispered a kiss at the corner of her mouth "—have to do with logic?"

"I don't want you to touch me like this."

"You want me to touch you," Hunter corrected. "But you can't explain it." In an expected move, he thrust his hands into her hair. "Try the unexplainable," he challenged before his lips closed over hers.

Power. It sped through her. Desire was a rush of heat. She could feel need sing through her as she stood motionless in his arms. She should have refused him. Lee was experienced in the art of refusals. There was suddenly no wit to evade, no strength to refuse.

For all his intensity, for all the force of his personality, the kiss was meltingly soft. Though his fingers were strong and firm in her hair, so firm if she'd tried to move away she'd have found herself trapped, his lips were as gentle and warm as the light that flickered on the table beside them. She didn't know when she reached for him, but her arms were around him, bodies merging, silk rustling. The quiet, intoxicating taste of wine was on his tongue. Lee drank it in. She could smell the candle wax and her own perfume. Her ordered, disciplined mind swam first with confusion, then with sensation after alluring sensation.

Her lips were cool but warmed quickly. Her body was tense but slowly relaxed. He enjoyed both changes. She wasn't a woman who gave herself freely or easily. He knew that just as he knew she wasn't a woman often taken by surprise.

She seemed very small against him, very fragile. He'd always treated fragility with great care. Even as the kiss grew deeper, even as his own need grew surprisingly greater, his mouth remained gentle on hers, teasing, requesting. He believed that lovemaking, from first touch to fulfillment, was an art. He believed that art could never be rushed. So, slowly, patiently, he showed her what might be, while his hands stayed only in her hair and his mouth stayed softly on her.

He was draining her. Lee could feel her will, her strength, her thoughts, seeping out of her. And as they drained away, a flood of sensation replenished what she lost. There was no dealing with it, no...explaining. It could only be experienced.

Pleasure this fluid couldn't be contained. Desire this strong couldn't be guided. It was the lack of control more than the flood of feeling that frightened her most. If she lost her control, she'd lose her purpose. Then she would flounder. With a murmured protest, she pulled away but found that while he freed her lips, he still held her.

Later, he thought, at some lonely, dark hour, he'd explore his own reaction. Now he was much more interested in hers. She looked at him as though she'd been struck—face pale, eyes dark. Though her lips parted, she said nothing. Under his fingers he could feel the light tremor that coursed through her—once, then twice.

"Some things can't be explained, even when they're understood." He said it softly, so softly she might have thought it a threat.

"I don't understand you at all." She put her hands on his forearms as if to draw him away. "I don't think I want to anymore."

He didn't smile as he let his hands slide down to her shoulders. "Perhaps not. You'll have a choice to make."

"No." Shaken, she stepped away and snatched up her purse. "The conference ends tomorrow and I go back to L.A." Suddenly angry, she turned to face him. "You'll go back to whatever hole it is you hide in."

He inclined his head. "Perhaps." It was best she'd put some distance between them. Very abruptly, he realized that if he'd held her a moment longer, he wouldn't have let her go. "We'll talk tomorrow."

She didn't question her own illogic, but shook her head. "No, we won't talk anymore."

He didn't correct her when she walked to the door, and he stood where he was when the door closed behind her. There was no need to contradict her; he knew they'd talk again. Lifting his glass of wine, Hunter gathered up the manuscript she'd forgotten and settled himself in a chair.

Chapter 4

Anger. Perhaps what Lee felt was simple anger, without other eddies and currents of emotion, but she wasn't certain whom she felt angry with.

What had happened the evening before could have been avoided—should have been, she corrected as she stepped out of the shower. Because she'd allowed Hunter to set the pace and the tone, she'd put herself in a vulnerable position *and* she'd wasted a valuable opportunity. If Lee had learned anything in her years as a reporter, it was that a wasted opportunity was the most destructive mistake in the business.

How much did she know of Hunter Brown that could be used in a concise, informative article? Enough for a paragraph, Lee thought in disgust. A very short paragraph.

She might have only one chance to make up for

lost time. Time lost because she'd let herself feel like a woman instead of thinking like a reporter. He'd led her along on a leash, she admitted bitterly, rubbing a towel over her dripping hair while the heat lamp in the ceiling warmed her skin. Instead of balking, she'd gone obediently where he'd taken her. And had missed the most important interview of her career. Lee tossed down the towel and stalked out of the steamy bathroom.

Telling herself she felt nothing but annoyance for him and for herself, Lee pulled on a robe before she sat down at the small writing desk. She still had some time before room service would deliver her first cup of coffee, but there wasn't any more time to waste. Business first...and last. She pulled out a pad and pencil.

HUNTER BROWN. Lee headed the top of the pad in bold letters and underlined the name. The problem had been, she admitted, that she hadn't approached Hunter—the assignment—logically, systematically. She could correct that now with a basic outline. She had, after all, seen him, spoken to him, asked him a few elementary questions. As far as she knew, no other reporter could make such a claim. It was time to stop berating herself for not tying everything up neatly in a matter of hours and make the slim advantage she still had work for her. She began to write in a decisive hand.

APPEARANCE. Not typical. Now there was a positive statement, she thought with a frown. In three bold strokes, she crossed out the words. Dark; lean, rangy build, she wrote. Like a long-distance runner, a cross-country skier. Her eyes narrowed as she brought his face to the foreground of her memory. Rugged face, offset by an air of intelligence. Most outstanding feature—eyes. Very dark, very direct, very...unnerving.

Was that editorializing? she asked herself. Would those long, quiet stares disturb everyone? Shrugging the question away, Lee continued to write. Tall, perhaps six-one, approximately a hundred sixty pounds. Very confident. Musician's hands, poet's mouth.

A bit surprised by her own description, Lee went on to her next category.

PERSONALITY. Enigmatic. Not enough, she decided, huffing slightly. Arrogant, self-absorbed, rude. Definitely editorializing. She set down her pen and took a deep breath, then picked it up again. A skilled, mesmerizing speaker, she admitted in print. Perceptive, cool, taciturn and open by turns, physical.

The last word had been a mistake, Lee discovered, as it brought back the memory of that long, soft, draining kiss, the gentleness of the mouth, the firmness of his hands. No, that wasn't for publication, nor would she need notes to bring back all the details, all the sensations. She would, however, be wise to remember that he was a man who moved quickly when he chose, a man who apparently took precisely what he wanted.

Humor? Yes, under the intensity there was humor in him. She didn't like recalling how he'd laughed at her, but when she had such a dearth of material, she needed every detail, uncomfortable or not.

She remembered every word he'd said on his philosophy of writing. But how could she translate something so intangible into a few clean, pragmatic sentences? She could say he thought of his work as an obligation. A vocation. It just wasn't enough, she thought in frustration. She needed his own words here, not a translation of his meaning. The simple truth was, she had to speak to him again.

Dragging a hand through her hair, she read over her orderly notes. She should have held the reins of the conversation from the very beginning. If she was an expert on anything, it was on channeling and steering talk along the lines she wanted. She'd interviewed subjects more closemouthed than Hunter, more hostile, but she couldn't remember any more frustrating.

Absently, she began to tap the end of her pencil against the table. It wasn't her job to be frustrated, but to be productive. It wasn't her job, she added, to allow herself to be so utterly seduced by an assignment.

She could have prevented the kiss. It still wasn't clear to Lee why she hadn't. She could have controlled her response to it. She didn't want to dwell on why she hadn't. It was much too easy to remember that long, strangely intense moment and in remembering, to feel it all again. If she was going to prevent herself from doing that, and remember instead all the reasons she'd come to Flagstaff, she had to put Hunter Brown firmly in the category of assignment and keep him there. For now, her biggest problem was how she was going to manage to see him again.

Professionally, she warned herself. But she couldn't sit still thinking of it, or him. Pacing, she tried to block

out the incredibly gentle feel of his mouth on hers.
And failed.

A flood of feeling; she'd never experienced anything like it. The weakness, the power—it was beyond
her to understand it. The longing, the need—how
could she know the way to control it?

If she understood him better perhaps... No. Lee
lifted her hairbrush, then set it down again. No, understanding Hunter would have nothing to do with
fighting her desire for him. She'd wanted to be
touched by him, and though she had no logical reason
for it, she'd wanted to be touched more than she'd
wanted to do her job. It was unprecedented, Lee admitted as she absently pushed bottles and jars around
on her dresser. When something was unprecedented,
you had to make up your own guidelines.

Uneasy, she glanced up and saw a pale woman with
sleepy eyes and unruly hair reflected in the glass. She
looked too young, too...fragile. No one ever saw her
without the defensive shield of grooming, but she
knew what was beneath the fastidiousness and gloss.
Fear. Fear of failure.

She'd built her confidence stone by meticulous
stone, until most of the time she believed in it herself.
But at moments like this, when she was alone, a little
weary, a little discouraged, the woman inside crept
out, and with her, all the tiny doubts and fears behind
that laboriously built wall.

She'd been trained from birth to be little more than
an intelligent, attractive ornament. Well-spoken, well-
groomed, well-disciplined. It was all her family ex-

pected of her. No, Lee corrected. It was *what* had been expected of her. In that respect, she'd already failed.

What trick of fate had made it so impossible for her to fit the mold she'd been fashioned for? Since childhood she'd known she needed more, yet it had taken her until after college to store up enough courage to break away from the road that would have led her from proper debutante to proper matron.

When she'd told her parents she wasn't going to be Mrs. Jonathan T. Willoby, but was leaving Palm Springs to live and work in Los Angeles, she'd been quaking inside. Not until later did she realize it had been their training that had seen her through the very difficult meeting. She'd been taught to remain cool and composed, never to raise her voice, never to show any vulgar signs of temper. When she'd spoken to them, she'd seemed perfectly sure of her own mind, while in truth she'd been terrified of leaving that comfortable gilt cage they'd been fashioning for her since before she was born.

Five years later, the fear had dulled, but it remained. Part of her drive to reach the top in her profession came from the very basic need to prove herself to her parents.

Foolish, she told herself, turning away from the vulnerability of the woman in the glass. She had nothing to prove to anyone, unless it was to herself. She'd come for a story, and that was her first, her only priority. The story was going to gel for her if she had to dog Hunter Brown's footsteps like a bloodhound.

Lee looked down at her notebook again, and at the

notes that filled less than a page. She'd have more
before the day was over, she promised herself. Much
more. He wouldn't get the upper hand again, nor
would he distract her from her purpose. As soon as
she'd dressed and had her morning coffee, she'd look
for Hunter. This time, she'd stay firmly behind the
wheel.

When she heard the knock, Lee glanced at the clock
beside her bed and gave a little sigh of frustration.
She was running behind schedule, something she
never permitted herself to do. She'd deliberately re-
quested coffee and rolls for nine o'clock so that she
could be dressed and ready to go when they were delivered. Now she'd have to rush to make certain she
had a couple of solid hours with Hunter before check-
out time. She wasn't going to miss an opportunity
twice.

Impatient with herself, she went to the door, drew
off the chain and pulled it open.

"You might as well eat nothing if you think you
can subsist on a couple of pieces of bread and some
jam." Before she could recover, Hunter swooped by
her, carrying her breakfast tray. "And an intelligent
woman never answers the door without asking who's
on the other side." Setting the tray on the table, he
turned to pin her with one of his long, intrusive stares.

She looked younger without the gloss of makeup
and careful style. The traces of fragility he'd already
sensed had no patina of sophistication over them now,
though her robe was silk and the sapphire color flattering. He felt a flare of desire and a simultaneous

protective twinge. Neither could completely deaden his anger.

She wasn't about to let him know how stunned she was to see him, or how disturbed she was that he was here alone with her when she was all but naked. "First a chauffeur, now a waiter," she said coolly, unsmiling. "You're a man of many talents, Hunter."

"I could return the compliment." Because he knew just how volatile his temper could be, he poured a cup of coffee. "Since one of the first requirements of a fiction writer is that he be a good liar, you're well on your way." He gestured to a chair, putting Lee uncomfortably in the position of visitor. As though she weren't the least concerned, she crossed the room and seated herself at the table.

"I'd ask you to join me, but there's only one cup." She broke a croissant in two and nibbled on it, unbuttered. "You're welcome to a roll." With a steady hand, she added cream to the coffee. "Perhaps you'd like to explain what you mean about my being a good liar."

"I suppose it's a requirement of a reporter as well." Hunter saw her fingers tense on the flaky bit of bread then relax, one by one.

"No." Lee took another bite of her roll as if her stomach hadn't just sunk to her knees. "Reporters deal in fact, not fiction." He said nothing, but the silent look demanded more of her than a dozen words would have. Taking her time, determined not to fumble again, she sipped at her coffee. "I don't remember mentioning that I was a reporter."

"No, you didn't mention it." He caught her wrist as she set down the cup. The grip of his fingers told her immediately just how angry he was. "You quite deliberately didn't mention it."

With a jerk of her head, she tossed the hair out of her eyes. If she'd lost, she wouldn't go down groveling. "It wasn't required that I tell you." Ignoring the fact that he held one of her hands prisoner, Lee picked up her croissant with the other and took a bite. "I paid my registration fee."

"And pretended to be something you're not."

She met his gaze without flinching. "Apparently, we both pretended to be something we weren't, right from the start."

He tilted his head at her reference to their initial meeting. "I didn't want anything from you. You, on the other hand, went beyond the harmless in your deception."

She didn't like the way it sounded when he said it—so petty, so dirty. And so true. If his fingers hadn't been biting into her wrist, she might have found herself apologizing. Instead, Lee held her ground. "I have a perfect right to be here and a perfect right to try to sell an article on any facet of this conference."

"And I," he said, so mildly her flesh chilled, "have a perfect right to my privacy, to the choice of speaking to a reporter or refusing to speak to one."

"If I'd told you that I was on staff at *Celebrity*," she threw back, making her first attempt to free her arm, "would you have spoken to me at all?"

He still held her wrist; he still held her eyes. For

several long seconds, he said nothing. "That's something neither of us will ever know now." He released her wrist so abruptly, her arm dropped to the table, clattering the cup. Lee found that she'd squeezed the flaky pastry into an unpalatable ball.

He frightened her. There was no use denying it even to herself. The force of his anger, so finely restrained, had tiny shocks of cold moving up and down her back. She didn't know him or understand him, nor did she have any way of being certain of what he might do. There was violence in his books; therefore, there was violence in his mind. Clinging to her composure, she lifted her coffee again, drank and tasted absolutely nothing.

"I'm curious to know how you found out." Good, her voice was calm, unhurried. She took the cup in both hands to cover the one quick tremor she couldn't control.

She looked like a kitten backed into a corner, Hunter observed. Ready to spit and scratch, even though her heart was pounding hard enough to be almost audible. He didn't want to respect her for it when he'd rather strangle her. He didn't want to feel a strong urge to touch the pale skin of her cheek. Being deceived by a woman was perhaps the only thing that still had the power to bring him to this degree of rage.

"Oddly enough, I took an interest in you, Lenore. Last night—" He saw her stiffen and felt a certain satisfaction. No, he wasn't going to let her forget that, any more than he could forget it himself. "Last night," he repeated slowly, waiting until her gaze lifted to his again, "I wanted to make love with you. I wanted to get beneath the careful layer of polish and discover you. When I had, you'd have looked as you do now. Soft, fragile, with your mouth naked and your eyes clouded."

Her bones were already melting, her skin already heating, and it was only words. He didn't touch her, didn't attempt to, but the sound of his voice flowed over her skin like the gentlest of caresses. "I don't—I had no intention of letting you make love to me."

"I don't believe in making love to a woman, only with." His eyes never left hers. She could feel her head begin to swim with passion, her breath tremble with it. "Only with," Hunter repeated. "When you left, I turned to the next best way of discovering you."

Lee gripped her hands together in her lap, knowing she had to control the shudders. How could a man have such power? And how could she fight it? Why did she feel as though they were already lovers, was it just the sense of inevitability that they would be, no matter what her choice? "I don't know what you mean." Her voice was no longer calm.

"Your manuscript."

Uncomprehending, she stared. She'd completely forgotten it the night before in her fear of him, and of herself. Anger and frustration had prevented her from remembering it that morning. Now, on top of a dazed desire, she felt the helplessness of a novice confronted by the master. "I never intended for you to read it," she began. Without thinking, she was shredding her napkin in her lap. "I don't have any aspirations toward being a novelist."

"Then you're a fool as well as a liar."

All sense of helplessness fled. No one, no one in all of her memory, had ever spoken to her like that. "I'm neither a fool nor a liar, Hunter. What I am is an excellent reporter. I want to write an exclusive, indepth and accurate article on you for our readers."

"Why do you waste your time writing gossip when you've got a novel to finish?"

She went rigid. The eyes that had been clouded with confused desire became frosty. "I don't write gossip."

"You can gloss over it, you can write it with style and intelligence, but it's still gossip." Before Lee could retort, he rose up so quickly, so furiously, her own words were swallowed. "You've no right working forty hours a week on anything but the novel you have inside you. Talent's a two-headed coin, Lenore, and the other side's obligation."

"I don't know what you're talking about." She rose, too, and found she could shout just as effectively as he. "I know my obligations, and one of them's to write a story on you for my magazine."

"And what about the novel?"

Flinging up her hands, she whirled away from him. "What about it?"

"When do you intend to finish it?"

Finish it? She should never have started it. Hadn't she told herself that a dozen times? "Damn it, Hunter, it's a pipe dream."

"It's good."

She turned back, her brows still drawn together with anger but the eyes beneath them suddenly wary. "What?"

"If it hadn't been, your camouflage would have worked very well." He drew out a cigarette while she stared at him. How could he be so patient, move so slowly, when she was ready to jump at every word? "I nearly called you last night to see if you had any more with you, but decided it would keep. I called my editor instead." Still calm, he blew out smoke. "When I gave the chapters to her to read, she recognized your name. Apparently she's quite a fan of *Celebrity*."

"You gave her..." Astonished, Lee dropped into the chair again. "You had no right to show anyone."

"At the time, I fully believed you were precisely what you'd led me to believe you were."

She stood again, then gripped the back of her chair. "I'm a reporter, not a novelist. I'd like you to get the manuscript from her and return it to me."

He tapped his cigarette in an ashtray, only then noticing her neatly written notes. As he skimmed them, Hunter felt twin surges of amusement and annoyance. So, she was trying to put him into a few tidy little slots. She'd find it more difficult than she'd imagined. "Why should I do that?"

"Because it belongs to me. You had no right to give it to anyone else."

"What are you afraid of?" he demanded.

Of failure. The words were almost out before Lee

managed to bite them back. "I'm not afraid of anything. I do what I'm best at, and I intend to continue doing it. What are you afraid of?" she retorted. "What are you hiding from?"

She didn't like the look in his eyes when he turned his head toward her again. It wasn't anger she saw there, nor was it arrogance, but something beyond both. "I do what I do best, Lenore." When he'd come into the room, he hadn't planned to do any more than rake her to the bone for her deception and berate her for wasting her talent. Now, as he watched her, Hunter began to think there was a better way to do that and at the same time learn more about her for his own purposes. He was a long way from finished with Lenore Radcliffe. "Just how important is doing a story on me to you?"

Alerted by the change in tone, Lee studied him cautiously. She'd tried everything else, she decided abruptly, perhaps she could appeal to his ego. "It's very important. I've been trying to learn something about you for over three months. You're one of the most popular and critically acclaimed writers of the decade. If you—"

He cut her off by merely lifting a hand. "If I decided to give you an interview, we'd have to spend a great deal of time together, and under my terms."

Lee heard the little warning bell, but ignored it. She could almost taste success. "We can hash out the terms beforehand. I keep my word, Hunter."

"I don't doubt that, once it's given." Crushing out his cigarette, Hunter considered the angles. Perhaps he was asking for trouble. Then again, he hadn't asked for any in quite some time. He was due. "How much more of the manuscript do you have completed?"

"That has nothing to do with this." When he merely lifted a brow and stared, she clenched her teeth. Humor him, Lee told herself. You're too close now. "About two hundred pages."

"Send the rest to my editor." He gave her a mild look. "I'm sure you have her name by now."

"What does that have to do with the interview?"

"It's one of the terms," Hunter told her easily. "I've plans for the week after next," he continued. "You can join me—with another copy of your manuscript."

"Join you? Where?"

"For two weeks I'll be camping in Oak Creek Canyon. You'd better buy some sturdy shoes."

"Camping?" She had visions of tents and mosquitoes. "If you're not leaving for your vacation right away, why can't we set up the interview a day or two before?"

"Terms," he reminded her. "My terms."

"You're trying to make this difficult."

"Yes." He smiled then, just a hint of amusement around his sculpted mouth. "You'll work for your exclusive, Lenore."

"All right." Her chin came up. "Where should I meet you and when?"

Now he smiled fully, appreciating determination when he saw it. "In Sedona. I'll contact you when

I'm certain of the date—and when my editor's let me know she's received the rest of your manuscript.''

"I hardly see why you're using that to blackmail me.''

He crossed to her then, unexpectedly combing his fingers through her hair. It was casual, friendly and uncannily intimate. ''Perhaps one of the first things you should know about me is I'm eccentric. If people accept their own eccentricities, they can justify anything they do. Anything at all.'' He ended the words by closing his mouth over hers.

He heard her suck in her breath, felt her stiffen. But she didn't struggle away. Perhaps she was testing herself, though he didn't think she could know she tested him, too. He wanted to carry her to the rumpled bed, slip off that thin swirl of silk and fit his body to hers. It would fit; somehow he already knew. She'd move with him, for him, as if they'd always been lovers. He knew, though he couldn't explain.

He could feel her melting into him, her lips growing warm and moist from his. They were alone and the need was like iron. Yet he knew, without understanding, that if they made love now, sated that need, he'd never see her again. They both had fears to face before they became lovers, and after.

Hunter gave himself the pleasure of one long, last kiss, drawing her taste into him, allowing himself to be overwhelmed, just for a moment, by the feel of her against him. Then he forced himself to level, forced himself to remember that they each wanted something from the other—secrets and an intimacy both would put into words in their own ways.

Drawing back, he let his hands linger only a moment on the curve of her cheek, the softness of her hair, while she said nothing. "If you can get through two weeks in the canyon, you'll have your story."

Leaving her with that, he turned and strolled out the door.

"If I can make it through two weeks," Lee muttered, pulling a heavy sweater out of her drawer. "I tell you, Bryan, I've never met anyone who says as little who can irritate me as much." Ten days back in L.A. hadn't dulled her fury.

Bryan fingered the soft wool of the sweater. "Lee, don't you have *any* grub-around clothes?"

"I bought some sweatshirts," she said under her breath. "I haven't spent a great deal of my time in a tent."

"Advice." Before another pair of the trim slacks could be packed into the knapsack Lee had borrowed from her, Bryan took her hand.

Lee lifted one thin coppery brow. "You know I detest advice."

Grinning, Bryan dropped down on the bed. "I know. That's why I can never resist dishing it out. Lee, really, I know you have a pair of jeans. I've *seen* you wear them." She brushed at the hair that escaped her braid. "Designer or not, take jeans, not seventy-five-dollar slacks. Invest in another pair or two," she went on while Lee frowned down at the clothes still in her free hand. "Put that gorgeous wool sweater back in your drawer and pick up a couple of flannel shirts. That'll take care of the nights if it turns cool. Now..."

Because Lee was listening with a frown of concentration, she continued. "Put in some T-shirts; blouses are for the office, not for hiking. Take at least one pair of shorts and invest in some good thick socks. If you had more time, I'd tell you to break in those new hiking boots, because they're going to make you suffer."

"The salesman said—"

"There's nothing wrong with them, Lee, except they've never been out of the box. Face it—" She stretched back among Lee's collection of pillows. "You've been too concerned about packing enough paper and pencils to worry about gear. If you don't want to make an ass of yourself, listen to momma."

With a quick hiss of breath, Lee replaced the sweater. "I've already made an ass of myself, several times." She slammed one of her dresser drawers. "He's not going to get the best of me during these next two weeks, Bryan. If I have to sleep out in a tent and climb rocks to get this story, then I'll do it."

"If you tried real hard, you could have fun at the same time."

"I'm not looking for fun. I'm looking for an exclusive."

"We're friends."

Though it was a statement, not a question, Lee

glanced over. "Yes." For the first time since she'd begun packing, she smiled. "We're friends."

"Then tell me what it is that bothers you about this guy. You've been ready to chew your nails for over a week." Though she spoke lightly, the concern leaked through. "You wanted to interview Hunter Brown, and you're going to interview Hunter Brown. How come you look like you're preparing for war?"

"Because that's how I feel." With anyone else, Lee would have evaded the question or turned cold. Because it was Bryan, she sat on the edge of the bed, twisting a newly purchased sweatshirt in her hands. "He makes me want what I don't want to want, feel what I don't want to feel. Bryan, I don't have room in my life for complications."

"Who does?"

"I know exactly where I'm going," Lee insisted, a bit too vehemently. "I know exactly how to get there. Somehow I have a feeling that Hunter's a detour."

"Sometimes a detour is more interesting than a planned route, and you get to the same place eventually."

"He looks at me as though he knows what I'm thinking. More, as if he knows what I thought yesterday, or last year. It's not comfortable."

"You've never looked for the comfortable," Bryan stated, pillowing her head on her folded arms. "You've always looked for a challenge. You've just never found one in a man before."

"I don't want one in a man." Violently, Lee stuffed

the sweatshirt into the knapsack. "I want them in my work."

"You don't have to go."

Lee lifted her head. "I'm going."

"Then don't go with your teeth gritted." Crossing her legs under her, Bryan sat up. She was as rumpled as Lee was tidy but seemed oddly suited to the luxurious pile of pillows around her. "This is a tremendous opportunity for you, professionally and personally. Oak Creek's one of the most beautiful canyons in the country. You'll have two weeks to be part of it. There's a man who doesn't bore or cater to you." She grinned at Lee's arch look. "You know damn well they do one or the other and you can't abide it. Enjoy the change of scene."

"I'm going to work," Lee reminded her. "Not to pick wildflowers."

"Pick a few anyway; you'll still get your story."

"And make Hunter Brown squirm."

Bryan gave her throaty laugh, tossing a pillow into the air. "If that's what you're set on doing, you'll do it. I'd feel sorry for the guy if he hadn't given me nightmares." After a quick grimace, her look softened into one of affection. "And Lee..." She laid her hand over her friend's. "If he makes you want something, take it. Life isn't crowded with offers. Give yourself a present."

Lee sat silently for a moment, then sighed. "I'm not sure if I'd be giving myself a present or a curse." Rising, she went to her dresser. "How many pairs of socks?"

* * *

"But is she pretty?" Sarah sat in the middle of the rug, one leg bent toward her while she tried valiantly to hook the other behind her neck. "*Really* pretty?"

Hunter dug into the basket of laundry. Sarah had scrupulously reminded him it was his turn to sort and fold. "I wouldn't use the word *pretty*. A carefully arranged basket of fruit's pretty."

Sarah giggled, then rolled and arched into a back bend. She liked nothing better than talking with her father, because no one else talked like him. "What word would you use then?"

Hunter folded a T-shirt with the name of a popular rock band glittered across it. "She has a rare, classic beauty that a lot of women wouldn't know precisely what to do with."

"But she does?"

He remembered. He wanted. "She does."

Sarah laid down on her back to snuggle with the dog that stretched out beside her. She liked the soft, warm feel of Santanas's fur, in much the same way she liked to close her eyes and listen to her father's voice. "She tried to fool you," Sarah reminded him. "You don't like it when people try to fool you."

"To her way of thinking, she was doing her job."

With one hand on the dog's neck, Sarah looked up at her father with big, dark eyes so much like his own. "You never talk to reporters."

"They don't interest me." Hunter came upon a pair of jeans with a widening hole in the knee. "Aren't these new?"

"Sort of. So why are you taking her camping with you?"

"Sort of new shouldn't have holes already, and I'm not taking her; she's coming with me."

Digging in her pocket, she came up with a stick of gum. She wasn't supposed to chew any because of her braces, so she fondled the wrapped piece instead. In six months, Sarah thought, she was going to chew a dozen pieces, all at once. "Because she's a reporter or because she has a rare, classic beauty?"

Hunter glanced down to see his daughter's eyes laughing at him. She was entirely too clever, he decided, and threw a pair of rolled socks at her. "Both, but mostly because I find her interesting and talented. I want to see how much I can find out about her, while she's trying to find out about me."

"You'll find out more," Sarah declared, idly tossing the socks up in the air. "You always do. I think it's a good idea," she added after a moment. "Aunt Bonnie says you don't see enough women, especially women who challenge your mind."

"Aunt Bonnie thinks in couples."

"Maybe she'll incite your simmering passion."

Hunter's hand paused on its way to the basket. "What?"

"I read it in a book." Expertly, she rolled so that her feet touched the floor behind her head. "This man met this woman, and they didn't like each other at first, but there was this strong physical attraction and this growing desire, and—"

"I get the picture." Hunter looked down at the

slim, dark-haired girl on the floor. She was his daughter, he thought. She was ten. How in God's name had they gotten involved in the subject of passion? "You of all people should know that things don't often happen in real life the way they do in books."

"Fiction's based on reality." Sarah grinned, pleased to throw one of his own quotes back at him. "But before you do fall in love with her, or have too much simmering passion, I want to meet her."

"I'll keep that in mind." Still watching her, Hunter held up three unmatched socks. "Just how does this happen every week?"

Sarah considered the socks a moment, then sat up. "I think there's a parallel universe in the dryer. On the other side of the door, at this very minute, someone else is holding up three unmatched socks."

"An interesting theory." Reaching down, Hunter grabbed her. As Sarah's laughter bounced off the lofted ceiling, he dropped her, bottom first, into the basket.

Chapter 5

It was like every western she'd ever seen. With the sun bright in her eyes, Lee could almost see outlaws outrunning posses and Indians hiding in wait behind rocks and buttes. If she let her imagination go, she could almost hear the hoofbeats ring against the rock-hard ground. Because she was alone in the car, she could let her imagination go.

The rich red mountains rose up into a painfully blue sky. There was a vastness that was almost outrageous in scope, with no lushness, with no need for any, with no patience for any. It made her throat dry and her heart thud.

There was green—the silvery green of sage clinging to the red, rocky soil and the deeper hue of junipers, which would give way to a sudden, seemingly planned sparseness. Yet the sparseness was rich in itself. The

space, the overwhelming space, left her stunned and
humble and oddly hungry for more. Everywhere there
were more rocky ridges, more color, more... Lee
shook her head. Just more.

Even when she came closer to town, the houses and
buildings couldn't compete with the openness. Stop
signs, streetlights, flower gardens, were inconsequential. Her car joined more cars, but five times the number would still have been insignificant. It was a view
you drank in, she thought, but its taste was hot and
packed a punch.

She liked Sedona immediately. Its tidy western flavor suited the fabulous backdrop instead of marring
it. She hadn't been sure anything could.

The main street was lined with shops with neat
signs and clean plate glass. She noticed lots of wood,
lots of bargains and absolutely no sense of urgency.
Sedona clung to the aura of town rather than city. It
seemed comfortable with itself and with the spectac-
ular spread of sky. Perhaps, Lee mused as she followed the directions to the rental-car drop-off, just
perhaps, she'd enjoy the next two weeks after all.

Since she was early for her arranged meeting time
with Hunter even after dealing with the paperwork on
her rental car, Lee decided she could afford to indulge
herself playing tourist. She had nearly an hour to vacation before work began again.

The liquid silver necklaces and turquoise earrings
in the shop windows tempted her, but she moved past
them. There'd be plenty of opportunities after this lit-

tle adventure for something frivolous—as a reward for success. For now, she was only passing time.

But the scent of fudge drew her. Slipping inside the little shop that claimed to sell the world's best, Lee bought a half pound. For energy, she told herself as the sample melted in her mouth. There was no telling what kind of food she'd get over the next two weeks. Hunter had very specifically told her when he contacted her by phone that he'd handle the supplies. The fudge, Lee told herself, would be emergency rations.

Besides, some of Bryan's advice had been valid enough. There was no use going into this thing thinking she'd be miserable and uncomfortable. There wasn't any harm getting into the spirit a bit, Lee decided as she strolled into a western-wear shop. If she viewed the next two weeks as a working vacation, she'd be much better off.

Though she toyed with conch belts for a few minutes, Lee rejected them. They wouldn't suit her, any more than the fringed or sequined shirts would. Perhaps she'd pick one up for Bryan before heading back to L.A. Anything Bryan put on suited her, Lee mused with something closer to a sigh than to envy. Bryan never had to feel restricted to the tailored, the simple or the proper.

Was it a matter of suitability, Lee wondered, or a matter of image? With a shrug, she ran a fingertip down the shoulder of a short suede jacket. Image or not, she'd locked herself into it for too long to change now. She didn't want to change, in any case, Lee reminded herself as she wandered through rows and rows of hats. She understood Lee Radcliffe just as she was.

Telling herself she'd stay only another minute, she set her knapsack at her feet. She wasn't particularly athletic. Lee tried on a dung-colored Stetson with a curved brim. She wasn't flighty. She exchanged the first hat for a smaller one with a spray of feathers in the band. What she was, was businesslike and down-to-earth. She dropped a black flat-brimmed hat on her head and studied the result. Sedate, she decided, smiling a little. Practical. Yes, if she were in the market for—

"You're wearing it all wrong."

Before Lee could react, two strong hands were tilting the hat farther down on her head. Critically, Hunter angled it slightly, then stepped away. "Yes, it's the perfect choice for you. The contrast with your hair and skin, that practical sort of dash." Taking her shoulders, her turned her toward the mirror, where both his image and hers looked back at her.

She saw the way his fingers held her shoulders, long and confident. She could see how small she looked pressing against him. In no more than an instant, Lee could feel the pleasure she wanted to ignore and the annoyance she had to concentrate on.

"I've no intention of buying it." Embarrassed, she drew the hat off and returned it to the shelf.

"Why not?"

"I've no need for it."

"A woman who buys only what she needs?" Amusement crossed his face even as anger crossed hers. "A sexist remark if I've ever heard one," Hunter continued before she could speak. "Still, it's a pity you won't buy it. It gives you a breezy air of confidence."

Ignoring that, Lee bent down and picked up her knapsack again. "I hope I haven't kept you waiting long. I got into town early and decided to kill some time."

"I saw you wander in here when I drove in. Even in jeans you walk as though you were wearing a three-piece suit." While she tried to work out if that had been a compliment, he smiled. "What kind did you buy?"

"What?" She was still frowning over his comment.

"Fudge." He glanced down at the bag. "What kind did you buy?"

Caught again, Lee thought, nearly resigned to it. "Some milk chocolate and some rocky road."

"Good choice." Taking her arm, he led her through the shop. "If you're determined to resist the hat, we may as well get started."

She noted the Jeep parked at the curb and narrowed her eyes. This was certainly the same one he'd had in Flagstaff. "Have you been staying in Arizona?"

He circled the hood, leaving her to climb in on her own. "I've had some business to take care of."

Her reporter's sense sharpened. "Research?"

He gave her that odd ghost of a smile. "A writer's always researching." He wouldn't tell her—yet—that his research on Lenore Radcliffe had led him to some intriguing conclusions. "You brought a copy of the rest of your manuscript?"

Unable to prevent herself, Lee shot him a look of intense dislike. "That was one of the conditions."

"So it was." Easily he backed up, then pulled into the thin stream of traffic. "What's your impression of Sedona?"

"I can see that the weather and the atmosphere would draw the tourist trade." She found it necessary to sit very erect and to look straight ahead.

"The same might be said of Maui or the South of France."

She couldn't stop her lips from curving, but turned to look out the side window. "It has the air of having been here forever, with very little change. The sense of space is fierce, not at all soothing, but it pulls you in. I suppose it makes me think of the people who first saw it from horseback or the seat of a wagon. I imagine some of them would have been compelled to build right away, to set up a community so that the vastness didn't overwhelm them."

"And others would have been drawn to the desert or the mountains so that the buildings wouldn't close them in."

As she nodded, it occurred to her that she might fit into the first group, and he into the second.

The road he took narrowed and twisted down. He didn't drive sedately, but with the air of a man who knew he could negotiate whatever curve was thrown at him. Lee gripped the door handle, determined not to comment on his speed. It was like taking the downhill rush of a roller coaster without having had the preparatory uphill climb. They whooshed down, a rock wall on one side, a spiraling drop on the other.

"Do you camp often?" Her knuckles were whitening on the handle, but though she had to shout to be heard she was satisfied that her voice was calm enough.

"Now and again."

"I'm curious..." She stopped and cleared her throat as Hunter whipped around a snaking turn. "Why camping?" Did the rocks in the sheer wall beside them ever loosen and tumble onto the road? She decided it was best not to think about it. "A man in your position could go anywhere and do anything he chose."

"This is what I chose," he pointed out.

"All right. Why?"

"There are times when everyone needs simplicity."

Her foot pressed down on the floorboard as if it were a brake pedal. "Isn't this just one more way you have of avoiding people?"

"Yes." His easy agreement had her turning her head to stare at him. He was amused to note that her hand loosened on the handle and that her concentration was on him now rather than the road. "It's also a way of getting away from my work. You never get away from writing, but there are times you need to get away from the trappings of writing."

Her gaze sharpened. Though her fingers itched for

her notebook, Lee had faith in her own powers of retention. "You don't like trappings."

"We don't always like what's necessary."

Oblivious to the speed and the curves now, Lee tucked one leg under her and turned toward him. That attracted him, Hunter reflected. The way she'd unconsciously drop that careful shield whenever something challenged her mind. That attracted him every bit as much as her cool, nineteenth-century beauty.

"What do you consider trappings as regards your profession?"

"The confinement of an office, the hum of a machine, the paperwork that's unavoidable but interferes with the story flow."

Odd, but that was precisely what she needed in order to maintain discipline. "If you could change it, what would you do?"

He smiled again. Hunter had never known anyone who thought in more basic terms or straighter lines. "I'd go back a few centuries to when I could simply travel and tell the story."

She believed him. Though he had wealth and fame and critical acclaim, Lee believed him. "None of the rest means anything to you, does it? The glory, the admiration?"

"Whose admiration?"

"Your readers and the critics."

He pulled off the road next to a small wooden building that served as a trading post. "I'm not indifferent to my readership, Lenore."

"But to the critics."

"I admire the orderliness of your mind," he said and stepped from the Jeep.

It was a good beginning, Lee thought, pleased, as she climbed out the passenger side. He'd already told her more than anyone else knew, and the two weeks had barely begun. If she could just keep him talking, learn enough generalities, then she could pin him down on specifics. But she'd have to pace herself. When you were dealing with a master of evasion, you had to tread carefully. She couldn't afford to relax.

"Do we have to check in?"

From behind her back Hunter grinned, while Lee struggled to pull out her knapsack. "I've already taken care of the paperwork."

"I see." Her pack was heavy, but she told herself she'd refuse any offer of assistance and carry it herself. A moment later, she saw it wouldn't be an issue. Hunter merely stood aside, watching as she wriggled into the shoulder straps. So much for chivalry, she thought, annoyed that he hadn't given her the opportunity to assert her independence. She caught the gleam in his eye. He read her mind much too easily.

"Want me to carry the fudge?"

She closed her fingers firmly over the bag. "I'll manage."

With his own gear on his back, Hunter started down a path, leaving her no choice but to follow. He moved as though he'd been walking dirt paths all his life—as if perhaps he'd cut a few of his own. Though she felt out of place in her hiking boots, Lee was determined to keep up and to make it look easy.

"You've camped here before?"

"Mmm-hmm."

"Why?"

He stopped, turning to fix her with that dark, intense stare that always took her breath away. "You only have to look."

She did and saw that the walls and peaks of the canyon rose up as if they'd never stop. They were a color and texture unique to themselves, enhanced by the snatches of green from rough, hardy trees and shrubs that seemed to grow out of the rock. As she had from the air, Lee thought of castles and fortresses, but without the distance the plane had given her, she couldn't be sure whether she was storming the walls or being enveloped by them.

She was warm. The sun was strong, even with the shade of trees that grew thickly at this elevation. Though she saw other people—children, adults, babies carried papoose-style—she felt no sense of crowding.

It's like a painting, she realized all at once. It's as though we're walking into a canvas. The feeling it gave her was both eerie and irresistible. She shifted the pack on her back as she kept pace with Hunter.

"I noticed some houses," she began. "I didn't realize people actually lived in the canyon."

"Apparently."

Sensing his mind was elsewhere, Lee lapsed into silence. She'd done too well to start pushing. For now, she'd follow Hunter, since he obviously knew where he was going.

It surprised her that she found the walk pleasant.

For years her life had been directed by deadlines, rush and self-imposed demands. If someone had asked her where she'd choose to spend two weeks relaxing, her mind would have gone blank. But when ideas had begun to come, roughing it in a canyon in Arizona wouldn't have made the top ten. She'd never have considered that the purity of air and the unimpeded arch of sky would be so appealing to her.

She heard a quiet, musical tinkle that took her several moments to identify. The creek, Lee realized. She could smell the water. The new sensation gave her a quick thrill. Her guide, and her project, continued to move at a steady pace in front of her. Lee banked down the urge to share her discovery with him. He'd only think her foolish.

Did she realize how totally out of her element she looked? Hunter wondered. It had taken him only one glance to see that the jeans and the boots she wore were straight out of the box. Even the T-shirt that fit softly over her torso was obviously boutiqueware rather than a department-store purchase. She looked like a model posing as a camper. She smelled expensive, exclusive. Wonderful. What kind of woman carried a worn knapsack and wore sapphire studs in her ears?

As her scent wafted toward him again, carried on the breeze, Hunter reminded himself that he had two weeks to find out. Whatever notes she would make on him, he'd be making an equal number on her. Perhaps both of them would have what they wanted before the time was up. Perhaps both of them would have cause to regret it.

He wanted her. It had been a long time since he'd wanted anything, anyone, that he didn't already have. Over the past days he'd thought often of her response to that long, lingering kiss. He'd thought of his own response. They'd learn about each other over the next two weeks, though they each had their own purposes. But nothing was free. They'd both pay for it.

The quiet soothed him. The towering walls of the canyon soothed him. Lee saw their ferocity, he their tranquillity. Perhaps they both saw what they needed to see.

"For a woman, and a reporter, you have an amazing capacity for silence."

The weight of her pack was beginning to take precedence over the novelty of the scenery. Not once had he asked if she wanted to stop and rest, not once had he even bothered to look back to see if she was still behind him. She wondered why he didn't feel the hole her eyes were boring into his back.

"You have an amazing capacity for the insulting compliment."

Hunter turned to look at her for the first time since they'd started out. There was a thin sheen of perspiration on her brow and her breath came quickly. It didn't detract an iota from her cool, innate beauty. "Sorry," he said, but didn't appear to be. "Have I been walking too fast? You don't look out of shape."

Despite the ache that ran down the length of her

back, Lee straightened. "I'm *not* out of shape." Her feet were killing her.

"The site's not much farther." Reaching down to his hip, he lifted the canteen and unscrewed the top. "It's perfect weather for hiking," he said mildly. "Mid-seventies, and there's a breeze."

Lee managed to suppress a scowl as she eyed the canteen. "Don't you have a cup?"

It took Hunter a moment to realize she was perfectly serious. Wisely, he decided to swallow the chuckle. "Packed away with the china," he told her soberly enough.

"I'll wait." She hooked her hands in the front straps of her knapsack to ease some of the weight.

"Suit yourself." While Lee looked on, Hunter drank deeply. If he sensed her resentment, he gave no sign as he capped the canteen again and resumed the walk.

Her throat was all the drier at the thought of water. He'd done it on purpose, she thought while she gritted her teeth. Did he think she'd missed that quick flash of humor in his eyes? It was just one more thing to pay him back for when the time came. Oh, she couldn't wait to write the article and expose Hunter Brown for the arrogant, coldhearted demigod he'd set himself up to be.

She wouldn't be surprised if he was walking her in circles, just to make her suffer. Bryan had been all too right about the boots. Lee had lost count of the number of campsites they'd passed, some occupied and some empty. If this was his way of punishing her for not revealing from the start that she worked for *Celebrity*, he was certainly doing an elaborate job.

Disgusted, exhausted, with her legs feeling less like flesh and more like rubber, she reached out and grabbed his arm. "Just why, when you obviously have a dislike for women and for reporters, did you agree to spend two weeks with me?"

"Dislike women?" His brows arched. "My likes and dislikes aren't as generalized as that, Lenore." Her skin was warm and slightly damp when he curled his fingers around the back of her neck. "Have I given you the impression I dislike you?"

She had to fight the urge to stretch like a cat under his hand. "I don't care what your personal feelings are toward me. This is business."

"For you." His fingers squeezed gently, bringing her an inch closer. "I'm on vacation. Do you know, your mouth's every bit as appealing now as it was the first time I saw it."

"I don't want to appeal to you." But her voice was breathy. "I want you to think of me only as a reporter."

The smile hovered at the edges of his mouth, around the corners of his eyes. "All right," he agreed. "In a minute."

Then he touched his lips to hers, as gently as he had the first time, and as devastatingly. She stood still, amazed to feel as intense a swirl of sensation as she had before. When he touched her, hardly touching her, it was as if she'd never been kissed before. A new discovery, a fresh beginning—how could it be?

The weight on her back seemed to vanish. The ache in her muscles turned into a deeper, richer ache that penetrated to the bone. Her lips parted, though she knew what she invited. Then his tongue joined with hers, slipping into the moistness, drinking up her flavor.

Lee felt the urgency scream through her body, but he was patient. So patient, she couldn't know what the patience cost him. He hadn't expected pain. No woman had ever brought him pain with desire. He hadn't expected the need to flame through him like brushfire, fast and out of control. Hunter had a vision, with perfect clarity, of what it would be like to take her there, on the ground, under the blazing sun with the canyon circling like castle walls around them and the sky like a cathedral dome.

But there was too much fear in her. He could sense it. Perhaps there was too much fear in him. When they came together, it might have the power to topple both their worlds.

"Your lips melt against mine, Lenore," he whispered. "It's all but impossible to resist."

She drew back, aroused, alarmed and all too aware of how helpless she'd been. "I don't want to repeat myself, Hunter," she managed. "And I don't want to amuse you with clichés, but this is business. I'm a reporter on assignment. If we're to make it through the next two weeks peacefully, it'd be wise to remember that."

"I don't know about the peace," he countered, "but we'll try your rules first."

Suspicious, but finding no room to argue, Lee followed him again. They walked out of the sunlight into the dim coolness of a stand of trees. The creek was distant but still audible. From somewhere to the left came the tinny sound of music from a portable radio. Closer at hand was the rustling of small animals. With a nervous look around, Lee convinced herself they were nothing more than squirrels and rabbits.

With the trees closing around them, they might have been anywhere. The sun filtered through, but softly, on the rough, uneven ground. There was a clearing, small and snug, with a circle of stones surrounding a long-dead campfire. Lee glanced around, fighting off the uneasiness. Somehow, she hadn't thought it would be this remote, this quiet, this...alone.

"There're shower and bathroom facilities a few hundred yards east," Hunter began as he slipped off his pack. "Primitive but adequate. The metal can's for trash. Be sure the lid's tightly closed or it'll attract animals. How's your sense of direction?"

Gratefully, she slipped out of her own pack and let it drop. "It's fine." Now, if she could just take off the boots and rest her feet.

"Good. Then you can gather some firewood while I set up the tent."

Annoyed with the order, she opened her mouth, then firmly shut it again with only a slight hiss. He wouldn't have any cause to complain about her. But as she started to stalk off, the rest of his sentence hit home.

"What do you mean *the* tent?"

He was already unfastening the straps of his pack. "I prefer sleeping in something in case it rains."

"*The* tent," Lee repeated, closing in on him. "As in singular?"

He didn't even spare her a look. "One tent, two sleeping bags."

She wasn't going to explode; she wasn't going to make a scene. After taking a deep breath, she spoke precisely. "I don't consider those adequate arrangements."

He didn't speak for a minute, not because he was choosing his words but because the unpacking occupied him more than the conversation. "If you want to sleep in the open, it's up to you." Hunter drew out a slim, folded piece of material that looked more like a bedsheet than a tent. "But when we decide to become lovers, the arrangements won't make any difference."

"We didn't come here to be lovers," Lee snapped back furiously.

"A reporter and an assignment," Hunter replied mildly. "Two sexless terms. They shouldn't have any problem sharing a tent."

Caught in her own logic, Lee turned and stalked away. She wouldn't give him the satisfaction of seeing her behave like a woman.

Hunter lifted his head and watched her storm off through the trees. She'd make the first move, he promised himself, suddenly angry. By God, he wouldn't touch her until she came to him.

While he set up camp, he tried to convince himself it was as easy as it sounded.

Chapter 6

Two sexless terms, Lee repeated silently as she scooped up some twigs. Bastard, she thought with grim satisfaction, was also a sexless term. It suited Hunter Brown to perfection. He had no business treating her like a fool just because she'd made a fool of herself already.

She wasn't going to give an inch. She'd sleep in the damn sleeping bag in the damn tent for the next thirteen nights without saying another word about it.

Thirteen, she thought, sending a malicious look over her shoulder. He'd probably planned that, too. If he thought she was going to make a scene, or curl up outside the tent to sleep in the open to spite him, he'd be disappointed. She'd be scrupulously professional, unspeakably cooperative and utterly sexless.

Before it was over, he'd think he'd been sharing his tent with a robot.

But she'd know better. Lee let out one long, frustrated breath as she scouted for more sticks. She'd know there was a man beside her in the night. A powerfully sexy, impossibly attractive man who could make her blood swim with no more than a look.

It wouldn't be easy to forget she was a woman over the next two weeks, when she'd be spending every night with a man who already had her nerves jumping.

Her job wasn't to make herself forget, Lee reminded herself, but to make certain *he* forgot. A challenge. That was the best way to look at it. It was a challenge she promised herself she'd succeed at.

With her arms full of sticks and twigs, Lee lifted her chin. She felt hot, dirty and tired. It wasn't an auspicious way to begin a war. Ignoring the ache, she squared her shoulders. She might have to sacrifice a round or two, but she'd win the battle. With a dangerous light in her eyes, she headed toward camp.

She had to be grateful his back was to her when she walked into the clearing. The tent was smaller, much, much smaller, than she'd imagined. It was fashioned from tough, lightweight material that looked nearly transparent. It arched, rounded rather than pointed at the peak, and low to the ground. So low, Lee noted, that she'd have to crawl to get inside. Once in, they'd be forced to sleep nearly elbow to elbow. Then and there, she determined to sleep like a rock. Unmoving.

The size of the tent preoccupied her, so that she didn't notice what Hunter was doing until she was almost beside him. Fresh rage broke out as she dropped her load of wood on the ground. "Just what the hell do you think you're doing?"

Unperturbed by the fury in her voice, Hunter glanced up. In one hand he held a large clear-plastic bag filled with makeup, in the other a flimsy piece of peach-colored material trimmed with ivory lace. "You did know we were going camping," he said mildly, "not to the Beverly Wilshire?"

The color she considered the curse of fair skin flooded her cheeks. "You have no right to go digging around in my things." She snatched the teddy out of his hand, then balled it in her fist.

"I was unpacking." Idly, he turned the makeup bag over to study it from both sides. "I thought you knew to bring only necessities. While I'll admit you have a very subtle, experienced way with this sort of thing—" he gestured with the bag "—eye shadow and lip gloss are excess baggage around a campfire." His voice was infuriatingly friendly, his eyes were only lightly amused. "I've seen you without any of it and had no cause to complain. You certainly don't have to bother with this on my account."

"You conceited jerk." Lee snatched the bag out of his hand. "I don't care if I look like a hag on your account." Taking the knapsack, she stuffed her belongings back inside. "It's *my* baggage, and I'll carry it."

"You certainly will."

"You officious sonofa—" She broke off, barely. "Just don't tell me how to run my life."

"Now, now, name-calling's no way to promote goodwill." Rising, Hunter held out a friendly hand. "Truce?"

Lee eyed him warily. "On what terms?"

He grinned. "That's what I like about you, Lenore, no easy capitulations. A truce with as little interference as possible on both sides. An amiable business arrangement." He saw her relax slightly and couldn't resist the temptation to ruffle her feathers again. "You won't complain about my coffee, and I won't complain when you wear that little scrap of lace to bed."

She gave him a cool smile as she took his hand. "I'm sleeping in my clothes."

"Fair enough." He gave her hand a quick squeeze. "I'm not. Let's see about that coffee."

As he often did, he left her torn between frustration and amusement.

When he put his mind to it, Lee was to discover, Hunter could make things easier. Without fuss, he had the campfire burning and the coffee brewing. Its scent alone was enough to soothe her temper. The economical way he went about it made her think more kindly of him.

There was no point in being at each other's throats for the next two weeks, she decided as she found a convenient rock to sit on. Relaxing might be out of the question, she mused, watching him take clever, compact cooking utensils out of the pack, but animosity wouldn't help, not with a man like Hunter. He was playing games with her. As long as she knew that and avoided the pitfalls, she'd get what she'd come for. So far, she'd allowed him to set the rules and change them at his whim. That would have to change. Lee hooked her hands around a raised knee.

"Do you go camping to get away from the pressure?"

Hunter didn't look back at her, but checked the lantern. So, they were going to start playing word games already. "What pressure?"

Lee might have sighed if she weren't so determined to be pleasantly professional. "There must be pressures from all sides in your line of work. Demands from your publisher, disagreements with your editor, a story that just won't gel the way you want it to, deadlines."

"I don't believe in deadlines."

There was something, Lee thought, and reached for her notepad. "But doesn't every writer face deadlines from time to time? And can't they be an enormous pressure when the story isn't flowing or you're blocked?"

"Writer's block?" Hunter poured coffee into a metal cup. "There's no such thing."

She glanced over for only a second, brow raised. "Oh, come on, Hunter, some very successful writers have suffered from it, even sought professional help.

There must have been a time in your career when you found yourself up against a wall.''

''You push the wall out of the way.''

Frowning, she accepted the cup he handed her. ''How?''

''By working through it.'' He had a jar of powdered milk, which she refused. ''If you don't believe in something, refuse to believe it exists, it doesn't, not for you.''

''But you write about things that couldn't possibly exist.''

''Why not?''

She stared at him, a dark, attractive man sitting on the ground drinking coffee from a metal cup. He looked so at ease with himself, so relaxed, that for a moment she found it difficult to connect him to the man who created stark terror out of words. ''Because there aren't monsters under the bed or demons in the closet.''

''There's demons in every closet,'' he disagreed mildly, ''some better hidden than others.''

''You're saying you believe in what you write about.''

''Every writer believes in what he writes. There'd be no purpose in it otherwise.''

''You think some—'' She didn't want to use the word *demon* again, and her hand moved in frustration as she sought the right phrase. ''Some evil force,'' Lee chose, ''can actually manipulate people?''

''It's more accurate to say I don't believe in anything. Possibilities.'' Did his eyes become darker, or was it her imagination? "There's no limit to possibilities, Lenore."

His eyes were too dark to read. If he was playing with her, baiting her, she couldn't tell. Uncomfortable, she shifted the topic. "When you sit down to write a story, you craft it, spending hours, days, on the angles and the edges, the same way a carpenter builds a cabinet."

He liked her analogy. Hunter sipped at the strong black coffee, enjoying the taste, enjoying the mingled scents of burning wood, summer and Lee's quiet perfume. "Telling a story's an art, writing's a craft."

Lee felt a quick kick of excitement. That was exactly what she was after, those concise little quotes that gave an insight into his character. "Do you consider yourself an artist, then, or a craftsman?"

He drank without hurry, noting that Lee had barely touched her coffee. The eagerness was with her again, her pen poised, her eyes fixed on his. He found he wanted her more when she was like this. He wanted to see that eager look on her face for him, for the man, not the writer. He wanted to sense the ripe anticipation, lover to lover, arms reaching, mouth softening.

If he were writing the script, he'd keep these two people from fulfilling each other's needs for some time yet. It was necessary to flesh them out a bit first, but the ache told him what he needed. Carefully he arranged another piece of wood on the fire.

"An artist by birth," he said at length, "a craftsman by choice."

"I know it's a standard question," she began, with a brisk professionalism that made him smile, "but where do you get your ideas?"

"From life."

She looked over again as he lit a cigarette. "Hunter, you can't convince me that the plot for *Devil's Due* came out of the everyday."

"If you take the everyday, twist it, add a few maybes, you can come up with anything."

"So you take the ordinary, twist it and come up with the extraordinary." Understanding this a bit better, she nodded, satisfied. "How much of yourself goes into your characters?"

"As much as they need."

Again it was so simply, so easily, said, she knew he meant it exactly. "Do you ever base one of your characters on someone you know?"

"From time to time." He smiled at her, a smile she neither trusted nor understood. "When I find someone intriguing enough. Do you ever get tired of writing about other people when you've got a world of characters in your own head?"

"It's my job."

"That's not an answer."

"I'm not here to answer questions."

"Why are you here?"

He was closer. Lee hadn't realized he'd moved. He was sitting just below her, obviously relaxed, slightly curious, in charge. "To do an interview with a successful, award-winning author."

"An award-winning author wouldn't make you nervous."

The pencil was growing damp in her hand. She could have cursed in frustration. "You don't."

"You lie too quickly, and not easily at all." His hands rested loosely on his knees as he watched her. The odd ring he wore glinted dully, gold and silver. "If I were to touch you, just touch you, right now, you'd tremble."

"You think too much of yourself," she told him, but rose.

"I think of you," he said, so quietly the pad slipped out of her hand, unnoticed. "You make me want, I make you nervous." He was looking into her again; she could almost feel it. "It should be an interesting combination over the next couple of weeks."

He wasn't going to intimidate her. He *wasn't* going to make her tremble. "The sooner you remember I'm going to be working for the next two weeks, the simpler things will be." Trying to sound haughty nearly worked. Lee wondered if he heard the slight catch in her voice.

"Since you're resigned to working," he said easily, "you can give me a hand starting dinner. After tonight, we'll take turns making meals."

She wasn't going to give him the satisfaction of telling him she knew nothing about cooking over a fire. He already knew. Neither would she give the satisfaction of being confused by his mercurial mood changes. Instead, Lee brushed at her bangs. "I'm going to wash up first."

Hunter watched her start off in the wrong direc tion, but said nothing. She'd find the shower facilities sooner or later, he figured. Things would be more interesting if neither of them gave the other an inch.

He wasn't sure, but Hunter thought he heard Lee swear from somewhere behind him. Smiling a little, he leaned back against the rock and finished his cigarette.

Groggy, stiff and sniffing the scent of coffee in the air, Lee woke. She knew exactly where she was—as far over on her side of the tent as she could get, deep into the sleeping bag Hunter had provided for her. And alone. It took her only seconds to sense that Hunter no longer shared the tent with her. Just as it had taken her hours the night before to convince herself it didn't matter that he was only inches away.

Dinner had been surprisingly easy. Easy, Lee realized as she stared at the ceiling of the tent, because Hunter's mood had shifted again when she'd returned to help him fix it. Amiable? No, she decided, cautiously stretching her cramped muscles. *Amiable* was too free a word when applied to Hunter. *Moderately friendly* was more suitable. Cooperative he hadn't been at all. He'd spent the evening hours reading by the light of his lamp, while she'd taken out a fresh notepad and begun what would be a journal on her two weeks in Oak Creek Canyon.

She found it helpful to write down her feelings. Lee had often used her manuscript in much the same fashion. She could say what she wanted, feel what she wanted, without ever taking the risk that anyone would read her words. Perhaps it hadn't worked out precisely that way with her book, since Hunter had read more of her neat double-spaced typing under the steady lamplight, but the journal would be for no one's eyes but her own.

In any case, she thought, it was to her advantage that he'd been occupied with her manuscript. She hadn't had to talk to him as the night had grown later, the darkness deeper. While he'd still been reading, she'd been able to crawl into the tent and squeeze herself into a corner. When he'd joined her, much later, it hadn't been necessary to exchange words in the intimacy of the tent. She'd made certain he'd thought her asleep—though sleep hadn't come for hours.

In the quiet, she'd listened to him breathe beside her. Quiet, steady. That was the kind of man he was. Lee had lain still, telling herself the closeness meant nothing. But this morning, she saw that her nails, which had begun to grow again, had been gnawed down.

The first night was bound to be the hardest, she told herself and sat up, dragging a hand through her hair. She'd survived it. Her problem now was how to get by him and to the showers, where she could change out of the clothes she'd slept in and fix her hair and face. Cautiously, she crept forward to peek through the tent flap.

He knew she was awake. Hunter had sensed it almost the moment she'd opened her eyes. He'd gotten up early to start coffee, knowing that if he'd had trouble sleeping beside her, he'd never have been able to handle waking with her.

He'd seen little more than the coppery mass of hair above the sleeping bag in the dim morning light of the tent. Because he'd wanted to touch it, draw her to him, wake her, he'd given himself some distance. Today he'd walk for miles and fish for hours. Lee could stick to her role of reporter, and by answering her questions he'd learn as much about her as she believed she was learning about him. That was his plan, Hunter reminded himself, and poured a second cup of coffee. He was better off remembering it.

"Coffee's hot," Hunter commented without turning around. Though she'd taken great care to be quiet, he'd heard Lee push the tent flap aside.

Biting back an oath, Lee scooped up her pack. The man had ears like a wolf. "I want to shower first," she mumbled.

"I told you that you didn't have to fix up your face for me." He began to arrange strips of bacon in a skillet. "I like it fine the way it is."

Infuriated, Lee scrambled to her feet. "I'm not fixing anything for you. Sleeping all night in my clothes tends to make me feel dirty."

"Probably sleep better without them." Hunter agreed mildly. "Breakfast's in fifteen minutes, so I'd move along if I wanted to eat."

Clutching her bag and her dignity, Lee strode off through the trees.

He wouldn't get to her so easily if she wasn't stiff

and grubby and half-starved, she thought, making her way along the path to the showers. God knows how he could be so cheerful after spending the night sleeping on the ground. Maybe Bryan had been right all along. The man was weird. Lee took her shampoo and her plastic case of French-milled soap and stepped into a shower stall.

The spot he'd chosen might be magnificent, the air might smell clean and pure, but a sleeping bag wasn't a feather bed. Lee stripped and hung her clothes over the door. She heard the water running in the stall next to hers and sighed. For the next two weeks she'd be sharing bathroom facilities. She might as well get used to it.

The water came out in a steady gush, lukewarm. Gritting her teeth, she stepped under. Today, she was going to begin to dig out a few more personal facts on Hunter Brown.

Was he married? She frowned, then deliberately relaxed her features. The question was for the article, not for herself. His marital status meant nothing to her.

He probably wasn't. She soaped her hair vigorously. What woman would put up with him? Besides, wouldn't a wife come along on camping trips even if she detested them? Would that kind of man marry anyone who didn't like precisely what he did?

What did he do for relaxation? Besides playing Daniel Boone in the woods, she added with a grim smile. Where did he live? Where had he grown up? What sort of childhood had he had?

The water streamed over her, sluicing away soap and shampoo. The curiosity she felt was purely professional. Lee found she had to remind herself of that a bit too often. She needed the whole man to do an incisive article. She needed the whole man...

Alarmed at her own thoughts, she opened her eyes wide, then swore when shampoo stung them. Damn the whole man! she thought fiercely. She'd take whatever pieces of him she could get and write an article that would pay him back, in spades, for all the trouble he'd caused her.

Clean, fragrant and shivering, she turned off the water. It wasn't until that moment that Lee remembered she hadn't brought a towel. Campground showers didn't lay in their own linen supply. Damn it, how was she supposed to remember everything?

Dripping, her chilled skin covered with gooseflesh, she stood in the middle of the stall and swore silently and pungently. For as long as she could stand it, Lee let the air dry her while she squeezed water out of her hair. Revenge, she thought, placing the blame squarely on Hunter's shoulders. Sooner or later, she'd have it.

She reached under the stall door for her pack and pulled out a fresh sweatshirt. Resigned, she dabbed at her wet face with the soft outside. Once she'd dragged it over her damp shoulders, she hunted up underwear. Though her clothes clung to her, her skin warmed. In front of the line of sinks and mirrors, she plugged in her blow-dryer and set to work on her hair.

In spite of him, Lee thought, not because of him, she spent more than her usual time perfecting her makeup. Satisfied, she repacked her portable hairdryer and left the showers, smelling lightly of jasmine.

Her scent was the first thing he sensed when she stepped back into the clearing. Hunter's stomach muscles tightened. As if he were unaffected, he finished off another cup of coffee, but he didn't taste it.

Calmer and much more at ease now, Lee stowed her pack before she walked toward the low-burning camp fire. On a small shelf of rocks beside it sat the skillet with the remainder of the bacon and eggs. She didn't have to taste them to know they were cold.

"Feel better?" Hunter asked conversationally.

"I feel fine." She wouldn't say one word about the food being cold and, Lee told herself as she scooped her breakfast onto a plate, she'd eat every bite. She'd give him no more cause to smirk at her.

While she nibbled on the bacon, Lee glanced over at him. He'd obviously showered earlier. His hair glinted in the sun and he smelled cleanly of soap without the interference of cologne or after-shave. A man didn't use after-shave if he didn't bother with a razor, Lee concluded, studying the shadow of stubble over his chin. It should've made him look unkempt, but somehow he managed to look oddly dashing. She concentrated on her cold eggs.

"Sleep well?"

"I slept fine," she lied, and gratefully washed down her breakfast with strong, hot coffee. "You?"

"Very well," he lied, and lit a cigarette. She was getting on nerves he hadn't known he had.

"Have you been up long?"

Since dawn, Hunter thought. "Long enough." He glanced down at her barely scuffed hiking boots and wondered how long it would take before her feet just gave out. "I plan to do some hiking today."

She wanted to groan but put on a bright smile. "Fine, I'd like to see some of the canyon while I'm here." Preferably in a Jeep, she thought, swallowing the last crumb of bacon. If there was one cliché she could now attest to, it was that the open air increased the appetite.

It took Lee perhaps half again as long to wash up the breakfast dishes with the plastic water container as it would've taken Hunter, but she already understood the unstated rule. One cooks, the other cleans.

By the time she was finished, he was standing impatiently, binocular and canteen straps crisscrossed over his chest and a light pack in one hand. This he shoved at her. Lee resisted the urge to shove it back at him.

"I want my camera." Without giving him a chance to complain, she dug it out of her own gear and slipped the small rectangle in the back pocket of her jeans. "What's in here?" she asked, adjusting the strap of the pack over her shoulder.

"Lunch."

Lee lengthened her stride to keep up with Hunter as he headed out of the clearing. If he'd packed a lunch, she'd have to resign herself to a very long day on her feet. "How do you know where you're going and how to get back?"

For the first time since she'd returned to camp smelling like fragility and flowers, Hunter smiled. "Landmarks, the sun."

"Do you mean moss growing on one side of a tree?" She looked around, hoping to find some point of reference for herself. "I've never trusted that sort of thing."

She wouldn't know east from west, either, he mused, unless they were discussing L.A. and New York. "I've got a compass, if that makes you feel better."

It did—a little. When you hadn't the faintest idea how something worked, you had to take it on faith. Lee was far from comfortable putting her faith in Hunter.

But as they walked, she forgot to worry about losing her way. The sun was a white flash of light, and though it was still shy of 9:00 A.M., the air was warm. She liked the way the light hit the red walls of the canyon and deepened the colors. The path inclined upward, narrow, pebbled with loose stones. She heard people laugh, and the sound carried so cleanly over the air, they might have been standing beside her.

Green became sparser as they climbed. What she saw now was scrubby bushes, dusty and faded, that forced their way out of thin ribbons of dirt in the rock. Curious, she broke off a spray of leaves. Their scent was strong, tangy and fresh. Then she found she had to dash to catch up with Hunter. It had been his idea to hike, but he didn't appear to be enjoying it. More, he looked like a man who had some urgent, unpleasant appointment to keep.

It might be a good time, Lee considered, to start a casual conversation that could lead to the kind of personal information she was shooting for. As the path became steadily steeper, she decided she'd better talk while she had the breath to do it. The sweatshirt had been a mistake, too. Her back was damp again, this time from sweat.

"Have you always preferred the outdoors?"

"For hiking."

Undaunted, she scowled at his back. "I suppose you were a Boy Scout."

"No."

"Your interest in camping and hiking is fairly new, then."

"No."

She had to grit her teeth to hold back a groan. "Did you go off and pitch a tent in the woods with your father when you were a boy?"

She'd have been interested in the amused expression on his face if she could have seen it. "No."

"You lived in the city, then."

She was clever, Hunter reflected. And persistent. He shrugged. "Yes."

At last, Lee thought. "What city?"

"L.A."

She tripped over a rock and nearly stumbled headlong into his back. Hunter never slackened his pace.

"L.A.?" she repeated. "You live in Los Angeles and still manage to bury yourself so that no one knows you're there?"

"I grew up in L.A.," he said mildly, "In a part of the city you'd have little occasion for visiting. Socially, Lenore Radcliffe, formerly of Palm Springs, wouldn't even know such neighborhoods existed."

That pulled her up short. Again, she had to dash to catch him, but this time she grabbed his arm and made him stop. "How do you know I came from Palm Springs?"

He watched her with the tolerant amusement she found both infuriating and irresistible. "I did my research. You graduated from U.C.L.A. with honors, after three years in a very classy Swiss boarding school. Your engagement to Jonathan Willoby, up-and-coming plastic surgeon, was broken when you accepted a position in *Celebrity*'s Los Angeles office."

"I was never engaged to Jonathan," she began furiously, then decisively bit her tongue. "You have no business probing into my life, Hunter. I'm doing the article, not you."

"I make it a habit to find out everything I can about anyone I do business with. We do have a business arrangement, don't we, Lenore?"

He was clever with words, she thought grimly. But so was she. "Yes, and it consists of my interviewing you, not the other way around."

"On my terms," Hunter reminded her. "I don't talk to anyone unless I know who they are." He reached out, touching the ends of her hair as he'd done once before. "I think I know who you are."

"You don't," she corrected, struggling against the need to back away from a touch that was barely a touch. "And you don't have to. But the more honest and open you are with me, the more honest the article I write will be."

He uncapped the canteen. When she refused his offer with a shake of her head, Hunter drank. "I am being honest with you." He secured the cap. "If I made it easier for you, you wouldn't get a true picture of who I am." His eyes were suddenly dark, intense and piercing. Without warning, he reached out. The power in his eyes made her believe he could quite easily sweep her off the path. Yet his hand skimmed down her cheek, light as rain. "You wouldn't understand what I am," he said quietly. "Perhaps, for my own reasons, I want you to."

She'd have been less frightened if he'd shouted at her, raged at her, grabbed at her. The sound of her own heartbeat vibrated in her head. Instinctively, she stepped back, escape her first and only thought. Her foot met empty space.

In an instant, she was caught against him, pressed body to body, so that the warmth from his seeped right into hers. The fear tripled so that she arched back, raising both hands to his chest.

"Idiot," he said, with an edge to his voice that made her head snap up. "Take a look behind you before you tell me to let you go."

Automatically, she turned her head to look over

her shoulder. Her stomach rose up to her throat, then plummeted. The hands that had been poised to push him away grabbed his shoulders until the fingers dug into his flesh. The view behind her was magnificent, sweeping and straight down.

"We—we walked farther up than I'd thought," she managed. And if she didn't sit down, very, very soon, she was going to disgrace herself.

"The trick is to watch where you're going." Hunter didn't move her away from the edge, but took her chin in his hand until their eyes met and held. "Always watch exactly where you're going, then you'll know how to fall."

He kissed her, just as unexpectedly as before, but not so gently. Not nearly so gently. This time, she felt the full force of the strength that had been only an undercurrent each other time his mouth had touched hers. If she'd pitched back and taken that dizzying fall, she'd have been no more helpless than she was at this moment, molded to him, supported by him, wrapped around him. The edge was close— inside her, behind her. Lee couldn't tell which would be more fatal. But she knew, helplessly, that either could break her.

He hadn't meant to touch her just then, but the demanding climb up the path hadn't deadened the need he'd woken with. He'd take this much, her taste, her softness, and make it last until she willingly turned to him. He wanted the sweetness she tried to gloss over, the fragility she tried to deny. And he wanted the strength that kept her pushing for more.

Yes, he thought he knew her and was very close to understanding her. He knew he wanted her.

Slowly, very slowly, for lingering mouth-to-mouth both soothed and excited him, Hunter drew her away. Her eyes were as clouded as his thoughts, her pulse as rapid as his. He shifted her until she was close to the cliff wall and away from the drop.

"Never step back unless you've looked over your shoulder first," he said quietly. "And don't step forward until you've tested the ground."

Turning, he continued up the path, leaving her to wonder if he'd been speaking of hiking or something entirely different.

Chapter 7

Lee wrote in her journal:

On the eighth day of this odd on-again off-again interview, I know more about Hunter and understand less. By turns, he's friendly, then distant. There's an aloof streak in him, bound so tightly around his private life that I've found no way through it. When I ask about his preference in books, he can go on indefinitely—apparently he has no real preference except for the written word itself. When I ask about his family, he just smiles and changes the subject or gives me one of those intense stares and says nothing. In either case, he keeps a cloak of mystery around his privacy.

He's possibly the most efficient man I've ever met. There's no waste of time, no extra movements and, infuriating to me, never a mistake, when it comes to starting a campfire or cooking a meal—such as they are. Yet, he's content to do absolutely nothing for hours at a time.

He's fastidious—the camp looks as if we've been here no more than a half hour rather than a week—yet he hasn't shaved in that amount of time. The beard should look scruffy, but somehow it looks so natural I find myself wondering if he didn't always have one.

Always, I've been able to find a category to slip an assignment into. An acquaintance into. Not with Hunter. In all this time, I've found no easy file for him.

Last night we had a heated discussion on Sylvia Plath, and this morning I found him paging through a comic book over coffee. When I questioned him on it, his answer was that he respected all forms of literature. I believed him. One of the problems I'm having on this assignment is that I find myself believing everything he says, no matter how contradictory the statement might be to another he makes. Can a total lack of consistency make someone consistent?

He's the most complex, frustrating, fascinating man I've ever known. I've yet to find a way of controlling the attraction he holds for me, or even the proper label for it. Is it physical? Hunter's very compelling physically. Is it intellectual? His mind has such odd twists and turns, it takes all my effort to follow them.

Either of these I believe I could handle successfully enough. Over the years, I've had to deal professionally with attractive, intelligent, charismatic men. It's a challenge, certainly, but here I have the uncomfortable feeling that I'm caught in the middle of a silent chess game and have already lost my queen.

My greatest fear at this moment is that I'm going to find myself emotionally involved.

Since the first day we walked up the canyon, he hasn't touched me. I can still remember exactly how I felt, exactly what the air smelled like at that moment. It's foolish, overly romantic and absolutely true.

Each night we sleep together in the same tent, so close I can feel his breath. Each morning I wake alone. I should be grateful that he isn't making this assignment any more difficult than it already is, and yet I find myself waiting to be held by him.

For over a week I've thought of little else but him. The more I learn, the more I want to know—for myself. Too much for myself.

Twice, I've woken in the middle of the night, aching, and nearly turned to him. Now, I wonder what would happen if I did. If I believed in the spells and forces Hunter writes of, I'd think one was on me. No one's ever made me want so much, feel so much. Fear so much. Every night, I wonder.

Sometimes Lee wrote of the scenery and her feelings about it. Sometimes, she wrote a play-by-play description of the day. But most of the time, more of the time, she wrote of Hunter. What she put down in her journal had nothing to do with her organized, precisely written notes for the article. She wouldn't permit it. What she didn't understand, and what she wouldn't write down in either space, was that she was losing sleep. And she was having fun.

Though he was cannily evasive on personal details, she was gathering information. Even now, barely halfway through the allotted time, Lee had enough for a solid, successful article—more, she knew, than she'd expected to gather. But she wanted even more, for her readers and, undeniably, for herself.

"I don't see how any self-respecting fish could be fooled by something like this." Lee fiddled with the small rubbery fly Hunter attached to her line.

"Myopic," Hunter countered, bending to choose his own lure. "Fish are notoriously nearsighted."

"I don't believe you." Clumsily, she cast off. "But this time *I'm* going to catch one."

"You'll need to get your fly in the water first." He glanced down at the line tangled on the bank of the creek before expertly casting his own.

He wouldn't even offer to help. After a week in his company, Lee had learned not to expect it. She'd also learned that if she wanted to compete with him in this, or in a discussion of eighteenth-century English literature, she had to get into the spirit of things.

It wasn't simple and it wasn't quick, but kneeling, Lee worked on the tangles until she was back to square one. She shot a look at Hunter, who appeared much too engrossed with the surface of the creek to notice her progress. By now, Lee knew better. He saw everything that went on around him, whether he looked or not.

Standing a few feet away, Lee tried again. This time, her lure landed with a quiet plop.

Hunter saw the rare, quick grin break out, but said nothing. She was, he'd learned, a woman who generally took herself too seriously. Yet he saw the sweetness beneath, and the warmth Lee tried to be so frugal with.

She had a low, smoky laugh she didn't use often enough. It only made him want to urge it out of her.

The past week hadn't been easy for her. Hunter hadn't intended it to be. You learned more about people by observing them in difficult situations than at a catered cocktail party. He was adding to the layers of the first impression he'd had, at the airport in Flagstaff. But he had layers still to go.

She could, unlike most people he knew, be comfortable with long spells of silence. It appealed to him. The more careless he became in his attire and appearance, the more meticulous she became in hers. It amused him to see her go off every morning and return with her makeup perfected and her hair carefully groomed. Hunter made sure they'd been mussed a bit by the end of the day.

Hiking, fishing. Hunter had seen to it that her jeans and boots were thoroughly broken in. Often, in the evening, he'd caught her rubbing her tired feet. When she was back in Los Angeles, sitting in her cozy office, she wouldn't forget the two weeks she'd spent in Oak Creek Canyon.

Now, Lee stood near the edge of the creek, a fishing rod held in both hands, a look of smug concentration on her face. He liked her for it—for her innate need to compete and for the vulnerability beneath the confidence. She'd stand there, holding the rod, until he called a halt to the venture. Back in camp, he knew she'd rub her hands with cream and they would smell lightly of jasmine and stay temptingly soft.

Since it was her turn to cook, she'd do it, though she still fumbled a bit with the utensils and managed to singe almost anything she put on the fire. He liked her for that, too—for the fact that she never gave up on anything.

Her curiosity remained unflagging. She'd question him, and he'd evade or answer as he chose. Then she'd grant him silence to read, while she wrote. Comfortable. Hunter found that she was an unusually comfortable woman in the quiet light of a camp fire. Whether she knew it or not, she relaxed then, writing in the journal, which intrigued him, or going over her daily notes for the article, which didn't.

He'd expected to learn about her during the two weeks together, knowing he'd have to give some information on himself in return. That, he considered, was an even enough exchange. But he hadn't expected to enjoy her companionship.

The sun was strong, the air almost still, with an early-morning taste to it. But the sky wasn't clear. Hunter wondered if she'd noticed the bank of clouds to the east and if she realized there'd be a storm by nightfall. The clouds held lightning. He simply sat cross-legged on the ground. It'd be more interesting if Lee found out for herself.

The morning passed in silence, but for the occasional voice from around them or the rustle of leaves. Twice Hunter pulled a trout out of the creek, throwing the second back because of size. He said nothing. Lee said nothing, but barely prevented herself from grinding her teeth. On every jaunt, he'd gone back to camp with fish. She'd gone back with a sore neck.

"I begin to wonder," she said, at length, "if you've put something on that lure that chases fish away."

He'd been smoking lazily and now he stirred himself to crush out the cigarette. "Want to change rods?"

She slanted him a look, taking in the slight amusement in his arresting face. When her muscles quivered, Lee stiffened them. Would she never become completely accustomed to the way her body reacted when they looked at each other? "No," she said coolly. "I'll keep this one. You're rather good at this sort of thing, for a boy who didn't go fishing."

"I've always been a quick study."

"What did your father do in L.A.?" Lee asked, knowing he would either answer in the most offhand way or evade completely.

"He sold shoes."

It took a moment, as she'd been expecting the latter. "Sold shoes?"

"That's right. In the shoe department of a moderately successful department store downtown. My mother sold stationery on the third floor." He didn't have to look at her to know she was frowning, her brows drawn together. "Surprised?"

"Yes," she admitted. "A bit. I suppose I imagined you'd been influenced by your parents to some extent and that they'd had some unusual career or interests."

Hunter cast off again with an agile flick of his wrist. "Before my father sold shoes, he sold tickets at the local theater; before that, it was linoleum, I think." His shoulders moved slightly before he turned to her. "He was a man trapped by financial circumstances into working, when he'd been born to dream. If he'd been born into affluence, he might've been a painter or a poet. As it was, he sold things and regularly lost his job because he wasn't suited to selling anything, not even himself."

Though he spoke casually, Lee had to struggle to distance herself emotionally. "You speak as though he's not living."

"I've always believed my mother died from overwork, and my father from lack of interest in life without her."

Sympathy welled up in her throat. She couldn't swallow at all. "When did you lose them?"

"I was eighteen. They died within six months of each other."

"Too old for the state to care for you," she murmured, "too young to be alone."

Touched, Hunter studied her profile. "Don't feel sorry for me, Lenore. I managed very well."

"But you weren't a man yet." No, she mused, perhaps he had been. "You had college to face."

"I had some help, and I waited tables for a while."

Lee remembered the wallet full of credit cards she'd

carried through college. Anything she'd wanted had always been at her fingertips. "It couldn't have been easy."

"It didn't have to be." He lit a cigarette, watching the clouds move slowly closer. "By the time I was finished with college, I knew I was a writer."

"What happened from the time you graduated from college to when your first book was published?"

He smiled through the smoke that drifted between them. "I lived, I wrote, I went fishing when I could."

She wasn't about to be put off so easily. Hardly realizing she did it, Lee sat down on the ground beside him. "You must've worked."

"Writing, though many disagree, is work." He had a talent for making the sharpest sarcasm sound mildly droll.

Another time, she might have smiled. "You know that's not what I mean. You had to have an income, and your first book wasn't published until nearly six years ago."

"I wasn't starving in a garret, Lenore." He ran a finger down the hand she held on the rod and felt a flash of pleasure at the quick skip of her pulse. "You'd just have been starting at *Celebrity* when *The Devil's Due* hit the stands. One might say our stars were on the rise at the same time."

"I suppose." She turned from him to look back at the surface of the creek again.

"You're happy there?"

Unconsciously, she lifted her chin. "I've worked my way up from gofer to staff reporter in five years."

"That's not an answer."

"Neither are most of yours," she mumbled.

"True enough. What're you looking for there?"

"Success," she said immediately. "Security."

"One doesn't always equal the other."

Her voice was as defiant as the look she aimed at him. "You have both."

"A writer's never secure," Hunter disagreed. "Only a foolish one expects to be. I've read all of the manuscript you brought."

Lee said nothing. She'd known he'd bring it up before the two weeks were over, but she'd hoped to put it off a bit longer. The faintest of breezes played with the ends of her hair while she sat, staring at the moving waters of the creek. Some of the pebbles looked like gems. Such were illusions.

"You know you have to finish it," he told her calmly. "You can't make me believe you're content to leave your characters in limbo, when you've drawn them so carefully. Your story's two-thirds told, Lenore."

"I don't have time," she began.

"Not good enough."

Frustrated, she turned to him again. "Easy for you to say from your little pinnacle of fame. I have a demanding full-time job. If I give it my time and my talent, there's no place I can go but up at *Celebrity*."

"Your novel needs your time and talent."

She didn't like the way he said it—as if she had no real choice. "Hunter, I didn't come here to discuss my work, but you and yours. I'm flattered that you

think my novel has some merit, but I have a job
to do.''

''Flattered?'' he countered. The deep, black gaze
pinned her again, and his hand closed over hers. ''No,
you're not. You wish I'd never seen your novel and
you don't want to discuss it. Even if you were convinced it was worthwhile, you'd still be afraid to put
it all on the line.''

The truth grated on her nerves and on her temper.
''My job is my first priority. Whether that suits you
or not doesn't matter. It's none of your business.''

''No, perhaps not,'' he said slowly, watching her.
''You've got a fish on your line.''

''I don't want you to—'' Eyes narrowing, she broke
off. ''What?''

''There's a fish on your line,'' he repeated. ''You'd
better reel it in.''

''I've got one?'' Stunned, Lee felt the rod jerk in
her hands. ''I've got one! Oh, God.'' She gripped the
rod in both hands again and watched the line jiggle.
''I've really caught one. What do I do now?''

''Reel it in,'' Hunter suggested again, leaning back
on the grass.

''Aren't you going to help?'' Her hands felt foolishly clumsy as she started to crank the reel. Hoping
leverage would give her some advantage, she scrambled to her feet. ''Hunter, I don't know what I'm doing. I might lose it.''

''Your fish,'' he pointed out. Grinning, he watched
her. Would she look any more exuberant if she'd been
given an interview with the president? Somehow,

Hunter didn't think so, though he was sure Lee would disagree. But then, she couldn't see herself at that moment, hair mussed, cheeks glowing, eyes wide and her tongue caught firmly between her teeth. The late-morning sunlight did exquisite things to her skin, and the quick laugh she gave when she pulled the struggling fish from the water ran over the back of his neck like soft fingers.

Desire moved lazily through him as he took his gaze up the long length of leg flattered by brief shorts, then over the subtle curves accented by the shifting of muscle under her shirt as she continued to fight with the fish, to her face, still flushed with surprise.

"Hunter!" She laughed as she held the still-wriggling fish high over the grass. "I did it."

It was nearly as big as the largest one he'd caught that week. He pursed his lips as he sized it up. It was tempting to compliment her, but he decided she looked smug enough already. "Gotta get it off the hook," he reminded her, shifting only slightly on his elbows.

"Off the hook?" Lee shot him an astonished look. "I don't want to touch it."

"You have to touch it to take it off the hook."

Lee lifted a brow. "I'll just toss it back in."

With a shrug, Hunter shut his eyes and enjoyed the faint breeze. The hell she would. "Your fish, not mine."

Torn between an abhorrence of touching the still-flopping fish and pride at having caught it, Lee stared down at Hunter. He wasn't going to help; that was painfully obvious. If she threw the fish back into the water, he'd smirk at her for the rest of the evening. Intolerable. And, she reasoned logically, wouldn't she still have to touch it to get rid of it? Setting her teeth, Lee reached out a hand for the catch of the day.

It was wet, slippery and cold. She pulled her hand back. Then, out of the corner of her eye, she saw Hunter grinning up at her. Holding her breath, Lee took the trout firmly in one hand and wiggled the hook out with the other. If he hadn't been looking at her, challenging her, she never would've managed it. With the haughtiest air at her disposal, she dropped the trout into the small cooler Hunter brought along on fishing trips.

"Very good." He closed the lid on the cooler before he reeled in his line. "That looks like enough for tonight's dinner. You caught a good-sized one, Lenore."

"Thank you." The words were icily polite and self-satisfied.

"It'll nearly be enough for both of us, even after you've cleaned it."

"It's as big as..." He was already walking back toward camp, so that she had to run to catch up with him and his statement. "*I* clean it?"

"Rule is, you catch, you clean."

She planted her feet, but he wasn't paying attention. "I'm not cleaning any fish."

"Then you don't eat any fish." His words were as offhand and careless as a shrug.

Abandoning pride, Lee caught at his arm. "Hunter,

you'll have to change the rule." She sighed, but convinced herself she wouldn't choke on the word. At least not very much. "Please."

He stopped, considering. "If I clean it, you've got to balance the scales—" the smile flickered over his face "—no pun intended, by doing me a favor."

"I can cook two nights in a row."

"I said a favor."

Her head turned sharply, but one look at his face had her laughing. "All right, what's the deal?"

"Why don't we leave it open-ended?" he suggested. "I don't have anything in mind at the moment."

This time, she considered. "It'll be negotiable?"

"Naturally."

"Deal." Turning her palms up, Lee wrinkled her nose. "Now I'm going to wash my hands."

She hadn't realized she could get such a kick out of catching a fish or out of cooking it herself over an open fire. There were other things Lee hadn't realized. She hadn't looked at the trim gold watch on her wrist in days. If she hadn't kept a journal, she probably wouldn't know what day it was. It was true that her muscles still revolted after a night in the tent and the shower facilities were an inconvenience at best, purgatory at worst, but despite herself she was relaxing.

For the first time in her memory, her day wasn't regimented, by herself or by anyone else. She got up when she woke, slept when she was tired and ate when she was hungry. For the moment, the word *deadline* didn't exist. That was something she hadn't allowed herself since the day she'd walked out of her parents' home in Palm Springs.

No matter how rapid Hunter could make her pulse by one of those unexpected looks, or how much desire for him simmered under the surface, she found him comfortable to be with. Because it was so unlikely, Lee didn't try to find the reasons. On this late afternoon, in the hour before dusk, she was content to sit by the fire and tend supper.

"I never knew anything could smell so good."

Hunter continued to pour a cup of coffee before he glanced over at her. "We cooked fish two days ago."

"Your fish," Lee pointed out, carefully turning the trout. "This one's mine."

He grinned, wondering if she remembered just how horrified she'd been the first time he'd suggested she pick up a rod and reel. "Beginner's luck."

Lee opened her mouth, ready with a biting retort, then saw the way he smiled at her. Not only did her retort vanish, but so did much of her defensive wall. She let out a long, quiet breath as she turned back to the skillet. The man became only more dangerous with familiarity. "If fishing depends on luck," she managed, "you've had more than your share."

"Everything depends on luck." He held out two plates. Lee slipped the sizzling trout onto them, then sat back to enjoy.

"If you believe that, what about fate? You've said more than once that we can fight against our fate, but we can't win."

He lifted a brow. That consistently sharp, consistently logical mind of hers never failed to impress him. "One works with the other." He tasted a bit of trout, noting that she'd been careful enough not to singe her own catch. "It's your fate to be here, with me. You were lucky enough to catch a fish for dinner."

"It sounds to me as though you twist things to your own point of view."

"Yes. Doesn't everyone?"

"I suppose." Lee ate, thoughtfully studying the view over his shoulder. Had anything ever tasted this wonderful? Would anything ever again? "But not everyone makes it work as well as you." Reluctantly, she accepted some of the dried fruit he offered. He seemed to have an unending supply, but Lee had yet to grow used to the taste or texture.

"If you could change one thing about your life, what would it be?"

Perhaps because he'd asked without preamble, perhaps because she was so unexpectedly relaxed, Lee answered without thinking. "I'd have more."

He didn't, as her parents had done, ask more what. Hunter only nodded. "We could say it's your fate to want it, and your luck to have it or not."

Nibbling on an apricot, she studied him. The lowering light and flickering fire cast his face in shadows. They suited him. The short, rough beard surrounded the poet's mouth, making it all the more compelling. He was a man a woman would never be able to ignore, never be able to forget. Lee wondered if he knew it. Then she nearly laughed. Of course he did. He knew entirely too much.

"What about you?" She leaned forward a bit, as she did whenever the answer was important. "What would you change?"

He smiled in the way that made her blood heat. "I'd take more," he said quietly.

She felt the shiver race up her spine, was all but certain Hunter could see it. Lee found she was compelled to remind herself of her job. "You know," she began easily enough, "you've told me quite a bit over this week, more in some ways than I'd expected, but much less in others." Steady again, she took another bite of trout. "I might understand you quite a bit better if you'd give me a run-through of a typical day."

He ate, enjoying the tender, open-air flavor. The clouds were rolling in, the breeze picking up. He wondered if she noticed. "There's no such thing as a typical day."

"You're evading again."

"Yeah."

"It's my job to pin you down."

He watched her over the rim of his coffee cup. "I like watching you do your job."

She laughed. It seemed he could always frustrate and amuse her at the same time. "Hunter, why do I have the feeling you're doing your best to make this difficult for me?"

"You're very perceptive." Setting his plate aside, he began to toy with the ends of her hair in a habit she could never take casually. "I have an image of a woman with a romantic kind of beauty and an orderly, logical mind.''

''Hunter—''

''Wait, I'm just fleshing her out. She's ambitious, full of nerves, highly sensuous without being fully aware of it.'' He could see her eyes change, growing as dark as the sky above them. ''She's caught in the middle of something she can't explain or understand. Things happen around her and she's finding it more and more difficult to distance herself from it. And there's a man, a man she desires but can't quite trust. He doesn't offer her the logical explanations she wants, but the illogic he offers seems terrifyingly close to the truth. If she puts her trust in him, she has to turn her back on most of what she believes is fact. If she doesn't, she'll be alone.''

He was talking to her, about her, for her. Lee knew her throat was dry and her palms were damp, but she didn't know if it was from his words or the light touch on the ends of her hair. ''You're trying to frighten me by weaving a plot around me.''

''I'm weaving a plot around you,'' Hunter agreed. ''Whether I frighten you or not depends on how successful I am with that plot. Shadows and storms are my business.'' As if on cue, lightning snaked out in the sky overhead. ''But all writers need a foil. Smooth, pale skin—'' He stroked the back of his hand up her cheek. ''Soft hair with touches of gold and fire. Against that I have darkness, wind, voices that speak from shadows. Logic against the impossible. The unspeakable against cool, polished beauty.''

She swallowed to relieve the dryness in her throat and tried to speak casually. "I suppose I should be flattered, but I'm not sure I want to see myself molded into a character in a horror story."

"That comes back to fate again, doesn't it?" Lightning ripped through the early dusk as their eyes met again. "I need you, Lenore," he murmured. "For the tale I have to tell—and more."

Nerves prickled along her skin, all the more frantically because of the relaxed hours. "It's going to rain." But her voice wasn't calm and even. Her senses were already swimming. When she started to rise, she found that her hand was caught in his and that he stood with her. The wind blew around her, stirring leaves, stirring desire. The light dimmed to shadow. Thunder rumbled.

What she saw in his eyes chilled her, then heated her blood so quickly she had no way to keep up with the change. The grip on her hand was light. Lee could've broken the hold if she'd had the will to do so. It was his look that drained the will from her. They stood there, hands touching, eyes locked, while the storm swirled like madness around them.

Perhaps life was made up of the choices Hunter had once spoken of. Perhaps luck swayed the balance. But at that moment, for hardly more than a heartbeat, Lee believed that fate ruled everything. She was meant to go to him, to give to him, with no more choice than one of the characters his imagination formed.

Then the sky opened. The rain poured out. The shock of the sudden drenching had Lee jolting back, breaking contact. Yet for several long seconds she stood still while water ran over her and lightning flashed in wicked bolts.

"Damn it!" But he knew she spoke to him, not the storm. "Now what am I supposed to do?"

Hunter smiled, barely resisting the urge to cup her face in his hands and kiss her until her legs gave way. "Head for drier land." He continued to smile despite the rain, the wind, the lightning.

Wet, edgy and angry, Lee crawled inside the tent. He's enjoying this, she thought, tugging on the sodden laces of her boots. There's nothing he likes better than to see me at my worst. It would probably take a week for the boots to dry out, she thought grimly as she managed to pry the first one off.

When Hunter slipped into the tent beside her, she said nothing. Concentrating on anger seemed the best solution. The pounding of the rain on the sides of the tent made the space inside seem to shrink. She'd never been more aware of him, or of herself. Water dripped uncomfortably down her neck as she leaned forward to pull off her socks.

"I don't suppose this'll last long."

Hunter pulled the sodden shirt over his head. "I wouldn't count on it stopping much before morning."

"Terrific." She shivered and wondered how the hell she was supposed to get out of the wet clothes and into dry ones.

Hunter turned the lantern he'd carried in with him down to a dim glow. "Relax and listen to it. It's different from rain in the city. There's no swish of tires on wet asphalt, no horns, no feet running on the side-walk.'' He took a towel out of his pack and began to dry her hair.

"I can do it.'' She reached up, but his hands continued to massage.

"I like to do it. Wet fire,'' he murmured. ''That's what your hair looks like now.''

He was so close she could smell the rain on him. The heat from his body called subtly, temptingly, to hers. Was the rain suddenly louder, or were her senses more acute? For a moment, she thought she could hear each individual drop as it hit the tent. The light was dim, a smoky gray that held touches of unreality. Lee felt as though she'd been running away from this one isolated spot all her life. Or perhaps she'd been running toward it.

"You need to shave,'' she murmured, and found that her hand was already reaching out to touch the untrimmed growth of beard on his face. "This hides too much. You're already difficult to know.''

"Am I?'' He moved the towel over her hair, soothing and arousing by turns.

"You know you are.'' She didn't want to turn away now, from the look that could infuse such warmth through her chilled, damp skin. Lightning flashed, illuminating the tent brilliantly before plunging it back into gloom. Yet, through the gloom she could see all she needed to, perhaps more than she wanted to. "It's my job to find out more, to find out everything.''

"And my right to tell you only what I want to.''

"We just don't look at things the same way.''

"No."

She took the towel and, half dreaming, began to dry his hair. "We have no business being together like this."

He hadn't known desire with claws. If he didn't touch her soon, he'd be ripped through. "Why?"

"We're too different. You look for the unexplainable, I look for the logical." But his mouth was so near hers, and his eyes held such power. "Hunter..." She knew what was going to happen, recognized the impossibility of it and the pain that was bound to follow. "I don't want this to happen."

He didn't touch her, though he was certain he'd soon be mad from the lack of it. "You have a choice."

"No." It was said quietly, almost on a sigh. "I don't think I do." She let the towel fall. She saw the flicker of lightning and waited, six long heartbeats, for the answering thunder. "Maybe neither one of us has a choice."

Her breath was already unsteady as she let her hands curl over his bare shoulders. There was strength there. She wanted to feel it, but had been afraid to. His eyes never left hers as she touched him. Though the force of need curled tight in his stomach, he'd let her set the pace this first time, this most important time.

Her fingers were long and smooth on his skin, cool, not so much hesitant as cautious. They ran down his arms, moving slowly over his chest and back until desire was taut as a bow poised for firing. The sound of the rain drummed in his head. Her face was pale and elegant in the gloomy light. The tent was suddenly too big. He wanted her in a space that was too small to move in unless they moved together.

She could hardly believe she could touch him this way, freely, openly, so that his skin quivered under the trace of her fingers. All the while, he watched her with a passion so fierce it would have terrified her if she hadn't been so dazed with her own need. Carefully, afraid to make the wrong move and break the mood for both of them, she touched her mouth to his.

The rough brush of beard was a stunning contrast to the softness of his lips. He gave back to her such feelings, such warmth, with no pressure. She'd never known anyone who could give without taking. This generosity was, to her, the ultimate seduction. In that moment, any reserve she'd clung to was washed away. Her arms went around his neck, her cheek pressed to his.

"Make love to me, Hunter."

He drew her away, only far enough so that they could see each other again. Wet hair curled around her face. Her eyes were as the sky had been an hour before. Dusky and clouded. "With."

Her lips curved. Her heart opened. He poured inside. "Make love with me."

Then his hands were framing her face, and the kiss was so gentle it drugged every cell of her body. She felt him tug the wet shirt from her, and shivered once before he warmed her. His body felt so strong against hers, so solid, yet his hands played over her with the care of a jeweler polishing a rare gem. He sighed when she touched him, so she touched once again, wanting to give pleasure as it was given to her.

She'd thought the panic would return, or at least the need to rush. But they'd been given all the time in the world. The rain could fall, the thunder bellow. It didn't involve them. She tasted hunger on his lips, but he held it in check. He'd sup slowly. Pleasure bubbled up inside her and came softly through her lips.

His mouth on her breast had the need leaping up to the next plane. Yet he didn't hurry, even when she arched against him. His tongue flicked, his teeth nibbled, until he could feel the crazed desire vibrating through her. She thought only of him now, Hunter knew it even as he struggled to hold the reins of his own passion. She'd have more. She'd take all. And so, by God, would he.

When she struggled with the snap of his jeans, he let her have her way. He wanted to be flesh-to-flesh with her, body-to-body, without barriers. In his mind, he'd already had her bare, like this, a dozen times. Her hair was cool and wet, her skin smooth and fragrant. Spring flowers and summer rain. The scents raced through him as her hands became more urgent.

Her breathing was ragged as she tugged the wet denim down his legs. She recognized strength, power and control. It was only the last she needed to break so that she could have what she ached for.

Wherever she could reach, she touched, she tasted, wallowing in pleasure each time she heard his breath tremble. Her shorts were drawn slowly down her body by strong, clever hands, until she wore nothing but the lacy triangle riding low on her hips. With his lips, he journeyed down, down her body, slowly, so that the bristle of beard awakened every pore. His tongue slid under the lace, making her gasp. Then, as abruptly as the storm had broken, Lee was lost in a morass of sensation too dark, too deep, to understand.

He felt her explode, and the power sang through him. He heard her call his name, and the greed to hear it again almost overwhelmed him. Bracing himself over her, Hunter held back that final, desperate need until she opened her eyes. She'd look at him when they came together. He'd promised himself that.

Dazed, trembling, frenzied, Lee stared at him. He looked invincible. "What do you want from me?"

His mouth swooped down on hers, and for the first time the kiss was hard, urgent, almost brutal with the force of passion finally unleashed. "Everything." He plunged into her, catapulting them both closer to the crest. "Everything."

Chapter 8

Dawn was clear as glass. Lee woke to it slowly, naked, warm and, for the first time in over a week, comfortable. And for the first time in over a week, she woke not precisely sure where she was.

Her head was pillowed in the curve of Hunter's shoulder, her body turned toward his of its own volition and by the weight of the arm held firmly around her. There was a drowsy feeling that was a mix of security and excitement. In all of her memory, she couldn't recall experiencing anything quite like it.

Before she was fully awake, she smelled the lingering fragrance of rain on his skin and remembered. In remembering, she took a deep, drinking breath of the scent.

It was like a dream, like something in some subliminal fantasy, or a scene that had come straight from the imagination. She'd never offered herself to anyone so freely before, or so completely. Never. Lee knew there'd never been anyone who'd tempted her to.

She could still remember the sensation of her lips touching his, and all doubt, all fear, melting away with the gentle contact.

Should she feel so content now that the rain had stopped and dawn was breaking? Fantasies were for that private hour of the night, not for the daylight. After all, it hadn't been a dream, and there'd be no pretending it had been. Perhaps she should be appalled that she'd given him exactly what he'd demanded: everything.

She couldn't. No, it was more than that, she realized. She wouldn't. Nothing, no one, would spoil what had happened, not even she herself.

Still, it might be best if he didn't realize quite yet how completely victorious he'd been. Lee let her eyes close and wrapped the sensation of closeness around her. For the next few days, there was no desk, no typewriter, no phone ringing with more demands. There'd be no self-imposed schedule. For the next few days, she was alone with her lover. Maybe the time had come to pick those wildflowers.

She tilted her head, wanting to look at him, trying not to wake him. Over the week they'd spent in such intimate quarters, she'd never seen him sleep. Every other morning he'd been up, already making coffee. She wanted the luxury of absorbing him when he was unaware.

Lee knew that most people looked more vulnerable

in sleep, more innocent, perhaps. Hunter looked just as dangerous, just as compelling, as ever. True, those dark, intense eyes were hidden, but knowing the lids could lift at any moment, and the eyes spear you with that peculiar power, didn't add innocence to his face, only more mystery.

Lee discovered she didn't want it to. She was glad he was more dangerous than the other men she'd known. In an odd way, she was glad he was more difficult. She hadn't fallen in love with the ordinary, the everyday, but with the unique.

Fallen in love. She ran the phrase around in her head, taking it apart and putting it back together again with the caution she was prone to. It triggered a trickle of unease. The phrase itself connoted bruises. Hadn't Hunter himself warned her to test the ground before she started forward? Even warned, she hadn't. Even seeing the pit, she hadn't checked her step. The tumble she'd taken had a soft fall. This time. Lee knew it was all too possible to stumble and be destroyed.

She wasn't going to think about it. Lee allowed herself the luxury of cuddling closer. She was going to find those wildflowers and enjoy each individual petal. The dream would end soon enough, and she'd be back to the reality of her life. It was, of course, what she wanted. For a while, she lay still, just listening to the silence.

The clever thing to do, she thought lazily, would be to hang their wet clothes out in the sun. Her boots certainly needed drying out, but in the meantime, she had her sneakers. She yawned, thinking she wanted a few moments to write in her journal as well. Hunter's breathing was slow and even. A smile curved her lips. She could do all that, then come back and wake him. Waking him, in whatever way she chose, was a lover's privilege.

Lover. Skimming her gaze over his face again, she wondered why she didn't feel any particular surprise at the word. Was it possible she'd recognized it from the beginning? Foolish, she told herself, and shook her head.

Slowly, she shifted away from him, then crawled to the front of the tent to peek out. Even as she reached for the flap, a hand closed around her ankle. Hunter pillowed his other hand under his head as he watched her.

"If you're going out like that, we won't keep everyone away from the campsite for long."

As she was naked, the haughty look she sent him lost something. "I was just looking out. I thought you were asleep."

He smiled, thinking she was the only woman who could make a viable stab at dignity while on her hands and knees in a tent, without a stitch on. The finger around her ankle stroked absently. "You're up early."

"I thought I'd hang these clothes out to dry."

"Very practical." Because he sensed she was feeling awkward, Hunter sat up and grabbed her arm, tugging until she tumbled back, sprawled over him. Content, he held her against him and sighed. "We'll do it later."

Unsure whether to laugh or complain, Lee blew the

hair out of her eyes as she propped herself on one elbow. "I'm not tired."

"You don't have to be tired to lie down." Then he rolled on top of her. "It's called relaxing."

As the planes of his body fit against the curves of hers, Lee felt the warmth seep in. A hundred tiny pulse points began to drum. "I don't think this has a lot to do with relaxing."

"No?" He'd wanted to see her like this, in the thin light of dawn with her hair mussed from his hands, her skin flushed from sleep, her limbs heavy from a night of loving and alert for more. He ran a hand down her with a surge of possession that wasn't quite comfortable, wasn't quite expected. "Then we'll relax later, too." He saw her lips form a gentle smile just before he brushed his over them.

Hunter didn't question that he wanted her just as urgently now as he had all the days and nights before. He rarely questioned feelings, because he trusted them. Her arms went around him, her lips parted. The completeness of her giving shot a shaft of heat through him that turned to a unified warmth. Lifting his head, Hunter looked down at her.

Milkmaid skin over a duchess's cheekbones, eyes like the sky at dusk and hair like copper shot with gold. Hunter gave himself the pleasure of looking at all of her, slowly.

She was small and sleek and smooth. He ran a fingertip along the curve of her shoulder and studied the contrast of his skin against hers. Fragile, delicate—but

he remembered how much strength there was inside her.

"You always look at me as if you know everything
there is to know about me."

The intensity in his eyes remained, as he caught her
hand in his. "Not enough. Not nearly enough." With
the lightest of touches, he kissed her shoulder, her
temple, then her lips.

"Hunter..." She wanted to tell him that no one had
ever made her feel this way before. She wanted to tell
him that no one had ever made her want so badly to
believe in magic and fairy tales and the simplicity of
love. But as she started to speak, courage deserted her.
She was afraid to risk, afraid to fail. Instead she
touched a hand to his cheek. "Kiss me again."

He understood there was something more, something he needed to know. But he understood, too, that
when something fragile was handled clumsily, it
broke. He did as she asked and savored the warm,
dark taste of her mouth.

Soft...sweet...silky. It was how he could make her
feel with only a kiss. The ground was hard and unyielding under the thin tent mattress, but it might have
been a luxurious pile of feathers. It was so easy to
forget where she was, when he was with her this way,
to forget a world existed outside that small space two
bodies required. He could make her float, and she'd
never known she'd wanted to. He could make her
ache, and she'd never known there could be pleasure
from it. He spoke against her mouth words she didn't

need to understand. She wanted and was wanted, needed and was needed. She loved...

With an inarticulate murmur of acceptance for whatever he could give, Lee drew him closer. Closer. The moment was all that mattered.

Deep, intoxicating, tender, the kiss went on and on and on.

Even an imagination as fluid as his hadn't fantasized anything so sweet, anything so soft. It was as though she melted into him, giving everything before he could ask. Once, only once, only briefly, it sped through his mind that he was as vulnerable as she. The unease came, flicking at the corner of his mind. Then her hands ran over him, stroking, and he accepted the weakness.

Only one other person had ever had the power to reach inside him and hold his heart. Now there were two. The time to deal with it was tomorrow. Today was for them alone.

Without hurry, he whispered kisses over her face. Perhaps it was a homage to beauty, perhaps it was much, much more. He didn't question his motives as he traced the slope of her cheek. There was an immediacy he'd never experienced before, but it didn't carry the urgency he'd expected. She was there for him as long as he needed. He understood that, without words.

"You smell of spring and rain," he murmured against her ear. "Why should that drive me mad?"

The words vibrated through her, as arousing as the

most intimate caress. Heavy-lidded, clouded, her eyes
met his. "Just show me. Show me again."

He loved her with such generosity. Each touch was
a separate pleasure, each kiss a luxurious taste. Patience—there was more patience in him than in her.
Her body was tossed between utter contentment and
urgency, until reason was something too vague to
grasp.

"Here—" He nibbled lightly at her breast, listening
to and allured by her unsteady breaths. "You're small
and soft. Here—" He took his hand over her hip to
her thigh. "You're taut and lean. I can't seem to touch
enough, taste enough." He drew the peak of her breast
into his mouth, so that she arched against him, center
to center.

"Hunter." His name was barely audible, but the
sound of it was enough to bring him to desperation.
"I need you."

God, had he wanted to hear that so badly? Struggling to understand what those three simple words had
triggered, he buried his mouth against her skin. But
he couldn't think, only feel. Only want. "You have
me."

With his hands and lips alone, he took her spiraling
over the first peak.

Her movements beneath him grew wild, her murmurs frenzied, but she was unaware. All Lee knew
was that they were flesh-to-flesh. This was the storm
he'd gentled the night before, the power unleashed,
the demands unsoftened. The tenderness became passion so quickly, she could only ride with it, blind to

her own power and her own demands. She was spinning too fast in the world they'd created to know how hungrily her mouth sought him, how sure were her own hands. She drew from him everything he drew from her. Again and again she took him to the edge, and again and again he clung, wanting more. And still more.

Greed. He'd never known this degree of greed. With the blood pounding in his head, singing in his veins, he molded his open mouth to hers. With his hands gripping her hips, he rolled until she lay over him. They were still mouth-to-mouth when they joined, and her gasp of pleasure rocketed through him.

Strength seemed to build, impossibly. She thought she could feel each individual muscle of her body coil and release as they moved together. Power called to power. Lee remembered the lightning, remembered the thunder, and lived it again. When the storm broke, she was clasped against him, as if the heat had fused them.

Minutes, hours, days. Lee couldn't have measured the time. Slowly, her body settled. Gradually, her heartbeat leveled. With her body pressed close to his, she could feel each breath he took and found a foolish satisfaction that the rhythm matched her own.

"A pity we wasted a week." Finding the effort to open his eyes too great, Hunter kept them closed as he combed his fingers through her hair.

She smiled a little, because he couldn't see. "Wasted?"

"If we'd started out this way, I'd've slept a lot better."

"Really?" Schooling her features, Lee lifted her head. "Have you had trouble sleeping?"

His eyelids opened lazily. "I've rarely found it necessary to get up at dawn, unless it's to write."

The surge of pleasure made her voice smug. She traced a fingertip over his shoulder. "Is that so?"

"You insisted on wearing that perfume to make me crazy."

"To make you crazy?" Folding her arms on his chest, she arched a brow. "It's a very subtle scent."

"Subtle." He ran a casual hand over her bottom. "Like a hammer in the solar plexus."

The laugh nearly escaped. "You were the one who insisted we share a tent."

"Insisted?" He gave her a mildly amused glance. "I told you I had no objection if you chose to sleep outside."

"Knowing I wouldn't."

"True, but I didn't expect you to resist me for so long."

Her head came up off her folded arms. "Resist you?" she repeated. "Are you saying you plotted this out like a scene in a book?"

Grinning, he pillowed his arms behind his head. God, he couldn't remember a time he'd felt so clean, so...complete. "It worked."

"Typical," she said, wishing she were insulted and trying her best to act as though she were. "I'm surprised there was room in here for the two of us and your inflated ego.''

''And your stubbornness.''

She sat up at the word, both brows disappearing under her tousled bangs. ''I suppose you thought I'd just '' her hand gestured in a quick circle ''—fall at your feet.''

Hunter considered this a moment, while he gave himself the pleasure of memorizing every curve of her body. ''It might've been nice, but I'd figured a few detours into the scenario.''

''Oh, had you?'' She wondered if he realized he was steadily digging himself into a hole. ''I bet we can come up with a great many more.'' Searching in her pack, Lee found a fresh T-shirt. ''Starting now.''

As she started to drag the shirt over her head, Hunter grabbed the hem and yanked. Lee tumbled down on top of him again, to find her mouth captured. When he let her surface, she narrowed her eyes. ''You think you're pretty clever, don't you?''

''Yeah.'' He caught her chin in his hand and kissed her again. ''Let's have breakfast.''

She swallowed a laugh, but her eyes gave her away. ''Bastard.''

''Okay, but I'm still hungry.'' He tugged her shirt down her torso before he started to dress.

Lying back, Lee strugggled into a pair of jeans. ''I don't suppose, now that the point's been made, we could finish out this week at a nice resort?''

Hunter dug out a fresh pair of socks. ''A resort?

Don't tell me you're having problems roughing it, Lenore.''

"I wouldn't say problems." She stuck a hand in one boot and found the inside damp. Resigned, she hunted for her sneakers. "But there is the matter of having fantasies about a hot tub and a soft bed." She pressed a hand to her lower back. "Wonderful fantasies."

"Camping does take a certain amount of strength and endurance," he said easily. "I suppose if you've reached your limit and want to quit—"

"I didn't say anything about quitting," she retorted. She set her teeth, knowing whichever way she went, she lost. "We'll finish out the damn two weeks," she mumbled, and crawled out of the tent.

Lee couldn't deny that the quality of the air was exquisite and the clarity of the sky more perfect than any she'd ever seen. Nor, if he'd asked, would she have told Hunter that she wanted to be back in Los Angeles. It was a matter of basic creature comforts, she thought. Like soaking in hot, fragrant water and stretching out on a firm, linen-covered mattress. Certainly, it wasn't more than most people wanted in their day-to-day lives. But then, she reflected, Hunter Brown wasn't most people.

"Fabulous, isn't it?" His arms came around her waist, drawing her back to his chest. He wanted her to see what he saw, feel what he felt. Perhaps he wanted it too much.

"It's a beautiful spot. It hardly seems real." Then she sighed, not entirely sure why. Would Los Angeles seem more real to her when this final week was up? At the very least, she understood the tall buildings and crowded streets. Here—here she seemed so small, and that top rung of the ladder seemed so vague and unimportant.

Abruptly, she turned and clung to him. "I hate to admit it, but I'm glad you brought me." She found she wanted to continue clinging, continue holding, so that there wouldn't be a time when she had to let go. Pushing away all thoughts of tomorrow, Lee told herself to remember the wildflowers. "I'm starving," she said, able to smile when she drew away. "It's your turn to cook."

"A small blessing."

Lee gave him a quick jab before they cleaned up the dishes they'd left out in the rain.

In his quick, efficient manner, Hunter had the campfire burning and bacon sizzling. Lee sat back, absorbing the scents while she watched him break eggs into the pan.

"We've been through a lot of eggs," she commented idly. "How do you manage to keep them fresh out here?"

Because she was watching his hands, she missed the quick smile. "Just one of the many mysteries of life. You'd better pass me a plate."

"Yes, but— Oh, look." The movement that had caught her eye turned out to be two rabbits, curious enough to bound to the edge of the clearing and watch. The mystery of the eggs was forgotten in the simple fascination of something she'd just begun to appreciate. "Every time I see one, I want to touch."

"If you managed to get close enough to touch, they'd show you they have very sharp teeth."

Shrugging, she dropped her chin to her knees and continued to stare back at the visitors. "The bunnies I think about don't bite."

Hunter reached for a plate himself. "Bunnies, fuzzy little squirrels and cute raccoons are nice to look at but foolish to handle. I remember having a long, heated argument with Sarah on the subject a couple of years ago."

"Sarah?" Lee accepted the plate he offered, but her attention was fully on him.

Until that moment, Hunter hadn't realized how completely he'd forgotten who she was and why she was there. To have mentioned Sarah so casually showed him he needed to keep personal feelings separate from professional agreements. "Someone very special," he told her as he scooped the remaining eggs onto his plate. He remembered his daughter's comment about simmering passion and falling in love. The smile couldn't be prevented. "I imagine she'd like to meet you."

Lee felt something cold squeeze her heart and fought to ignore it. They'd said nothing about commitment, nothing about exclusivity. They were adults. She was responsible for her own emotions and their consequences. "Would she?" Taking the first bite of eggs, she tasted nothing. Her eyes were drawn to the ring on his finger. It wasn't a wedding band, but...

She had to ask, she had to know before things went any further.

"The ring you wear," she began, satisfied her voice was even. "It's very unusual. I've never seen another quite like it."

"You shouldn't." He ate with the ease of a man completely content. "My sister made it."

"Sister?" If her name was Sarah...

"Bonnie raises children and makes jewelry," Hunter went on. "I'm not sure which comes first."

"Bonnie." Nodding, she forced herself to continue eating. "Is she your only sister?"

"There were just the two of us. For some odd reason, we got along very well." He remembered those early years when he was struggling to learn how to be both father and mother to Sarah. He smiled. "We still do."

"How does she feel about what you do?"

"Bonnie's a firm believer that everyone should do exactly what suits them. As long as they're married, with a half-dozen children." He grinned, recognizing the unspoken question in Lee's eyes. "In that area, I've disappointed her." He paused for a moment, the grin fading. "Do you think I could make love with you if I had a wife waiting for me at home?"

She dropped her gaze to her plate. Why could he always read her when she couldn't read him? "I still don't know very much about you."

He didn't know if he consciously made the decision at that moment or if he'd been ready to make it all along. "Ask," he said simply.

Lee looked up at him. It no longer mattered if she needed to know for herself or for her job. She just needed to know. "You've never been married?"

"No."

"Is that an outgrowth of your need for privacy?"

"No, it's an outgrowth of not finding anyone who could deal with the way I live and my obligations."

Lee mulled this over, thinking it a rather odd way to phrase it. "Your writing?"

"Yes, there's that."

She started to press further, then decided to change directions. Personal questions could be reciprocated with personal questions. "You said you hadn't always wanted to be a writer, but were born to be one. What made you realize it?"

"I don't think it was a matter of realizing, but of accepting." Understanding that she wanted something specific, he drew out a cigarette, studying the tip. He was no more certain why he was answering than Lee was why she was asking. "It must've been in my first year of college. I'd written stories ever since I could remember, but I was dead set on a career as an athlete. Then I wrote something that seemed to trigger it. It was nothing fabulous," he added thoughtfully. "A very basic plot, simple background, but the characters pulled me in. I knew them as well as I knew anyone. There was nothing else for me to do."

"It must've been difficult. Publishing isn't an easy field. Even when you break in, it isn't particularly lucrative unless you write best-sellers. With your parents gone, you had to support yourself."

"I had experience waiting tables." He smiled, a bit more easily now. "And detested it. Sometimes you have to put it all on the line, Lenore. So I did."

"How did you support yourself from the time you graduated from college until you broke through with *The Devil's Due*?"

"I wrote."

Lee shook her head, forgetting the half-full plate on her lap. "The articles and short stories couldn't have brought in very much. And that was your first book."

"No, I'd had a dozen others before it." Blowing out a stream of smoke, he reached for the coffeepot. "Want some?"

She leaned forward a bit, her brows drawing together. "Look, Hunter, I've been researching you for months. I might not have gotten much, but I know every book, every article and every short story you've written, including the majority of your college work. There's no way I'd've missed a dozen books."

"You know everything Hunter Brown's written," he corrected and poured himself coffee.

"That's precisely what I said."

"You didn't research Laura Miles."

"Who?"

He sipped, enjoying the coffee and the conversation more than he'd anticipated. "A great many writers use pseudonyms. Laura Miles was mine."

"A woman's name?" Confused on one level, reporter's instincts humming on another, she frowned at him. "You wrote a dozen books before *The Devil's Due* under a woman's name?"

"Yeah. One of the problems with writing is that the name alone can project a certain perception of the author." He offered her the last piece of bacon. "Hunter Brown wasn't right for what I was doing at the time."

Lee let out a frustrated breath. "What were you doing?"

"Writing romance novels." He flicked his cigarette into the fire.

"Writing... *You?*"

He studied her incredulous face before he leaned back. He was used to criticism of genre fiction and, more often than not, amused by it. "Do you object to the genre in general, or to my writing in it?"

"I don't—" Confused, she broke off to try to gather her thoughts. "I just can't picture you writing happy-ever-after love stories. Hunter, I just finished *Silent Scream*. I kept my bedroom door locked for a week." She dragged a hand through her hair as he quietly watched her. "Romances?"

"Most novels have some kind of relationship with them. A romance simply focuses on it, rather than using it as a subplot or a device."

"But didn't you feel you were wasting your talent?" Lee knew his skill in drawing the reader in from the first page, from the first sentence. "I understand there being a matter of putting food on the table, but—"

"No." He cut her off. "I never wrote for the money, Lenore, any more than the novel you're writing is done for financial gain. As far as wasting my talent, you shouldn't look down your nose at something you don't understand.''

''I'm sorry, I don't mean to be condescending. I'm just—'' Helplessly, she shrugged. ''I'm just surprised. No, I'm astonished. I see those colorful little paperbacks everywhere, but—''

''You never considered reading one,'' he finished. ''You should, they're good for you.''

''I suppose, for simple entertainment.''

He liked the way she said it, as though it were something to be enjoyed in secret, like a child's lollipop. ''If a novel doesn't entertain, it isn't a novel and it's wasted your time. I imagine you've read *Jane Eyre, Rebecca, Gone with the Wind, Ivanhoe.*''

''Yes, of course.''

''Romances. A lot of the same ingredients are in those colorful little paperbacks.''

He was perfectly serious. At that moment, Lee would've given up half the books in her personal library for the chance to read one Laura Miles story. ''Hunter, I want to print this.''

''Go ahead.''

Her mouth was already open for the argument she'd expected. ''Go ahead?'' she repeated. ''You don't care?''

''Why should I? I'm not ashamed of the work I did as Laura Miles. In fact...'' He smiled, thinking back. ''I'm rather pleased with most of it.''

''Then why—'' She shook her head as she began to absently nibble on cold bacon. ''Damn it, Hunter, why haven't you ever said so before? Laura Miles is as much a deep, dark secret as everything else about you."

"I never met a reporter I chose to tell before." He rose, stretching, and enjoyed the wide blue expanse of sky. Just as he'd never met a woman he'd have chosen to live with before. Hunter was beginning to wonder if one had very much to do with the other. "Don't complicate the simple, Lenore," he told her, thinking aloud. "It usually manages to complicate itself."

Setting her plate aside, she stood in front of him. "One more question, then."

He brought his gaze back down to hers. She hadn't bothered to fuss with her hair or makeup that morning, as she had from the first morning of the trip. For a moment, he wondered if the reporter was too anxious for the story or the woman was too involved with the man. He wished he knew. "All right," he agreed. "One more question."

"Why me?"

How did he answer what he didn't know? How did he answer what he was hesitant to ask himself? Framing her face, he brought his lips to hers. Long, lingering, and very, very new. "I see something in you," Hunter murmured, holding her face still so that he could study it. "I want something from you. I don't know what either one is yet, and maybe I never will. Is that answer enough?"

She put her hands on his wrists and felt his life pump through them. It was almost possible to believe hers pumped through them, too. "It has to be."

Chapter 9

Standing high on the bluff, Lee could see down the canyon, over the peaks and pinnacles, beyond the rich red buttes to the sheer-faced walls. There were pictures in them. People, creatures, stories. They pleased her all the more because she hadn't realized she could find them.

She hadn't known land could be so demanding, or so compelling. Not knowing that, how could she have known she would feel at home so far away from the world she knew or the life she'd made?

Perhaps it was the mystery, the awesomeness—the centuries of work nature had done to form beauty out of rock, the centuries it had yet to work. Weather had landscaped, carved and created without pampering. It might have been the quiet she'd learned to listen to, the quiet she'd learned to hear more than she'd ever heard sound before. Or it might have been the man she'd discovered in the canyon, who was slowly, inevitably dominating every aspect of her life in much the same way wind, water and sun dominated the shape of everything around her. He wouldn't pamper, either.

They'd been lovers only a matter of days, yet he seemed to know just where her strengths lay, and her weaknesses. She learned about him, step by gradual step, always amazed that each new discovery came so naturally, as though she'd always known. Perhaps the intensity came from the briefness. Lee could almost accept that theory, but for the timelessness of the hours they spent together.

In two days, she'd leave the canyon, and the man, and go back to being the Lee Radcliffe she'd molded herself into over the years. She'd step back into the rhythm, write her article and go on to the next stage of her career.

What choice was there? Lee asked herself as she stood with the afternoon sun beating down on her. In L.A., her life had direction, it had purpose. There, she had one goal: to succeed. That goal didn't seem so important here and now, where just being, just breathing, was enough, but this world wasn't the one she would live in day after day. Even if Hunter had asked, even if she'd wanted to, Lee couldn't go on indefinitely in this unscheduled, unplanned existence. Purpose, she wondered. What would her purpose be here? She couldn't dream by the campfire forever.

But two days. She closed her eyes, telling herself

that everything she'd done and everything she'd seen would be forever implanted in her memory. Did the time left have to be so short? And the time ahead of her loomed so long.

"Here." Hunter came up alongside her, holding out a pair of binoculars. "You should always see as far as you can."

She took them, with a smile for the way he had of putting things. The canyon zoomed closer, abruptly becoming more personal. She could see the water rushing by in the creek, rushing with a sound too distant to be heard. Why had she never noticed how unique each leaf on a tree could be? She could see other campers loitering near their sites or mingling with the day tourists on paths. Lee let the binoculars drop. They brought intrusion too close.

"Will you come back next year?" She wanted to be able to picture him there, looking out over the endless space, remembering.

"If I can."

"It won't have changed," she murmured. If she came back, five, ten years from then, the creek would still snake by, the buttes would still stand. But she couldn't come back. With an effort, she shook off the mood and smiled at him. "It must be nearly lunchtime."

"It's too hot to eat up here." Hunter wiped at the sweat on his brow. "We'll go down and find some shade."

"All right." She could see the dust plume up from his boots as he walked. "Someplace near the creek."

She glanced to the right. "Let's go this way, Hunter. We haven't walked down there yet."

He hesitated only a moment. "Fine." Holding her hand, he took the path she'd chosen.

The walk down was always easier than the walk up. That was another invaluable fact Lee had filed away during the last couple of weeks. And Hunter, though he held her hand, didn't guide or lead. He simply walked his own way. Just as he'd walk his own way in forty-eight hours, she mused, and stretched her stride to keep pace with him.

"Will you start on your next book as soon as you get back?"

Questions, he thought. He'd never known anyone with such an endless supply of questions. "Yes."

"Are you ever afraid you'll, well, dry up?"

"Always."

Interested, she stopped a moment. "Really?" She'd considered him a man without any fear at all. "I'd have thought that the more success you achieved, the more confident you'd become."

"Success is a deity that's never satisfied." She frowned, a bit uncomfortable with his description. "Every time I face that first blank page, I wonder how I'll ever get through a beginning, middle and end."

"How do you?"

He began to walk again, so that she had to keep up or be left behind. "I tell the story. It's as simple and as miserably complex as that."

So was he, she reflected, that simple, that complex.

Lee thought over his words as she felt the temperature gradually change with the decrease in elevation.

It seemed tidier in this section of the canyon. Once she thought she heard the purr of a car's engine, a sound she hadn't heard in days. The trees grew thicker, the shade more generous. How strange, she reflected, to have those sheer, unforgiving walls at her back and a cozy little forest in front of her. More unreality? Then, glancing down, she saw a patch of small white flowers. Lee picked three, leaving the rest for someone else. She hadn't come for them, she remembered as she tucked them in her hair, but she was glad, so very glad, to have found them.

"How's this?" He turned to see her secure the last flower in her hair. The need for her, the complete her, rose inside of him so swiftly it took his breath away. Lenore. He had no trouble understanding why the man in Poe's verse had mourned the loss of her to the point of madness. "You grow lovelier. Impossible." Hunter touched a fingertip to her cheek. Would he, too, grow mad from mourning the loss of her?

Her face, lifted to the sun, needed nothing more than the luminescence of her skin to make it exquisite. But how long, he wondered, how long would she be content to shun the polish? How long would it be before she craved the life she'd begun to carve out for herself?

Lee didn't smile, because his eyes prevented her. He was looking into her again, for something... Something. She wasn't certain, even if she'd known what it was, that she could give him the answer he wanted. Instead, she did what he'd once done. Placing her hands on his shoulders, she touched her mouth to his. With her eyes squeezed shut, she dropped her head onto his chest.

How could she leave? How could she not? There seemed to be no direction she could go and not lose something essential. "I don't believe in magic," she murmured, "but if I did, I'd say this was a magic place. Now, in the day, it's quiet. Sleeping, perhaps. But at night, the air would be alive with spirits."

He held her closer as he rested his neck on top of her head. Did she realize how romantic she was? he wondered. Or just how hard she fought not to be? A week ago, she might have had such a thought, but she'd never have said it aloud. A week from now... Hunter bit back a sigh. A week from now, she'd give no more thought to magic.

"I want to make love with you here," he said quietly. "With the sunlight streaming through the leaves and onto your skin. In the evening, just before the dew falls. At dawn, when the light's caught somewhere between rose and gray."

Moved, ruled by love, she smiled up at him. "And at midnight, when the moon's high and anything's possible."

"Anything's always possible." He kissed one cheek, then the other. "You only have to believe it."

She laughed, a bit shakily. "You almost make me believe it. You make my knees weak."

His grin flashed as he swept her up in his arms. "Better?"

Would she ever feel this free again? Throwing her arms around his neck, Lee kissed him with all the feeling that welled inside her. "Yes. And if you don't put me down, I'll want you to carry me back to camp."

The half smile touched his lips. "Decided you aren't hungry after all?"

"Since I doubt you've got anything in that bag but dried fruit and sunflower seeds, I don't have any illusions about lunch."

"I've still got a couple pieces of fudge."

"Let's eat."

Hunter dropped her unceremoniously on the ground. "It shows the woman's basic lust centers around food."

"Just chocolate," Lee disagreed. "You can have my share of the sunflower seeds."

"They're good for you." Digging into the pack, he pulled out some small clear-plastic bags.

"I can handle the raisins," Lee said unenthusiastically. "But I can do without the seeds."

Shrugging, Hunter popped two in his mouth. "You'll be hungry before dinner."

"I've been hungry before dinner for two weeks," she tossed back, and began to root through the pack herself for the fudge. "No matter how good seeds and nuts and little dried pieces of apricot are for you, they don't take the place of red meat—" she found a small square of fudge "—or chocolate."

Hunter watched her close her eyes in pure pleasure as she chewed the candy. "Hedonist."

"Absolutely." Her eyes were laughing when she opened them. "I like silk blouses, French champagne and lobster with warm butter sauce." She sighed as she sat back, wondering if Hunter had any emotional attachment to the last piece of fudge. "I especially enjoy them after I've worked all week to justify having them."

He understood that, perhaps too well. She wasn't a woman who wanted to be taken care of, nor was he a man who believed anyone should have a free ride. But what future was there in a relationship when two people couldn't acclimate to each other's life-style? He'd never imposed his on anyone else, nor would be permit anyone to sway him from his own. And yet, now that he felt the clock ticking the hours away, the days away, he wondered if it would be as simple to go back, alone, as he'd once expected it to be.

"You enjoy living in the city?" he asked casually.

"Of course." It wasn't possible to tell him that she hated the thought of going back, alone, to what she'd always thought was perfect for her. "My apartment's twenty minutes from the magazine."

"Convenient." And practical, he mused. It seemed she would always choose the practical, even if she had a whim for the fanciful. He opened the canteen and drank. When he passed it to Lee, she accepted. She'd learned to make a number of adjustments.

"I suppose you work at home."

"Yes."

She touched a hand absently to one of the flowers in her hair. "That takes discipline. I think most people need the structure of an office away from their living space to accomplish anything.''

''You wouldn't.''

She looked over then, wishing they could talk about more personal things without bringing on that quiet sense of panic. Better that they talked of work or the weather, or of nothing at all. ''No?''

''You'd drive yourself harder than any supervisor or time clock.'' He bit into an apple slice. ''If you put your mind to it, you'd have that manuscript finished within a month.''

Restlessly, she moved her shoulders. ''If I worked eight hours a day, without any other obligations.''

''The story's your only obligation.''

She held back a sigh. She didn't want to argue or even debate, not when they had so little time left together. Yet if they didn't discuss her work, she might not be able to prevent herself from talking about her feelings. That was a circle without any meeting point.

''Hunter, as a writer, you can feel that way about a book. I suppose you have to. I have a job, a career that demands blocks of time and a great deal of my attention. I can't simply put that into hiatus while I speculate on my chances of getting a manuscript published.''

''You're afraid to risk it.''

It was a direct hit to her most sensitive area. Both of them knew her anger was a defense. ''What if I am? I've worked hard for my position at *Celebrity*. Everything I've done there, and every benefit I've re-

ceived, I've earned on my own. I've already taken
enough risks.''

"By not marrying Jonathan Willoby?''

The fury leaped into her eyes quickly, interesting
him. So, it was still a sore point, Hunter realized. A
very sore point.

"Do you find that amusing?'' Lee demanded.
"Does the fact that I reneged on an unspoken agreement appeal to your sense of humor?''

"Not particularly. But it intrigues me that you'd
consider it possible to renege on something unspoken.''

From the meticulous way she recapped the canteen,
he gauged just how angry she was. Her voice was cool
and detached, as he hadn't heard it for days. "My
family and the Willobys have been personally and
professionally involved for years. The marriage was
expected of me and I knew it from the time I was
sixteen.''

Hunter leaned back against the trunk of a tree until
he was comfortable. "And at sixteen you didn't consider that sort of expectation antiquated?''

"How could you possibly understand?'' Fuming,
she rose. The nerves that had been dormant for days
began to jump again. Hunter could almost see them
spring to life. "You said your father was a dreamer
who made his living as a salesman. My father was a
realist who made his living socializing and delegating.
He socialized with the Willobys. He delegated me to
complete the social and professional merger with them
by marrying Jonathan.'' Even now, the tidy, unemo-

tional plans gave her a twinge of distaste. "Jonathan was attractive, intelligent, already successful. My father never considered that I'd object."

"But you did," Hunter pointed out. "Why do you continue to insist on paying for something that was your right?"

Lee whirled to him. It was no longer possible for her to answer coolly, to rebuff with aloofness. "Do you know what it cost me not to do what was expected of me? Everything I did, all my life, was ultimately for their approval."

"Then you did something for yourself." Without hurry, he rose to face her. "Is your career for yourself, Lenore, or are you still trying to win their approval?"

He had no right to ask, no right to make her search for the answer. Pale, she turned away from him. "I don't want to discuss this with you. It's none of your concern."

"Isn't it?" Abruptly as angry as she, Hunter spun her around again. "Isn't it?" he repeated.

Her hands curled around his arms—whether in protest or for support, she wasn't certain. Now, she thought, now perhaps she'd reached that edge where she had to make a stand, no matter how unsteady the ground under her feet. "My life and the way I live it are my business, Hunter."

"Not anymore."

"You're being ridiculous." She threw back her head, the better to meet his eyes. "This argument doesn't even have a point."

Something was building inside him so quickly he

didn't have a chance to fight it or reason it through.
"You're wrong."

She was beginning to tremble without knowing
why. Along with the anger came the quick panic she
recognized too well. "I don't know what you want."

"You." She was crushed against him before she
understood her own reaction. "All of you."

His mouth closed over hers with none of the gentle
patience he usually showed. Lee felt a lick of fear that
was almost immediately swallowed by raging need.

He'd made her feel passion before, but not so
swiftly. Desire had burst inside her before, but not so
painfully. Everything was as it always was whenever
he touched her, and yet everything was so different.

Was it anger she felt from him? Frustration? Passion? She only knew that the control he mastered so
finely was gone. Something strained inside him, something more primitive than he'd let free before. This
time, they both knew it could break loose. Her blood
swam with the panicked excitement of anticipation.

Then they were on the ground, with the scent of
sun-warmed leaves and cool water. She felt his beard
scrape over her cheek before he buried his mouth in
her throat. Whatever drove him left her no choice but
to race with him to the end that waited for both of
them.

He didn't question his own desperation. He
couldn't. If she held off sharing certain pieces of herself with him, she still shared her body willingly. He
wanted more, all, though he told himself it wasn't reasonable. Even now, as he felt her body heat and melt

for him, he knew he wouldn't be satisfied. When would she give her feelings to him as freely? For the first time in his life, he wanted too much.

He struggled back to the edge of reason, resisting the wave after wave of need that raged through him. This wasn't the time, the place or the way. In his mind, he knew it, but emotion battled to betray him. Still holding her close, he buried his face in her hair and waited for the madness to pass.

Stunned, as much by his outburst of passion as by her unquestioning response, Lee lay still. Instinctively, she stroked a hand down his back to soothe. She knew him well enough to understand that his temper was rarely unguarded. Now she knew why.

Hunter lifted his head to look at her, seeing on a surge of self-disgust that her eyes were wary again. The flowers had fallen from her hair. Taking one, he pressed it into her hand. "You're much too fragile to be handled so clumsily."

His eyes were so intense, so dark, it was impossible for her to relax again. Against his back, her fingers curled and uncurled. There was a warning somewhere in her brain that he wanted more than she'd expected him to want, more than she knew how to give. Play it light, Lee ordered herself, and deliberately stilled the movement of her fingers. She smiled, though her eyes remained cautious.

"I should've waited until we were back in the tent before I made you angry."

Understanding what she was trying to do, Hunter lifted a brow. Under his voice, and hers, was a strain both of them pretended not to hear. "We can go back now. I can toss you around a bit more."

As the panic subsided, she sent him a mild glance. "I'm stronger than I look."

"Yeah?" He sent her a smile of his own. He had the long hours of night to think about what had happened and what he was going to do about it. "Show me."

More confident than she should've been, Lee pushed against him, intent on rolling him off her. He didn't budge. The look of calm amusement on his face had her doubling her efforts. Breathless, unsuccessful, she lay back and frowned at him. "You're heavier than you look," she complained. "It must be all those sunflower seeds."

"Your muscles are full of chocolate," he corrected.

"I only had one piece," she began.

"Today. By my count, you've polished off—"

"Never mind." Her brow arched elegantly. The nerves in her stomach hadn't completely subsided. "If you want to talk about unhealthy habits, you're the one who smokes too much."

He shrugged, accepting the truth. "Everyone's entitled to one vice."

Her grin became wicked, then sultry. "Is that your only one?"

If she'd planned to make her mouth irresistible, she'd succeeded. Hunter lowered his to nibble at the sweetness. "I've never been one to consider pleasures vices."

Sighing, she linked her arms around his neck. They

didn't have enough time left to waste it arguing, or even thinking. "Why don't we go back to the tent so you can show me what you mean?"

He laughed softly and shifted to kiss the curve of her shoulder. Her laugh echoed his, then Lee's smile froze when she glanced down the length of his body to what stood at their feet.

Fear ripped through her. She couldn't have screamed. Her short, unpainted nails dug into Hunter's back.

"What—" He lifted his head. Her face was ice-white and still. Though her body was rigid beneath his, there was lively fear in the hands that dug into his back. Muscles tense, he turned to look in the direction she was staring. "Damn." The word was hardly out of his mouth before a hundred pounds of fur and muscle leaped on him. This time, Lee's scream tore free.

Adrenaline born of panic gave her the strength to send the three of them rolling to the edge of the bank. As she struck out blindly, Lee heard Hunter issue a sharp command. A whimper followed it.

"Lenore." Her shoulders were gripped before she could spring to her feet. In her mind, the only thought was to find a weapon to defend them. "It's all right." Without giving her a choice, Hunter held her close. "It's all right, I promise. He won't hurt you."

"My God, Hunter, it's a wolf!" Every nightmare she'd ever read or heard about fangs and claws spun in her mind. With her arms wrapped around him to protect him, as much as for protection for herself, Lee turned her head. Silver eyes stared back at her from a silver coat.

"No." He felt the fresh fear jump through her and continued to soothe. "He's only half wolf."

"We've got to do something." Should they run? Should they sit perfectly still? "He attacked—"

"Greeted," Hunter corrected. "Trust me, Lenore. He's not vicious." Annoyed and resigned, Hunter held out a hand. "Here, Santanas."

A bit embarrassed at having lost control of himself, the dog crawled forward, head down. Speechless, Lee watched Hunter stroke the thick silver-gray fur.

"He's usually better behaved," Hunter said mildly. "But he hasn't seen me for nearly two weeks."

"Seen you?" She pressed herself closer to Hunter. "But..." Logic began to seep through her panic as she saw the dog lick Hunter's extended hand. "You called him by name," she said shakily. "What did you call him?"

Before Hunter could answer, there was a rustling in the trees behind them. Lee had nearly mustered the breath to scream again when another voice, young and high, shouted out. "Santanas! You come back here. I'm going to get in trouble."

"Damn right," Hunter mumbled under his breath.

Lee drew back far enough to look into Hunter's face. "Just what the hell's going on?"

"A reunion," he said simply.

Puzzled, with her heart still pounding in her ears, Lee watched the girl break through the trees. The dog's tail began to thump the ground.

"Santanas!" She stopped, her dark braids whipping back and forth. Smiling, she uninhibitedly showed her braces. "Whoops." The quick exclamation trailed off as Lee was treated to a long intense stare that was hauntingly familiar. The girl stuck her hands in the pockets of cutoff jeans, scuffing the ground with battered sneakers. "Well, hi." Her gaze shifted to Hunter briefly before it focused on Lee again. "I guess you wonder what I'm doing here."

"We'll get into that later," Hunter said in a tone both females recognized as basic male annoyance.

"Hunter—" Lee drew farther away, traces of anger and anxiety working their way through the confusion. She couldn't bring herself to look away from the dark, dark eyes of the girl who stared at her. "What's going on here?"

"Apparently a lesson in manners should be," he returned easily. "Lenore, the creature currently sniffing at your hand is Santanas, my dog." At the gesture of his hand, the large, lean animal sat and lifted a friendly paw. Dazed, Lee found herself taking it while she turned to watch the dog's master. She saw Hunter's gaze travel beyond her with a smile that held both irony and pride. "The girl rudely staring at you is Sarah. My daughter."

Chapter 10

Daughter...Sarah...

Lee turned her head to meet the dark, direct eyes that were a duplicate of Hunter's. Yes, they were a duplicate. It struck her like a blast of air. He had a child? This lovely, slender girl with a tender mouth and braids secured by mismatched rubber bands was Hunter's daughter? So many opposing emotions moved through her that she said nothing. Nothing at all.

"Sarah." Hunter spoke into the drumming silence. "This is Ms. Radcliffe."

"Sure, I know, the reporter. Hi."

Still sitting on the ground, with the dog now sniffing around her shoulder, Lee felt like a complete fool. "Hello." She hoped the word wasn't as ridiculously formal as it sounded to her.

"Dad said I shouldn't call you pretty because pretty was like a bowl of fruit." Sarah didn't tilt her head as one might to study from a new angle, but Lee had the impression she was being weighed and dissected like a still life. "I like your hair," Sarah declared. "Is it a real color?"

"A definite lesson in manners," Hunter put in, more amused than annoyed. "I'm afraid Sarah's a bit of a brat."

"He always says that." Sarah moved thin, expressive shoulders. "He doesn't mean it, though."

"Until today." He ruffled the dog's fur, wondering just how he would handle the situation. Lee was still silent, and Sarah's eyes were all curiosity. "Take Santanas back to the house. I assume Bonnie's there."

"Yeah. We came back yesterday because I remembered I had a soccer game and she had an inspiration and couldn't do anything with it in Phoenix with all the kids running around like monkeys."

"I see." And though he did, perfectly, Lee was left floundering in the dark. "Go ahead, then, we'll be right along."

"Okay. Come on, Santanas." Then she shot Lee a quick grin. "He looks pretty ferocious, but he doesn't bite." As the girl darted away, Lee wondered if she'd been speaking of the dog or her father. When she was once again alone with Hunter, Lee remained still and silent.

"I'll apologize for the rudeness of my family, if you'd like."

Family. The word struck her, a dose of reality that

flung her out of the dream. Rising, Lee meticulously dusted off her jeans. "There's no need." Her voice was cool, almost chill. Her muscles were wire-taut. "Since the game's over, I'd like you to drive me into Sedona so I can arrange for transportation back to L.A."

"Game?" In one long, easy motion, he came to his feet, then took her hand, stopping its nervous movement. It was a gesture that had become so much of a habit, neither of them noticed. "There's no game, Lenore."

"Oh, you played it very well." The hurt she wouldn't permit in her voice showed clearly in her eyes. Her hand remained cold and rigid in his. "So well, in fact, I completely forgot we were playing."

Patience deserted him abruptly and without warning. Anger he could handle, with more anger or with amusement. But hurt left him with no defense, no attack. "Don't be an idiot. Whatever game there was ended a few nights ago in the tent."

"Ended." Tears sprang to her eyes, stunning her. Furiously she blinked them back, filled with self-disgust, but not before he'd seen them. "No, it never ended. You're an excellent strategist, Hunter. You seemed to be so open with me that I didn't think you were holding anything back." She jerked her hand from his, longing for the luxury of dissolving into those hot, cleansing tears. "How could you?" she demanded. "How could you touch me that way and lie?"

"I never lied to you." His voice was as calm as hers, his eyes were as full of passion.

"You have a child." Something snapped inside her, so that she had to grip her hands together to prevent herself from wringing them. "You have a half-grown daughter you never mentioned to me. You told me you'd never been married."

"I haven't been," he said simply, and waited for the inevitable questions.

They leaped into her mind, but Lee found she couldn't ask them. She didn't want to know. If she was to put him out of her life immediately and completely, she couldn't ask. "You said her name once, and when I asked, you avoided answering."

"Who asked?" he countered. "You or the reporter?"

She paled, and her step away from him said more than a dozen words.

"If that was an unfair question," he said, feeling his way carefully, "I'm sorry."

Lee stifled a bitter answer. He'd just said it all. "I want to go back to Sedona. Will you drive me, or do I have to arrange for a car?"

"Stop this." He gripped her shoulders before she could back farther away. "You've been a part of my life for a few days; Sarah's been my life for ten years. I take no risks with her." She saw the fury come and go in his eyes as he fought against it. "She's off the record, do you understand? She stays off the record. I won't have her childhood disturbed by photographers dogging her at soccer games or hanging from trees at school picnics. Sarah's not an item for the glossy pages of any magazine.''

"Is that what you think of me?" she whispered. "We've come no further than that?" She swallowed a mixture of pain and betrayal. "Your daughter won't be mentioned in any article I write. You have my word. Now let me go."

She wasn't speaking only of the hands that held her there, and they both knew it. He felt a bubble of panic he'd never expected, a twist of guilt that left him baffled. Frustrated, he stared down at her. He'd never realized she could be a complication. "I can't." It was said with such simplicity her skin iced. "I want you to understand, and I need time for that."

"You've had nearly two weeks to make me understand, Hunter."

"Damn it, you came here as a reporter." He paused, as if waiting for her to confirm or deny, but she said nothing. "What happened between us wasn't planned or expected by either one of us. I want you to come back with me to my home."

Somehow she met his eyes levelly. "I'm still a reporter."

"We have two days left in our agreement." His voice softened, his hands gentled. "Lenore, spend those two days with me at home, with my daughter."

"You have no problem asking for everything, do you?"

"No." She was still holding herself away from him. No matter how badly he wanted to, Hunter knew better than to try to draw her closer. Not yet. "It's important to me that you understand. Give me two days.''

She wanted to say no. She wanted to believe she could deny him even that and turn away, go away, without regrets. But there'd be regrets, Lee realized, if she went back to L.A. without taking whatever was left. "I can't promise to understand, but I'll stay two more days."

Though she was reluctant, he held her hand to his lips. "Thank you. It's important to me."

"Don't thank me," she murmured. The anger had slipped away so quietly, she couldn't recall it. "Things have changed."

"Things changed days ago." Still holding her hand, he drew her in the direction Sarah had gone. "I'll come back for the gear."

Now that the first shock had passed, the second occurred to her. "But you live here in the canyon."

"That's right."

"You mean to tell me you have a house, with hot and cold running water and a normal bed, but you chose to spend two weeks in a tent?"

"It relaxes me."

"That's just dandy," she muttered. "You've had me showering with lukewarm water and waking up with aching muscles, when you knew I'd've given a week's pay for one tub bath."

"Builds character," he claimed, more comfortable with her annoyance.

"The hell it does. You did it deliberately." She stopped, turning to him as the sun dappled light through the trees. "You did it all deliberately to see just how much I could tolerate."

"You were very impressive." He smiled infuriatingly. "I admit I never expected you to last out a week, much less two."

"You sonofa—"

"Don't get cranky now," he said easily. "You can take as many baths as you like over the next couple of days." He swung a friendly arm over her shoulder before she could prevent it. And he'd have time, he thought, to explain to her about Sarah. Time, he hoped, to make her understand. "I'll even see to it that you have that red meat you've been craving."

Fury threatened. Control strained. "Don't you dare patronize me."

"I'm not; you're not a woman a man could patronize." Though she mistrusted his answer, his voice was bland with sincerity and he wasn't smiling. "I'm enjoying you and, I suppose, the foul-up of my own plans. Believe me, I hadn't intended for you to find out I lived a couple miles from the campsite in quite this way."

"Just how did you intend for me to find out?"

"By offering you a quiet candlelight dinner on our last night. I'd hoped you'd see the—ah—humor in the situation."

"You'd've been wrong," she said precisely, then caught sight of the house cocooned in the trees.

It was smaller than she'd expected, but with the large areas of glass in the wood, it seemed to extend into the land. It made her think of dolls' houses and fairy tales, though she didn't know why. Dolls' houses were tidy and formal and laced with gingerbread. Hunter's house was made up of odd angles and unexpected peaks. A porch ran across the front, where the roof arched to a high pitch. Plants spilled over the banister—bloodred geraniums in jade-green pots. The roof sloped down again, then ran flat over a parallelogram with floor-to-ceiling windows. On the patio that jutted out from it, a white wicker chair lay overturned next to a battered soccer ball.

The trees closed in around it. Closed it in, Lee thought. Protected, sheltered, hid. It was like a house out of a play, or... Stopping, she narrowed her eyes and studied it again. ''This is Jonas Thorpe's house in *Silent Scream*.''

Hunter smiled, rather pleased she'd seen it so quickly. ''More or less. I wanted to put him in isolation, miles away from what would normally be considered civilized, but in reality, the only safe place left.''

''Is that how you look at it?'' she wondered aloud. ''As the only safe place left?''

''Often.'' Then a shriek, which after a heart-stopping moment Lee identified as laughter, ripped through the silence. It was followed by an excited bout of barking and a woman's frazzled voice. ''Then there're other times,'' Hunter murmured as he led Lee toward the front door.

Even as he opened it, Sarah came bounding out. Unsure of her own feelings, Lee watched the girl throw her arms around her father's waist. She saw

Hunter stroke a hand over the dark hair at the crown of Sarah's head.

"Oh, Dad, it's so funny! Aunt Bonnie was making a bracelet out of glazed dough and Santanas ate it—or he chewed on it until he found out it tasted awful."

"I'm sure Bonnie thinks it's a riot."

Her eyes, so like her father's, lit with a wicked amusement that would've made a veteran fifth-grade teacher nervous. "She said she had to take that sort of thing from art critics, but not from half-breed wolves. She said she'd make some tea for Lenore, but there aren't any cookies because we ate them yesterday. And she said—"

"Never mind, we'll find out for ourselves." He stepped back so that Lee could walk into the house ahead of him. She hesitated for a moment, wondering just what she was walking into, and his eyes lit with the same wicked amusement as Sarah's. They were quite a pair, Lee decided, and stepped forward.

She hadn't expected anything so, well, normal in Hunter Brown's home. The living room was airy, sunny in the afternoon light. *Cheerful.* Yes, Lee realized, that was precisely the word that came to mind. No shadowy corners or locked doors. There were wildflowers in an enameled vase and plump pillows on the sofa.

"Were you expecting witches' brooms and a satin-lined coffin?" he murmured in her ear.

Annoyed, she stepped away from him. "Of course not. I suppose I didn't expect you to have something quite so...domesticated."

He arched a brow at the word. "I am domesticated."

Lee looked at him, at the face that was half rugged, half aristocratic. On one level, perhaps, she mused. But only on one.

"I guess Aunt Bonnie's got the mess in the kitchen pretty well cleaned up." Sarah kept one arm around her father as she gave Lee another thorough going-over. "She'd like to meet you because Dad doesn't see nearly enough women and never talks to reporters. So maybe you're special because he decided to talk to you."

While she spoke, she watched Lee steadily. She was only ten, but already she'd sensed there was something between her father and this woman with the dark-blue eyes and nifty hair. What she didn't know was exactly how she felt about it yet. In the manner of her father, Sarah decided to wait and see.

Equally unsure of her own feelings, Lee went with them into the kitchen. She had an impression of sunny walls, white trim and confusion.

"Hunter, if you're going to keep a wolf in the house, you should at least teach him to appreciate art. Hi, I'm Bonnie."

Lee saw a tall, thin woman with dark-brown shoulder-length hair streaked liberally with blond. She wore a purple T-shirt with faded pink printing over cutoffs as ragged as her niece's. Her bare feet were tipped at the toes with hot-pink polish. Studying her thin model's face, Lee couldn't be sure if she was years older than Hunter or years younger. Automatically she

held out her hand in response to Bonnie's out-
stretched one.

"How do you do?"

"I'd be doing a lot better if Santanas hadn't tried
to make a snack of my latest creation." She held up
a golden-brown half circle with ragged ends. "Just
lucky for him it was a dreadful idea. Anyway, sit."
She gestured to a table piled with bowls and canisters
and dusted the flour. "I'm making tea."

"You didn't turn the kettle on," Sarah pointed out,
and did so herself.

"Hunter, the child's always picking on details. I
worry about her."

With a shrug of acceptance, he picked up what
looked like a small doughnut and might, with imagination, have been an earring. "You're finding gold
and silver too traditional to work with these days?"

"I thought I might start a trend." When Bonnie
smiled, she became abruptly and briefly stunning. "In
any case, it was a small failure. Probably cost you less
than three dollars in flour. Sit," she repeated as she
began to transfer the mess from the table to the
counter behind her. "So, how was the camping trip?"

"Enlightening. Wouldn't you say, Lenore?"

"Educational," she corrected, but thought the last
half hour had been the most educational of all.

"So, you work for *Celebrity*." Bonnie's long,
twisted gold earrings swung when she walked, much
like Sarah's braids. "I'm a faithful reader."

"That's because she's had a couple of embarrass-
ingly flattering write-ups."

"Write-ups?" Lee watched Bonnie dust her flour-covered hands on her cutoffs.

Hunter smiled as he watched his sister reach for a tin of tea and send others clattering to the counter. "Professionally she's known as B. B. Smithers."

The name rang a bell. For years, B. B. Smithers had been considered the queen of avant-garde jewelry. The elite, the wealthy and the trendy flocked to her for personal designs. They paid, and paid well, for her talent, her creativity, and the tiny Bs etched into the finished product. Lee stared at the thin, somewhat clumsy woman with something close to wonder. "I've admired your work."

"But you wouldn't wear it," Bonnie put in with a smile as she shoved tumbled boxes and tins out of her way. "No, it's the classics for you. What a fabulous face. Do you want lemon in your tea? Do we have any lemons, Hunter?"

"Probably not."

Taking this in stride, Bonnie set the teapot on the table to let the tea steep. "Tell me, Lenore, how did you talk the hermit into coming out of his cave?"

"By making him furious, I believe."

"That might work." She sat down across from Lee as Sarah walked to her father's side. Her eyes were softer than her brother's, less intense, but not, Lee thought, less perceptive. "Did the two weeks playing pioneer in the canyon give you the insight to write an article on him?"

"Yes." Lee smiled, because there was humor in

Bonnie's eyes. "Plus I gained a growing affection for box springs and mattresses."

The quick, stunning smile flashed again. "My husband takes the children camping once a year. That's when I go to Elizabeth Arden's for the works. When we come home, both of us feel we've accomplished several small miracles."

"Camping's not so bad," Sarah commented in her father's defense.

"Is that so?" He patted her bottom as he drew her closer. "Why is it that you always have this all-consuming desire to visit Bonnie in Phoenix whenever I start packing gear?"

She giggled, and her arm went easily around his shoulder. "Must be coincidence," she said in a dry tone that echoed his. "Did he make you go fishing?" Sarah wanted to know. "And sit around for just *hours*?"

Lee watched Hunter's brow lift before she answered. "Actually, he did, ah, suggest fishing several days running."

"Ugh" was Sarah's only comment.

"But I caught a bigger fish than he did."

Unimpressed, Sarah shook her head. "It's awfully boring." She sent her father an apologetic glance. "I guess somebody's got to do it." Leaning her head against her father's, she smiled at Lee. "Mostly he's never boring, he just likes some weird stuff. Like fishing and beer."

"Sarah doesn't consider Hunter's shrunken-head

collection at all unusual.'' Bonnie picked up the tea-pot. ''Are you having some?'' she asked her brother.

''I'll pass. Sarah and I'll go and break camp.''

''Take your wolf with you,'' Bonnie told him as she poured tea into Lee's cup. ''He's still on my hit list. By the way, a couple of calls from New York came in for you yesterday.''

''They'll keep.'' As he rose, he ran a careless hand down Lee's hair, a gesture not lost on either of the other females in the room. ''I'll be back shortly.''

She started to offer her help, but it was so comfortable in the sunny, cluttered kitchen, and the tea smelled like heaven. ''All right.'' She saw the proprietary hand Sarah put on her father's arm and thought it just as well to stay where she was.

Together, father and daughter walked to the back door. Hunter whistled for the dog, then they were gone.

Bonnie stirred her tea. ''Sarah adores her father.''

''Yes.'' Lee thought of the way they'd looked, side by side.

''And so do you.''

Lee had started to lift her cup; now it only rattled in the saucer. ''I beg your pardon?''

''You're in love with Hunter,'' Bonnie said mildly. ''I think it's marvelous.''

She could've denied it—vehemently, icily, laughingly, but hearing it said aloud seemed to put her in some kind of trance. ''I don't—that is, it doesn't...'' Lee stopped, realizing she was running the spoon handle through her hands. ''I'm not sure how I feel.''

"A definite symptom. Does being in love worry you?"

"I didn't say I was." Again, Lee stopped. Could anyone make evasions with those soft doe eyes watching? "Yes, it worries me a lot."

"Only natural. I used to fall in and out of love like some people change clothes. Then I met Fred." Bonnie laughed into her tea before she sipped. "I went around with a queasy stomach for weeks."

Lee pressed a hand to her own before she rose. Tea wasn't going to help. She had to move. "I have no illusions about Hunter and myself," she said, more firmly than she'd expected to. "We have different priorities, different tastes." She looked through the kitchen window to the high red walls far beyond the clustering trees. "Different lives. I have to get back to L.A."

Bonnie calmly continued to drink tea. "Of course." If Lee heard the irony, she didn't respond to it. "There are people who have it fixed in their heads that in order to have a relationship, the two parties involved must be on the same wavelength. If one adores sixteenth-century French poetry and the other detests it, there's no hope." She noticed Lee's frown but continued, lightly. "Fred's an accountant who gets a primal thrill out of interest rates." She wiped absently at a smudge of flour on the table. "Statistically, I suppose we should've divorced years ago."

Lee turned back, unable to be angry, unable to smile. "You're a great deal like Hunter, aren't you?"

"I suppose. Is your mother Adreanne Radcliffe?"

Though she no longer wanted it, Lee came back to the table for her tea. "Yes."

"I met her at a party in Palm Springs two, no, must've been three years ago. Yes, three," Bonnie said decisively, "because I was still nursing Carter, my youngest, and he's currently terrorizing everyone at nursery school. Just last week he tried to cook a goldfish in a toy oven. You're not at all like your mother, are you?"

It took a moment for Lee to catch up. She set down her tea again, untasted. "Aren't I?"

"Do you think you are?" Bonnie tossed her tousled, streaked hair behind her shoulder. "I don't mean any offense, but she wouldn't know what to say to anyone not born to the blue, so to speak. I'd've considered her a very sheltered woman. She's very lovely; you certainly appear to've inherited her looks. But that seems to be all."

Lee stared down at her tea. How could she explain that, because of the strong physical resemblance between her and her mother, she'd always figured there were other resemblances. Hadn't she spent her childhood and adolescence trying to find them, and all of her adult life trying to repress them? A sheltered woman. She found it a terrifying phrase, and too close to what she herself could have become.

"My mother has standards," she answered, at length. "She never seems to have any trouble living up to them."

"Oh, well, everyone should do what they do best." Bonnie propped her elbows on the table, lacing her fingers so that the three rings on her right hand gleamed and winked. "According to Hunter, the thing you do best is write. He mentioned your novel to me."

The irritation came so quickly Lee hadn't the chance to mask it. "He's the kind of man who can't admit when he's made a mistake. I'm a reporter, not a novelist."

"I see." Still smiling blandly, Bonnie dropped her chin onto her laced fingers. "So, what are you going to report about Hunter?"

Was there a challenge under the smile? A trace of mockery? Whatever there was at the edges, Lee couldn't help but respond to it. Yes, she thought again, Bonnie Smithers was a great deal like her brother.

"That he's a man who considers writing both a sacred duty and a skilled profession. That he has a sense of humor that's often so subtle it takes you hours to catch up. That he believes in choices and luck with the same stubbornness that he believes in fate." Pausing, she lifted her cup. "He values the written word, whether it's in comic books or Chaucer, and he works desperately hard to do what he considers his job: to tell the story."

"I like you."

Cautiously, Lee smiled. "Thank you."

"I love my brother," Bonnie went on easily. "More than that, I admire him, for personal and professional reasons. You understand him. Not everyone would."

"Understand him?" Lee shook her head. "It seems to me that the more I find out about him, the less I understand. He's shown me more beauty in a pile of rocks than I'd ever have found for myself, yet he writes about horror and fears.''

"And you consider that a contradiction?'' Bonnie shrugged as she leaned back in her chair. "It's just that Hunter sees both sides of life very clearly. He writes about the dark side because it's the most intriguing.''

"Yet he lives...'' Lee gestured as she glanced around the kitchen.

"In a cozy little house nestled in the woods.''

The laugh came naturally. "I wouldn't precisely call it cozy, but it's certainly not what you'd expect from the country's leading author of horror and occult fiction.''

"The country's leading author of horror and occult fiction has a child to raise.''

"Yes.'' Lee's smile faded. "Yes, Sarah. She's lovely.''

"Will she be in your article?''

"No.'' Again, she lifted her gaze to Bonnie's. "No, Hunter made it clear he objected to that.''

"She's the focal point of his life. If he seems a bit overprotective in certain ways, believe me, it's a completely unselfish act.'' When Lee merely nodded, Bonnie felt a stirring of sympathy. "He hasn't told you about her?''

"No, nothing.''

There were times Bonnie's love and admiration for Hunter became clouded with frustration. A great many times. This woman was in love with him, was one

step away from being irrevocably committed to him.
Any fool could see it, Bonnie mused. Any fool except
Hunter. "As I said, there are times he's overly pro-
tective. He has his reasons, Lenore."

"And will you tell me what they are?"

She was tempted. It was time Hunter opened that
part of his life, and she was certain this was the
woman he should open it to. "The story's Hunter's,"
Bonnie said at length. "You should hear it from him."
She glanced around idly as she heard the Jeep pull up
in the drive. "They're back."

"I guess I'm glad you brought her back," Sarah
commented as they drove the last mile toward home.

"You guess?" Hunter turned his head, to see his
daughter looking pensively through the windshield.

"She's beautiful, like a princess." For the first time
in months, Sarah worried her braces with her tongue.
"You like her a lot, I can tell."

"Yes, I like her a lot." He knew every nuance of
his daughter's voice, every expression, every gesture.
"That doesn't mean I like you any less."

Sarah gave him one long look. She needed no other
words from him to reaffirm love. "I guess you have
to like me," she decided, half teasing, "'cause we're
stuck with each other. But I don't think she does."

"Why shouldn't Lenore like you?" Hunter countered, able to follow her winding statement without
any trouble.

"She doesn't smile much."

Not enough, he silently agreed, but more each day. "When she relaxes, she does."

Sarah shrugged, unconvinced. "Well, she looked at me awful funny."

"Your grammar's deteriorating."

"She did."

Hunter frowned a bit as he turned into the dirt drive to their house. "It's only that she was surprised. I hadn't mentioned you to her."

Sarah stared at him a moment, then put her scuffed sneakers on the dash. "That wasn't very nice of you."

"Maybe not."

"You'd better apologize."

He sent his daughter a mild glance. "Really?"

She patted Santanas's head when he leaned over the back of her seat and dropped it on her shoulder. "Really. You always make me apologize when I'm rude."

"I didn't consider that you were any of her business." At first, Hunter amended silently. Things changed. Everything changed.

"You always make me apologize, even when I make up excuses," Sarah pointed out unmercifully. When they pulled up by the house, she grinned at him. "And even when I hate apologizing."

"Brat," he mumbled, setting the brake.

With a squeal of laughter, Sarah launched herself at him. "I'm glad you're home."

He held her close a moment, absorbing her scent— youthful sweat, grass and flowery shampoo. It seemed impossible that ten years had passed since he'd first held her. Then she'd smelled of powder and fragility

and fresh linen. It seemed impossible that she was
half-grown and the time had been so short.

"I love you, Sarah."

Content, she cuddled against him a moment, then,
lifting her head, she grinned. "Enough to make pizza
for dinner?"

He pinched her subtly pointed chin. "Maybe just
enough for that."

Chapter 11

When Lee thought of family dinners, she thought of quiet meals at a glossy mahogany table laid with heavy Georgian silver, meals where conversation was subdued and polite. It had always been that way for her.

Not this dinner.

The already confused kitchen became chaotic while Sarah dashed around, half dancing, half bobbing, as she filled her father in on every detail of the past two weeks. Oblivious to the noise, Bonnie used the kitchen phone to call home and check in with her husband and children. Santanas, forgiven, lay sprawled on the floor, dozing. Hunter stood at the counter, preparing what Sarah claimed was the best pizza in the stratosphere. Somehow he managed to keep up with his daughter's disjointed conversation, answer the questions Bonnie tossed at him and cook at the same time.

Feeling like oil poured heedlessly on a rub of churning water, Lee began to clear the table. If she didn't do something, she decided, she'd end up standing in the middle of the room with her head swiveling back and forth, like a fan at a tennis match.

"I'm supposed to do that."

Awkwardly, Lee set down the teapot she'd just lifted and looked at Sarah. "Oh." Stupid, she berated herself. Haven't you any conversation for a child?

"You can help, I guess," Sarah said after a moment. "But if I don't do my chores, I don't get my allowance." Her gaze slid to her father, then back again. "There's this album I want to buy. You know, the Total Wrecks."

"I see." Lee searched her mind for even a wispy knowledge of the group but came up blank.

"They're actually not as bad as the name makes them sound," Bonnie commented on her way out to the kitchen. "Anyway, Hunter won't dock your pay if you take on an assistant, Sarah. It's considered good business sense."

Turning his head, Hunter caught his sister's quick grin before she waltzed out of the room. "I suppose Lee should earn her supper as well," he said easily. "Even if it isn't red meat."

The smile made it difficult for her to casually lift the teapot again.

"You'll like the pizza better," Sarah stated confidently. "He puts *everything* on it. Anytime I have friends over for dinner, they always want Dad's pizza.'' As she continued to clear the table, Lee tried to imagine Hunter competently preparing meals for several young, chattering girls. She simply couldn't. ''I think he was a cook in another life.''

Good Lord, Lee thought, did the child already have views on reincarnation?

''The same way you were a gladiator,'' Hunter said dryly.

Sarah laughed, childlike again. ''Aunt Bonnie was a slave sold at an Arabian auction for thousands and thousands of drachmas.''

''Bonnie has a very fluid ego.''

With a clatter, Sarah set the cups in the sink. ''I think Lenore must've been a princess.''

With a damp cloth in her hands, Lee looked up, not certain if she should smile.

''A medieval princess,'' Sarah went on. ''Like with King Arthur.''

Hunter seemed to consider the idea a moment, while he studied his daughter and the woman under discussion. ''It's a possibility. One of those delicate jeweled crowns and filmy veils would suit her.''

''And dragons.'' Obviously enjoying the game, Sarah leaned back against the counter, the better to imagine Lee in a flowing pastel gown. ''A knight would have to kill at least one full-grown male dragon before he could ask for her hand.''

''True enough,'' Hunter murmured, thinking that dragons came in many forms.

''Dragons aren't easy to kill.'' Though she spoke

lightly, Lee wondered why her stomach was quivering. It was entirely too easy to imagine herself in a great torchlit hall, with jewels winking from her hair and from the bodice of a rich silk gown.

"It's the best way to prove valor," Sarah told her, nibbling on a slice of green pepper she'd snitched from her father. "A princess can't marry just anyone, you know. The king would either give her to a worthy knight, or marry her off to a neighboring prince so he could have more land with peace and prosperity."

Incredibly, Lee pictured her father, staff in hand, decreeing that she would marry Jonathan of Willoby.

"I bet you never had to wear braces."

Cast from one century to another in the blink of an eye, Lee merely stared. Sarah was frowning at her with the absorbed, absorbing concentration she could have inherited only from Hunter. It was all so foolish, Lee thought. Knights, princesses, dragons. For the first time, she was able to smile naturally at the slim, dark girl who was a part of the man she loved.

"Two years."

"You did?" Interest sprang into Sarah's solemn face. She stepped forward, obviously to get a better look at Lee's teeth. "It worked good," she decided. "Did you hate them?"

"Every minute."

Sarah giggled, so that the silver flashed. "I don't mind too much, 'cept I can't chew gum." She sent a sulky look over her shoulder in Hunter's direction. "Not even one stick."

"Neither could I." Ever, she thought, but didn't

add it. Gum chewing was not permitted in the Radcliffe household.

Sarah studied her another moment, then nodded. "I guess you can help me set the table, too."

Acceptance, Lee was to discover, was just that simple.

The sun was streaming into the kitchen while they ate. It was rich and golden, without those harsh, stunning flashes of white she remembered from the cliffs of the canyon. She found it peaceful, despite all the talk and laughter and arguments swimming around her.

Her fantasies had run to eating a thick, rare steak and a crisp chef's salad in a dimly lit, quiet restaurant where the hovering waiter saw that your glass of Bordeaux was never empty. She found herself in a bright, noisy kitchen, eating pizza stringy with cheese, chunky with slices of green pepper and mushroom, spiced with pepperoni and hot sausage. And while she did, she found herself agreeing with Sarah's accolade. The best in the stratosphere.

"If only Fred could learn how to make one of these." Bonnie cut into her second slice with the same dedication she'd cut into her first. "On a good day he makes a superior egg salad, but it's not the same."

"With a family the size of yours," Hunter commented, "you'd need to set up an assembly line. Five hungry children could keep a pizzeria hopping."

"And do," Bonnie agreed. "In a bit less than seven months, it'll be six."

She grinned as Hunter's knife paused. "Another?"

"Another." Bonnie winked across the table at her niece. "I always said I'd have half a dozen kids," she said casually to Lee. "People should do what they do best."

Hunter reached over to take her hand. Lee saw the fingers interlock. "Some might call it overachievement."

"Or sibling rivalry," she tossed back. "I'll have as many kids as you do best-sellers." With a laugh, she squeezed her brother's hand. "It takes us about the same length of time to produce."

"When you bring the baby to visit, she should sleep in my room." Sarah bit off another mouthful of pizza.

"She?" Hunter ruffled her hair before he started to eat again.

"It'll be a girl." With the confidence of youth, Sarah nodded. "Aunt Bonnie already has three boys, so another girl makes it even."

"I'll see what I can do," Bonnie told her. "Anyway, I'll be heading back in the morning. Cassandra, she's my oldest," she put in for Lee's benefit, "has decided she wants a tattoo." She closed her eyes as she leaned back. "Ah, it's nice to be needed."

"A tattoo?" Sarah wrinkled her nose. "That's gross. Cassie's nuts."

"Fred and I are forced to agree."

Interested, Hunter lifted his wine. "Where does she want it?"

"On the curve of her right shoulder. She insists it'll be very tasteful."

"Dumb." Sarah handed out the decree with a

shrug. "Cassie's thirteen," she added, rolling her eyes. "Boy, is she a case."

Lee choked back a laugh at both the facial and verbal expressions. "How will you handle it?"

Bonnie only smiled. "Oh, I think I'll take her to the tattoo parlor."

"But you wouldn't—" Lee broke off, seeing Bonnie's liberally streaked hair and shoulder-length earrings. Perhaps she would.

With a laugh, Bonnie patted Lee's hand. "No, I wouldn't. But it'll be a lot more effective if Cassie makes the decision herself—which she will, the minute she gets a good look at all those nasty little needles."

"Sneaky," Sarah approved with a grin.

"Clever," Bonnie corrected.

"Same thing." With her mouth half-full, she turned to Lee. "There's always a crisis at Aunt Bonnie's house," she said confidentially. "Did you have brothers and sisters?"

"No." Was that wistfulness she saw in the child's eyes? She'd often had the same wish herself. "There was only me."

"I think it's better to have them, even though it gets crowded." She slanted her father a guileless smile. "Can I have another piece?"

The rest of the evening passed, not quietly but, for all the noise, peacefully. Sarah dragged her father outside for soccer practice, which Bonnie declined, grinning. Her condition, she claimed, was too delicate. Lee, over her protests, found herself drafted. She learned, though her aim was never very accurate, to kick a ball with the side of her foot and bounce it off her head. She enjoyed it, which surprised her, and didn't feel like a fool, which surprised her more.

Dusk came quickly, then a dark that flickered with fireflies. Though her eyes were heavy, Sarah groaned about going to bed until Hunter agreed to carry her up on his back. Lee didn't have to be told it was a nightly ritual; she only had to see them together.

He'd said Sarah was his life, and though she'd only seen them together for a matter of hours, Lee believed it.

She'd never have expected the man whose books she'd read to be a devoted father, content to spend his time with a ten-year-old girl. She'd never have imagined him here, in a house so far away from the excitement of the city. Even the man she'd grown to know over the past two weeks didn't quite fit the structure of being parent, disciplinarian and mentor to a ten-year-old. Yet he was.

If she superimposed the image of Sarah's father over those of her lover and the author of *Silent Scream,* they all seemed to meld into one. The problem was dealing with it.

Righting the overturned chair on the patio, Lee sat. She could hear Sarah's sleepy laughter drift through the open window above her. Hunter's voice, low and indistinct, followed it. It was an odd way to spend her last hours with Hunter, here in his home, only a few miles from the campsite where they'd become lovers.

And yes, she realized as she stared up at the stars, friends. She very much wanted to be his friend.

Now, when she wrote the article, she'd be able to do so with knowledge of both sides of him. It was what she'd come for. Lee closed her eyes because the stars were suddenly too bright. She was going back with much more and, because of it, much less.

"Tired?"

Opening her eyes, she looked up at Hunter. This was how she'd always remember him, cloaked in shadows, coming out of the darkness. "No. Is Sarah asleep?"

He nodded, coming around behind her to put his hands on her shoulders. This was where he wanted her. Here, when night was closing in. "Bonnie, too."

"You'd work now," she guessed. "When the house was quiet and the windows dark."

"Yes, most of the time. I finished my last book on a night like this." He hadn't been lonely then, but now... "Let's walk. The moon's full.

"Afraid? I'll give you a talisman." He slipped his ring off his pinky, sliding it onto her finger.

"I'm not superstitious," she said loftily, but curled her fingers into her palm to hold the ring in place.

"Of course you are." He drew her against his side as they walked. "I like the night sounds."

Lee listened to them—the faintest breeze through the trees, the murmur of water, the singsong of insects. "You've lived here a long time." As the day had passed, it had become less feasible to think of his living anywhere else.

"Yes. I moved here the year Sarah was born."

"It's a lovely spot."

He turned her into his arms. Moonlight spilled over her, silver, jewellike in her hair, marbling her skin, darkening her eyes. "It suits you," he murmured. He ran a hand through her hair, then watched it fall back into place. "The princess and the dragon."

Her heart had already begun to flutter. Like a teenager's, Lee thought. He made her feel like a girl on her first date. "These days women have to kill their own dragons."

"These days—" his mouth brushed over hers "—there's less romance. If these were the Dark Ages, and I came upon you in a moonlit wood, I'd take you because it was my right. I'd woo you because I'd have no choice." His voice darkened like the shadows in the trees surrounding them. "Let me love you now, Lenore, as if it were the first time."

Or the last, she thought dimly as his lips urged her to soften, to yield, to demand. With his arms around her, she could let her consciousness go. Imagine and feel. Lovemaking consisted of nothing more. Even as her head tilted back in submission, her arms strengthened around him, challenging him to take whatever he wanted, to give whatever she asked.

Then his hands were on her face, gently, as gently as they'd ever been, memorizing the slope and angle of her bones, the softness of her skin. His lips followed, tasting, drinking in each separate flavor. The pleasure that could come so quickly ran liquid through her. Bonelessly, she slid with him to the ground.

He'd wanted to love her like this, in the open, with the moon silvering the trees and casting purple shadows. He'd wanted to feel her muscles coil and go fluid under the touch of his hand. What she gave to him now was something out of his own dreams and much, much more real than anything he'd ever had. Slowly, he undressed her, while his lips and the tips of his fingers both pleasured and revered her. This would be the night when he gave her all of him and when he asked for all of her.

Moonlight and shadows washed over her, making his heart pound in his ears. He heard the creek bubble nearby to mix with her quiet sighs. The woods smelled of night. And so, as she buried his face against her neck, did she.

She felt the surging excitement in him, the growing, straining need that swept her up. Willingly, she went into the whirlpool he created. There the air was soft to the touch and streaked with color. There she would stay, endlessly possessed.

His skin was warm against hers. She tasted, her head swimming from pleasure, power and newly awakened dizzying speed. Ravenous for more, she raced over him, acutely aware of every masculine tremble beneath her, every drawn breath, every murmur of her name.

Silver and shadows. Lee felt them every bit as tangibly as she saw them flickering around her. The silver streak of power. The dark shadow of desire. With them, she could take him to that trembling precipice.

When he swore, breathlessly, she laughed. Their

needs were tangled together, twining tighter. She felt it. She celebrated it.

The air seemed to still, the breeze pause. The sounds that had grown to one long din around them seemed to hush. The fingers tangled in her hair tightened desperately. In the silence, their eyes met and held, moment after moment.

Her lips curved as she opened for him.

She could have slept there, effortlessly, with the bare ground beneath her, the sky overhead and his body pressed to hers. She might have slept there, endlessly, like a princess under a spell, if he hadn't drawn her up into his arms.

"You fall asleep like a child," he murmured. "You should be in bed. My bed."

Lee sighed, content to stay where she was. "Too far."

With a low laugh, he kissed the hollow between her neck and shoulder. "Should I carry you?"

"Mmm." She nestled against him. "'Kay."

"Not that I object, but you might be a bit disconcerted if Bonnie happened to walk downstairs while I was carrying you in, naked."

She opened her eyes, so that her irises were dusky blue slits under her lashes. Reality was returning. "I guess we have to get dressed."

"It might be advisable." His gaze skimmed over her, then back to her face. "Should I help you?"

She smiled. "I think that we might have the same

result with you dressing me as we do with you undressing me."

"An interesting theory." Hunter reached over her for the brief strip of ivory lace.

"But this isn't the time to test it out." Lee plucked her panties out of his hand and wiggled into them. "How long have we been out here?"

"Centuries."

She shot him a look just before her head disappeared into her shirt. She wasn't completely certain he was exaggerating. "The least I deserve after these past two weeks is a real mattress."

He took her hand, pressing her palm to his lips. "You're welcome to share mine."

Lee curled her fingers around his briefly, then released them. "I don't think that's wise."

"You're worried about Sarah."

It wasn't a question. Lee took her time, making certain all the clouds of romance were out of her head before she spoke. "I don't know a great deal about children, but I imagine she's unprepared for someone sharing her father's bed."

Silence lay for a moment, like the eye of a storm. "I've never brought a woman to our home before."

The statement caused her to look at him quickly, then, just as quickly, look away. "All the more reason."

"All the more reason for many things." He dressed without speaking while Lee stared out into the trees. So beautiful, she thought. And more and more distant.

"You wanted to ask me about Sarah, but you didn't."

She moistened her lips. "It's not my business."

Her chin was captured quickly, not so gently. "Isn't it?" he demanded.

"Hunter—"

"This time you'll have the answer without asking." He dropped his hand, but his gaze never faltered. She needed nothing else to tell her the calm was over. "I met a woman, almost a dozen years ago. I was writing as Laura Miles by then, so that I could afford a few luxuries. Dinner out occasionally, the theater now and then. I was still living in L.A., alone, enjoying my work and the benefits it brought me. She was a student in her last year. Brains and ambition she had in abundance, money she didn't have at all. She was on scholarship and determined to be the hottest young attorney on the West Coast."

"Hunter, what happened between you and another woman all those years ago isn't my business."

"Not just another woman. Sarah's mother."

Lee began to pull at the tuft of grass by her side. "All right, if it's important for you to tell me, I'll listen."

"I cared about her," he continued. "She was bright, lovely and full of dreams. Neither of us had ever considered becoming too serious. She still had law school to finish, the bar to pass. I had stories to tell. But then, no matter how much we plan, fate has a way of taking over."

He drew out a cigarette, thinking back, remembering each detail. His tiny, cramped apartment with the leaky plumbing, the battered typewriter with its hiccuping carriage, the laughter from the couple next door that would often seep through the thin walls.

"She came by one afternoon. I knew something was wrong because she had afternoon classes. She was much too dedicated to skip classes. It was hot, one of those sultry, breathless days. The windows were up, and I had a little portable fan that stirred the air around without doing much to cool it. She'd come to tell me she was pregnant."

He could remember the way she'd looked if he concentrated. But he never chose to. But whether he chose to or not, he'd always be able to remember the tone of her voice when she'd told him. Despair, laced with fury and accusation.

"I said I cared about her, and that was true. I didn't love her. Still, our parents' values do trickle down. I offered to marry her." He laughed then, not humorously, but not, Lee reflected, bitterly. It was the laugh of a man who'd accepted the joke life had played on him. "She refused, almost as angry with the solution I'd offered as she was with the pregnancy. She had no intention of taking on a husband and a child when she had a career to carve out. It might be difficult to understand, but she wasn't being cold, simply practical, when she asked me to pay for the abortion."

Lee felt all of her muscles contract. "But, Sarah—"

"That's not the end of the story." Hunter blew out a stream of smoke and watched it fade into darkness. "We had a memorable fight, threats, accusations,

blame-casting. At the time, I couldn't see her end of
it, only the fact that she had part of me inside her that
she wanted to dispose of. We parted then, both of us
furious, both of us desperate enough to know we each
needed time to think."

She didn't know what to say, or how to say it.
"You were young," she began.

"I was twenty-four," Hunter corrected. "I'd long
since stopped being a boy. I was—we were—responsible for our own actions. I didn't sleep for two days.
I thought of a dozen answers and rejected them all,
over and over. Only one thing stuck with me in that
whole sweaty, terrified time. I wanted the child. It's
not something I can explain, because I did enjoy my
life, the lack of responsibilities, the possibility of becoming really successful. I simply knew I had to have
the child. I called her and asked her to come back.

"We were both calmer the second time, and both
more frightened than either of us had ever been in our
lives. Marriage couldn't be considered, so we set it
aside. She didn't want the child, so we dealt with that.
I did. That was something a bit more complex to deal
with. She needed freedom from the responsibility
we'd made together, and she needed money. In the
end, we resolved it all."

Dry-mouthed, Lee turned to him. "You paid her."

He saw, as he'd expected to see, the horror in her
eyes. When he continued, his voice was calm, but it
took a great deal of effort to make it so. "I paid all
the medical expenses, her living expenses up until she

delivered, and I gave her ten thousand dollars for my daughter.''

Stunned, heartsick, Lee stared at the ground. "How could she—''

"We each wanted something. In the only way open, we gave it to each other. I've never resented that young law student for what she did. It was her choice, and she could've taken another without consulting me.''

"Yes." She tried to understand, but all Lee could see was that slim, dark little girl. "She chose, but she lost.''

It meant everything just to hear her say it. "Sarah's been mine, only mine, from the first moment she breathed. The woman who carried her gave me a priceless gift. I only gave her money.''

"Does Sarah know?''

"Only that her mother had choices to make.''

"I see." She let out a long breath. "The reason you're so careful about keeping publicity away from her is to keep speculation away.''

"One of them. The other is simply that I want her to have the uncomplicated life every child's entitled to.''

"You didn't have to tell me." She reached a hand for his. "I'm glad you did. It can't have been easy for you, raising a baby by yourself.''

There was nothing but understanding in her eyes now. Every taut muscle in his body relaxed as if she'd stroked them. He knew now, with utter certainty, that she was what he'd been waiting for. "No, not easy, but always a pleasure.'' His fingers tightened on hers. ''Share it with me, Lenore.''

Her thoughts froze. ''I don't know what you mean.''

''I want you here, with me, with Sarah. I want you here with the other children we'll have together.'' He looked down at the ring he'd put on her hand. When his eyes came back to hers, she felt them reach inside her. ''Marry me.''

Marry? She could only stare at him blankly while the panic quietly built and built. ''You don't—you don't know what you're asking.''

''I do,'' he corrected, holding her hand more firmly when she tried to draw it away. ''I've asked only one other woman, and that out of obligation. I'm asking you because you're the first and only woman I've ever loved. I want to share your life. I want you to share mine.''

Panic steadily turned into fear. He was asking her to change everything she'd aimed for. To risk everything. ''Our lives are too far apart,'' she managed. ''I have to go back. I have my job.''

''A job you know you weren't made for.'' Urgency slipped into his voice as he took her shoulders. ''You know you were made to write about the images you have in your head, not about other people's social lives and tomorrow's trends.''

''It's what I know!'' Trembling, she jerked away from him. ''It's what I've been working for.''

''To prove a point. Damn it, Lenore, do something for yourself. For yourself.''

"It is for myself," she said desperately. You love him, a voice shouted inside her. Why are you pushing away what you need, what you want? Lee shook her head, as if to block the voice out. Love wasn't enough, needs weren't enough. She knew that. She had to remember it. "You're asking me to give it all up, every hard inch I've climbed in five years. I have a life in L.A., I know who I am, where I'm going. I can't live here and risk—"

"Finding out who you really are?" he finished. He wouldn't allow despair. He barely controlled anger. "If it was only myself, I'd go anywhere you liked, live anywhere that suited you, even if I knew it was a mistake. But there's Sarah. I can't take her away from the only home she's ever known."

"You're asking for everything again." Her voice was hardly a whisper, but he'd never heard anything more clearly. "You're asking me to risk everything, and I can't. I won't."

He rose, so that shadows shifted around him. "I'm asking you to risk everything," he agreed. "Do you love me?" And by asking, he'd already risked it all.

Torn by emotions, pushed by fear, she stared at him. "Yes. Damn you, Hunter, leave me alone."

She streaked back toward the house until the darkness closed in between them.

Chapter 12

"If you're not going to break for lunch, at least take this." Bryan held out one of her inexhaustible supply of candy bars.

"I'll eat when I've finished the article." Lee kept her eyes on the typewriter and continued to pound at the keys, lightly, rhythmically.

"Lee, you've been back for two days and I haven't seen you so much as nibble on a Danish." And her photographer's eye had seen beneath the subtle use of cosmetics to the pale bruises under Lee's eyes. That must've been some interview, she thought, as the brisk, even clickity-click of the typewriter keys went on.

"Not hungry." No, she wasn't hungry any more than she was tired. She'd been working steadily on Hunter's article for the better part of forty-eight hours.

It was going to be perfect, she promised herself. It was going to be polished like a fine piece of glass. And oh, God, when she finished it, *finished it*, she'd have purged her system of him.

She'd gripped that thought so tightly, it often skidded away.

If she'd stayed... If she went back...

The oath came quickly, under her breath, as her fingers faltered. Meticulously, Lee reversed the carriage to make the correction. She couldn't go back. Hadn't she made that clear to Hunter? She couldn't just toss everything over her shoulder and go. But the longer she stayed away, the larger the hole in her life became. In the life, Lee was ruthlessly reminded, that she'd so carefully carved out for herself.

So she'd work in a nervous kind of fury until the article was finished. Until, she told herself, it was all finished. Then it would be time to take the next step. When she tried to think of that next step, her mind went stunningly, desperately blank. Lee dropped her hands into her lap and stared at the paper in front of her.

Without a word, Bryan bumped the door with her hip so that it closed and muffled the noise. Dropping down into the chair across from Lee, she folded her hands and waited a beat. ''Okay, now why don't you tell me the story that's not for publication?''

Lee wanted to be able to shrug and say she didn't have time to talk. She was under a deadline, after all. The article was under a deadline. But then, so was her life. Drawing a breath, she turned in her chair. She didn't want to see the neat, clever little words she'd typed. Not now.

"Bryan, if you'd taken a picture, one that required a great deal of your time and all of your skill to set up, then once you'd developed it, it had come out in a completely different way than you'd planned, what would you do?"

"I'd take a good hard look at the way it had come out," she said immediately. "There'd be a good possibility I should've planned it that way in the first place."

"But wouldn't you be tempted to go back to your original plans? After all, you'd worked very, very hard to set it up in a certain way, wanting certain specific results."

"Maybe, maybe not. It'd depend on just what I'd seen when I looked at the picture." Bryan sat back, crossing long, jeans-clad legs. "What's in your picture, Lee?"

"Hunter." Her troubled gaze shifted, and locked on Bryan's. "You know me."

"As well as you let anyone know you."

With a short laugh, Lee began to push at a paper clip on her desk. "Am I as difficult as all that?"

"Yeah." Bryan smiled a bit to soften the quick answer. "And, I've always thought, as interesting. Apparently, Hunter Brown thinks the same thing."

"He asked me to marry him." The words came out in a jolt that left both women staring.

"Marry?" Bryan leaned forward. "As in 'till death do us part'?"

"Yes."

"Oh." The word came out like a breath of air as Bryan leaned back again. "Fast work." Then she saw Lee's unhappy expression. Just because Bryan didn't smell orange blossoms when the word *marriage* came up was no reason to be flippant. "Well, how do you feel? About Hunter, I mean."

The paper clip twisted in Lee's fingers. "I'm in love with him."

"Really?" Then she smiled, because it sounded nice when said so simply. "Did all this happen in the canyon?"

"Yes." Lee's fingers moved restlessly. "Maybe it started to happen before, when we were in Flagstaff. I don't know anymore."

"Why aren't you happy?" Bryan narrowed her eyes as she did when checking the light and angle. "When the man you love, really love, wants to build a life with you, you should be ecstatic."

"How do two people build a life together when they've both already built separate ones, completely different ones?" Lee demanded. "It isn't just a matter of making more room in the closet or shifting furniture around." The end of the paper clip broke off in her fingers as she rose. "Bryan, he lives in Arizona, in the canyon. I live in L.A."

Lifting booted feet, Bryan rested them on Lee's polished desk, crossing her ankles. "You're not going to tell me it's all a matter of geography."

"It just shows how impossible it all is!" Angry, Lee whirled around. "We couldn't be more different, almost opposites. I do things step-by-step, Hunter goes in leaps and bounds. Damn it, you should see his house. It's like something out of a sophisticated fairy tale. His sister's B. B. Smithers—'' Before Bryan could fully register that, Lee was blurting out, ''He has a daughter.''

''A daughter?'' Her attention fully caught, Bryan dropped her feet again. ''Hunter Brown has a child?''

Lee pressed her fingers to her eyes and waited for calm. True, it wouldn't have come out if she hadn't been so agitated, and she'd never discuss such personal agitations with anyone but Bryan, but now she had to deal with it. ''Yes, a ten-year-old girl. It's important that it not be publicized.''

''All right.''

Lee needed no promises from Bryan. Trying to calm herself, she took a quiet breath. ''She's bright, lovely and quite obviously the center of his life. I saw something in him when they were together, something incredibly beautiful. It scared the hell out of me.''

''Why?''

''Bryan, he's capable of so much talent, brilliance, emotion. He's put them together to make a complete success of himself, in all ways.''

''That bothers you?''

''I don't know what I'm capable of. I only know I'm afraid I'd never be able to balance it all out, make it all work.''

Bryan said something short, quick and rude. ''You won't marry him because you don't think you can juggle? You should know yourself better.''

"I thought I did." Shaking her head, she took her seat again. "It's ridiculous, in the first place," she said more briskly. "Our lives are miles apart."

Bryan glanced out the window at the tall, sleek building that was part of Lee's view of the city. "So, he can move to L.A. and close the distance."

"He won't." Swallowing, Lee looked at the pages on her desk. The article was finished, she knew it, just as she knew that if she didn't let it go, she'd polish it to death. "He belongs there. He wants to raise his daughter there. I understand that."

"So, you move to the canyon. Great scenery."

Why did it always sound so simple, so plausible, when spoken aloud? The little trickle of fear returned, and her voice firmed. "My job's here."

"I guess it comes down to priorities, doesn't it?" Bryan knew she wasn't being sympathetic, just as she knew it wasn't sympathy that Lee needed. Because she cared a great deal, she spoke without any compassion. "You can keep your job and your apartment in L.A. and be miserable. Or you can take a few chances."

Chances. Lee ran a finger down the slick surface of her desk. But you were supposed to test the ground before you stepped forward. Even Hunter had said that. But... She looked at the mangled paper clip in the center of her spotless blotter. How long did you test it before you took the jump?

It was barely two weeks later that Lee sat in her apartment in the middle of the day. She was so rarely

there during the day, during the week, that she somehow expected everything to look different. Everything
looked precisely the same. Even, she was forced to
admit, herself. Yet nothing was.

Quit. She tried to digest the word as she dealt with
the panic she'd held off the past few days. There was
a leafy, blooming African violet on the table in front
of her. It was well-tended, as every area of her life
had been well-tended. She'd always water it when the
soil was dry and feed it when it required nourishing.
As she stared at the plant, Lee knew she would never
be capable of pulling it ruthlessly out by the roots.
But wasn't that what she'd done to herself?

Quit, she thought again, and the word reverberated
in her brain. She'd actually handed in her resignation,
served her two weeks' notice and summarily turned
her back on her steadily thriving career—ripped out
its roots.

For what? she demanded of herself as panic trick-
led through. To follow some crazy dream that had
planted itself in her mind years ago. To write a book
that would probably never be published. To take a
ridiculous risk and plunge headlong into the unknown.

Because Hunter had said she was good. Because
he'd fed that dream, just as she fed the violet. More
than that, Lee thought, he'd made it impossible for her
to stop thinking about the "what ifs" in her life. And
he was one of them. The most important one of them.

Now that the step was taken and she was here, alone
in her impossibly quiet midweek, midmorning apartment, Lee wanted to run. Out there were people, noise,

distractions. Here, she'd have to face those "what-ifs." Hunter would be the first.

He hadn't tried to stop her when she left the morning after he'd asked her to marry him. He'd said nothing when she'd made her goodbyes to Sarah. Nothing at all. Perhaps they'd both known that he'd said all there was to say the night before. He'd looked at her once, and she'd nearly wavered. Then Lee had climbed into the car with Bonnie, who'd driven her to the airport that was one step closer to L.A.

He hadn't phoned her since she'd returned. Had she expected him to? Lee wondered. Maybe she had, but she'd hoped he wouldn't. She didn't know how long it would take before she'd be able to hear his voice without going to pieces.

Glancing down, she stared at the twisted gold-and-silver ring on her hand. Why had she kept it? It wasn't hers. It should've been left behind. It was easy to tell herself she'd simply forgotten to take it off in the confusion, but it wasn't the truth. She'd known the ring was still on her finger as she packed, as she walked out of Hunter's house, as she stepped into the car. She just hadn't been capable of taking it off.

She needed time, and it was time, Lee realized, that she now had. She had to prove something again, but not to her parents, not to Hunter. Now there was only herself. If she could finish the book. If she could give it her very best and really finish it...

Rising, Lee went to her desk, sat down at the typewriter and faced the fear of the blank page.

* * *

Lee had known pressure in her work on *Celebrity*. The minutes ticking away while deadlines drew closer and closer. There was the pressure of making not-so-fascinating seem fascinating, in a limited space, and of having to do it week after week. And yet, after nearly a month of being away from it, and having only herself and the story to account for, Lee had learned the full meaning of pressure. And of delight.

She hadn't believed—truly believed—that it would be possible for her to sit down, hour after hour, and finish a book she'd begun on a whim so long ago. And it was true that for the first few days she'd met with nothing but frustration and failure. There'd been a ring of terror in her head. Why had she left a job where she was respected and knowledgeable to stumble in the dark this way?

Time after time, she was tempted to push it all aside and go back, even if it would mean starting over at *Celebrity*. But each time, she could see Hunter's face—lightly mocking, challenging and somehow encouraging.

"It takes a certain amount of stamina and endurance. If you've reached your limit and want to quit..."

The answer was no, just as grimly, just as determinedly as it had been in that little tent. Perhaps she'd fail. She shut her eyes as she struggled to deal with the thought. Perhaps she'd fail miserably, but she wouldn't quit. Whatever happened, she'd made her own choice, and she'd live with it.

The longer she worked, the more of a symbol those typewritten pages became. If she could do this, and do it well, she could do anything. The rest of her life balanced on it.

By the end of the second week, Lee was so absorbed she rarely noticed the twelve- and fourteen-hour days she was putting in. She plugged in her phone machine and forgot to return the calls as often as she forgot to eat.

It was as Hunter had once said. The characters absorbed her, drove her, frustrated and delighted her. As time passed, Lee discovered she wanted to finish the story, not only for her sake but for theirs. She wanted, as she'd never wanted before, for these words to be read. The excitement of that, and the dread, kept her going.

She felt a queer little thrill when the last word was typed, a euphoria mixed with an odd depression. She'd finished. She'd poured her heart into her story. Lee wanted to celebrate. She wanted to weep. It was over. As she pressed her fingers against her tired eyes, she realized abruptly that she didn't even know what day it was.

He'd never had a book race so frantically, so quickly. Hunter could barely keep up with his own zooming thoughts. He knew why, and flowed with it because he had no choice. The main character of this story was Lenore, though her name would be changed to Jennifer. She was Lenore, physically, emotionally, from the elegantly groomed red-gold hair to the nervously bitten fingernails. It was the only way he had of keeping her.

It had cost him more than she'd ever know to let her go. When he'd watched her climb into the car, he'd told himself she wouldn't stay away. She couldn't. If he was wrong about her feelings for him, then he'd been wrong about everything in his life.

Two women had crashed into his life with importance. The first, Sarah's mother, he hadn't loved, yet she'd changed everything. After that, she'd gone away, unable to find it possible to mix her ambition with a life that included children and commitment.

Lee, he loved, and she'd changed everything again. She, too, had gone away. Would she stay away, for the same reasons? Was he fated to bind himself to women who wouldn't share the tie? He wouldn't believe it.

So he'd let her go, aches and fury under the calm. She'd be back.

But a month had passed, and she hadn't come. He wondered how long a man could live when he was starving.

Call her. Go after her. You were a fool to ever let her go. Drag her back if necessary. You need her. You need...

His thoughts ran this way like clockwork. Every day at dusk. Every day at dusk, Hunter fought the urge to follow through on them. He needed; God, he needed. But if she didn't come to him willingly, he'd never have what he needed, only the shell of it. He looked down at his naked finger. She hadn't left everything behind. It was more, much more, than a piece of metal that she'd taken with her.

He'd given her a talisman, and she'd kept it. As long as she had it, she didn't sever the bond. Hunter was a man who believed in fate, omens and magic.

"Dinner's ready." Sarah stood in the doorway, her hair pulled back in a ponytail, her narrow face streaked with a bit of flour.

He didn't want to eat. He wanted to go on writing. As long as the story moved through him, he had a part of Lenore with him. Just as, whenever he stopped, the need to have all of her tore him apart. But Sarah smiled at him.

"Nearly ready," she amended. She came into the room, barefoot. "I made this meat loaf, but it looks more like a pancake. And the biscuits." She grinned, shrugging. "They're pretty hard, but we can put some jam or something on them." Sensing his mood, she wrapped her arms around his neck, resting her cheek against his. "I like it better when you cook."

"Who turned her nose up at the broccoli last night?"

"It looks like little trees that got sick." She wrinkled her nose, but when she drew back from him, her face was serious. "You really miss her a lot, huh?"

He could've evaded with anyone else. But this was Sarah. She was ten. She knew him inside out. "Yeah, I miss her a lot."

Thinking, Sarah fiddled with the hair that fell over his forehead. "I guess maybe you wanted her to marry you."

"She turned me down."

Her brows lowered, not so much from annoyance

that anyone could say no to her father, but in concentration. Donna's father hardly had any hair at all, she thought, touching Hunter's again, and Kelly's dad's stomach bounced over his belt. Shelley's mother never got jokes. She didn't know anybody who was as neat to look at or as neat to be with as her dad. Anybody would want to marry him. When she'd been little, she'd wanted to marry him herself. But of course, she knew now that was just silly stuff.

Her brows were still drawn together when she brought her gaze to his. "I guess she didn't like me."

He heard everything just as clearly as if she'd spoken her thoughts aloud. He was greatly touched, and not a little impressed. "Couldn't stand you."

Her eyes widened, then brightened with laughter. "Because I'm such a brat."

"Right. I can barely stand you myself."

"Well." Sarah huffed a moment. "She didn't look stupid, but I guess she is if she wouldn't marry you." She cuddled against him, and knowing it was to comfort, Hunter warmed with love. "I liked her," Sarah murmured. "She was nice, kinda quiet, but really nice when she smiled. I guess you love her."

"Yes, I do." He didn't offer her any words of reassurance—it's different from the way I love you, you'll always be my little girl. Hunter simply held her, and it was enough. "She loves me, too, but she has to make her own life."

Sarah didn't understand that, and personally thought it was foolish, but decided not to say so. "I guess I wouldn't mind if she decided to marry you after all.

It might be nice to have somebody who'd be like a mother.''

He lifted a brow. She never asked about her own mother, knowing with a child's intuition, he supposed, that there was nothing to ask about. "Aren't I?''

"You're pretty good," she told him graciously. "But you don't know a whole lot about lady stuff." Sarah sniffed the air, then grinned. "Meat loaf's done.''

"Overdone, from the smell of it.''

"Picky, picky." She jumped off his lap before he could retaliate. "I hear a car coming. You can ask them to dinner so we can get rid of all the biscuits.''

He didn't want company, Hunter thought as he watched his daughter dash out of the room. An evening with Sarah was enough, then he'd go back to work. After switching off his machine, he rose to go to the door. It was probably one of her friends, who'd talked her parents into dropping by on their way home from town. He'd brush them off, as politely as he could manage, then see if anything could be done about Sarah's meat loaf.

When he opened the door, she was standing there, her hair caught in the light of a late summer's evening. He was, quite literally, knocked breathless.

"Hello, Hunter." How calm a voice could sound, Lee thought, even when a heart's hammering against ribs. "I'd've called, but your number's unlisted." When he said nothing, Lee felt her heart move from her ribs to her throat. Somehow, she managed to speak over it. "May I come in?''

Silently, he stepped back. Perhaps he was dreaming, like the character in "The Raven." All he needed was a bust of Pallas and a dying fire.

She'd used up nearly all of her courage just coming back. If he didn't speak soon, they'd end up simply staring at each other. Like a nervous speaker about to lecture on a subject she hadn't researched, Lee cleared her throat. "Hunter..."

"Hey, I think we'd better just give the biscuits to Santanas because—" Sarah stopped her headlong flight into the room. "Well, gee."

"Sarah, hello." Lee was able to smile now. The child looked so comically surprised, not cool and distant like her father.

"Hi." Sarah glanced uncertainly from one adult to the other. She supposed they were going to make a mess of things. Aunt Bonnie said that people who loved each other usually made a mess of things, for at least a little while. "Dinner's ready. I made meat loaf. It's probably not too bad."

Understanding the invitation, Lee grasped at it. At least it would give her more time before Hunter tossed her out again. "It smells wonderful."

"Okay, come on." Imperiously, Sarah held out her hand, waiting until Lee took it. "It doesn't look very good," she went on, as she led Lee into the kitchen. "But I did everything I was supposed to."

Lee looked at the flattened meat loaf and smiled. "Better than I could do."

"Really?" Sarah digested this with a nod. "Well, Dad and I take turns." And if they got married, Sarah figured, she'd only have to cook every third day. "You'd better set another place," she said lightly to her father. "The biscuits didn't work, but we've got potatoes."

The three of them sat down, very much as if it were the natural thing to do. Sarah served, carrying on a babbling conversation that alleviated the need for either adult to speak to the other. They each answered her, smiled, ate, while their thoughts were in a frenzy.

He doesn't want me anymore.

Why did she come?

He hasn't even spoken to me.

What does she want? She looks lovely. So lovely.

What can I do? He looks wonderful. So wonderful.

Sarah lifted the casserole containing the rest of the meat loaf. "I'll give this to Santanas." Like most children, she detested leftovers—unless it was spaghetti. "Dad has to do the dishes," she explained to Lee. "You can help him if you like." After she'd dumped Santanas's dinner in his bowl, she danced out of the room. "See you later."

Then they were alone, and Lee found she was gripping her hands together so tightly they were numb. Deliberately, she unlaced her fingers. He saw the ring, still on her finger, and felt something twist, loosen, then tighten again in his chest.

"You're angry," she said in that same calm, even voice. "I'm sorry, I shouldn't have come this way."

Hunter rose and began to stack dishes. "No, I'm not angry." Anger was possibly the only emotion he hadn't experienced in the last hour. "Why did you?"

"I..." Lee looked down helplessly at her hands. She should help him with the dishes, keep busy, stay natural. She didn't think her legs would hold her just yet. "I finished the book," she blurted out.

He stopped and turned. For the first time since she'd opened the door, she saw that hint of a smile around his mouth. "Congratulations."

"I wanted you to read it. I know I could've mailed it—I sent a copy on to your editor—but..." She lifted her eyes to his again. "I didn't want to mail it. I wanted to give it to you. Needed to."

Hunter put the dishes in the sink and came back to the table, but he didn't sit. He had to stand. If this was what she'd come for, all she'd come for, he wasn't certain he could face it. "You know I want to read it. I expect you to autograph the first copy for me."

She managed a smile. "I'm not as optimistic as that, but you were right. I had to finish it. I wanted to thank you for showing me." Her lips remained curved, but the smile left her eyes. "I quit my job."

He hadn't moved, but it seemed that he suddenly became very still. "Why?"

"I had to try to finish the book. For me." If only he'd touch her, just her hand, she wouldn't feel so cold. "I knew if I could do that, I could do anything. I needed to prove that to myself before I..." Lee trailed off, not able to say it all. "I've been reading your work, your earlier work as Laura Miles."

If he could just touch her... But once he did, he'd never let her go again. "Did you enjoy it?"

"Yes." There was enough lingering surprise in her voice to make him smile. "I'd never have believed there could be a similarity of styles between a romance novel and a horror story, but there was. Atmosphere, tension, emotion." Taking a deep breath, she stood so that she could face him. It was perhaps the most difficult step she'd taken so far. "You understand how a woman feels. It shows in your work."

"*Writer*'s a word without gender."

"Still, it's a rare gift, I think, for a man to be able to understand and appreciate the kinds of emotions and insecurities that go on inside a woman." Her eyes met his again, and this time held. "I'm hoping you can do the same with me."

He was looking into her again. She could feel it.

"It's more difficult when your own emotions are involved."

She gripped her fingers together, tightly. "Are they?"

He didn't touch her, not yet, but she thought she could almost feel his hand against her cheek. "Do you need me to tell you I love you?"

"Yes, I—"

"You've finished your book, quit your job. You've taken a lot of risks, Lenore." He waited. "But you've yet to put it all on the line."

Her breath trembled out. No, he'd never make things easy for her. There'd always be demands, expectations. He'd never pamper. "You terrified me when you asked me to marry you. I thought about it a great deal, like the small child thinks about a dark closet. I don't know what's in there—it might be dream or nightmare. You understand that.''

"Yes." Though it hadn't been a question. "I understand that.''

She breathed a bit easier. "I used what I had in L.A. as an excuse because it was logical, but it wasn't the real reason. I was just afraid to walk into that closet.''

"And are you still?''

"A little.'' It took more effort than she'd imagined to relax her fingers. She wondered if he knew it was the final step. She held out her hand. "But I want to try. I want to go there with you.''

His fingers laced with hers, and she felt the nerves melt away. Of course he knew. "It won't be dream or nightmare, Lenore. Every minute of it will be real.''

She laughed then, because his hand was in hers. "Now you're really trying to scare me." Stepping closer, she kissed him softly, until desire built to a quiet roar. It was so easy, like sliding into a warm, clear stream. "You won't scare me off,'' she whispered.

The arms around her were tight, but she barely noticed. "No, I won't scare you off." He breathed in the scent of her hair, wallowed in the texture of it. She'd come to him. Completely. "I won't let you go, either. I've waited too long for you to come back.''

"You knew I would,'' she murmured.

"I had to, I'd've gone mad otherwise.''

She closed her eyes, content, but with a thrill of

excitement underneath. "Hunter, if Sarah doesn't, that is, if she isn't able to adjust..."

"Worried already." He drew her back. "Sarah gave me a pep talk just this evening. You do, I assume, know quite a bit about lady stuff?"

"Lady stuff?"

He drew her back just a bit farther, to look her up and down. "Every inch the lady. You'll do, Lenore, for me, and for Sarah."

"Okay." She let out a long breath, because as usual, she believed him. "I'd like to be with you when you tell her."

"Lenore." Framing her face, he kissed both cheeks, gently, with a hint of a laugh beneath. "She already knows."

A brow lifted. "Her father's daughter."

"Exactly." He grabbed her, swinging her around once in a moment of pure, irrepressible joy. "The lady's going to find it interesting living in a house with real and imaginary monsters."

"The lady can handle that," she tossed back. "And anything else you dream up."

"Is that so?" He shot her a wicked look—amusement, desire, knowledge—as he released her. "Then let's get these dishes done and I'll see what I can do."

* * * * *

One Summer

Chapter 1

The room was dark. Pitch-dark. But the man named Shade was used to the dark. Sometimes he preferred it. It wasn't always necessary to see with your eyes. His fingers were both clever and competent, his inner eye as keen as a knife blade.

There were times, even when he wasn't working, when he'd sit in a dark room and simply let images form in his mind. Shapes, textures, colors. Sometimes they came clearer when you shut your eyes and just let your thoughts flow. He courted darkness, shadows, just as relentlessly as he courted the light. It was all part of life, and life—its images—was his profession.

He didn't always see life as others did. At times it was harsher, colder, than the naked eye could see— or wanted to. Other times it was softer, more lovely, than the busy world imagined. Shade observed it, grouped the elements, manipulated time and shape, then recorded it his way. Always his way.

Now, with the room dark and the sound of recorded jazz coming quiet and disembodied from the corner, he worked with his hands and his mind. Care and timing. He used them both in every aspect of his work. Slowly, smoothly, he opened the capsule and transferred the undeveloped film onto the reel. When the light-tight lid was on the developing tank, he set the timer with his free hand, then pulled the chain that added the amber light to the room.

Shade enjoyed developing the negative and making the print as much as, sometimes more than, he enjoyed taking the photograph. Darkroom work required precision and accuracy. He needed both in his life. Making the print allowed for creativity and experimentation. He needed those as well. What he saw, what he felt about what he saw, could be translated exactly or left as an enigma. Above all, he needed the satisfaction of creating something himself, alone. He always worked alone.

Now, as he went through each precise step of developing—temperature, chemicals, agitation, timing—the amber light cast his face into shadows. If Shade had been looking to create the image of photographer at work, he'd never have found a clearer statement than himself.

His eyes were dark, intense now as he added the stop bath to the tank. His hair was dark as well, too long for the convention he cared nothing about. It brushed over his ears, the back of his T-shirt, and fell over his forehead nearly to his eyebrows. He never gave much thought to style. His was cool, almost cold, and rough around the edges.

His face was deeply tanned, lean and hard, with strong bones dominating. His mouth was taut as he concentrated. There were lines spreading out finely from his eyes, etched there by what he'd seen and what he'd felt about it. Some would say there'd already been too much of both.

The nose was out of alignment, a result of a professional hazard. Not everyone liked to have his picture taken. The Cambodian soldier had broken Shade's nose, but Shade had gotten a telling picture of the city's devastation, of the waste. He still considered it an even exchange.

In the amber light, his movements were brisk. He had a rangy, athletic body, the result of years in the field—often a foreign, unfriendly field—miles of legwork and missed meals.

Even now, years after his last staff assignment for *International View,* Shade remained lean and agile. His work wasn't as grueling as it had been in his early years in Lebanon, Laos, Central America, but his pattern hadn't changed. He worked long hours, sometimes waiting endlessly for just the right shot, sometimes using a roll of film within minutes. If his style and manner were aggressive, it could be said that they'd kept him alive and whole during the wars he'd recorded.

The awards he'd won, the fee he now commanded, remained secondary to the picture. If no one had paid

him or recognized his work, Shade would still have
been in the darkroom, developing his film. He was
respected, successful and rich. Yet he had no assistant
and continued to work out of the same darkroom he'd
set up ten years before.

When Shade hung his negatives up to dry, he already had an idea which ones he'd print. Still, he
barely glanced at them, leaving them hanging as he
unlocked the darkroom door and stepped out. Tomorrow his outlook would be fresher. Waiting was an
advantage he hadn't always had. Right now he wanted
a beer. He had some thinking to do.

He headed straight for the kitchen and grabbed a
cold bottle. Popping off the lid, he tossed it into the
can his once-a-week housekeeper lined with plastic.
The room was clean, not particularly cheerful with the
hard whites and blacks, but then it wasn't dull.

After he tilted the bottle back, he chugged the beer
down, draining half. He lit a cigarette, then took the
beer to the kitchen table where he leaned back in a
chair and propped his feet on the scrubbed wood surface.

The view out the kitchen window was of a not-so-
glamorous L.A. It was a little seamy, rough, sturdy
and tough. The early-evening light couldn't make it
pretty. He could've moved to a glossier part of town,
or out to the hills, where the lights of the city at night
looked like a fairy tale. Shade preferred the small
apartment that looked out over the unpampered streets
of a city known for glitz. He didn't have much patience with glitz.

Bryan Mitchell. She specialized in it.

He couldn't deny that her portraits of the rich, famous and beautiful were well done—even excellent ones of their kind. There was compassion in her photographs, humor and a smooth sensuality. He wouldn't even deny that there was a place for her kind of work in the field. It just wasn't his angle. She reflected culture, he went straight for life.

Her work for *Celebrity* magazine had been professional, slick and often searing in its way. The larger-than-life people she'd photographed had often been cut down to size in a way that made them human and approachable. Since she'd decided to freelance, the stars, near-stars and starmakers she'd photographed for the glossy came to her. Over the years, she'd developed a reputation and style that had made her one of them, part of the inner, select circle.

It could happen to a photographer, he knew. They could come to resemble their own themes, their own studies. Sometimes what they tried to project became a part of them. Too much a part. No, he didn't begrudge Bryan Mitchell her state of the art. Shade simply had doubts about working with her.

He didn't care for partnerships.

Yet those were the terms. When he'd been approached by *Life-style* to do a pictorial study of America, he'd been intrigued. Photo essays could make a strong, lasting statement that could rock and jar or soothe and amuse. As a photographer, he had sought to do that. *Life-style* wanted him, wanted the strong, sometimes concise, sometimes ambiguous emotions his pictures could portray. But they also wanted a counterbalance. A woman's view.

He wasn't so stubborn that he didn't see the point and the possibilities. Yet it irked him to think that the assignment hinged on his willingness to share the summer, his van and the credit with a celebrity photographer. And with a woman at that. Three months on the road with a female who spent her time perfecting snapshots of rock stars and personalities. For a man who'd cut his professional teeth in war-torn Lebanon, it didn't sound like a picnic.

But he wanted to do it. He wanted the chance to capture an American summer from L.A. to New York, showing the joy, the pathos, the sweat, the cheers and disappointments. He wanted to show the heart, even while he stripped it to the bone.

All he had to do was say yes, and share the summer with Bryan Mitchell.

''Don't think about the camera, Maria. Dance.'' Bryan lined up the forty-year-old ballet superstar in her viewfinder. She liked what she saw. Age? Touches of it, but years meant nothing. Grit, style, elegance. Endurance—most of all, endurance. Bryan knew how to catch them all and meld them.

Maria Natravidova had been photographed countless times over her phenomenal twenty-five-year career. But never with sweat running down her arms and dampening her leotard. Never with the strain showing. Bryan wasn't looking for the illusions dancers live with, but the exhaustion, the aches that were the price of triumph.

She caught Maria in a leap, legs stretched parallel to the floor, arms flung wide in perfect alignment. Drops of moisture danced from her face and shoulders; muscles bunched and held. Bryan pressed the shutter, then moved the camera slightly to blur the motion.

That would be the one. She knew it even as she finished off the roll of film.

"You make me work," the dancer complained as she slid into a chair, blotting her streaming face with a towel.

Bryan took two more shots, then lowered her camera. "I could've dressed you in costume, backlit you and had you hold an arabesque. That would show that you're beautiful, graceful. Instead I'm going to show that you're a strong woman."

"And you're a clever one." Maria sighed as she let the towel drop. "Why else do I come to you for the pictures for my book?"

"Because I'm the best." Bryan crossed the studio and disappeared into a back room. Maria systematically worked a cramp out of her calf. "Because I understand you, admire you. And—" she brought out a tray, two glasses and a pitcher clinking with ice "—because I squeeze oranges for you."

"Darling." With a laugh, Maria reached for the first glass. For a moment, she held it to her high forehead, then drank deeply. Her dark hair was pulled back severely in a style only good bones and flawless skin could tolerate. Stretching out her long, thin body in the chair, she studied Bryan over the rim of her glass.

Maria had known Bryan for seven years, since the photographer had started at *Celebrity* with the assignment to take pictures of the dancer backstage. The dancer had been a star, but Bryan hadn't shown awe. Maria could still remember the young woman with the thick honey-colored braid and bib overalls. The elegant prima ballerina had found herself confronted with candid eyes the color of pewter, an elegant face with slanting cheekbones and a full mouth. The tall, athletic body had nearly been lost inside the baggy clothes. She'd worn ragged sneakers and long, dangling earrings.

Maria glanced down at the dingy Nikes Bryan wore. Some things didn't change. At first glance, you'd categorize the tall, tanned blonde in sneakers and shorts as typically California. Looks could be deceiving. There was nothing typical about Bryan Mitchell.

Bryan accepted the stare as she drank. "What do you see, Maria?" It interested her to know. Conceptions and preconceptions were part of her trade.

"A strong, smart woman with talent and ambition." Maria smiled as she leaned back in the chair. "Myself, nearly."

Bryan smiled. "A tremendous compliment."

Maria acknowledged this with a sweeping gesture. "There aren't many women I like. Myself I like, and so, you. I hear rumors, my love, about you and that pretty young actor."

"Matt Perkins." Bryan didn't believe in evading or

pretending. She lived, by choice, in a town fueled by rumors, fed by gossip. "I took his picture, had a few dinners."

"Nothing serious?"

"As you said, he's pretty." Bryan smiled and chewed on a piece of ice. "But there's barely room enough for his ego and mine in his Mercedes."

"Men." Maria leaned forward to pour herself a second glass.

"Now you're going to be profound."

"Who better?" Maria countered. "Men." She said the word again, savoring it. "I find them tedious, childish, foolish and indispensable. Being loved... sexually, you understand?"

Bryan managed to keep her lips from curving. "I understand."

"Being loved is exhilarating, exhausting. Like Christmas. Sometimes I feel like the child who doesn't understand why Christmas ends. But it does. And you wait for the next time."

It always fascinated Bryan how people felt about love, how they dealt with it, groped for it and avoided it. "Is that why you never married, Maria? You're waiting for the next time?"

"I married dance. To marry a man, I would have to divorce dance. There's no room for two for a woman like me. And you?"

Bryan stared into her drink, no longer amused. She understood the words too well. "No room for two," she murmured. "But I don't wait for the next time."

"You're young. If you could have Christmas every day, would you turn away from it?"

Bryan moved her shoulders. "I'm too lazy for Christmas every day."

"Still, it's a pretty fantasy." Maria rose and stretched. "You've made me work long enough. I have to shower and change. Dinner with my choreographer."

Alone, Bryan absently ran a finger over the back of her camera. She didn't often think about love and marriage. She'd been there already. Once a fantasy was exposed to reality, it faded, like a photo improperly fixed. Permanent relationships rarely worked, and still more rarely worked well.

She thought of Lee Radcliffe, married to Hunter Brown for nearly a year, helping to raise his daughter and pregnant with her first child. Lee was happy, but then she'd found an extraordinary man, one who wanted her to be what she was, even encouraged her to explore herself. Bryan's own experience had taught her that what's said and what's felt can be two opposing things.

Your career's as important to me as it is to you. How many times had Rob said that *before* they'd been married? *Get your degree. Go for it.*

So they'd gotten married, young, eager, idealistic. Within six months he'd been unhappy with the time she'd put into her classes and her job at a local studio. He'd wanted his dinner hot and his socks washed. Not so much to ask, Bryan mused. To be fair, she had to say that Rob had asked for little of her. Just too much at the time.

They'd cared for each other, and both had tried to make adjustments. Both had discovered they'd wanted different things for themselves—different things from each other, things neither could be, neither could give.

It would've been called an amicable divorce—no fury, no bitterness. No passion. A signature on a legal document, and the dream had been over. It had hurt more than anything Bryan had ever known. The taint of failure had stayed with her a long, long time.

She knew Rob had remarried. He was living in the suburbs with his wife and their two children. He'd gotten what he'd wanted.

And so, Bryan told herself as she looked around her studio, had she. She didn't just want to be a photographer. She was a photographer. The hours she spent in the field, in her studio, in the darkroom, were as essential to her as sleep. And what she'd done in the six years since the end of her marriage, she'd done on her own. She didn't have to share it. She didn't have to share her time. Perhaps she was a great deal like Maria. She was a woman who ran her own life, made her own decisions, personally and professionally. Some people weren't made for partnerships.

Shade Colby. Bryan propped her feet on Maria's chair. She might just have to make a concession there. She admired his work. So much so, in fact, that she'd plunked down a heady amount for his print of an L.A. street scene at a time when money had been a large concern. She'd studied it, trying to analyze and guess at the techniques he'd used for setting the shot and making the print. It was a moody piece, so much gray, so little light. And yet, Bryan had sensed a certain grit in it, not hopelessness, but ruthlessness. Still, admiring his work and working with him were two different things.

They were based in the same town, but they moved in different circles. For the most part, Shade Colby didn't move in any circles. He kept to himself. She'd seen him at a handful of photography functions, but they'd never met.

He'd be an interesting subject, she reflected. Given enough time, she could capture that air of aloofness and earthiness on film. Perhaps if they agreed to take the assignment she'd have the chance.

Three months of travel. There was so much of the country she hadn't seen, so many pictures she hadn't taken. Thoughtfully, she pulled a candy bar out of her back pocket and unwrapped it. She liked the idea of taking a slice of America, a season, and pulling the images together. So much could be said.

Bryan enjoyed doing her portraits. Taking a face, a personality, especially a well-known one, and finding out what lay behind it was fascinating. Some might find it limited, but she found it endlessly varied. She could take the tough female rock star and show her vulnerabilities, or pull the humor from the cool, regal megastar. Capturing the unexpected, the fresh—that was the purpose of photography to her.

Now she was being offered the opportunity to do

the same thing with a country. The people, she thought. So many people.

She wanted to do it. If it meant sharing the work, the discoveries, the fun, with Shade Colby, she still wanted to do it. She bit into the chocolate. So what if he had a reputation for being cranky and remote? She could get along with anyone for three months.

"Chocolate makes you fat and ugly."

Bryan glanced up as Maria swirled back into the room. The sweat was gone. She looked now as people expected a prima ballerina to look. Draped in silk, studded with diamonds. Cool, composed, beautiful.

"It makes me happy," Bryan countered. "You look fantastic, Maria."

"Yes." Maria brushed a hand down the draping silk at her hip. "But then it's my job to do so. Will you work late?"

"I want to develop the film. I'll send you some test proofs tomorrow."

"And that's your dinner?"

"Just a start." Bryan took a huge bite of chocolate. "I'm sending out for pizza."

"With pepperoni?"

Bryan grinned. "With everything."

Maria pressed a hand to her stomach. "And I eat with my choreographer, the tyrant, which means I eat next to nothing."

"And I'll have a soda instead of a glass of Taittinger. We all have our price to pay."

"If I like your proofs, I'll send you a case."

"Of Taittinger?"

"Of soda." With a laugh, Maria swept out.

An hour later, Bryan hung her negatives up to dry. She'd need to make the proofs to be certain, but out of more than forty shots, she'd probably print no more than five.

When her stomach rumbled, she checked her watch. She'd ordered the pizza for seven-thirty. Well timed, she decided as she left the darkroom. She'd eat and go over the prints of Matt she'd shot for a layout in a glossy. Then she could work on the one she chose until the negatives of Maria were dry. She began rummaging through the two dozen folders on her desk— her personal method of filing—when someone knocked at the studio door.

"Pizza," she breathed, greedy. "Come on in. I'm starving." Plopping her enormous canvas bag on the desk, Bryan began to hunt for her wallet. "This is great timing. Another five minutes and I might've just faded away. Shouldn't miss lunch." She dropped a fat, ragged notebook, a clear plastic bag filled with cosmetics, a key ring and five candy bars on the desk. "Just set it down anywhere, I'll find the money in a minute." She dug deeper into the bag. "How much do you need?"

"As much as I can get."

"Don't we all." Bryan pulled out a worn man's billfold. "And I'm desperate enough to clean out the safe for you, but…" She trailed off as she looked up and saw Shade Colby.

He gave her face a quick glance, then concentrated on her eyes. "What would you like to pay me for?"

"Pizza." Bryan dropped the wallet onto the desk with half the contents of her purse. "A case of starvation and mistaken identity. Shade Colby." She held out her hand, curious and, to her surprise, nervous. He looked more formidable when he wasn't in a crowd. "I recognize you," she continued, "but I don't think we've met."

"No, we haven't." He took her hand and held it while he studied her face a second time. Stronger than he'd expected. He always looked for the strength first, then the weaknesses. And younger. Though he knew she was only twenty-eight, Shade had expected her to look harder, more aggressive, glossier. Instead, she looked like someone who'd just come in from the beach.

Her T-shirt was snug, but she was slim enough to warrant it. The braid came nearly to her waist and made him speculate on how her hair would look loose and free. Her eyes interested him—gray edging toward silver, and almond-shaped. They were eyes he'd like to photograph with the rest of her face in shadow. She might carry a bag of cosmetics, but it didn't look as if she used any of them.

Not vain about her appearance, he decided. That would make things simpler if he decided to work with her. He didn't have the patience to wait while a woman painted and groomed and fussed. This one wouldn't. And she was assessing him even as he assessed her. Shade accepted that. A photographer, like any artist, looked for angles.

"Am I interrupting your work?"

"No, I was just taking a break. Sit down."

They were both cautious. He'd come on impulse. She wasn't certain how to handle him. Each decided to bide their time before they went beyond the polite, impersonal stage. Bryan remained behind her desk. Her turf, his move, she decided.

Shade didn't sit immediately. Instead, he tucked his hands in his pockets and looked around her studio. It was wide, well lit from the ribbon of windows. There were baby spots and a blue backdrop still set up from an earlier session in one section. Reflectors and umbrellas stood in another, with a camera still on a tripod. He didn't have to look closely to see that the equipment was first-class. But then, first-class equipment didn't make a first-class photographer.

She liked the way he stood, not quite at ease, but ready, remote. If she had to choose now, she'd have photographed him in shadows, alone. But Bryan insisted on knowing the person before she made a portrait.

How old was he? she wondered. Thirty-three, thirty-five. He'd already been nominated for a Pulitzer when she'd still been in college. It didn't occur to her to be intimidated.

"Nice place," he commented before he dropped into the chair opposite the desk.

"Thanks." She tilted her chair so that she could study him from another angle. "You don't use a studio of your own, do you?"

"I work in the field." He drew out a cigarette. "On

the rare occasion I need a studio, I can borrow or rent one easily enough.''

Automatically she hunted for an ashtray under the chaos on her desk. "You make all your own prints?''

"That's right.''

Bryan nodded. On the few occasions at *Celebrity* when she'd been forced to entrust her film to someone else, she hadn't been satisfied. That had been one of the major reasons she'd decided to open her own business. "I love darkroom work.''

She smiled for the first time, causing him to narrow his eyes and focus on her face. What kind of power was that? he wondered. A curving of lips, easy and relaxed. It packed one hell of a punch.

Bryan sprang up at the knock on the door. "At last.''

Shade watched her cross the room. He hadn't known she was so tall. Five-ten, he estimated, and most of it leg. Long, slender, bronzed leg. It wasn't easy to ignore the smile, but it was next to impossible to ignore those legs.

Nor had he noticed her scent until she moved by him. Lazy sex. He couldn't think of another way to describe it. It wasn't floral, it wasn't sophisticated. It was basic. Shade drew on his cigarette and watched her laugh with the delivery boy.

Photographers were known for their preconceptions; it was part of the trade. He'd expected her to be sleek and cool. That was what he'd nearly resigned himself to working with. Now it was a matter of re-arranging his thinking. Did he want to work with a woman who smelled like twilight and looked like a beach bunny?

Turning away from her, Shade opened a folder at random. He recognized the subject a box-office queen with two Oscars and three husbands under her belt. Bryan had dressed her in glitters and sparkles. Royal trappings for royalty. But she hadn't shot the traditional picture.

The actress was sitting at a table jumbled with pots and tubes of lotions and creams, looking at her own reflection in a mirror and laughing. Not the poised, careful smile that didn't make wrinkles, but a full, robust laugh that could nearly be heard. It was up to the viewer to speculate whether she laughed at her reflection or an image she'd created over the years.

"Like it?" Carrying the cardboard box, Bryan stopped beside him.

"Yeah. Did she?"

Too hungry for formalities, Bryan opened the lid and dug out the first piece. "She ordered a sixteen-by-twenty-four for her fiancé. Want a piece?"

Shade looked inside the box. "They miss putting anything on here?"

"Nope." Bryan searched in a drawer of her desk for napkins and came up with a box of tissues. "I'm a firm believer in overindulgence. So…" With the box opened on the desk between them, Bryan leaned back in her chair and propped up her feet. It was time, she decided, to get beyond the fencing stage. "You want to talk about the assignment?"

Shade took a piece of pizza and a handful of tissues. "Got a beer?"

"Soda—diet or regular." Bryan took a huge, satisfying bite. "I don't keep liquor in the studio. You end up having buzzed clients."

"We'll skip it for now." They ate in silence a moment, still weighing each other. "I've been giving a lot of thought to doing this photo essay."

"It'd be a change for you." When he only lifted a brow, Bryan wadded a tissue and tossed it into the trash can. "Your stuff overseas—it hit hard. There was sensitivity and compassion, but for the most part, it was grim."

"It was a grim time. Everything I shoot doesn't have to be pretty."

This time she lifted a brow. Obviously he didn't think much of the path she'd taken in her career. "Everything I shoot doesn't have to be raw. There's room for fun in art."

He acknowledged this with a shrug. "We'd see different things if we looked through the same lens."

"That's what makes each picture unique." Bryan leaned forward and took another piece.

"I like working alone."

She ate thoughtfully. If he was trying to annoy her, he was right on target. If it was just an overflow of his personality, it still wouldn't make things any easier. Either way, she wanted the assignment, and he was part of it. "I prefer it that way myself," she said slowly. "Sometimes there has to be compromise.

You've heard of compromise, Shade. You give, I give. We meet somewhere close to the middle."

She wasn't as laid-back as she looked. Good. The last thing he needed was to go on the road with someone so mellow she threatened to mold. Three months, he thought again. Maybe. Once the ground rules were set. "I map out the route," he began briskly. "We start here in L.A. in two weeks. Each of us is responsible for their own equipment. Once we're on the road, each of us goes our own way. You shoot your pictures, I shoot mine. No questions."

Bryan licked sauce from her finger. "Anyone ever question you, Colby?"

"It's more to the point whether I answer." It was said simply, as it was meant. "The publisher wants both views, so he'll have them. We'll be stopping off and on to rent a darkroom. I'll look over your negatives."

Bryan wadded more tissue. "No, you won't." Lazily, she crossed one ankle over the other. Her eyes had gone to slate, the only outward show of a steadily growing anger.

"I'm not interested in having my name attached to a series of pop-culture shots."

To keep herself in control, Bryan continued to eat. There were things, so many clear, concise things, she'd like to say to him. Temper took a great deal of energy, she reminded herself. It usually accomplished nothing. "The first thing I'll want written into the contract is that each of our pictures carries our own bylines. That way neither of us will be embarrassed by the other's work. I'm not interested in having the public think I have no sense of humor. Want another piece?''

''No.'' She wasn't soft. The skin on the inside of her elbow might look soft as butter, but the lady wasn't. It might annoy him to be so casually insulted, but he preferred it to spineless agreement. ''We'll be gone from June fifteenth until after Labor Day.'' He watched her scoop up a third piece of pizza. ''Since I've seen you eat, we'll each keep track of our own expenses.''

''Fine. Now, in case you have any odd ideas, I don't cook and I won't pick up after you. I'll drive my share, but I won't drive with you if you've been drinking. When we rent a darkroom, we trade off as to who uses it first. From June fifteenth to after Labor Day, we're partners. Fifty-fifty. If you have any problems with that, we'll hash it out now, before we sign on the dotted line.''

He thought about it. She had a good voice, smooth, quiet, nearly soothing. They might handle the close quarters well enough—as long as she didn't smile at him too often and he kept his mind off her legs. At the moment, he considered that the least of his problems. The assignment came first, and what he wanted for it, and from it.

''Do you have a lover?''

Bryan managed not to choke on her pizza. ''If that's an offer,'' she began smoothly, ''I'll have to decline. Rude, brooding men just aren't my type.''

Inwardly he acknowledged another hit; outwardly

his face remained expressionless. "We're going to be living in each other's pockets for three months." She'd challenged him, whether she realized it or not. Whether he realized it or not, Shade had accepted. He leaned closer. "I don't want to hassle with a jealous lover chasing along after us or constantly calling while I'm trying to work."

Just who did he think she was? Some bimbo who couldn't handle her personal life? She made herself pause a moment. Perhaps he'd had some uncomfortable experiences in his relationships. His problem, Bryan decided.

"I'll worry about my lovers, Shade." Bryan bit into her crust with a vengeance. "You worry about yours." She wiped her fingers on the last of the tissue and smiled. "Sorry to break up the party, but I've got to get back to work."

He rose, letting his gaze skim up her legs before he met her eyes. He was going to take the assignment. And he'd have three months to figure out just how he felt about Bryan Mitchell. "I'll be in touch."

"Do that."

Bryan waited until he'd crossed the room and shut the studio door behind him. With uncommon energy, and a speed she usually reserved for work, she jumped up and tossed the empty cardboard box at the door.

It promised to be a long three months.

Chapter 2

She knew exactly what she wanted. Bryan might've been a bit ahead of the scheduled starting date for the American Summer project for *Life-style*, but she enjoyed the idea of being a step ahead of Shade Colby. Petty, perhaps, but she did enjoy it.

In any case, she doubted a man like him would appreciate the timeless joy of the last day of school. When else did summer really start, but with that one wild burst of freedom?

She chose an elementary school because she wanted innocence. She chose an inner-city school because she wanted realism. Children who would step out the door and into a limo weren't the image she wanted to project. This school could've been in any city across the country. The kids who'd bolt out the door would be all kids. People who looked at the photograph, no matter what their age, would see something of themselves.

Bryan gave herself plenty of time to set up, choosing and rejecting half a dozen vantage points before she settled on one. It wasn't possible or even advisable to stage the shoot. Only random shots would give her what she wanted—the spontaneity and the rush.

When the bell rang and the doors burst open, she got exactly that. It was well worth nearly being trampled under flying sneakers. With shouts and yells and whistles, kids poured out into the sunshine.

Stampede. That was the thought that went through her mind. Crouching quickly, Bryan shot up, catching the first rush of children at an angle that would convey speed, mass and total confusion.

Let's go, let's go! It's summer and every day's Saturday. September was years away. She could read it on the face of every child.

Turning, she shot the next group of children head-on. In the finished spot, they'd appear to be charging right out of the page of the magazine. On impulse, she shifted her camera for a vertical shot. And she got it. A boy of eight or nine leaped down the flight of steps, hands flung high, a grin splitting his face. Bryan shot him in midair while he hung head and shoulders above the scattering children. She'd captured the boy filled with the triumph of that magic, golden road of freedom spreading out in all directions.

Though she was dead sure which shot she'd print for the assignment, Bryan continued to work. Within ten minutes, it was over.

Satisfied, she changed lenses and angles. The school was empty now, and she wanted to record it that way. She didn't want the feel of bright sunlight here, she decided as she added a low-contrast filter. When she developed the print, Bryan would "dodge" the light in the sky by holding something over that section of the paper to keep it from being overexposed. She wanted the sense of emptiness, of waiting, as a contrast to the life and energy that had just poured out of the building. She'd exhausted a roll of film before she straightened and let the camera hang by its strap.

School's out, she thought with a grin. She felt that charismatic pull of freedom herself. Summer was just beginning.

Since resigning from the staff of *Celebrity*, Bryan had found her work load hadn't eased. If anything, she'd found herself to be a tougher employer than the magazine. She loved her work and was likely to give it all of her day and most of her evenings. Her ex-husband had once accused her of being obsessed not with her camera, but by it. It was something she'd neither been able to deny nor defend. After two days of working with Shade, Bryan had discovered she wasn't alone.

She'd always considered herself a meticulous craftsman. Compared to Shade, she was lackadaisical. He had a patience in his work that she admired even as it set her teeth on edge. They worked from entirely different perspectives. Bryan shot a scene and conveyed her personal viewpoint—her emotions, her feel-

ings about the image. Shade deliberately courted am-
biguity. While his photographs might spark off a
dozen varied reactions, his personal view almost always remained his secret. Just as everything about him
remained half shadowed.

He didn't chat, but Bryan didn't mind working in
silence. It was nearly like working alone. His long,
quiet looks could be unnerving, however. She didn't
care to be dissected as though she were in a viewfinder.

They'd met twice since their first encounter in her
studio, both times to argue out their basic route and
the themes for the assignment. She hadn't found him
any easier, but she had found him sharp. The project
meant enough to both of them to make it possible for
them to do as she'd suggested—meet somewhere in
the middle.

After her initial annoyance with him had worn off,
Bryan had decided they could become friends over the
next months—professional friends, in any case. Then,
after two days of working with him, she'd known it
would never happen. Shade didn't induce simple emotions like friendship. He'd either dazzle or infuriate.
She didn't choose to be dazzled.

Bryan had researched him thoroughly, telling herself her reason was routine. You didn't go on the road
with a man you knew virtually nothing about. Yet the
more she'd found out—rather, the more she hadn't
found out—the deeper her curiosity had become.

He'd been married and divorced in his early twen-
ties. That was it—no anecdotes, no gossip, no right

and wrong. He covered his tracks well. As a photographer for *International View*, Shade had spent a total of five years overseas. Not in pretty Paris, London and Madrid, but in Laos, Lebanon, Cambodia. His work there had earned him a Pulitzer nomination and the Overseas Press Club Award.

His photographs were available for study and dissection, but his personal life remained obscure. He socialized rarely. What friends he had were unswervingly loyal and frustratingly closemouthed. If she wanted to learn more about him, Bryan would have to do it on the job.

Bryan considered the fact that they'd agreed to spend their last day in L.A. working at the beach a good sign. They'd decided on the location without any argument. Beach scenes would be an ongoing theme throughout the essay—California to Cape Cod.

At first they walked along the sand together, like friends or lovers, not touching but in step with each other. They didn't talk, but Bryan had already learned that Shade didn't make idle conversation unless he was in the mood.

It was barely ten, but the sun was bright and hot. Because it was a weekday morning, most of the sun- and water-seekers were the young or the old. When Bryan stopped, Shade kept walking without either of them saying a word.

It was the contrast that had caught her eye. The old woman was bundled in a wide, floppy sun hat, a long beach dress and a crocheted shawl. She sat under an umbrella and watched her granddaughter—dressed only in frilly pink panties—dig a hole in the sand beside her. Sun poured over the little girl. Shadow blanketed the old woman.

She'd need the woman to sign a release form. Invariably, asking someone if you could take her picture stiffened her up, and Bryan avoided it whenever it was possible. In this case it wasn't, so she was patient enough to chat and wait until the woman had relaxed again.

Her name was Sadie, and so was her granddaughter's. Before she'd clicked the shutter the first time, Bryan knew she'd title the print *Two Sadies*. All she had to do was get that dreamy, faraway look back in the woman's eyes.

It took twenty minutes. Bryan forgot she was uncomfortably warm as she listened, thought and reasoned out the angles. She knew what she wanted. The old woman's careful self-preservation, the little girl's total lack of it, and the bond between them that came with blood and time.

Lost in reminiscence, Sadie forgot about the camera, not noticing when Bryan began to release the shutter. She wanted the poignancy—that's what she'd seen. When she printed it, Bryan would be merciless with the lines and creases in the grandmother's face, just as she'd highlight the flawlessness of the toddler's skin.

Grateful, Bryan chatted a few more minutes, then noted the woman's address with the promise of a print. She walked on, waiting for the next scene to unfold.

Shade had his first subject as well, but he didn't

chat. The man lay facedown on a faded beach towel. He was red, flabby and anonymous. A businessman taking the morning off, a salesman from Iowa—it didn't matter. Unlike Bryan, he wasn't looking for personality, but for the sameness of those who grilled their bodies under the sun. There was a plastic bottle of tanning lotion stuck in the sand beside him and a pair of rubber beach thongs.

Shade chose two angles and shot six times without exchanging a word with the snoring sunbather. Satisfied, he scanned the beach. Three yards away, Bryan was casually stripping out of her shorts and shirt. The sleek red maillot rose tantalizing high at the thighs. Her profile was to him as she stepped out of her shorts. It was sharp, well defined, like something sculpted with a meticulous hand.

Shade didn't hesitate. He focused her in his viewfinder, set the aperture, adjusted the angle no more than a fraction and waited. At the moment when she reached down for the hem of her T-shirt, he began to shoot.

She was so easy, so unaffected. He'd forgotten anyone could be so totally unselfconscious in a world where self-absorption had become a religion. Her body was one long lean line, with more and more exposed as she drew the shirt over her head. For a moment, she tilted her face up to the sun, inviting the heat. Something crawled into his stomach and began to twist, slowly.

Desire. He recognized it. He didn't care for it.

It was, he could tell himself, what was known in

the trade as a decisive moment. The photographer
thinks, then shoots, while watching the unfolding
scene. When the visual and the emotional elements
come together—as they had in this case, with a
punch—there was success. There were no replays
here, no reshooting. Decisive moment meant exactly
that, all or nothing. If he'd been shaken for a instant,
it only proved he'd been successful in capturing that
easy, lazy sexuality.

Years before, he'd trained himself not to become
overly emotional about his subjects. They could eat
you alive. Bryan Mitchell might not look as though
she'd take a bite out of a man, but Shade didn't take
chances. He turned away from her and forgot her. Almost.

It was more than four hours later before their paths
crossed again. Bryan sat in the sun near a concession
stand, eating a hot dog buried under mounds of mustard and relish. On one side of her she'd set her camera bag, on the other a can of soda. Her narrow red
sunglasses shot his reflection back at him.

"How'd it go?" she asked with her mouth full.

"All right. Is there a hot dog under that?"

"Mmm." She swallowed and gestured toward the
stand. "Terrific."

"I'll pass." Reaching down, Shade picked up her
warming soda and took a long pull. It was orange and
sweet. "How the hell do you drink this stuff?"

"I need a lot of sugar. I got some shots I'm pretty
pleased with." She held out a hand for the can. "I
want to make prints before we leave tomorrow."

"As long as you're ready at seven."

Bryan wrinkled her nose as she finished off her hot dog. She'd rather work until 7:00 A.M. than get up that early. One of the first things they'd have to iron out on the road was the difference in their biological schedules. She understood the beauty and power of a sunrise shot. She just happened to prefer the mystery and color of sunset.

"I'll be ready." Rising, she brushed sand off her bottom, then pulled her T-shirt over her suit. Shade could've told her she was more modest without it. The way the hem skimmed along her thighs and drew the eyes to them was nearly criminal. "As long as you drive the first shift," she continued. "By ten I'll be functional."

He didn't know why he did it. Shade was a man who analyzed each movement, every texture, shape, color. He cut everything into patterns, then reassembled them. That was his way. Impulse wasn't. Yet he reached out and curled his fingers around her braid without thinking of the act or the consequences. He just wanted to touch.

She was surprised, he could see. But she didn't pull away. Nor did she give him that small half smile women used when a man couldn't resist touching what attracted him.

Her hair was soft; his eyes had told him that, but now his fingers confirmed it. Still, it was frustrating not to feel it loose and free, not to be able to let it play between his fingers.

He didn't understand her. Yet. She made her living

recording the elite, the glamorous, the ostentatious, yet she seemed to have no pretensions. Her only jewelry was a thin gold chain that fell to her breasts. On the end was a tiny ankh. Again, she wore no makeup, but her scent was there to tantalize. She could, with a few basic female touches, have turned herself into something breathtaking, but she seemed to ignore the possibilities and rely on simplicity. That in itself was stunning.

Hours before, Bryan had decided she didn't want to be dazzled. Shade was deciding at that moment that he didn't care to be stunned. Without a word, he let her braid fall back to her shoulder.

"Do you want me to take you back to your apartment or your studio?"

So that was it? He'd managed to tie her up in knots in a matter of seconds, and now he only wanted to know where to dump her off. "The studio." Bryan reached down and picked up her camera bag. Her throat was dry, but she tossed the half-full can of soda into the trash. She wasn't certain she could swallow. Before they'd reached Shade's car, she was certain she'd explode if she didn't say something.

"Do you enjoy that cool, remote image you've perfected, Shade?"

He didn't look at her, but he nearly smiled. "It's comfortable."

"Except for the people who get within five feet of you." Damned if she wouldn't get a rise out of him. "Maybe you take your own press too seriously," she suggested. "Shade Colby, as mysterious and intriguing as his name, as dangerous and as compelling as his photographs.''

This time he did smile, surprising her. Abruptly he looked like someone she'd want to link hands with, laugh with. ''Where in hell did you read that?''

''*Celebrity*,'' she muttered, ''April, five years ago. They did an article on the photo sales in New York. One of your prints sold for seventy-five hundred at Sotheby's.''

''Did it?'' His gaze slid over her profile. ''You've a better memory than I.''

Stopping, she turned to face him. ''Damn it, I bought it. It's a moody, depressing, fascinating street scene that I wouldn't have given ten cents for if I'd met you first. And if I wasn't so hooked on it, I'd pitch it out the minute I get home. As it is, I'll probably have to turn it to face the wall for six months until I forget that the artist behind it is a jerk.''

Shade watched her soberly, then nodded. ''You make quite a speech once you're rolling.''

With one short, rude word, Bryan turned and started toward the car again. As she reached the passenger side and yanked open the door, Shade stopped her. ''Since we're essentially going to be living together for the next three months, you might want to get the rest of it out now.''

Though she tried to speak casually, it came out between her teeth. ''The rest of what?''

''Whatever griping you have to do.''

She took a deep breath first. She hated to be angry. Invariably it exhausted her. Resigned to it, Bryan curled her hands around the top of the door and leaned toward him. "I don't like you. I'd say it's just that simple, but I can't think of anyone else I don't like."

"No one?"

"No one."

For some reason, he believed her. He nodded, then dropped his hands over hers on top of the door. "I'd rather not be lumped in a group in any case. Why should we have to like each other?"

"It'd make the assignment easier."

He considered this while holding her hands beneath his. The tops of hers were soft, the palms of his hard. He liked the contrast, perhaps too much. "You like things easy?"

He made it sound like an insult, and she straightened. Her eyes were on a level with his mouth, and she shifted slightly. "Yes. Complications are just that. They get in the way and muck things up. I'd rather shovel them aside and deal with what's important."

"We've had a major complication before we started."

She might've concentrated on keeping her eyes on his, but that didn't prevent her from feeling the light, firm pressure of his hands. It didn't prevent her from understanding his meaning. Since it was something they'd meticulously avoided mentioning from the beginning, Bryan lunged at it, straight on.

"You're a man and I'm a woman."

He couldn't help but enjoy the way she snarled it at him. "Exactly. We can say we're both photogra-

phers and that's a sexless term.'' He gave her the bar-
est hint of a smile. ''It's also bullshit.''

''That may be,'' she said evenly. ''But I intend to
handle it, because the assignment comes first. It helps
a great deal that I don't like you.''

''Liking doesn't have anything to do with chemistry.''

She gave him an easy smile because her pulse was
beginning to pound. ''Is that a polite word for lust?''

She wasn't one to dance around an issue once she'd
opened it up. Fair enough, he decided. ''Whatever you
call it, it goes right back to your complication. We'd
better take a good look at it, then shove it aside.''

When his fingers tightened on hers, she dropped her
gaze to them. She understood his meaning, but not his
reason.

''Wondering what it would be like's going to distract both of us,'' Shade continued. She looked up
again, wary. He could feel her pulse throb where his
fingers brushed her wrist, yet she'd made no move to
pull back. If she had... There was no use speculating;
it was better to move ahead. ''We'll find out. Then
we'll file it, forget it and get on with our job.''

It sounded logical. Bryan had a basic distrust of
anything that sounded quite so logical. Still, he'd been
right on target when he'd said that wondering would
be distracting. She'd been wondering for days. His
mouth seemed to be the softest thing about him, yet
even that looked hard, firm and unyielding. How
would it feel? How would it taste?

She let her gaze wander back to it, and the lips

curved. She wasn't certain if it was amusement or sarcasm, but it made up her mind.

"All right." How intimate could a kiss be when a
car door separated them?

They leaned toward each other slowly, as if each
waited for the other to draw back at the last moment.
Their lips met lightly, passionlessly. It could've ended
then, with each of them shrugging the other off in
disinterest. It was the basic definition of a kiss. Two
pairs of lips meeting. Nothing more.

Neither one would be able to say who changed it,
whether it was calculated or accidental. They were
both curious people, and curiosity might have been
the factor. Or it might have been inevitable. The texture of the kiss changed so slowly that it wasn't possible to stop it until it was too late for regrets.

Lips opened, invited, accepted. Their fingers clung.
His head tilted, and hers, so that the kiss deepened.
Bryan found herself pressing against the hard, unyielding door, searching for more, demanding it, as
her teeth nipped at his bottom lip. She'd been right.
His mouth was the softest thing about him. Impossibly
soft, unreasonably luxurious as it heated on hers.

She wasn't used to wild swings of mood. She'd
never experienced anything like it. It wasn't possible
to lie back and enjoy. Wasn't that what kisses were
for? Up to now, she'd believed so. This one demanded
all her strength, all her energy. Even as it went on,
she knew when it ended she'd be drained. Wonderfully, totally drained. While she reveled in the excitement, she could anticipate the glory of the aftermath.

He should've known. Damn it, he should've known she wasn't as easy and uncomplicated as she looked. Hadn't he looked at her and ached? Tasting her wasn't going to alleviate any of it, only heighten it. She could undermine his control, and control was essential to his art, his life, his sanity. He'd developed and perfected it over years of sweat, fear and expectations. Shade had learned that the same calculated control he used in the darkroom, the same careful logic he used to set up a shot, could be applied to a woman successfully. Painlessly. One taste of Bryan and he realized just how tenuous control could be.

To prove to himself, perhaps to her, that he could deal with it, he allowed the kiss to deepen, grow darker, moister. Danger hovered, and perhaps he courted it.

He might lose himself in the kiss, but when it was over, it would be over, and nothing would be changed.

She tasted hot, sweet, strong. She made him burn. He had to hold back, or the burn would leave a scar. He had enough of them. Life wasn't as lovely as a first kiss on a hot afternoon. He knew better than most.

Shade drew away, satisfying himself that his control was still in place. Perhaps his pulse wasn't steady, his mind not perfectly clear, but he had control.

Bryan was reeling. If he'd asked her a question, any question, she'd have had no answer. Bracing herself against the car door, she waited for her equilibrium to return. She'd known the kiss would drain her. Even now, she could feel her energy flag.

He saw the look in her eyes, the soft look any man

would have to struggle to resist. Shade turned away from it. "I'll drop you at the studio."

As he walked around the car to his side, Bryan dropped down on the seat. File it and forget it, she thought. Fat chance.

She tried. Bryan put so much effort into forgetting what Shade had made her feel that she worked until 3:00 A.M. By the time she'd dragged herself back to her apartment, she'd developed the film from the school and the beach, chosen the negatives she wanted to print and perfected two of them into what she considered some of her best work.

Now she had four hours to eat, pack and sleep. After building herself an enormous sandwich, Bryan took out the one suitcase she'd been allotted for the trip and tossed in the essentials. Groggy with fatigue, she washed down bread, meat and cheese with a great gulp of milk. None of it felt too steady on her stomach, so she left her partially eaten dinner on the bedside table and went back to her packing.

She rummaged in the top of her closet for the box with the prim man-tailored pajamas her mother had given her for Christmas. Definitely essential, she decided as she dropped them on the disordered pile of lingerie and jeans. They were sexless, Bryan mused. She could only hope she felt sexless in them. That afternoon she'd been forcibly reminded that she was a woman, and a woman had some vulnerabilities that couldn't always be defended.

She didn't want to feel like a woman around Shade

again. It was too perilous, and she avoided perilous situations. Since she wasn't the type to make a point of her femininity, there should be no problem.

She told herself.

Once they were started on the assignment, they'd be so wound up in it that they wouldn't notice if the other had two heads and four thumbs.

She told herself.

What had happened that afternoon was simply one of those fleeting moments the photographer sometimes came across when the moment dictated the scene. It wouldn't happen again, because the circumstances would never be the same.

She told herself.

And then she was finished thinking of Shade Colby. It was nearly four, and the next three hours were all hers, the last she had left to herself for a long time. She'd spend them the way she liked best. Asleep. Stripping, Bryan let her clothes fall in a heap, then crawled into bed without remembering to turn off the light.

Across town, Shade lay in the dark. He hadn't slept, although he'd been packed for hours. His bag and his equipment were neatly stacked at the door. He was organized, prepared and wide-awake.

He'd lost sleep before. The fact didn't concern him, but the reason did. Bryan Mitchell. Though he'd managed to push her to the side, to the back, to the corner of his mind throughout the evening, he couldn't quite get her out.

He could dissect what had happened between them that afternoon point by point, but it didn't change one essential thing. He'd been vulnerable. Perhaps only for an instant, only a heartbeat, but he'd been vulnerable. That was something he couldn't afford. It was something he wouldn't allow to happen a second time.

Bryan Mitchell was one of the complications she claimed she liked to avoid. He, on the other hand, was used to them. He'd never had any problem dealing with complications. She'd be no different.

He told himself.

For the next three months, they'd be deep into a project that should totally involve all their time and energy. When he worked, he was well able to channel his concentration on one point and ignore everything else. That was no problem.

He told himself.

What had happened had happened. He still believed it was best done away with before they started out—best that they did away with the speculation and the tension it could cause. They'd eliminated the tension.

He told himself.

But he couldn't sleep. The ache in his stomach had nothing to do with the dinner that had grown cold on his plate, untouched.

He had three hours to himself, then he'd have three months of Bryan. Closing his eyes, Shade did what he was always capable of doing under stress. He willed himself to sleep.

Chapter 3

Bryan was up and dressed by seven, but she wasn't ready to talk to anyone. She had her suitcase and tripod in one hand, with two camera bags and her purse slung crosswise over her shoulders. As Shade pulled up to the curb, she was walking down the stairs and onto the sidewalk. She believed in being prompt, but not necessarily cheerful.

She grunted to Shade; it was as close to a greeting as she could manage at that hour. In silence, she loaded her gear into his van, then kicked back in the passenger seat, stretched out her legs and closed her eyes.

Shade looked at what he could see of her face behind round, amber-lensed sunglasses and under a battered straw hat. "Rough night?" he asked, but she was already asleep. Shaking his head, he released the

brake and pulled out into the street. They were on
their way.

Shade didn't mind long drives. They gave him a
chance to think or not think, as he chose. In less than
an hour, he was out of L.A. traffic and heading north-
east on the interstate. He liked riding into the rising
sun with a clear road ahead. Light bounced off the
chrome on the van, shimmered on the hood and sliced
down on the road signs.

He planned to cover five or six hundred miles that
day, leading up toward Utah, unless something interesting caught his eye and they stopped for a shoot.
After this first day, he saw no reason for them to be
mileage-crazy. It would hamper the point of the assignment. They'd drive as they needed to, working
toward and around the definite destinations they'd ultimately agreed on.

He had a route that could easily be altered, and no
itinerary. Their only time frame was to be on the East
Coast by Labor Day. He turned the radio on low and
found some gritty country music as he drove at a
steady, mile-eating pace. Beside him, Bryan slept.

If this was her routine, he mused, they wouldn't
have any problems. As long as she was asleep, they
couldn't grate on each other's nerves. Or stir each
other's passion. Even now he wondered why thoughts
of her had kept him restless throughout the night.
What was it about her that had worried him? He didn't
know, and that was a worry in itself.

Shade liked to be able to put his finger on things
and pick a problem apart until the pieces were small

enough to rearrange to his preference. Even though she was quiet, almost unobtrusive, at the moment, he didn't believe he'd be able to do that with Bryan Mitchell.

After his decision to take the assignment, he'd made it his business to find out more about her. Shade might guard his personal life and snarl over his privacy, but he wasn't at a loss for contacts. He'd known of her work for *Celebrity*, and her more inventive and personalized work for magazines like *Vanity* and *In Touch*. She'd developed into something of a cult artist over the years with her offbeat, often radical photographs of the famous.

What he hadn't known was that she was the daughter of a painter and a poet, both eccentric and semi-successful residents of Carmel. She'd been married to an accountant before she was twenty, and divorced him three years later. She dated with an almost studied casualness, and she had vague plans about buying a beach house at Malibu. She was well liked, respected and, by all accounts, dependable. She was often slow in doing things—a combination of her need for perfection and her belief that rushing was a waste of energy.

He'd found nothing surprising in his research, and no clue as to his attraction to her. But a photographer, a successful one, was patient. Sometimes it was necessary to come back to a subject again and again until you understood your own emotion toward it.

As they crossed the border into Nevada, Shade lit

a cigarette and rolled down his window. Bryan stirred, grumbled, then groped for her bag.

"Morning." Shade sent her a brief, sidelong look.

"Mmm-hmm." Bryan rooted through the bag, then gripped the chocolate bar in relief. With two quick rips, she unwrapped it and tossed the trash in her purse. She usually cleaned it out before it overflowed.

"You always eat candy for breakfast?"

"Caffeine." She took a huge bite and sighed. "I prefer mine this way." Slowly, she stretched, torso, shoulders, arms, in one long, sinuous move that was completely unplanned. It was, Shade thought ironically, one definitive clue as to the attraction. "So where are we?"

"Nevada." He blew out a stream of smoke that whipped out the open window. "Just."

Bryan folded her legs under her as she nibbled on the candy bar. "It must be about my shift."

"I'll let you know."

"Okay." She was content to ride as long as he was content to drive. She did, however, give a meaningful glance at the radio. Country music wasn't her style. "Driver picks the tunes."

He shrugged his acceptance. "If you want to wash that candy down with something, there's some juice in a jug in the back."

"Yeah?" Always interested in putting something into her stomach, Bryan unfolded herself and worked her way into the back of the van.

She hadn't paid any attention to the van that morning, except for a bleary scan that told her it was black and well cared-for. There were padded benches along each side that could, if you weren't too choosy, be suitable for beds. Bryan thought the pewter carpet might be the better choice.

Shade's equipment was neatly secured, and hers was loaded haphazardly into a corner. Above, glossy ebony cabinets held some essentials. Coffee, a hot plate, a small teakettle. They'd come in handy, she thought, if they stopped in any campgrounds with electric hookups. In the meantime, she settled for the insulated jug of juice.

"Want some?"

He glanced in the rearview mirror to see her standing, legs spread for balance, one hand resting on the cabinet. "Yeah."

Bryan took two jumbo plastic cups and the jug back to her seat. "All the comforts of home," she commented with a jerk of her head toward the back. "Do you travel in this much?"

"When it's necessary." He heard the ice thump against the cup and held out his hand. "I don't like to fly. You lose any chance you'd have at getting a shot at something on the way." After flipping his cigarette out the window, he drank his juice. "If it's an assignment within five hundred miles or so, I drive."

"I hate to fly." Bryan propped herself in the V between the seat and the door. "It seems I'm forever having to fly to New York to photograph someone who can't or won't come to me. I take a bottle of Dramamine, a supply of chocolate bars, a rabbit's foot and a socially significant, educational book. It covers all the bases.''

''The Dramamine and the rabbit's foot, maybe.''

''The chocolate's for my nerves. I like to eat when I'm tense. The book's a bargaining point.'' She shook her cup so the ice clinked. ''I feel like I'm saying— see, I'm doing something worthwhile here. Let's not mess it up by crashing the plane. Then, too, the book usually puts me to sleep within twenty minutes.''

The corner of Shade's mouth lifted, something Bryan took as a hopeful sign for the several thousand miles they had to go. ''That explains it.''

''I have a phobia about flying at thirty thousand feet in a heavy tube of metal with two hundred strangers, many of whom like to tell the intimate details of their lives to the person next to them.'' Propping her feet on the dash, she grinned. ''I'd rather drive across country with one cranky photographer who makes it a point to tell me as little as possible.''

Shade sent her a sidelong look and decided there was no harm in playing the game as long as they both knew the rules. ''You haven't asked me anything.''

''Okay, we'll start with something basic. Where'd Shade come from? The name, I mean.''

He slowed down, veering off toward a rest stop. ''Shadrach.''

Her eyes widened in appreciation. ''As in Meshach and Abednego in the Book of Daniel?''

''That's right. My mother decided to give each of her offspring a name that would roll around a bit. I've a sister named Cassiopeia. Why Bryan?''

"My parents wanted to show they weren't sexist."

The minute the van stopped in a parking space, Bryan hopped out, bent from the waist and touched her palms to the asphalt—much to the interest of the man climbing into the Pontiac next to her. With the view fuddling his concentration, it took him a full thirty seconds to fit his key in the ignition.

"God, I get so stiff!" She stretched up, standing on her toes, then dropped down again. "Look, there's a snack bar over there. I'm going to get some fries. Want some?"

"It's ten o'clock in the morning."

"Almost ten-thirty," she corrected. "Besides, people eat hash browns for breakfast. What's the difference?"

He was certain there was one, but didn't feel like a debate. "You go ahead. I want to buy a paper."

"Fine." As an afterthought, Bryan climbed back inside and grabbed her camera. "I'll meet you back here in ten minutes."

Her intentions were good, but she took nearly twenty. Even as she approached the snack bar, the formation of the line of people waiting for fast food caught her imagination. There were perhaps ten people wound out like a snake in front of a sign that read Eat Qwik.

They were dressed in baggy Bermudas, wrinkled sundresses and cotton pants. A curvy teenager had on a pair of leather shorts that looked as though they'd been painted on. A woman six back from the stand fanned herself with a wide-brimmed hat banded with a floaty ribbon.

They were all going somewhere, all waiting to get there, and none of them paid any attention to anyone else. Bryan couldn't resist. She walked up the line one way, down it another, until she found her angle.

She shot them from the back so that the line seemed elongated and disjointed and the sign loomed promisingly. The man behind the counter serving food was nothing more than a vague shadow that might or might not have been there. She'd taken more than her allotted ten minutes before she joined the line herself.

Shade was leaning against the van reading the paper when she returned. He'd already taken three calculated shots of the parking lot, focusing on a line of cars with license plates from five different states. When he glanced up, Bryan had her camera slung over her shoulder, a giant chocolate shake in one hand and a jumbo order of fries smothered in ketchup in the other.

"Sorry." She dipped into the box of fries as she walked. "I got a couple of good shots of the line at the snack bar. Half of summer's hurry up and wait, isn't it?"

"Can you drive with all that?"

"Sure." She swung into the driver's side. "I'm used to it." She balanced the shake between her thighs, settled the fries just ahead of it and reached out a hand for the keys.

Shade glanced down at the breakfast snuggled between very smooth, very brown legs. "Still willing to share?"

Bryan turned her head to check the rearview as she backed out. "Nope." She gave the wheel a quick turn and headed toward the exit. "You had your chance." With one competent hand steering, she dug into the fries again.

"You eat like that, you should have acne down to your navel."

"Myths," she announced, and zoomed past a slower-moving sedan. With a few quick adjustments, she had an old Simon and Garfunkel tune pouring out of the radio. "That's music," she told him. "I like songs that give me a visual. Country music's usually about hurting and cheating and drinking."

"And life."

Bryan picked up her shake and drew on the straw. "Maybe. I guess I get tired of too much reality. Your work depends on it."

"And yours often skirts around it."

Her brows knit, then she deliberately relaxed. In his way, he was right. "Mine gives options. Why'd you take this assignment, Shade?" she asked suddenly. "Summer in America exemplifies fun. That's not your style."

"It also equals sweat, crops dying from too much sun and frazzled nerves." He lit another cigarette. "More my style?"

"You said it, I didn't." She swirled the chocolate in her mouth. "You smoke like that, you're going to die."

"Sooner or later." Shade opened the paper again and ended the conversation.

Who the hell was he? Bryan asked herself as she leveled the speed at sixty. What factors in his life had brought out the cynicism as well as the genius? There was humor in him—she'd seen it once or twice. But he seemed to allow himself only a certain degree and no more.

Passion? She could attest firsthand that there was a powder keg inside him. What might set it off? If she was certain of one thing about Shade Colby, it was that he held himself in rigid control. The passion, the power, the fury—whatever label you gave it—escaped into his work, but not, she was certain, into his personal life. Not often, in any case.

She knew she should be careful and distant; it would be the smartest way to come out of this long-term assignment without scars. Yet she wanted to dig into his character, and she knew she'd have to give in to the temptation. She'd have to press the buttons and watch the results, probably because she didn't like him and was attracted to him at the same time.

She'd told him the truth when she'd said that she couldn't think of anyone else she didn't like. It went hand in hand with her approach to her art—she looked into a person and found qualities, not all of them admirable, not all of them likable, but something, always something, that she could understand. She needed to do that with Shade, for herself. And because, though she'd bide her time telling him, she wanted very badly to photograph him.

"Shade, I want to ask you something else."

He didn't glance up from the paper. "Hmm?"

"What's your favorite movie?"

Half annoyed at the interruption, half puzzled at the question, he looked up and found himself wondering yet again what her hair would look like out of that thick, untidy braid. "What?"

"Your favorite movie," she repeated. "I need a clue, a starting point."

"For what?"

"To find out why I find you interesting, attractive and unlikable."

"You're an odd woman, Bryan."

"No, not really, though I have every right to be." She stopped speaking a moment as she switched lanes. "Come on, Shade, it's going to be a long trip. Let's humor each other on the small points. Give me a movie."

"*To Have and Have Not.*"

"Bogart and Bacall's first together." It made her smile at him in the way he'd already decided was dangerous. "Good. If you'd named some obscure French film, I'd have had to find something else. Why that one?"

He set the paper aside. So she wanted to play games. It was harmless, he decided. And they still had a long day ahead of them. "On-screen chemistry, tight plotting and camera work that made Bogart look like the consummate hero and Bacall the only woman who could stand up to him."

She nodded, pleased. He wasn't above enjoying heroes, fantasies and bubbling relationships. It might've been a small point, but she could like him for it. "Movies fascinate me, and the people who make them. I suppose that was one of the reasons I jumped at the chance to work for *Celebrity*. I've lost count of the number of actors I've shot, but when I see them up on the screen, I'm still fascinated."

He knew it was dangerous to ask questions, not because of the answers, but because of the questions you'd be asked in return. Still, he wanted to know. "Is that why you photograph the beautiful people? Because you want to get close to the glamour?"

Because she considered it a fair question, Bryan decided not to be annoyed. Besides, it made her think about something that had simply seemed to evolve, almost unplanned. "I might've started out with something like that in mind. Before long, you come to see them as ordinary people with extraordinary jobs. I like finding that spark that's made them the chosen few."

"Yet for the next three months you're going to be photographing the everyday. Why?"

"Because there's a spark in all of us. I'd like to find it in a farmer in Iowa, too."

So he had his answer. "You're an idealist, Bryan."

"Yes." She gave him a frankly interested look. "Should I be ashamed of it?"

He didn't like the way the calm, reasonable question affected him. He'd had ideals of his own once, and he knew how much it hurt to have them rudely taken away. "Not ashamed," he said after a moment. "Careful."

They drove for hours. In midafternoon, they switched positions and Bryan skimmed through Shade's discarded paper. By mutual consent, they left the freeway and began to travel over back roads. The pattern became sporadic conversations and long silences. It was early evening when they crossed the border into Idaho.

"Skiing and potatoes," Bryan commented. "That's all I can think of when I think of Idaho." With a shiver, she rolled up her window. Summer came slower in the north, especially when the sun was low. She gazed out the glass at the deepening twilight.

Sheep, hundreds of them, in what seemed like miles of gray or white bundles, were grazing lazily on the tough grass that bordered the road. She was a woman of the city, of freeways and office buildings. It might've surprised Shade to know she'd never been this far north, nor this far east except by plane.

The acres of placid sheep fascinated her. She was reaching for her camera when Shade swore and hit the brakes. Bryan landed on the floor with a plop.

"What was that for?"

He saw at a glance that she wasn't hurt, not even annoyed, but simply curious. He didn't bother to apologize. "Damn sheep in the road."

Bryan hauled herself up and looked out the windshield. There were three of them lined unconcernedly across the road, nearly head to tail. One of them turned its head and glanced up at the van, then looked away again.

"They look like they're waiting for a bus," she

decided, then grabbed Shade's wrist before he could lean on the horn. "No, wait a minute. I've never touched one."

Before Shade could comment, she was out of the van and walking toward them. One of them shied a few inches away as she approached, but for the most part, the sheep couldn't have cared less. Shade's annoyance began to fade as she leaned over and touched one. He thought another woman might look the same as she stroked a sable at a furrier. Pleased, tentative and oddly sexual. And the light was good. Taking his camera, he selected a filter.

"How do they feel?"

"Soft—not as soft as I'd thought. Alive. Nothing like a lamb's-wool coat." Still bent over, one hand on the sheep, Bryan looked up. It surprised her to be facing a camera. "What's that for?"

"Discovery." He'd already taken two shots, but he wanted more. "Discovery has a lot to do with summer. How do they smell?"

Intrigued, Bryan leaned closer to the sheep. He framed her when her face was all but buried in the wool. "Like sheep," she said with a laugh, and straightened. "Want to play with the sheep and I'll take your picture?"

"Maybe next time."

She looked as if she belonged there, on the long deserted road surrounded by stretches of empty land, and it puzzled him. He'd thought she set well in L.A., in the center of the glitz and illusions.

"Something wrong?" She knew he was thinking of

her, only of her, when he looked at her like that. She wished she could've taken it a step further, yet was oddly relieved that she couldn't.

"You acclimate well."

Her smile was hesitant. "It's simpler that way. I told you I don't like complications."

He turned back to the truck, deciding he was thinking about her too much. "Let's see if we can get these sheep to move."

"But, Shade, you can't just leave them on the side of the road." She jogged back to the van. "They'll wander right back out. They might get run over."

He gave her a look that said he clearly wasn't interested. "What do you expect me to do? Round 'em up?"

"The least we can do is get them back over the fence." As if he'd agreed wholeheartedly, Bryan turned around and started back to the sheep. As he watched, she reached down, hauled one up and nearly toppled over. The other two bleated and scattered.

"Heavier than they look," she managed, and began to stagger toward the fence strung along the shoulder of the road while the sheep she carried bleated, kicked and struggled. It wasn't easy, but after a test of wills and brute strength, she dropped the sheep over the fence. With one hand, she swiped at the sweat on her forehead as she turned to scowl at Shade. "Well, are you going to help or not?"

He'd enjoyed the show, but he didn't smile as he leaned against the van. "They'll probably find the hole in the fence again and be back on the road in ten minutes."

"Maybe they will," Bryan said between her teeth as she headed for the second sheep. "But I'll have done what should be done."

"Idealist." he said again.

With her hands on her hips, she whirled around. "Cynic."

"As long as we understand each other." Shade straightened. "I'll give you a hand."

The others weren't as easily duped as the first. It took Shade several exhausting minutes to catch number two, with Bryan running herd. Twice he lost his concentration and his quarry because her sudden husky laughter distracted him.

"Two down and one to go," he announced as he set the sheep free in pasture.

"But this one looks stubborn." From opposite sides of the road, the rescuers and the rescuee studied each other. "Shifty eyes," Bryan murmured. "I think he's the leader."

"She."

"Whatever. Look, just be nonchalant. You walk around that side, I'll walk around this side. When we have her in the middle, wham!"

Shade sent her a cautious look. "Wham?"

"Just follow my lead." Tucking her thumbs in her back pockets, she strolled across the road, whistling.

"Bryan, you're trying to outthink a sheep."

She sent him a bland look over her shoulder. "Maybe between the two of us we can manage to."

He wasn't at all sure she was joking. His first urge was to simply get back in the van and wait until she'd finished making a fool of herself. Then again, they'd already wasted enough time. Shade circled around to the left as Bryan moved to the right. The sheep eyed them both, swiveling her head from side to side.

"Now!" Bryan shouted, and dived.

Without giving himself the chance to consider the absurdity, Shade lunged from the other side. The sheep danced delicately away. Momentum carrying them both, Shade and Bryan collided, then rolled together onto the soft shoulder of the road. Shade felt the rush of air as they slammed into each other, and the soft give of her body as they tumbled together.

With the breath knocked out of her, Bryan lay on her back, half under Shade. His body was very hard and very male. She might not have had her wind, but Bryan had her wit. She knew if they stayed like this, things were going to get complicated. Drawing in air, she stared up into his face just above her.

His look was contemplative, considering and not altogether friendly. He wouldn't be a friendly lover, that she knew instinctively. It was in his eyes—those dark, deepset eyes. He was definitely a man to avoid having a personal involvement with. He'd overwhelm quickly, completely, and there'd be no turning back. She had to remind herself that she preferred easy relationships, as her heart started a strong, steady rhythm.

"Missed," she managed to say, but didn't try to move away.

"Yeah." She had a stunning face, all sharp angles and soft skin. Shade could nearly convince himself that his interest in it was purely professional. She'd photograph wonderfully from any angle, in any light. He could make her look like a queen or a peasant, but she'd always look like a woman a man would want. The lazy sexuality he could sense in her would come across in the photograph.

Just looking at her, he could plot half a dozen settings he'd like to shoot her in. And he could think of dozens of ways he'd like to make love to her. Here was first, on the cool grass along the roadside with the sun setting behind them and no sound.

She saw the decision in his eyes, saw it in time to avoid the outcome. But she didn't. She had only to shift away, only to protest with one word or a negative movement. But she didn't. Her mind told her to, arguing with an urge that was unarguably physical. Later, Bryan would wonder why she hadn't listened. Now, with the air growing cool and the sky darkening, she wanted the experience. She couldn't admit that she wanted him.

When he lowered his mouth to hers, there wasn't any of the light experimentation of the first time. Now he knew her and wanted the full impact of her passion. Their mouths met greedily, as if each one were racing the other to delirium.

Her body heated so quickly that the grass seemed to shimmer like ice beneath her. She wondered it didn't melt. It was a jolt that left her bewildered. With a small sound in her throat, Bryan reached for more.

His fingers were in her hair, tangled in the restriction
of her braid as if he didn't choose, or didn't dare, to
touch her yet. She moved under him, not in retreat but
in advance. Hold me, she seemed to demand. Give me
more. But he continued to make love only to her
mouth. Devastatingly.

She could hear the breeze; it tickled through the
grass beside her ear and taunted her. He'd give spar-
ingly of himself. She could feel it in the tenseness of
his body. He'd hold back. While his mouth stripped
away her defenses, one by one, he held himself apart.
Frustrated, Bryan ran her hands up his back. She'd
seduce.

Shade wasn't used to the pressure to give, to the
desire to. She drew from him a need for merging he'd
thought he'd beaten down years before. There seemed
to be no pretenses in her—her mouth was warm and
eager, tasting of generosity. Her body was soft and
agile, tempting. Her scent drifted around him, sexual,
uncomplicated. When she said his name, there seemed
to be no hidden meaning. For the first time in too long
for him to remember, he wanted to give, unheedingly,
boundlessly.

He held himself back. Pretenses, he knew, could be
well hidden. But he was losing to her. Even though
Shade was fully aware of it, he couldn't stop it. She
drew and drew from him, with a simplicity that
couldn't be blocked. He might've sworn against it,
cursed her, cursed himself, but his mind was beginning to swim. His body was throbbing.

They both felt the ground tremble, but it didn't oc-

cur to either of them that it was anything but their
own passion. They heard the noise, the rumble, growing louder and louder, and each thought it was inside
his or her own head. Then the wind rocketed by them
and the truck driver gave one long, rude blast of the
horn. It was enough to jolt them back to sanity. Feeling real panic for the first time, Bryan scrambled to
her feet.

"We'd better take care of that sheep and get going." She swore at the breathiness of her own voice
and wrapped her arms protectively around herself.
There was a chill in the air, she thought desperately.
That was all. "It's nearly dark."

Shade hadn't realized how deep the twilight had
become. He'd lost track of his surroundings—something he never allowed to happen. He'd forgotten that
they were on the side of the road, rolling in the grass
like a couple of brainless teenagers. He felt the lick
of anger, but stemmed it. He'd nearly lost control
once. He wouldn't lose it now.

She caught the sheep on the other side of the road,
where it grazed, certain that both humans had lost interest. It bleated in surprised protest as she scooped it
up. Swearing under his breath, Shade stalked over and
grabbed the sheep from her before Bryan could take
another tumble. He dumped it unceremoniously in the
pasture.

"Satisfied now?" he demanded.

She could see the anger in him, no matter how
tightly he reined it in. Her own bubbled. She'd had
her share of frustrations as well. Her body was puls-

ing, her legs were unsteady. Temper helped her to forget them.

"No," she tossed back. "And neither are you. It seems to me that should prove to both of us that we'd better keep a nice, clean distance."

He grabbed her arm as she started to swing past. "I didn't force you into anything, Bryan."

"Nor I you," she reminded him. "I'm responsible for my own actions, Shade." She glanced down at the hand that was curled around her arm. "And my own mistakes. If you like to shift blame, it's your prerogative."

His fingers tightened on her arm, briefly, but long enough for her eyes to widen in surprise at the strength and the depth of his anger. No, she wasn't used to wild swings of mood in herself or to causing them in others.

Slowly, and with obvious effort, Shade loosened his grip. She'd hit it right on the mark. He couldn't argue with honesty.

"No," he said a great deal more calmly. "I'll take my share, Bryan. It'll be easier on both of us if we agree to that nice, clean distance."

She nodded, steadier. Her lips curved into a slight smile. "Okay." Lighten up, she warned herself, for everyone's sake. "It'd have been easier from the beginning if you'd been fat and ugly."

He'd grinned before he'd realized it. "You too."

"Well, since I don't suppose either of us is willing to do anything about that particular problem, we just have to work around it. Agreed?'' She held out her hand.

''Agreed.''

Their hands joined. A mistake. Neither of them had recovered from the jolt to their systems. The contact, however casual, only served to accentuate it. Bryan linked her hands behind her back. Shade dipped his into his pockets.

''Well...'' Bryan began, with no idea where to go.

''Let's find a diner before we head into camp. Tomorrow's going to start early.''

She wrinkled her nose at that but started toward her side of the truck. ''I'm starving,'' she announced, and pretended she was in control by propping her feet on the dash. ''Think we'll find something decent to eat soon, or should I fortify myself with a candy bar?''

''There's a town about ten miles down this road.'' Shade turned on the ignition. His hand was steady, he told himself. Or nearly. ''Bound to be a restaurant of some kind. Probably serve great lamb chops.''

Bryan looked at the sheep grazing beside them, then sent Shade a narrowed-eyed glance. ''That's disgusting.''

''Yeah, and it'll keep your mind off your stomach until we eat.''

They bumped back onto the road and drove in silence. They'd made it over a hump, but each of them knew there'd be mountains yet to struggle over. Steep, rocky mountains.

Chapter 4

Bryan recorded vacationers floating like corks in the Great Salt Lake. When the shot called for it, she used a long or a wide-angle lens to bring in some unusual part of the landscape. But for the most part, Bryan concentrated on the people.

In the salt flats to the west, Shade framed race car enthusiasts. He angled for the speed, the dust, the grit. More often than not, the people included in his pictures would be anonymous, blurred, shadowy. He wanted only the essence.

Trips to large cities and through tidy suburbs used up rolls of film. There were summer gardens, hot, sweaty traffic jams, young girls in thin dresses, shirtless men, and babies in strollers being pushed along sidewalks and in shopping malls.

Their route through Idaho and Utah had been wind-

ing, but steady. Neither was displeased with the pace
or the subjects. For a time, after the turbulent detour
on the country road in Idaho, Bryan and Shade worked
side by side in relative harmony. They concentrated
on their own subjects, but they did little as a team.

They'd already taken hundreds of pictures, a fraction of which would be printed and still a smaller fraction published. Once it occurred to Bryan that the pictures they'd taken far outnumbered the words they'd
spoken to each other.

They drove together up to eight hours a day, stopping along the way whenever it was necessary or desirable to work. And they worked as much as they
drove. Out of each twenty-four hours, they were together an average of twenty. But they grew no closer.
It was something either of them might have accomplished with the ease of a friendly gesture or a few
casual words. It was something both of them avoided.

Bryan learned it was possible to keep an almost
obsessive emotional distance from someone while
sharing a limited space. She also learned a limited
space made it very difficult to ignore what Shade had
once termed chemistry. To balance the two, Bryan
kept her conversations light and brief and almost exclusively centered on the assignment. She asked no
more questions. Shade volunteered no more information.

By the time they crossed the border into Arizona,
at the end of the first week, she was already finding
it an uncomfortable way to work.

It was hot. The sun was merciless. The van's air-conditioning helped, but just looking out at the endless desert and faded sage made the mouth dry. Bryan had an enormous paper cup filled with soda and ice. Shade drank bottled iced tea as he drove.

She estimated that they hadn't exchanged a word for fifty-seven miles. Nor had they spoken much that morning when they'd set up to shoot, each in separate territory, at Glen Canyon in Utah. Bryan might be pleased with the study she'd done of the cars lined up at the park's entrance, but she was growing weary of their unspoken agreement of segregation.

The magazine had hired them as a team, she reminded herself. Each of them would take individual pictures, naturally, but there had to be some communication if the photo essay were to have any cohesion. There had to be some blending if the final result was the success both of them wanted. Compromise, she remembered with a sigh. They'd forgotten the operative word.

Bryan thought she knew Shade well enough at this point to be certain he'd never make the first move. He was perfectly capable of driving thousands of miles around the country without saying her name more than once a day. As in, Pass the salt, Bryan.

She could be stubborn. Bryan thought about it as she brooded out the window at the wide stretches of Arizona. She could be just as aloof as he. And, she admitted with a grimace, she could bore herself to death within another twenty-four hours.

Contact, she decided. She simply couldn't survive without some kind of contact. Even if it was with a hard-edged, casually rude cynic. Her only choice was to swallow her pride and make the first move herself. She gritted her teeth, gnawed on ice and thought about it for another ten minutes.

"Ever been to Arizona?"

Shade tossed his empty bottle into the plastic can they used for trash. "No."

Bryan pried off one sneaker with the toe of the other. If at first you don't succeed, she told herself. "They filmed *Outcast* in Sedona. Now that was a tough, thinking-man's Western," she mused, and received no response. "I spent three days there covering the filming for *Celebrity*." After adjusting her sun visor, she sat back again. "I was lucky enough to miss my plane and get another day. I spent it in Oak Creek Canyon. I've never forgotten it—the colors, the rock formations."

It was the longest speech she'd made in days. Shade negotiated the van around a curve and waited for the rest.

Okay, she thought, she'd get more than one word out of him if she had to use a crowbar. "A friend of mine settled there. Lee used to work for *Celebrity*. Now she's a novelist with her first book due out in the fall. She married Hunter Brown last year."

"The writer?"

Two words, she thought, smug. "Yes, have you read his stuff?"

This time Shade merely nodded and pulled a cigarette out of his pocket. Bryan began to sympathize with dentists who had to coax a patient to open wide.

"I've read everything he's written, then I hate myself for letting his books give me nightmares."

"Good horror fiction's supposed to make you wake up at 3:00 A.M. and wonder if you've locked your doors."

This time she grinned. "That sounds like something Hunter would say. You'll like him."

Shade merely moved his shoulders. He'd agreed to the stop in Sedona already, but he wasn't interested in taking flattering, commercial pictures of the occult king and his family. It would, however, give Shade the break he needed. If he could dump Bryan off for a day or two with her friends, he could take the time to get his system back to normal.

He hadn't had an easy moment since the day they'd started out of L.A. Every day that went by only tightened his nerves and played havoc with his libido. He'd tried, but it wasn't possible to forget she was there within arm's reach at night, separated from him only by the width of the van and the dark.

Yes, he could use a day away from her, and that natural, easy sexuality she didn't even seem aware of.

"You haven't seen them for a while?" he asked her.

"Not in months." Bryan relaxed, more at ease now that they'd actually begun a two-way conversation. "Lee's a good friend. I've missed her. She'll have a baby about the same time her book comes out."

The change in her voice had him glancing over. There was something softer about her now. Almost wistful.

"A year ago, we were both still with *Celebrity*, and now…" She turned to him, but the shaded glasses hid her eyes. "It's odd thinking of Lee settled down with a family. She was always more ambitious than me. It used to drive her crazy that I took everything with such a lack of intensity."

"Do you?"

"Just about everything," she murmured. Not you, she thought to herself. I don't seem to be able to take you easily. "It's simpler to relax and live," she went on, "than to worry about how you'll be living next month."

"Some people have to worry *if* they'll be living next month."

"Do you think the fact they worry about it changes things?" Bryan forgot her plan to make contact, forgot the fact that she'd been groping for some sort of compromise from him. He'd seen more than she'd seen of the world, of life. She had to admit that he'd seen more than she wanted to see. But how did he feel about it?

"Being aware can change things. Looking out for yourself's a priority some of us haven't a choice about."

Some of us. She noted the phrase but decided not to pounce on it. If he had scars, he was entitled to keep them covered until they'd faded a bit more.

"Everyone worries from time to time," she decided. "I'm just not very good at it. I suppose it comes from my parents. They're…" She trailed off and laughed. It occurred to him he hadn't heard her laugh in days, and that he'd missed it. "I guess they're what's termed bohemians. We lived in this little house in Carmel that was always in varying states of disrepair. My father would get a notion to take out a wall or put in a window, then in the middle of the project, he'd get an inspiration, go back to his canvases and leave the mess where it lay."

She settled back, no longer aware that she was doing all the talking and Shade all the listening. "My mother liked to cook. Trouble was, you'd never know what mood she'd be in. You might have grilled rattlesnake one day, cheeseburgers the next. Then, when you least expected it, there'd be gooseneck stew."

"Gooseneck stew?"

"I ate at the neighbors' a lot." The memory brought on her appetite. Taking out two candy bars, she offered one to Shade. "How about your parents?"

He unwrapped the candy absently while he paced his speed to the state police car in the next lane. "They retired to Florida. My father fishes and my mother runs a craft shop. Not as colorful as yours, I'm afraid."

"Colorful." She thought about it, and approved. "I never knew they were unusual until I'd gone away to college and realized that most kids' parents were grown-up and sensible. I guess I never realized how much I'd been influenced by them until Rob pointed out things like most people preferring to eat dinner at six, rather than scrounging for popcorn or peanut butter at ten o'clock at night."

"Rob?"

She glanced over quickly, then straight ahead. Shade listened too well, she decided. It made it too easy to say more than you intended. "My ex-husband." She knew she shouldn't still see the "ex" as a stigma; these days it was nearly a status symbol. For Bryan, it was the symbol that proved she hadn't done what was necessary to keep a promise.

"Still sore?" He'd asked before he could stop himself. She made him want to offer comfort, when he'd schooled himself not to become involved in anyone's life, anyone's problem.

"No, it was years ago." After a quick shrug, she nibbled on her candy bar. Sore? she thought again. No, not sore, but perhaps she'd always be just a little tender. "Just sorry it didn't work out, I suppose."

"Regrets are more a waste of time than worrying."

"Maybe. You were married once, too."

"That's right." His tone couldn't have been more dismissive. Bryan gave him a long, steady look.

"Sacred territory?"

"I don't believe in rehashing the past."

This wound was covered with scar tissue, she mused. She wondered if it troubled him much, or if he'd truly filed it away. In either case, it wasn't her business, nor was it the way to keep the ball rolling between them.

"When did you decide to become a photographer?" That was a safe topic, she reflected. There shouldn't be any tender points.

"When I was five and got my hands on my father's new thirty-five-millimeter. When he had the film developed, he discovered three close-ups of the family dog. I'm told he didn't know whether to congratulate me or give me solitary confinement when they turned out to be better than any of his shots.''

Bryan grinned. ''What'd he do?''

''He bought me a camera of my own.''

''You were way ahead of me,'' she commented. ''I didn't have any interest in cameras until high school. Just sort of fell into it. Up until then, I'd wanted to be a star.''

''An actress?''

''No.'' She grinned again. ''A star. Any kind of a star, as long as I had a Rolls, a gold lamé dress and a big tacky diamond.''

He had to grin. She seemed to have the talent for forcing it out of him. ''An unassuming child.''

''No, materialistic.'' She offered him her drink, but he shook his head. ''That stage coincided with my parents' return-to-the-earth period. I guess it was my way of rebelling against people who were almost impossible to rebel against.''

He glanced down at her ringless hands and her faded jeans. ''Guess you got over it.''

''I wasn't made to be a star. Anyway, they needed someone to take pictures of the football team.'' Bryan finished off the candy bar and wondered how soon they could stop for lunch. ''I volunteered because I had a crush on one of the players.'' Draining her soda, she dumped the cup in with Shade's bottle. ''After the first day, I fell in love with the camera and forgot all about the defensive lineman.''

"His loss."

Bryan glanced over, surprised by the offhand compliment. "That was a nice thing to say, Colby. I didn't think you had it in you."

He didn't quite defeat the smile. "Don't get used to it."

"Heaven forbid." But she was a great deal more pleased than his casual words warranted. "Anyway, my parents were thrilled when I became an obsessive photographer. They'd lived with this deadly fear that I had no creative drives and would end up being a smashing business success instead of an artist."

"So now you're both."

She thought about it a moment. Odd how easy it was to forget about one aspect of her work when she concentrated so hard on the other. "I suppose you're right. Just don't mention it to Mom and Dad."

"They won't hear it from me."

They both saw the construction sign at the same time. Whether either of them realized it, their minds followed the same path. Bryan was already reaching for her camera when Shade slowed and eased off the road. Ahead of them, a road crew patched, graded and sweated under the high Arizona sun.

Shade walked off to consider the angle that would show the team and machinery battling against the erosion of the road. A battle that would be waged on roads across the country each summer as long as roads existed. Bryan homed in on one man.

He was bald and had a yellow bandanna tied around his head to protect the vulnerable dome of his scalp.

His face and neck were reddened and damp, his belly sagging over the belt of his work pants. He wore a plain white T-shirt, pristine compared to the colorful ones slashed with sayings and pictures the workmen around him had chosen.

To get in close she had to talk to him and deal with the comments and grins from the rest of the crew. She did so with an aplomb and charm that would've caused a public relations expert to rub his hands together. Bryan was a firm believer that the relationship between the photographer and the subject showed through in the final print. So first, in her own way, she had to develop one.

Shade kept his distance. He saw the men as a team—the sunburned, faceless team that worked roads across the country and had done so for decades. He wanted no relationship with any of them, nothing that would color the way he saw them as they stood, bent and dug.

He took a telling shot of the grime, dust and sweat. Bryan learned that the foreman's name was Al and he'd worked for the road commission for twenty-two years.

It took her a while to ease her way around his self-consciousness, but once she got him talking about what the miserable winter had done to his road, everything clicked. Sweat dribbled down his temple. When he reached up with one beefy arm to swipe at it, Bryan had her picture.

The impulsive detour took them thirty minutes. By

the time they piled back in the van, they were sweating as freely as the laborers.

"Are you always so personal with strangers?" Shade asked her as he switched on the engine and the air-conditioning.

"When I want their picture, sure." Bryan opened the cooler and pulled out one of the cold cans she'd stocked, and another bottle of iced tea for Shade. "You get what you wanted?"

"Yeah."

He'd watched her at work. Normally they separated, but this time he'd been close enough to see just how she went about her job. She'd treated the road man with more respect and good humor than many photographers showed their hundred-dollar-an-hour models. And she hadn't done it just for the picture, though Shade wasn't sure she realized it. She'd been interested in the man—who he was, what he was and why.

Once, a long time before, Shade had had that kind of curiosity. Now he strapped it down. Knowing involved you. But it wasn't easy, he was discovering, to strap down his curiosity about Bryan. Already she'd told him more than he'd have asked. Not more than he wanted to know, but more than he'd have asked. It still wasn't enough.

For nearly a week he'd backed off from her—just as far as it was possible under the circumstances. He hadn't stopped wanting her. He might not like to rehash the past, but it wasn't possible to forget that last molten encounter on the roadside.

He'd closed himself off, but now she was opening

him up again. He wondered if it was foolish to try to fight it, and the attraction they had for each other. It might be better, simpler, more logical, to just let things progress to the only possible conclusion.

They'd sleep together, burn the passion out and get back to the assignment.

Cold? Calculated? Perhaps, but he'd do nothing except follow the already routed course. He knew it was important to keep the emotions cool and the mind sharp.

He'd let his emotions fuddle his logic and his perception before. In Cambodia, a sweet face and a generous smile had blinded him to treachery. Shade's fingers tightened on the wheel without his realizing it. He'd learned a lesson about trust then—it was only the flip side of betrayal.

"Where've you gone?" Bryan asked quietly. A look had come into his eyes that she didn't understand, and wasn't certain she wanted to understand.

He turned his head. For an instant she was caught in the turmoil, in the dark place he remembered too well and she knew nothing about. Then it was over. His eyes were remote and calm. His fingers eased on the wheel.

"We'll stop in Page," he said briefly. "Get some shots of the boats and tourists on Lake Powell before we go down to the canyon."

"All right."

He hadn't been thinking of her. Bryan could comfort herself with that. She hoped the look that had come into his eyes would never be applied to her.

Even so, she was determined that sooner or later she'd discover the reason for it.

She could've gotten some good technical shots of the dam. But as they passed through the tiny town of Page, heading for the lake, Bryan saw the high golden arches shimmering behind waves of heat. It made her grin. Cheeseburgers and fries weren't just summer pastimes. They'd become a way of life. Food for all seasons. But she couldn't resist the sight of the familiar building settled low below the town, almost isolated, like a mirage in the middle of the desert.

She rolled down her window and waited for the right angle. "Gotta eat," she said as she framed the building. "Just gotta." She clicked the shutter.

Resigned, Shade pulled into the lot. "Get it to go," he ordered as Bryan started to hop out. "I want to get to the marina."

Swinging her purse over her shoulder, she disappeared inside. Shade didn't have the chance to become impatient before she bounded back out again with two white bags. "Cheap, fast and wonderful," she told him as she slid back into her seat. "I don't know how I'd make it through life if I couldn't get a cheeseburger on demand."

She pulled out a wrapped burger and handed it to him.

"I got extra salt," she said over her first taste of fries. "Mmm, I'm starving."

"You wouldn't be if you'd eat something besides a candy bar for breakfast."

"I'd rather be awake when I eat," she mumbled, involved in unwrapping her burger.

Shade unwrapped his own. He hadn't asked her to bring him anything. He'd already learned it was typical of her to be carelessly considerate. Perhaps the better word was *naturally*. But it wasn't typical of him to be moved by the simple offer of a piece of meat in a bun. He reached in a bag and brought out a paper napkin. "You're going to need this."

Bryan grinned, took it, folded her legs under her and dug in. Amused, Shade drove leisurely to the marina.

They rented a boat, what Bryan termed a putt-putt. It was narrow, open and about the size of a canoe. It would, however, carry them, and what equipment they chose, out on the lake.

She liked the little marina, with its food stands and general stores with displays of suntan oil and bathing suits. The season was in full swing; people strolled by dressed in shorts and cover-ups, in hats and sunglasses. She spotted a teenage couple, brown and gleaming, on a bench, licking at dripping ice-cream cones. Because they were so involved with each other, Bryan was able to take some candid shots before the paperwork on the rental was completed.

Ice cream and suntans. It was a simple, cheerful way to look at summer. Satisfied, she secured her camera in its bag and went back to Shade.

"Do you know how to drive a boat?"

He sent her a mild look as they walked down the dock. "I'll manage."

A woman in a neat white shirt and shorts gave them a rundown, pointing out the life jackets and explaining the engine before she handed them a glossy map of the lake. Bryan settled herself in the bow and prepared to enjoy herself.

"The nice thing about this," she called over the engine, "is it's so unexpected." She swept one arm out to indicate the wide expanse of blue.

Red-hued mesas and sheer rock walls rose up steeply to cradle the lake, settled placidly where man had put it. The combination was fascinating to her. Another time, she might've done a study on the harmony and power that could result in a working relationship between human imagination and nature.

It wasn't necessary to know all the technical details of the dam, of the labor force that built it. It was enough that it was, that they were here—cutting through water that had once been desert, sending up a spray that had once been sand.

Shade spotted a tidy cabin cruiser and veered in its direction. For the moment, he'd navigate and leave the camera work to Bryan. It'd been a long time since he'd spent a hot afternoon on the water. His muscles began to relax even as his perception sharpened.

Before he was done, he'd have to take some pictures of the rocks. The texture in them was incredible, even in their reflection on the water. Their colors, slashed against the blue lake, made them look surreal. He'd make the prints sharp and crisp to accent the incongruity. He edged a bit closer to the cabin cruiser as he planned the shot for later.

Bryan took out her camera without any definite plan. She hoped there'd be a party of people, perhaps greased up against the sun. Children maybe, giddy with the wind and water. As Shade steered, she glanced toward the stern and lifted the camera quickly. It was too good to be true.

Poised at the stern of the cruiser was a hound— Bryan couldn't think of any other description for the floppy dog. His big ears were blowing back, and his tongue was lolling as he stared down at the water. Over his chestnut fur was a bright orange life vest.

"Go around again!" she yelled to Shade.

She waited impatiently for the angle to come to her again. There were people on the boat, at least five of them, but they no longer interested her. Just the dog, she thought, as she gnawed on her lip and waited. She wanted nothing but the dog in the life jacket leaning out and staring down at the water.

There were towering mesas just behind the boat. Bryan had to decide quickly whether to work them in or frame them out. If she'd had more time to think... She opted against the drama and settled on the fun. Shade had circled the trim little cruiser three times before she was satisfied.

"Wonderful!" With a laugh, Bryan lowered her camera. "That one print's going to be worth the whole trip."

He veered off to the right. "Why don't we see what else we can dig up, anyway?"

They worked for two hours, shifting positions after the first. Stripped to the waist as defense against the heat, Shade knelt at the bow and focused in on a tour boat. The rock wall rose in the background, the water shimmered cool and blue. Along the rail the people were no more than a blur of color. That's what he wanted. The anonymity of tours, and the power of what drew the masses to them.

While Shade worked, Bryan kept the speed low and looked at everything. She'd decided after one glimpse of his lean, tanned torso that it'd be wiser for her to concentrate on the scenery. If she hadn't, she might've missed the cove and the rock island that curved over it.

"Look." Without hesitating, she steered toward it, then cut the engines until the boat drifted in its own wake. "Come on, let's take a swim." Before he could comment, she'd hopped out in the ankle-deep water and was securing the lines with rocks.

Wearing a snug tank top and drawstring shorts, Bryan dashed down to the cove and sank in over her head. When she surfaced, laughing, Shade was standing on the island above her. "Fabulous," she called out. "Come on, Shade, we haven't taken an hour to play since we started."

She was right about that. He'd seen to it. Not that he hadn't needed to relax, but he'd thought it best not to around her. He knew, even as he watched her smoothly treading in the rock-shadowed water, that it was a mistake. Yet he'd told himself it was logical to stop fighting what would happen between them. Following the logic, he walked down to the water.

"It's like opening a present," she decided, shifting

onto her back to float briefly. "I had no idea I was being slowly boiled until I stepped in here." With a sigh, she dipped under the water and rose again so that it flowed from her face. "There was a pond a few miles away from home when I was a kid. I practically lived there in the summer."

The water was seductive, almost painfully so. As Shade lowered himself into it, he felt the heat drain, but not the tension. Sooner or later, he knew, he'd have to find an outlet for it.

"We did a lot better here than I expected to." Lazily she let the water play through her fingers. "I can't wait to get to Sedona and start developing." She tossed her dripping braid behind her back. "And sleep in a real bed."

"You don't seem to have any trouble sleeping." One of the first things he'd noticed was that she could fall asleep anywhere, anytime, and within seconds of shutting her eyes.

"Oh, it's not the sleeping, it's the waking up." And waking up only a few feet away from him, morning after morning—seeing his face shadowed by a night's growth of beard, dangerously attractive, seeing his muscles ripple as he stretched, dangerously strong. No, she couldn't deny that the accommodations occasionally gave her a few twinges.

"You know," she began casually, "the budget could handle a couple of motel rooms every week or so—nothing outrageous. A real mattress and a private shower, you know. Some of those campgrounds we've stopped in advertise hot water with their tongues in their cheeks.''

He had to smile. It hadn't given him much pleasure to settle for tepid water after a long day on the road. But there was no reason to make it too easy on her. ''Can't handle roughing it, Bryan?''

She stretched out on her back again, deliberately kicking water up and over him. ''Oh, I don't mind roughing it,'' she said blandly. ''I just like to do it on my own time. And I'm not ashamed to say I'd rather spend the weekend at the Beverly Wilshire than rubbing two sticks together in the wilderness.'' She closed her eyes and let her body drift. ''Wouldn't you?''

''Yeah.'' With the admission, he reached out, grabbed her braid and tugged her head under.

The move surprised her, but it pleased her as well, even as she came up sputtering. So he was capable of a frivolous move from time to time. It was something else she could like him for.

''I'm an expert on water games,'' she warned him as she began to tread again.

''Water suits you.'' When had he relaxed? He couldn't pinpoint the moment when the tension began to ease from him. There was something about her— laziness? No, that wasn't true. She worked every bit as hard as he, though in her own fashion. *Easiness* was a better word, he decided. She was an easy woman, comfortable with herself and whatever surroundings she found herself in.

''It looks pretty good on you, too.'' Narrowing her

eyes, Bryan focused on him—something she'd avoided for several days. If she didn't allow herself a clear look, it helped bank down on the feelings he brought out in her. Many of them weren't comfortable, and Shade had been right. She was a woman who liked to be comfortable. But now, with the water lapping cool around her and the only sound that of boats putting in the distance, she wanted to enjoy him.

His hair was damp and tangled around his face, which was as relaxed as she'd ever seen it. There didn't seem to be any secrets in his eyes just now. He was nearly too lean, but there were muscles in his forearms, in his back. She already knew just how strong his hands were. She smiled at him because she wasn't sure just how many quiet moments they'd share.

"You don't let up on yourself enough, Shade."

"No?"

"No. You know..." She floated again, because treading took too much effort. "I think deep down, really deep down, there's a nice person in you."

"No, there isn't."

But she heard the humor in his voice. "Oh, it's buried in there somewhere. If you let me do your portrait, I'd find it."

He liked the way she floated in the water; there was absolutely no energy expended. She lay there, trusting buoyancy. He was nearly certain that if she lay quietly for five minutes, she'd be asleep. "Would you?" he murmured. "I think we can both do without that."

She opened her eyes again, but had to squint against

the sun to see him. It was at his back, glaring. "Maybe you can, but I've already decided to do it—once I know you better."

He circled her ankle with his finger, lightly. "You have to have my cooperation to do both."

"I'll get it." The contact was more potent than she could handle. She'd tensed before she could stop it. And so, she realized after a long ten seconds, had he. Casually, she let her legs drop. "The water's getting cold." She swam toward the boat with smooth strokes and a racing heart.

Shade waited a moment. No matter what direction he took with her, he always ended up in the same place. He wanted her, but wasn't certain he could handle the consequences of acting on that desire. Worse now, she was perilously close to becoming his friend. That wouldn't make things any easier on either of them.

Slowly, he swam out of the cove and toward the boat, but she wasn't there. Puzzled, he looked around and started to call, but then he saw her perched high on the rock.

She'd unbraided her hair and was brushing it dry in the sun. Her legs were folded under her, her face tilted up. The thin summer clothes she wore were drenched and clung to every curve. She obviously didn't care. It was the sun she sought, the heat, just as she'd sought the cool water only moments before.

Shade reached in his camera bag and attached his long lens. He wanted her to fill the viewfinder. He focused and framed her. For the second time, her careless sexuality gave him a staggering roundhouse punch. He was a professional, Shade reminded himself as he set the depth of field. He was shooting a subject, that was all.

But when she turned her head and her eyes met his through the lens, he felt the passion sizzle—from himself and from her. They held each other there a moment, separated, yet irrevocably joined. He took the picture, and as he did, Shade knew he was recording a great deal more than a subject.

A bit steadier, Bryan rose and worked her way down the curve of the rock. She had to remind herself to play it lightly—something that had always come easily to her. "You didn't get a release form, Colby," she reminded him as she dropped her brush into her oversize bag.

Reaching out, he touched her hair. It was damp, hanging rich and heavy to her waist. His fingers curled into it, his eyes locked on hers. "I want you."

She felt her legs liquefy, and heat started somewhere in the pit of her stomach and spread out to her fingertips. He was a hard man, Bryan reminded herself. He wouldn't give, but take. In the end, she'd need him to do both.

"That's not good enough for me," she said steadily. "People want all the time—a new car, a color TV. I have to have more than that."

She stepped around him and into the boat. Without a word, Shade joined her and they drifted away from the cove. As the boat picked up speed, both of them wondered if Shade could give any more than what he'd offered.

Chapter 5

Bryan had romanticized Oak Creek Canyon over the years since she'd been there. When she saw it again, she wasn't disappointed. It had all the rich strength, all the colors, she'd remembered.

Campers would be pocketed through it, she knew. They'd be worth some time and some film. Amateur and serious fishermen by the creek, she mused, with their intense expressions and colorful lures. Evening campfires with roasting marshmallows. Coffee in tin cups. Yes, it would be well worth the stop.

They planned to stay for three days, working, developing and printing. Bryan was itching to begin. But before they drove into town to handle the details, they'd agreed to stop in the canyon where Bryan could see Lee and her family.

"According to the directions, there should be a little

dirt road leading off to the right just beyond a trading post.''

Shade watched for it. He, too, was anxious to begin. Some of the shots he'd taken were pulling at him to bring them to life. He needed the concentration and quiet of a darkroom, the solitude of it. He needed to let his creativity flow, and hold in his hands the results.

The picture of Bryan sitting on the island of rock. He didn't like to dwell on that one, but he knew it would be the first roll he developed.

The important thing was that he'd have the time and the distance he'd promised himself. Once he dropped her at her friends'—and he was certain they'd want her to stay with them—he could go into Sedona, rent a darkroom and a motel room for himself. After living with her for twenty-four hours a day, he was counting on a few days apart to steady his system.

They'd each work on whatever they chose—the town, the canyon, the landscape. That gave him room. He'd work out a schedule for the darkroom. With luck, they wouldn't so much as see each other for the next three days.

''There it is,'' Bryan told him, though he'd already seen the narrow road and slowed for it. She looked at the steep, tree-lined road and shook her head. ''God, I'd never have pictured Lee here. It's so wild and rough and she's...well, elegant.''

He'd known a few elegant women in his life. He'd lived with one. Shade glanced at the terrain. ''What's she doing here, then?''

"She fell in love," Bryan said simply, and leaned forward. "There's the house. Fabulous."

Glass and style. That's what she thought of it. It wasn't the distinguished town house she would have imagined for Lee, but Bryan could see how it would suit her friend. There were flowers blooming, bright red-orange blossoms she couldn't identify. The grass was thick, the trees leafy.

In the driveway were two vehicles, a dusty late-model Jeep and a shiny cream-colored sedan. As they pulled up behind the Jeep, a huge silver-gray form bounded around the side of the house. Shade swore in sheer astonishment.

"That must be Santanas." Bryan laughed, but gave the dog a wary once-over with her door firmly closed.

Fascinated, Shade watched the muscles bunch as the dog moved. But the tail was wagging, the tongue lolling. Some pet, he decided. "It looks like a wolf."

"Yeah." She continued to look out the window as the dog paced up and down the side of the van. "Lee tells me he's friendly."

"Fine. You go first."

Bryan shot him a look that he returned with a casual smile. Letting out a deep breath, Bryan opened the door. "Nice dog," she told him as she stepped out, keeping one hand on the handle of the door. "Nice Santanas."

"I read somewhere that Brown raised wolves," Shade said carelessly as he stepped out of the opposite side.

"Cute," Bryan mumbled, and cautiously offered her hand for the dog to sniff.

He did so, and obviously liked her, because he knocked her to the ground in one bounding leap. Shade was around the van before Bryan had a chance to draw a breath. Fear and fury had carried him, but whatever he might've done was stopped by the sound of a high whistle.

"Santanas!" A young girl darted around the house, braids flying. "Cut it out right now. You're not supposed to knock people down."

Caught in the act, the huge dog plopped down on his belly and somehow managed to look innocent. "He's sorry." The girl looked at the tense man looming over the dog and the breathless woman sprawled beside him. "He just gets excited when company comes. Are you Bryan?"

Bryan managed a nod as the dog dropped his head on her arm and looked up at her.

"It's a funny name. I thought you'd look funny too, but you don't. I'm Sarah."

"Hello, Sarah." Catching her wind, Bryan looked up at Shade. "This is Shade Colby."

"Is that a real name?" Sarah demanded.

"Yeah." Shade looked down as the girl frowned up at him. He wanted to scold her for not handling her dog, but found he couldn't. She had dark, serious eyes that made him want to crouch down and look into them from her level. A heartbreaker, he decided. Give her ten years, and she'll break them all.

"Sounds like something from one of my dad's

books. I guess it's okay.'' She grinned down at Bryan
and shuffled her sneakers in the dirt. Both she and her
dog looked embarrassed. "I'm really sorry Santanas
knocked you down. You're not hurt or anything, are
you?''

Since it was the first time anyone had bothered to
ask, Bryan thought about it. "No.''

"Well, maybe you won't say anything to my dad.''
Sarah flashed a quick smile and showed her braces.
"He gets mad when Santanas forgets his manners.''

Santanas swiped an enormous pink tongue over
Bryan's shoulder.

"No harm done,'' she decided.

"Great. We'll go tell them you're here.'' She was
off in a bound. The dog clambered up and raced after
her without giving Bryan a backward look.

"Well, it doesn't look like Lee's settled for a dull
life,'' Bryan commented.

Shade reached down and hauled her to her feet.
He'd been frightened, he realized. Seriously frightened
for the first time in years, and all because a little girl's
pet had knocked down his partner.

"You okay?''

"Yeah.'' With quick swipes, she began to brush the
dirt off her jeans. Shade ran his hands up her arms,
stopping her cold.

"Sure?''

"Yes, I...'' She trailed off as her thoughts twisted
into something incoherent. He wasn't supposed to
look at her like that, she thought. As though he really
cared. She wished he'd look at her like that again, and

again. His fingers were barely touching her arms. She wished he'd touch her like that again. And again.

"I'm fine," she managed finally. But it was hardly more than a whisper, and her eyes never left his.

He kept his hands on her arms. "That dog had to weigh a hundred and twenty."

"He didn't mean any harm." Why, she wondered vaguely, were they talking about a dog, when there really wasn't anything important but him and her?

"I'm sorry." His thumb skimmed over the inside of her elbow, where the skin was as soft as he'd once imagined. Her pulse beat like an engine. "I should've gotten out first instead of playing around." If she'd been hurt... He wanted to kiss her now, right now, when he was thinking only of her and not the reasons that he shouldn't.

"It doesn't matter," she murmured, and found that her hands were resting on his shoulders. Their bodies were close, just brushing. Who had moved? "It doesn't matter," she said again, half to herself, as she leaned closer. Their lips hovered, hesitated, then barely touched. From the house came the deep, frantic sound of barking. They drew back from each other with something close to a jerk.

"Bryan!" Lee let the door slam behind her as she came onto the porch. It wasn't until she'd already called out that she noticed how intent the two people in her driveway were on each other.

With a quick shudder, Bryan took another step back before she turned. Too many feelings, was all she could think. Too many feelings, too quickly.

"Lee." She ran over, or ran away—she wasn't certain. All she knew was, at that moment she needed someone. Grateful, she felt herself closed in Lee's arms. "Oh, God, it's so good to see you."

The greeting was just a little desperate. Lee took a long look over Bryan's shoulder at the man who remained several paces back. Her first impression was that he wanted to stay that way. Separate. What had Bryan gotten herself into? she wondered, and gave her friend a fierce hug.

"I've got to look at you," Bryan insisted, laughing now as the tension drained. The elegant face, the carefully styled hair—they were the same. But the woman wasn't. Bryan could feel it before she glanced down to the rounded swell beneath Lee's crisp summer dress.

"You're happy." Bryan gripped Lee's hands. "It shows. No regrets?"

"No regrets." Lee took a long, hard study. Bryan looked the same, she decided. Healthy, easy, lovely in a way that seemed exclusively her own. The same, she thought, but for the slightest hint of trouble in her eyes. "And you?"

"Things are good. I've missed you, but I feel better about it after seeing you here."

With a laugh, Lee slipped her arm around Bryan's waist. If there was trouble, she'd find the source. Bryan was hopeless at hiding anything for long. "Come inside. Sarah and Hunter are making iced tea." She sent a significant look in Shade's direction and felt Bryan tense. Just a little, but Lee felt it and knew she'd already found the source.

Bryan cleared her throat. "Shade."

He moved forward, Lee thought, like a man who was used to testing the way.

"Lee Radcliffe—Lee Radcliffe Brown," Bryan corrected, and relaxed a bit. "Shade Colby. You remember when I spent the money I'd saved for a new car on one of his prints."

"Yes, I told you you were crazy." Lee extended her hand and smiled, but her voice was cool. "It's nice to meet you. Bryan's always admired your work."

"But you haven't," he returned, with more interest and respect than he'd intended to feel.

"I often find it harsh, but always compelling," Lee said simply. "Bryan's the expert, not me."

"Then she'd tell you that we don't take pictures for experts."

Lee nodded. His handshake had been firm—not gentle, but far from cruel. His eyes were precisely the same. She'd have to reserve judgment for now. "Come inside, Mr. Colby."

He'd intended to simply drop Bryan off and move along, but he found himself accepting. It wouldn't hurt, he rationalized, to cool off a bit before he drove into town. He followed the women inside.

"Dad, if you don't put more sugar in it, it tastes terrible."

As they walked into the kitchen, they saw Sarah

with her hands on her hips, watching her father mop up around a pitcher of tea.

"Not everyone wants to pour sugar into their system the way you do."

"I do." Bryan grinned when Hunter turned. She thought his work brilliant—often cursing him for it in the middle of the night, when it kept her awake. She thought he looked like a man one of the Brontë sisters would have written about—strong, dark, brooding. But more, he was the man who loved her closest friend. Bryan opened her arms to him.

"It's good to see you again." Hunter held her close, chuckling when he felt her reach behind him to the plate of cookies Sarah had set out. "Why don't you gain weight?"

"I keep trying," Bryan claimed, and bit into the chocolate chip cookie. "Mmm, still warm. Hunter, this is Shade Colby."

Hunter put down his dishcloth. "I've followed your work," he told Shade as they shook hands. "It's powerful."

"That's the word I'd use to describe yours."

"Your latest had me too paranoid to go down to the basement laundry room for weeks," Bryan accused Hunter. "I nearly ran out of clothes."

Hunter grinned, pleased. "Thanks."

She glanced around the sunlit kitchen. "I guess I expected your house to have cobwebs and creaking boards."

"Disappointed?" Lee asked.

"Relieved."

With a laugh, Lee settled at the kitchen table with Sarah on her left and Bryan across from her. "So how's the project going?"

"Good." But Lee noticed she didn't look at Shade as she spoke. "Maybe terrific. We'll know more once we develop the film. We've made arrangements with one of the local papers for the use of a darkroom. All we have to do is drive into Sedona, check in and get a couple of rooms. Tomorrow, we work."

"Rooms?" Lee set down the glass Hunter handed her. "But you're staying here."

"Lee." Bryan gave Hunter a quick smile as he offered the plate of cookies. "I wanted to see you, not drop in bag and baggage. I know both you and Hunter are working on new books. Shade and I'll be up to our ears in developing fluid."

"How are we supposed to visit if you're in Sedona?" Lee countered. "Damn it, Bryan, I've missed you. You're staying here." She laid a hand on her rounded stomach. "Pregnant women have to be pampered."

"You should stay," Shade put in before Bryan could comment. "It might be the last chance for quite a while for a little free time."

"We've a lot of work to do," Bryan reminded him.

"It's a short drive into town from here. That won't make any difference. We're going to need to rent a car, in any case, so we can both be mobile."

Hunter studied the man across the room. Tense, he thought. Intense. Not the sort of man he'd have picked for the free-rolling, slow-moving Bryan, but it wasn't his place to judge. It was his place, and his talent, to observe. What was between them was obvious to see. Their reluctance to accept it was just as obvious. Calmly, he picked up his tea and drank.

"The invitation applies to both of you."

Shade glanced over with an automatic polite refusal on the tip of his tongue. His eyes met Hunter's. They were both intense, internalized men. Perhaps that's why they understood each other so quickly.

I've been there before, Hunter seemed to say to him with a hint of a smile. *You can run fast but only so far.*

Shade sensed something of the understanding, and something of the challenge. He glanced down to see Bryan giving him a long, cool look.

"I'd love to stay," he heard himself say. Shade crossed to the table and sat.

Lee looked over the prints in her precise, deliberate way. Bryan paced up and down the terrace, ready to explode.

"Well?" she demanded. "What do you think?"

"I haven't finished looking through them yet."

Bryan opened her mouth, then shut it again. It wasn't like her to be nervous over her work. She knew the prints were good. Hadn't she put her sweat and her heart into each of them?

More than good, she told herself as she yanked a chocolate bar out of her pocket. These prints ranked with her best work. It might've been the competition with Shade that had pushed her to produce them. It might've been the need to feel a bit smug after some of the comments he'd made on her particular style of work. Bryan didn't like to think she was base enough to resort to petty rivalry, but she had to admit that now she was. And she wanted to win.

She and Shade had lived in the same house, worked in the same darkroom for days, but had managed to see almost nothing of each other. A neat trick, Bryan thought ruefully. Perhaps it had worked so well because they'd both played the same game. Hide and don't seek. Tomorrow they'd be back on the road.

Bryan found that she was anxious to go even while she dreaded it. And she wasn't a contrary person, Bryan reminded herself almost fiercely. She was basically straightforward and...well, yes, she was amiable. It was simply her nature to be. So why wasn't she with Shade?

"Well."

Bryan whirled around as Lee spoke. "Well?" she echoed, waiting.

"I've always admired your work, Bryan. You know that." In her tidy way, Lee folded her hands on the wrought-iron table.

"But?" Bryan prompted.

"But these are the best." Lee smiled. "The very best you've ever done."

Bryan let out the breath she'd been holding and crossed to the table. Nerves? Yes, she had them. She didn't care for them. "Why?"

"I'm sure there're a lot of technical reasons—the light and the shading, the cropping."

Impatiently, Bryan shook her head. "Why?"

Understanding, Lee chose a print. "This one of the old woman and the little girl on the beach. Maybe it's my condition," she said slowly as she studied it again, "but it makes me think of the child I'll have. It also makes me remember I'll grow old, but not too old to dream. This picture's powerful because it's so basically simple, so straightforward and so incredibly full of emotion. And this one..."

She shuffled the prints until she came to the one of the road worker. "Sweat, determination, honesty. You know when you look at this face that the man believes in hard work and paying his bills on time. And here, these teenagers. I see youth just before those inevitable changes of adulthood. And this dog." Lee laughed as she looked at it. "The first time I looked, it just struck me as cute and funny, but he looks so proud, so, well, human. You could almost believe the boat was his."

While Bryan remained silent, Lee tidied the prints again. "I could go over each one of them with you, but the point is, each one of them tells a story. It's only one scene, one instant of time, yet the story's there. The feelings are there. Isn't that the purpose?"

"Yes." Bryan smiled as her shoulders relaxed. "That's the purpose."

"If Shade's pictures are half as good, you'll have a wonderful essay."

"They will be," Bryan murmured. "I saw some of his negatives in the darkroom. They're incredible."

Lee lifted a brow and watched Bryan devour chocolate. "Does that bother you?"

"What? Oh, no, no, of course not. His work is his work—and in this case it'll be part of mine. I'd never have agreed to work with him if I hadn't admired him."

"But?" This time Lee prompted with a raised brow and half smile.

"I don't know, Lee, he's just so—so perfect."

"Really?"

"He never fumbles," Bryan complained. "He always knows exactly what he wants. When he wakes up in the morning, he's perfectly coherent, he never misses a turn on the road. He even makes decent coffee."

"Anyone would detest him for that," Lee said dryly.

"It's frustrating, that's all."

"Love often is. You are in love with him, aren't you?"

"No." Genuinely surprised, Bryan stared over at Lee. "Good God, I hope I've more sense than that. I have to work hard at even liking him."

"Bryan, you're my friend. Otherwise what I'm calling concern would be called prying."

"Which means you're going to pry," Bryan put in.

"Exactly. I've seen the way the two of you tiptoe around each other as if you're terrified that if you happened to brush up against each other there'd be spontaneous combustion."

"Something like that."

Lee reached out and touched her hand. "Bryan, tell me."

Evasions weren't possible. Bryan looked down at the joined hands and sighed. "I'm attracted," she admitted slowly. "He's different from anyone I've known, mostly because he's just not the type of man I'd normally socialize with. He's very remote, very serious. I like to have fun. Just fun."

"Relationships have to be made up of more than just fun."

"I'm not looking for a relationship." On this point she was perfectly clear. "I date so I can go dancing, go to a party, listen to music or see a movie. That's it. The last thing I want is all the tension and work that goes into a relationship."

"If someone didn't know you, they'd say that was a pretty shallow sentiment."

"Maybe it is," Bryan tossed back. "Maybe I am."

Lee said nothing, just tapped a finger on the prints.

"That's my work," Bryan began, then gave up. A lot of people might take what she said at face value, not Lee. "I don't want a relationship," she repeated, but in a quieter tone. "Lee, I've been there before, and I'm lousy at it."

"Relationship equals two," Lee pointed out. "Are you still taking the blame?"

"Most of the blame was mine. I was no good at being a wife."

"At being a certain kind of wife," Lee corrected.

"I imagine there's only a handful of definitions in the dictionary."

Lee only raised a brow. "Sarah has a friend whose mother is wonderful. She keeps not just a clean house, but an interesting one. She makes jelly, takes the minutes at the P.T.A. and runs a Girl Scout troop. The woman can take a colored paper and some glue and create a work of art. She's lovely and helps herself stay that way with exercise classes three times a week. I admire her a great deal, but if Hunter had wanted those things from me, I wouldn't have his ring on my finger."

"Hunter's special," Bryan murmured.

"I can't argue with that. And you know why I nearly ruined it with him—because I was afraid I'd fail at building and maintaining a relationship."

"It's not a matter of being afraid." Bryan shrugged her shoulders. "It's more a matter of not having the energy for it."

"Remember who you're talking to," Lee said mildly.

With a half laugh, Bryan shook her head. "All right, maybe it's a matter of being cautious. *Relationship*'s a very weighty word. *Affair*'s lighter," she said consideringly. "But an affair with a man like Shade's bound to have tremendous repercussions."

That sounded so cool, Bryan mused. When had she started to think in such logical terms? "He's not an easy man, Lee. He has his own demons and his own way of dealing with them. I don't know whether he'd share them with me, or if I'd want him to."

"He works at being cold," Lee commented. "But

I've seen him with Sarah. I admit the basic kindness in him surprised me, but it's there."

"It's there," Bryan agreed. "It's just hard to get to."

"Dinner's ready!" Sarah yanked open the screen door and let it hit the wall with a bang. "Shade and I made spaghetti, and it's terrific."

It was. During the meal, Bryan watched Shade. Like Lee, she'd noticed his easy relationship with Sarah. It was more than tolerance, she decided as she watched him laugh with the girl. It was affection. It hadn't occurred to her that Shade could give his affection so quickly or with so few restrictions.

Maybe I should be a twelve-year-old with braces, she decided, then shook her head at her own thought pattern. She didn't want Shade's affection. His respect, yes.

It wasn't until after dinner that she realized she was wrong. She wanted a great deal more.

It was the last leisurely evening before the group separated. On the front porch they watched the first stars come out and listened to the first night sounds begin. By that time the next evening, Shade and Bryan would be in Colorado.

Lee and Hunter sat on the porch swing with Sarah nestled between them. Shade stretched out in a chair just to the side, relaxed, a little tired, and mentally satisfied after his long hours in the darkroom. Still, as he sat talking easily to the Browns, he realized that he'd needed this visit as much as, perhaps more than, Bryan.

He'd had a simple childhood. Until these past days, he'd nearly forgotten just how simple, and just how solid. The things that had happened to him as an adult had blocked a great deal of it out. Now, without consciously realizing it, Shade was drawing some of it back.

Bryan sat on the first step, leaning back against a post. She joined in the conversation or distanced herself from it as she chose. There was nothing important being said, and the easiness of the conversation made the scene that much more appealing. A moth battered itself against the porch light, crickets called, and the breeze rippled through the full leaves of the surrounding trees. The sounds made a soothing conversation of their own.

She liked the way Hunter had his arm across the back of the swing. Though he spoke to Shade, his fingers ran lightly over his wife's hair. His daughter's head rested against his chest, but once in a while, she'd reach a hand over to Lee's stomach as if to test for movement. Though she hadn't been consciously setting the scene, it grew in front of her eyes. Unable to resist, Bryan slipped inside.

When she returned a few moments later, she had her camera, tripod and light stand.

"Oh, boy." Sarah took one look and straightened primly. "Bryan's going to take our picture."

"No posing," Bryan told her with a grin. "Just keep talking," she continued before anyone could protest. "Pretend I'm not even here. It's so perfect," she began to mutter to herself as she set up. "I don't know why I didn't see it before."

"Let me give you a hand."

Bryan glanced up at Shade in surprise, and nearly refused before she stopped the words. It was the first time he'd made any attempt to work with her. Whether it was a gesture to her or to the affection he'd come to feel for her friends, she wouldn't toss it back at him. Instead, she smiled and handed him her light meter.

"Give me a reading, will you?"

They worked together as though they'd been doing so for years. Another surprise, for both of them. She adjusted her light, already calculating her exposure as Shade gave her the readings. Satisfied, Bryan checked the angle and framing through the viewfinder, then stepped back and let Shade take her place.

"Perfect." If she was looking for a lazy summer evening and a family content with it and one another, she could've done no better. Stepping back, Shade leaned against the wall of the house. Without thinking about it, he continued to help by distracting the trio on the swing.

"What do you want, Sarah?" he began as Bryan moved behind the camera again. "A baby brother or a sister?"

As she considered, Sarah forgot her enchantment with being photographed. "Well..." Her hand moved to Lee's stomach again. Lee's hand closed over it spontaneously. Bryan clicked the shutter. "Maybe a brother,'' she decided. ''My cousin says a little sister can be a real pain.''

As Sarah spoke Lee leaned her head back, just slightly, until it rested on Hunter's arm. His fingers brushed her hair again. Bryan felt the emotion well up in her and blur her vision. She took the next shot blindly.

Had she always wanted that? she wondered as she continued to shoot. The closeness, the contentment that came with commitment and intimacy? Why had it waited to slam into her now, when her feelings toward Shade were already tangled and much too complicated? She blinked her eyes clear and opened the shutter just as Lee turned her head to laugh at something Hunter said.

Relationship, she thought as the longing rose up in her. Not the easy, careless friendships she'd permitted herself, but a solid, demanding, sharing relationship. That was what she saw through the viewfinder. That was what she discovered she needed for herself. When she straightened from the camera, Shade was beside her.

''Something wrong?''

She shook her head and reached over to switch off the light. ''Perfect,'' she announced with a casualness that cost her. She gave the family on the swing a smile. ''I'll send you a print as soon as we stop and develop again.''

She was trembling. Shade was close enough to see it. He turned and dealt with the camera and tripod himself. ''I'll take this up for you.''

She turned to tell him no, but he was already carrying it inside. "I'd better pack my gear," she said to Hunter and Lee. "Shade likes to leave at uncivilized hours."

When she went inside, Lee leaned her head against Hunter's arm again. "They'll be fine," he told her. "She'll be fine."

Lee glanced toward the doorway. "Maybe."

Shade carried Bryan's equipment up to the bedroom she'd been using and waited. The moment she came in with the light, he turned to her. "What's wrong?"

Bryan opened the case and packed her stand and light. "Nothing. Why?"

"You were trembling." Impatient, Shade took her arm and turned her around. "You're still trembling."

"I'm tired." In its way, it was true. She was tired of having her emotions sneak up on her.

"Don't play games with me, Bryan. I'm better at it than you."

God, could he have any idea just how much she wanted to be held at that moment? Would he have any way of understanding how much she'd give if only he'd hold her now? "Don't push it, Shade."

She should've known he wouldn't listen. With one hand, he cupped her chin and held her face steady. The eyes that saw a great deal more than he was entitled to looked into hers. "Tell me."

"No." She said it quietly. If she'd been angry, insulted, cold, he'd have dug until he'd had it all. He couldn't fight her this way.

"All right." He backed off, dipping his hands into

his pockets. He'd felt something out on the porch, something that had pulled at him, offered itself to him. If she'd made one move, the slightest move, he might have given her more at that moment than either of them could imagine. "Maybe you should get some sleep. We'll leave at noon."

"Okay." Deliberately she turned away to pack up the rest of her gear. "I'll be ready."

He was at the door before he felt compelled to turn around again. "Bryan, I saw your prints. They're exceptional."

She felt the first tears stream down her face and was appalled. Since when did she cry because someone acknowledged her talent? Since when did she tremble because a picture she was taking spoke to her personally?

She pressed her lips together for a moment and continued to pack without turning around. "Thanks."

Shade didn't linger any longer. He closed the door soundlessly on his way out.

Chapter 6

By the time they'd passed through New Mexico and into Colorado, Bryan felt more in tune with herself. In part, she thought that the break in Oak Creek Canyon had given her too much time for introspection. Though she often relied heavily on just that in her work, there were times when it could be self-defeating.

At least that's what she'd been able to convince herself of after she and Shade had picked up the routine of drive and shoot and drive some more.

They weren't looking for cities and major events on this leg. They sought out small, unrecognizable towns and struggling ranches. Families that worked with the land and one another to make ends meet. For them, summer was a time of hard, endless work to prepare for the rigors of winter. It wasn't all fun, all games, all sun and sand. It was migrant workers waiting to pick August peaches, and gardens being weeded and tended to offset the expense of winter vegetables.

They didn't consider Denver, but chose instead places like Antonito. They didn't go after the big, sprawling cattle spreads, but the smaller, more personal operations.

Bryan had her first contact with a cattle branding on a dusty little ranch called the Bar T. Her preconception of sweaty, loose-limbed cowboys rounding 'em up and heading 'em out wasn't completely wrong. It just didn't include the more basic aspects of branding—such as the smell of burned flesh and the splash of blood as potential bulls were turned into little steers.

She was, she discovered as her stomach heaved, a city girl at heart.

But they got their pictures. Cowboys with bandannas over their faces and spurs on their boots. Some of them laughed, some of them swore. All of them worked.

She learned the true meaning of *workhorse* as she watched the men push their mounts through their paces. The sweat of a horse was a heavy, rich smell. It hung thickly in the air with the sweat of men.

Bryan considered her best shot a near-classic study of a man taking hold of his leisure time with both hands. The young cowboy was rangy and ruddy, which made him perfect for what she was after. His chambray shirt was dark with patches of sweat down the front, down the back and spreading from under the arms. More sweat mixed with dust ran down his face. His work boots were creased and caked with grime. The back pocket of his jeans was worn from the constant rub against a round can of chewing tobacco. With his hat tilted back and his bandanna tied loosely around his throat, he straddled the fence and lifted an icy can of beer to his lips.

Bryan thought when the picture was printed you'd almost be able to see his Adam's apple move as he swallowed. And every woman who looked at it, she was certain, would be half in love. He was the mystic, the swashbuckler, the last of the knights. Having that picture in her camera nearly made up for almost losing her lunch over the branding.

She'd seen Shade home right in on it and known his pictures would be gritty, hard and detailed. Yet she'd also seen him focusing in on a young boy of eleven or twelve as he'd ridden in his first roundup with all the joy and innocence peculiar to a boy of that age. His choice had surprised her, because he rarely went for the lighter touch. It was also, unfortunately for her state of mind, something else she could like him for. There were others.

He hadn't made any comment when she'd turned green and distanced herself for a time from what was going on in the small enclosed corral where calves bawled for their mothers and let out long, surprised wails when knife and iron were applied. He hadn't said a word when she'd sat down in the shade until she was certain her stomach would stay calm. Nor had

he said a word when he'd handed her a cold drink.
Neither had she.

That night they camped on Bar T land. Shade had
given her space since they'd left Arizona, because she
suddenly seemed to need it. Oddly, he found he didn't.
In the beginning, it had always been Bryan who'd all
but forced him into conversations when he'd have
been content to drive in silence for hours. Now he
wanted to talk to her, to hear her laugh, to watch the
way her hands moved when she became enthusiastic
about a certain point. Or to watch the way she
stretched, easily, degree by inching degree, as her
voice slowed.

Something undefinable had shifted in both of them
during their time in Oak Creek. Bryan had become
remote, when she'd always been almost too open for
his comfort. He found he wanted her company, when
he'd always been solitary. He wanted, though he
didn't fully comprehend why, her friendship. It was a
shift he wasn't certain he cared for, or even understood. In any case, because the opposing shifts had
happened in both of them simultaneously, it brought
them no closer.

Shade had chosen the open space near a fast-
running creek for a campsite for no reason other than
that it appealed to him. Bryan immediately saw other
possibilities.

"Look, I'm going down to wash off." She was as
dusty as the cowboys she'd focused on all afternoon.
It occurred to her, not altogether pleasantly, that she
might smell a bit too much like the horses she'd

watched. "It's probably freezing, so I'll make it fast and you can have a turn."

Shade pried the top off a beer. Perhaps they hadn't rounded up cattle, but they'd been on their feet and in the sun for almost eight hours. "Take your time."

Bryan grabbed a towel and a cake of soap and dashed off. The sun was steadily dropping behind the mountains to the west. She knew enough of camping by now to know how quickly the air would cool once the sun went down. She didn't want to be wet and naked when it did.

She didn't bother to glance around before she stripped off her shirt. They were far enough away from the ranch house that none of the men would wander out that way at sunset. Shade and she had already established the sanctity of privacy without exchanging a word on the subject.

Right now, she thought as she wiggled out of her jeans, the cowboys they'd come to shoot were probably sitting down to an enormous meal—red meat and potatoes, she mused. Hot biscuits with plenty of butter. Lord knows they deserved it, after the day they'd put in. And me, too, she decided, though she and Shade were making do with cold sandwiches and a bag of chips.

Slim, tall and naked, Bryan took a deep breath of the pine-scented air. Even a city girl, she thought as she paused a moment to watch the sunset, could appreciate all this.

Gingerly she stepped into the cold knee-high water and began to rinse off the dust. Strange, she didn't mind the chill as much as she once had. The drive across America was bound to leave its mark. She was glad of it.

No one really wanted to stay exactly the same throughout life. If her outlook changed and shifted as they traveled, she was fortunate. The assignment was giving her more than the chance for professional exposure and creative expression. It was giving her experiences. Why else had she become a photographer, but to see things and understand them?

Yet she didn't understand Shade any better now than when they'd started out. Had she tried? In some ways, she thought, as she glided the soap over her arms. Until what she saw and understood began to affect her too deeply and too personally. Then she'd backed off fast.

She didn't like to admit it. Bryan shivered and began to wash more swiftly. The sun was nearly set. Self-preservation, she reminded herself. Perhaps her image was one of take what comes and make the best of it, but she had her phobias as well. And she was entitled to them.

It had been a long time since she'd been hurt, and that was because of her own deceptively simple maneuvering. If she stood at a crossroads and had two routes, one smooth, the other rocky, with a few pits, she'd take the smooth one. Maybe it was less admirable, but she'd always felt you ended up in the same place with less energy expended. Shade Colby was a rocky road.

In any case, it wasn't just a matter of her choice.

They could have an affair—a physically satisfying, emotionally shallow affair. It worked well for a great many people. But...

He didn't want to be involved with her any more than she did with him. He was attracted, just as she was, but he wasn't offering her any more than that. If he ever did... She dropped that line of thought like a stone. Speculation wasn't always healthy.

The important thing was that she felt more like herself again. She was pleased with the work she'd done since they'd left Arizona, and was looking forward to crossing over into Kansas the next day. The assignment, as they'd both agreed from the outset, was the first priority.

Wheat fields and tornadoes, she thought with a grin. Follow the yellow brick road. That was what Kansas brought to her mind. She knew better now, and looked forward to finding the reality. Bryan was beginning to enjoy having her preconceptions both confirmed and blown to bits.

That was for tomorrow. Right now it was dusk and she was freezing.

Agile, she scrambled up the small bank and reached for the towel. Shade could wash up while she stuffed herself with whatever was handy in the cupboards. She pulled on a long-sleeved oversize shirt and reached up to button it. That's when she saw the eyes.

For a moment she only stared with her hands poised at the top button. Then she saw there was more to it than a pair of narrow yellow eyes peering out of the lowering light. There was a sleek, muscled body and a set of sharp, white teeth only a narrow creek bed away.

Bryan took two steps back, tripped over her own tangled jeans and let out a scream that might've been heard in the next county.

Shade was stretched out in a folding chair beside the small campfire he'd built on impulse. He'd enjoyed himself that day—the rough-and-ready atmosphere, the baking sun and cold beer. He'd always admired the camaraderie that went hand in hand with people who work outdoors.

He needed the city—it was in his blood. For the most part, he preferred the impersonal aspects of people rushing to their own places, in their own time. But it helped to touch base with other aspects of life from time to time.

He could see now, even after only a few weeks on the road, that he'd been getting stale. He hadn't had the challenge of his early years. That get-the-shot-and-stay-alive sort of challenge. He didn't want it. But he'd let himself become too complacent with what he'd been doing.

This assignment had given him the chance to explore himself as well as his country. He thought of his partner with varying degrees of puzzlement and interest. She wasn't nearly as simple or laid-back as he'd originally believed. Still, she was nearly 180 degrees removed from him. He was beginning to understand her. Slowly, but he was beginning to.

She was sensitive, emotional and inherently kind. He was rarely kind, because he was careful not to be.

She was comfortable with herself, easily amused and candid. He'd learned long ago that candor can jump back on you with teeth.

But he wanted her—because she was different or in spite of it, he wanted her. Forcing himself to keep his hands off her in all the days and nights that had passed since that light, interrupted kiss in Hunter Brown's driveway was beginning to wear on him. He had his control to thank for the fact that he'd been able to, the control that he honed so well that it was nearly a prison.

Shade tossed his cigarette into the fire and leaned back. He wouldn't lose that control, or break out of that prison, but that didn't mean that sooner or later he and Bryan wouldn't be lovers. He meant it to happen. He would simply bide his time until it happened his way. As long as he was holding the reins, he wouldn't steer himself into the mire.

When he heard her scream, a dozen agonizing images rushed into his head, images that he'd seen and lived through, images that only someone who had could conjure up. He was out of the chair and running before he'd fully realized they were only memories.

When he got to her, Bryan was scrambling up from the tumble she'd taken. The last thing she expected was to be hauled up and crushed against Shade. The last thing she expected was exactly what she needed. Gasping for air, she clung to him.

"What happened?" Her own panic muffled her ears to the thread of panic in his voice. "Bryan, are you hurt?"

"No, no. It scared me, but it ran away." She pushed her face against his shoulder and just breathed. "Oh, God, Shade."

"What?" Gripping her by the elbows, he pulled her back far enough to see her face. "What scared you?"

"A cat."

He wasn't amused. His fear turned to fury, tangibly enough that Bryan could see the latter even before he cursed her. "Damn it! What kind of fool are you?" he demanded. "Letting out a scream like that over a cat."

She drew air in and out, in and out, and concentrated on her anger—genuine fear was something she didn't care for. "Not a house cat," she snapped. She was still shaken, but not enough to sit back and be called a fool. "It was one of those...I don't know." She lifted a hand to push at her hair and dropped it again when it trembled. "I have to sit down." She did so with a plop on the grass.

"A bobcat?" Calmer, Shade crouched down beside her.

"I don't know. Bobcat, cougar—I wouldn't know the difference. It was a hell of a lot bigger than any tabby." She lowered her head to her knees. Maybe she'd been frightened before in her life, but she couldn't remember anything to compare with this. "He just stood over there, staring at me. I thought— I thought he was going to jump over the creek. His teeth..." She shuddered and shut her eyes. "Big," she managed, no longer caring if she sounded like a simpleminded fool. "Real big."

"He's gone now." His fury turned inward. He should've known she wasn't the kind of woman who jumped at shadows. He knew what it was to be afraid and to feel helpless with it. This time he cursed himself as he slipped an arm around her. "The way you screamed, he's ten miles away and still running."

Bryan nodded but kept her face buried against her knees. "I guess he wasn't that big, but they look different out of the zoo. I just need a minute to pull myself together."

"Take your time."

He found he didn't mind offering comfort, though it was something he hadn't done in a long time. The air was cool, the night still. He could hear the sound of the water rushing by in the creek. For a moment he had a quick flash of the Browns' porch, of the easy family portrait on the swing. He felt a touch of the same contentment here, with his arm around Bryan and night closing in.

Overhead a hawk screeched, out for its first flight of the night. Bryan jolted.

"Easy," Shade murmured. He didn't laugh at her reaction, or even smile. He soothed.

"I guess I'm a little jumpy." With a nervous laugh, she lifted her hand to push at her hair again. It wasn't until then that Shade realized she was naked beneath the open, billowing shirt.

The sight of her slim, supple body beneath the thin, fluttering material sent the contentment he'd felt sky-rocketing into need. A need, he discovered only in that instant, that was somehow exclusively for her—not just for a woman with a lovely face, a desirable body, but for Bryan.

"Maybe we should get back and..." She turned her head and found her eyes only inches from his. In his, she saw everything he felt. When she started to speak again, he shook his head.

No words. No words now. Only needs, only feelings. He wanted that with her. As his mouth closed over hers, he gave her no choice but to want it as well.

Sweetness? Where had it come from and how could she possibly turn away from it? They'd been together nearly a month, but she'd never suspected he had sweetness in him. Nor had she known just how badly she'd needed to find it there.

His mouth demanded, but so slowly, so subtly, that she was giving before she was aware of it. Once she'd given, she couldn't take away again. She felt his hand, warm and firm on her bare skin, but she sighed in pleasure, not in protest. She'd wanted him to touch her, had waited for it, had denied her waiting. Now she leaned closer. There'd be no denying.

He'd known she'd feel like this—slim, strong, smooth. A hundred times, he'd imagined it. He hadn't forgotten that she'd taste like this—warm, tempting, generous. A hundred times, he'd tried not to remember.

This time she smelled of the creek, fresh and cool. He could bury his face in her throat and smell the summer night on her. He kissed her slowly, leaving her lips for her throat, her throat for her shoulder. As he lingered there, he gave himself the pleasure of discovering her body with his fingertips.

It was torture. Exquisite. Agonizing. Irresistible. Bryan wanted it to go on, and on and on. She drew him closer, loving the hard, lean feel of his body against hers, the brush of his clothes against her skin, the whisper of his breath across it. And through it all, the quick, steady beat of his heart near hers.

She could smell the work of the day on him, the faint tang of healthy sweat, the traces of dust he hadn't yet washed off. It excited her with memories of the way his muscles had bunched beneath his shirt when he'd climbed onto a fence for a better angle. She could remember exactly how he'd looked then, though she'd pretended to herself that she hadn't seen, hadn't needed to.

She wanted his strength. Not the muscles, but the inner strength she'd sensed in him from the start. The strength that had carried him through what he'd seen, what he'd lived with.

Yet wasn't it that strength that helped to harden him, to separate him emotionally from the people around him? With her mind whirling, her body pulsing, she struggled to find the answer she needed.

Wants weren't enough. Hadn't she told him so herself? God, she wanted him. Her bones were melting from the desire for him. But it wasn't enough. She only wished she knew what was.

"Shade..." Even when she tried to speak, he cut her off with another long, draining kiss.

She wanted him to drain her. Mind, body, soul. If

he did, there'd be no question and no need for answers. But the questions were there. Even as she held him to her, they were there.

"Shade," she began again.

"I want to make love with you." He lifted his head, and his eyes were so dark, so intense, it was almost impossible to believe his hands were so gentle. "I want to feel your skin under my hand, feel your heart race, watch your eyes."

The words were quiet, incredibly calm when his eyes were so passionate. More than the passion and demand in his eyes, the words frightened her.

"I'm not ready for this." She barely managed the words as she drew away from him.

He felt the needs rise and the anger begin. It took all his skill to control both. "Are you saying you don't want me?"

"No." She shook her head as she drew her shirt together. When had it become so cold? she wondered. "No, lying's foolish."

"So's backing away from something we both want to happen."

"I'm not sure I do. I can't be logical about this, Shade." She gathered her clothes quickly and hugged them against her as she stood. "I can't think something like this through step-by-tep the way you do. If I could, it'd be different, but I can only go with my feelings, my instincts."

There was a deadly calm around him when he rose. The control he'd nearly forfeited to her was back in place. Once more he accepted the prison he'd built for himself. "And?"

She shivered without knowing if it was from the cold without or the cold within. "And my feelings tell me I need more time." When she looked up at him again, her face was honest, her eyes were eloquent. "Maybe I do want this to happen. Maybe I'm just a little afraid of how much I want you."

He didn't like her use of the word *afraid*. She made him feel responsible, obliged. Defensive. "I've no intention of hurting you."

She gave herself a moment. Her breathing was easier, even if her pulse was still unsteady. Whether he knew it or not, Shade had already given her the distance she needed to resist him. Now she could look at him, calmer. Now she could think more clearly.

"No, I don't think you do, but you could, and I have a basic fear of bruises. Maybe I'm an emotional coward. It's not a pretty thought, but it might be true." With a sigh, she lifted both hands to her hair and pushed it back. "Shade, we've a bit more than two months left on the road. I can't afford to spend it being torn up inside because of you. My instincts tell me you could very easily do that to me, whether you planned on it or not."

She knew how to back a man into a corner, he thought in frustration. He could press, relieve the knot she'd tightened in his stomach. And by doing so, he'd run the risk of having her words echo back at him for a long time to come. It'd only taken a few words from her to remind him what it felt like to be responsible for someone else.

"Go back to the van," he told her, turning away to strip off his shirt. "I have to clean up."

She started to speak, then realized there was nothing more she could say. Instead, she left him to follow the thin, moonlit trail back to the van.

Chapter 7

Wheat fields. Bryan's preconception wasn't slashed as they drove through the Midwest, but reinforced. Kansas was wheat fields.

Whatever else Bryan saw as they crossed the state, it was the endless, rippling gold grass that captivated her, first and last. Color, texture, shape, form. Emotion. There were towns, of course, cities with modern buildings and plush homes, but in seeing basic Americana, grain against sky, Bryan saw it all.

Some might have found the continuous spread of sun-ripened grain waving, acre after acre, monotonous. Not Bryan. This was a new experience for a woman of the city. There were no jutting mountains, no glossy towering buildings, no looping freeways, to break the lines. Here was space, just as awesome as the terrain of Arizona, but lusher, and somehow calmer. She could look at it and wonder.

In the fields of wheat and acres of corn, Bryan saw the heart and the sweat of the country. It wasn't always an idyllic scene. There were insects, dirt, grimy machinery. People worked here with their hands, with their backs.

In the cities, she saw the pace and energy. On the farms, she saw a schedule that would have made a corporate executive wilt. Year after year, the farmer gave himself to the land and waited for the land to give back.

With the right angle, the proper light, she could photograph a wheat field and make it seem endless, powerful. With evening shadows, she could give a sense of serenity and continuity. It was only grass, after all, only stalks growing to be cut down, processed, used. But the grain had a life and a beauty of its own. She wanted to show it as she saw it.

Shade saw the tenuous, inescapable dependence of man on nature. The planter, keeper and harvester of the wheat, was irrevocably tied to the land. It was both his freedom and his prison. The man riding the tractor in the Kansas sunlight, damp with healthy sweat, lean from years of labor, was as dependent on the land as the land was on him. Without man, the wheat might grow wild, it might flourish, but then it would wither and die. It was the tie Shade sensed, and the tie he meant to record.

Still, perhaps for the first time since they'd left L.A., he and Bryan weren't shooting as separate entities. They might not have realized it yet, but their feelings, perceptions and needs were drawing them closer to the same mark.

They made each other think. How did she see this scene? How did he feel about this setting? Where before each of them had considered their photographs separately, now subtly, unconsciously, they began to do two things that would improve the final result: compete and consult.

They'd spent a day and a night in Dodge City for the Fourth of July celebrations in what had once been a Wild West town. Bryan thought of Wyatt Earp, of Doc Holliday and the desperadoes who had once ridden through town, but she'd been drawn to the street parade that might've been in Anytown, U.S.A.

It was here, caught up in the pageantry and the flavor, that she'd asked Shade his opinion of the right angle for shooting a horse and rider, and he in turn had taken her advice on capturing a tiny, bespangled majorette.

The step they'd taken had been lost in the moment to both of them. But they'd stood side by side on the curb as the parade had passed, music blaring, batons flying. Their pictures had been different—Shade had looked for the overview of holiday parades while Bryan had wanted individual reactions. But they'd stood side by side.

Bryan's feelings for Shade had become more complex, more personal. When the change had begun or how, she couldn't say. But because her work was most often a direct result of her emotions, the pictures she took began to reflect both the complexity and the intimacy. Their view of the same wheat field might be radically different, but Bryan was determined that when their prints were set side by side, hers would have equal impact.

She'd never been an aggressive person. It just wasn't her style. But Shade had tapped a need in her to compete—as a photographer, and as a woman. If she had to travel in close quarters for weeks with a man who ruffled her professional feathers and stirred her feminine needs, she had to deal with him directly—on both counts. Directly, she decided, but in her own fashion and her own time. As the days went on, Bryan wondered if it would be possible to have both success and Shade without losing something vital.

She was so damn calm! It drove him crazy. Every day, every hour, they spent together pushed Shade closer to the edge. He wasn't used to wanting anyone so badly. He didn't enjoy finding out he could, and that there was nothing he could do about it. Bryan put him in the position of needing, then having to deny himself. There were times he nearly believed she did so purposely. But he'd never known anyone less likely to scheme than Bryan. She wouldn't think of it—and if she did, she'd consider it too much bother.

Even now, as they drove through the Kansas twilight, she was stretched out in the seat beside him, sound asleep. It was one of the rare times she'd left her hair loose. Full, wavy and lush, it was muted to a dull gold in the lowering light. The sun had given her skin all the color it needed. Her body was relaxed, loose like her hair. Shade wondered if he'd ever had the capability to let his mind and body go so enviably limp. Was it that that tempted him, that drove at him? Was he simply pushed to find that spark of energy she could turn on and off at will? He wanted to set it to life. For himself.

Temptation. The longer he held himself back, the more intense it became. To have her. To explore her. To absorb her. When he did—he no longer used the word *if*—what cost would there be? Nothing was free.

Once, he thought as she sighed in sleep. Just once. His way. Perhaps the cost would be high, but he wouldn't be the one to pay it. His emotions were trained and disciplined. They wouldn't be touched. There wasn't a woman alive who could make him hurt.

His body and his mind tensed as Bryan slowly woke. Groggy and content to be so, she yawned. The scent of smoke and tobacco stung the air. On the radio was low, mellow jazz. The windows were half open, so that when she shifted, the slap of wind woke her more quickly than she'd have liked.

It was fully dark now. Surprised, Bryan stretched and stared out the window at a moon half covered by clouds. "It's late," she said on another yawn. The first thing she remembered as her mind cleared of sleep was that they hadn't eaten. She pressed a hand to her stomach. "Dinner?"

He glanced at her just long enough to see her shake

back her hair. It rippled off her shoulders and down her back. As he watched, he had to fight back the urge to touch it. "I want to get over the border tonight."

She heard it in his voice—the tension, the annoyance. Bryan didn't know what had prompted it, nor at the moment did she want to. Instead, she lifted a brow. If he was in a hurry to get to Oklahoma and was willing to drive into the night to get there, it was his business. She'd stocked a cabinet in the back of the van with a few essentials just for moments like this. Bryan started to haul herself out of her seat when she heard the long blare of a horn and the rev of an engine.

The scarred old Pontiac had a hole in the muffler you could've tossed a baseball through. The sound of the engine clattered like a badly tuned plane. It swerved around the van at a dangerous speed, fishtailed, then bolted ahead, radio blaring. As Shade swore, Bryan got a glimpse that revealed the dilapidated car was packed with kids.

"Saturday night in July," she commented.

"Idiots," he said between his teeth as he watched the taillights weave.

"Yeah." She frowned as she watched the car barrel ahead, smoke streaming. "They were just kids, I hope they don't..."

Even as she thought it, it happened. The driver decided to press his luck by passing another car over the double yellow lines. The truck coming toward him laid on the horn and swerved. Bryan felt her blood freeze.

Shade was already hitting the brakes as the Pontiac

screeched back into its own lane. But it was out of control. Skidding sideways, the Pontiac kissed the fender of the car it had tried to pass, then flipped into a telephone pole.

The sound of screaming tires, breaking glass and smashing metal whirled in her head. Bryan was up and out of the van before Shade had brought it to a complete stop. She could hear a girl screaming, others weeping. Even as the sounds shuddered through her, she told herself it meant they were alive.

The door on the passenger's side was crushed against the telephone pole. Bryan rushed to the driver's side and wrenched at the handle. She smelled the blood before she saw it. "Good God," she whispered as she managed to yank the door open on the second try. Then Shade was beside her, shoving her aside.

"Get some blankets out of the van," he ordered without looking at her. It had only taken him one glance at the driver to tell him it wasn't going to be pretty. He shifted enough to block Bryan's view, then reached in to check the pulse in the driver's throat as he heard her run back to the van. Alive, he thought, then blocked out everything but what had to be done. He worked quickly.

The driver was unconscious. The gash on his head was serious, but it didn't worry Shade as much as the probability of internal injuries. And nothing worried him as much as the smell of gas that was beginning to sweeten the air. Under other circumstances, Shade would've been reluctant to move the boy. Now there was no choice. Locking his arms under the boy's arms, Shade hauled him out. Even as Shade began to drag him, the driver of the truck ran over and took the boy's legs.

"Got a CB in the truck," he told Shade breathlessly. "Called for an ambulance."

With a nod, Shade laid the boy down. Bryan was already there with the first blanket.

"Stay here. The car's going to go up." He said it calmly. Without a backward glance, he went back to the crippled Pontiac.

Terror jolted through her. Within seconds, Bryan was at the car beside him, helping to pull the others out of the wreck.

"Get back to the van!" Shade shouted at her as Bryan half carried a sobbing girl. "Stay there!"

Bryan spoke soothingly, covered the girl with a blanket, then rushed back to the car. The last passenger was also unconscious. A boy, Bryan saw, of no more than sixteen. She had to half crawl into the car to reach him. By the time she'd dragged him to the open door, she was drenched and exhausted. Both Shade and the truck driver carried the other injured passengers. Shade had just set a young girl on the grass when he turned and saw Bryan struggling with the last victim.

Fear was instant and staggering. Even as he started to run, his imagination worked on him. In his mind, Shade could see the flash of the explosion, hear the sound of bursting metal and shattering, flying glass. He knew exactly what it would smell like the moment the gas ignited. When he reached Bryan, Shade scooped up the unconscious boy as though he were weightless.

"Run!" he shouted at her. Together, they raced away from the Pontiac.

Bryan didn't see the explosion. She heard it, but more, she felt it. The whoosh of hot air slammed into her back and sent her sprawling onto the grassy shoulder of the road. There was a whistle of metal as something hot and twisted and lethal flew overhead. One of the teenagers screamed and buried her face in her hands.

Stunned, Bryan lay prone a moment, waiting to catch her breath. Over the sound of fire, she could hear the whine of sirens.

"Are you hurt?" Shade half dragged her up to her knees. He'd seen the flying slice of metal whiz by her head. Hands that had been rock steady moments before trembled as they gripped her.

"No." Bryan shook her head and, finding her balance, turned to the whimpering girl beside her. A broken arm, she realized as she tucked the blanket under the girl's chin. And the cut on her temple would need stitches. "Take it easy," Bryan murmured, pulling out a piece of gauze from the first-aid box she'd brought from the van. "You're going to be fine. The ambulance is coming. Can you hear it?"

As she spoke, she pressed the gauze against the wound to stop the bleeding. Her voice was calm, but her fingers trembled.

"Bobby." Tears ran down the girl's face as she clung to Bryan. "Is Bobby all right? He was driving."

Bryan glanced over and looked directly at Shade before she lowered her gaze to the unconscious boy. "He's going to be fine," she said, and felt helpless.

Six young, careless children, she thought as she scanned those sitting or lying on the grass. The driver of the other car sat dazedly across from them, holding a rag to the cut on his own head. For a moment, a long, still moment, the night was quiet—warm, almost balmy. Stars were brilliant overhead. Moonlight was strong and lovely. Thirty feet away, what was left of the Pontiac crackled with flame. Bryan slipped her arm around the shoulders of the girl and watched the lights of the ambulance speed up the road.

As the paramedics began to work, another ambulance and the fire department were called. For twenty minutes, Bryan sat by the young girl, talking to her, holding her hand while her injuries were examined and tended to.

Her name was Robin. She was seventeen. Of the six teenagers in the car, her boyfriend, Bobby, was the oldest at nineteen. They'd only been celebrating summer vacation.

As Bryan listened and soothed, she glanced up to see Shade calmly setting his camera. Astonished, she watched as he carefully focused and framed in the injured. Dispassionately, he recorded the scene of the accident, the victims and what was left of the car. As astonishment faded, Bryan felt the fury bubble inside her. When Robin was carried to the second ambulance, Bryan sprang up.

"What the hell are you doing?" She grabbed his shoulder, spoiling a shot. Still calm, Shade turned to her and gave her one quick study.

She was pale. Her eyes showed both strain and fury. And, he thought, a dull sheen of shock. For the first time since he'd known her, Shade saw how tense her body could be. "I'm doing my job," he said simply, and lifted the camera again.

"Those kids are bleeding!" Bryan grabbed his shoulder again, swinging herself around until she was face-to-face with him. "They've got broken bones. They're hurt and they're frightened. Since when is your job taking pictures of their pain?"

"Since I picked up a camera for pay." Shade let the camera swing by its strap. He'd gotten enough, in any case. He didn't like the feeling in his own stomach, the tension behind his eyes. Most of all, he didn't like the look in Bryan's as she stared at him. Disgust. He shrugged it off.

"You're only willing to take pictures of fun in the sun for this assignment, Bryan. You saw the car, those kids. That's part of it too. Part of life. If you can't handle it, you'd better stick to your celebrity shots and leave the real world alone."

He'd taken two steps toward the van when Bryan was on him again. She might avoid confrontations as a matter of habit, take the line of least resistance as often as possible, but there were times when she'd fight. When she did, she used everything.

"I can handle it." She wasn't pale any longer; her face glowed with anger. Her eyes gleamed with it. "What I can't handle are the vultures who love picking at bones, making a profit off misery in the name of art. There were six people in that car. *People*," she repeated, hissing at him. "Maybe they were foolish, maybe they deserved what happened, but I'll be damned if I'm going to judge. Do you think it makes you a better photographer, a better artist, because you're cold enough, you're *professional* enough, to freeze their pain on printing paper? Is this the way you look for another Pulitzer nomination?"

She was crying now, too angry, too churned up by what she'd seen, to be aware of the tears streaming down her cheeks. Yet somehow the tears made her look stronger. They thickened her voice and gave it impact. "I'll tell you what it makes you," she went on when Shade remained silent. "It makes you empty. Whatever compassion you were born with died somewhere along the way, Shade. I'm sorry for you."

She left him standing in the middle of the road by the shell of the car.

It was nearly 3:00 A.M. Shade had learned that the mind was at its most helpless in those early hours of the morning. The van was dark and quiet, parked in a small campground just over the Oklahoma border. He and Bryan hadn't exchanged a word since the accident. Each had prepared for bed in silence, and though both of them had lain awake for some time, neither had spoken. Now they slept, but only Bryan slept dreamlessly.

There'd been a time, during the first months after his return from Cambodia, that Shade had had the dream regularly. Over the years it had come to him less and less. Often he could force himself awake and fight the dream off before it really took hold. But now, in the tiny Oklahoma campground, he was powerless.

He knew he was dreaming. The moment the figures and shapes began to form in his mind, Shade understood it wasn't real—that it wasn't real any longer. It didn't stop the panic or the pain. The Shade Colby in the dream would go through the same motions he'd gone through all those years ago, leading to the same end. And in the dream there were no soft lines, no mists to lessen the impact. He saw it as it had happened, in strong sunlight.

Shade came out of the hotel and onto the street with Dave, his assistant. Between them, they carried all their luggage and equipment. They were going home. After four months of hard, often dangerous work in a city torn, ravaged and smoldering, they were going home. It had occurred to Shade that they were calling it close—but he'd called it close before. Every day they stayed on added to the risk of getting out at all. But there'd always been one more picture to take, one more statement to make. And there'd been Sung Lee.

She'd been so young, so eager, so wise. As a contact in the city, she'd been invaluable. She'd been just as invaluable to Shade personally. After a bumpy, unpleasant divorce from a wife who'd wanted more glamour and less reality, Shade had needed the long, demanding assignment. And he'd needed Sung Lee.

She was devoted, sweet, undemanding. When he'd taken her to bed, Shade had finally been able to block out the rest of the world and relax. His only regret in going back home was that she wouldn't leave her country.

As they'd stepped out on the street, Shade had been thinking of her. They'd said their goodbyes the night before, but he was thinking of her. Perhaps if he hadn't been, he'd have sensed something. He'd asked himself that hundreds of times in the months that followed.

The city was quiet, but it wasn't peaceful. The tension in the air could erupt at any time. Those who were getting out were doing so in a hurry. Tomorrow, the next day, the doors might be closed. Shade took one last look around as they started toward their car. One last picture, he'd thought, of the calm before the storm.

A few careless words to Dave and he was alone, standing on the curb pulling his camera out of its case. He laughed as Dave swore and struggled with the luggage on his way to the car. Just one last picture. The next time he lifted his camera to shoot, it would be on American soil.

"Hey, Colby!" Young, grinning, Dave stood beside the car. He looked like a college student on spring break. "How about taking one of a future award-winning photographer on his way out of Cambodia?"

With a laugh, Shade lifted his camera and framed

in his assistant. He remembered exactly the way he'd looked. Blond, tanned, a bit gangly, with a crooked front tooth and a faded USC T-shirt.

He took the shot. Dave turned the key in the lock.

"Let's go home," his assistant yelled the instant before the car exploded.

"Shade. Shade!" Heart pounding, Bryan shook him. "Shade, wake up, it's a dream." He grabbed her hard enough to make bruises, but she kept talking. "It's Bryan, Shade. You're having a dream. Just a dream. We're in Oklahoma, in your van. Shade." She took his face in her hands and felt the skin cold and damp. "Just a dream," she said quietly. "Try to relax. I'm right here."

He was breathing too quickly. Shade felt himself straining for air and forced himself to calm. God, he was cold. He felt the warmth of Bryan's skin under his hands, heard her voice, calm, low, soothing. With an oath, he dropped back down again and waited for the shuddering to stop.

"I'll get you some water."

"Scotch."

"All right." The moonlight was bright enough. She found the plastic cup and the bottle and poured. Behind her, she heard the flare of his lighter and the hiss as it caught paper and tobacco. When Bryan turned, he was sitting up on the bunk, resting back against the side of the van. She had no experience with whatever trauma haunted Shade, but she did know how to soothe nerves. She handed him the drink, then, without asking, sat beside him. She waited until he'd taken the first sip.

"Better?"

He took another sip, a deeper one. "Yeah."

She touched his arm lightly, but the contact was made. "Tell me."

He didn't want to speak of it, not to anyone, not to her. Even as the refusal formed on his lips, she increased the grip on his arm.

"We'll both feel better if you do. Shade..." She had to wait again, this time for him to turn and look at her. Her heartbeat was steadier now, and so, as her fingers lay over his wrist, was his. But there was still a thin sheen of sweat drying on his skin. "Nothing gets better and goes away if you hold it in."

He'd held it in for years. It'd never gone away. Perhaps it never would. Maybe it was the quiet understanding in her voice, or the late hour, but he found himself talking.

He told her of Cambodia, and though his voice was flat, she could see it as he had. Ripe for explosion, crumbling, angry. Long, monotonous days punctuated by moments of terror. He told her how he'd reluctantly taken on an assistant and then learned to appreciate and enjoy the young man fresh out of college. And Sung Lee.

"We ran across her in a bar where most of the journalists hung out. It wasn't until a long time later that I put together just how convenient the meeting was. She was twenty, beautiful, sad. For nearly three

months, she gave us leads she supposedly learned
from a cousin who worked at the embassy.''

"Were you in love with her?''

"No.'' He drew on his cigarette until there was
nothing left but filter. "But I cared. I wanted to help
her. And I trusted her.''

He dropped his cigarette into an ashtray and concentrated on his drink. The panic was gone. He'd
never realized he could talk about it calmly, think
about it calmly. "Things were heating up, and the
magazine decided to pull its people out. We were going home. We were coming out of the hotel, and I
stopped to take a couple of shots. Like a tourist.'' He
swore and drained the rest of the Scotch. "Dave got
to the car first. It'd been booby-trapped.''

"Oh, my God.'' Without realizing it, she moved
closer to him.

"He was twenty-three. Carried a picture of the girl
he was going to marry.''

"I'm sorry.'' She laid her head against his shoulder,
wound her arm around him. "I'm so sorry.''

He braced himself against the flood of sympathy.
He wasn't ready for it. "I tried to find Sung Lee. She
was gone; her apartment was empty. It turned out that
I'd been her assignment. The group she'd worked for
had let things leak through so I'd relax and trust her.
They'd intended to make a statement by blowing away
an important American reporter. They'd missed me.
An assistant photographer on his first overseas assignment didn't make any impact. The kid died for nothing.''

And he'd watched the car explode, she thought. Just as he'd watched the car explode tonight. What had it done to him—then and now? Was that why, she wondered, he'd coolly taken out his camera and recorded it all? He was so determined not to feel.

"You blame yourself," she murmured. "You can't."

"He was a kid. I should've looked out for him."

"How?" She shifted so that they were face-to-face again. His eyes were dark, full of cold anger and frustration. She'd never forget just how they looked at that moment. "How?" she repeated. "If you hadn't stopped to take those pictures, you'd have gotten into the car with him. He'd still be dead."

"Yeah." Suddenly weary, Shade ran his hands over his face. The tension was gone, but not the bitterness. Perhaps that's what he was weary of.

"Shade, after the accident—"

"Forget it."

"No." This time she had his hand caught in hers. "You were doing what you had to, for your own reasons. I said I wouldn't judge those kids, but I was judging you. I'm sorry."

He didn't want her apology, but she gave it. He didn't want her to cleanse him, but she was washing away the guilt. He'd seen so much—too much—of the dark side of human nature. She was offering him the light. It tempted him and it terrified him.

"I'll never see things as you do," he murmured. After a moment's hesitation, he laced his fingers with hers. "I'll never be as tolerant."

Puzzled, she frowned as they stared at each other. "No, I don't think you will. I don't think you have to."

"You were right earlier when you said my compassion was dead. I haven't any." She started to speak, but he shook his head. "I haven't any patience, very little sympathy."

Did he look at his own pictures? she wondered. Didn't he see the carefully harnessed emotion in them? But she said nothing, letting him make whatever point he needed to.

"I stopped believing in intimacy, genuine intimacy, permanency, between two people a long time ago. But I do believe in honesty."

She might've drawn away from him. There was something in his voice that warned her, but she stayed where she was. Their bodies were close. She could feel his heartbeat steady as hers began to race. "I think permanency works for some people." Was that her voice? she wondered, so calm, so practical. "I stopped looking for it for myself."

Isn't that what he'd wanted to hear? Shade looked down at their joined hands and wondered why her words left him dissatisfied. "Then it's understood that neither of us wants or needs promises."

Bryan opened her mouth, amazed that she wanted to object. She swallowed. "No promises," she managed. She had to think, had to have the distance to manage it. Deliberately she smiled. "I think we both could use some sleep, though."

He tightened his grip on her hand as she started to

move. Honesty, he'd said. Though the words weren't easy for him, he'd say what he meant. He looked at her a long time. What was left of the moonlight showered her face and shadowed her eyes. Caught in his, her hand was steady. Her pulse wasn't.

"I need you, Bryan."

There were so many things he could have said, and to any of them she'd have had an answer. Wants— no, wants weren't enough. She'd already told him. Demands could be refused or shrugged off.

Needs. Needs were deeper, warmer, stronger. A need was enough.

He didn't move. He waited. Watching him, Bryan knew he'd let her take the step toward or away. Choices. He was a man who demanded them for himself, yet he was also capable of giving them. How could he know she'd had none the moment he'd spoken?

Slowly, she drew her hand from his. Just as slowly, she lifted both hands to his face and brought her mouth to his. With their eyes open, they shared a long, quiet kiss. It was a move that both offered and took.

She offered, with her hands light on his skin. She took, with her mouth warm and certain. He accepted. He gave. And then in the same instant, they both forgot the rules.

Her lashes fluttered down, her lips parted. Mindlessly he pulled her against him until their bodies were crushed close. She didn't resist, but went with him as they slid from the bunk and onto the rug.

She'd wanted this—the triumph and the weakness

of being touched by him. She'd wanted the glory of
letting herself go, of allowing her longings freedom.
With his mouth hungry on hers, there was no need to
think, no need to hold back what she'd wanted so
desperately to give him. Only to him.

Take more. Her mind was reeling from the demands
of her body. Take all. She could feel him tug at the
wide neck of her sleep shirt until her shoulder was
bare and vulnerable to his mouth. Still more. She
skimmed her hands up his back, naked and warm from
the night breeze flowing in the windows.

He wasn't easy as a lover. Hadn't she known it?
There was no patience in him. Hadn't he told her?
She'd known it before, but she was already aware that
she'd never know relaxation with Shade. He drove her
quickly, thoroughly. While she experienced all, she
had no time to luxuriate in separate sensations. Masses
of them swirled around, inside her.

Tastes…his lips, his skin—dark flavor. Scents…
flowers, flesh—sweet and pungent. Textures…the nap
of the rug rubbing against her legs, the hard brush of
his palm, the soft warmth of his mouth. Sounds…her
heartbeat pounding in her head, the murmur of her
name in his whisper. She could see shadows, moonlight, the gleam of his eyes before his mouth took hers
again. Everything merged and mixed together until
they were one overpowering sensation. Passion.

He pulled the shirt lower until her arms were
pinned. For a moment, she was helpless as he trailed
his lips down her breast, pausing to taste, taste thor-

oughly, with lips, tongue, teeth. Some women would've found him merciless.

Perhaps it was the sound of her moan that made him linger when he was driven to hurry on. She was so slender, so smooth. The moonlight filtered in so that he could see where her tan gave way to paler, more vulnerable skin. Once he'd have turned away from vulnerability, knowing the dangers of it. Now it drew him—the softness of it. Her scent was there, clinging to the underside of her breast where he could taste as well as smell it. Sexy, tempting, subtle. It was as she was, and he was lost.

He felt his control slip, skid away from him. Ruthlessly, he brought it back. They would make love once—a hundred times that night—but he'd stay in control. As he was now, he thought as she arched under him. As he'd promised himself he would be, always. He would drive her, but he would not, could not, be driven by her.

Pulling the material down, he explored every inch of her mercilessly. He would show no mercy to either of them. Already she was beyond thought and he knew it. Her skin was hot, and somehow softer with the heat; her scent intensified with it. He could run those hungry, openmouthed kisses wherever he chose.

Her hands were free. Energy and passion raced together inside her. She tumbled over the first peak, breathless and strong. Now she could touch, now she could enrage him, entice him, weaken him. She moved quickly, demanding when he'd expected surrender. It was too sudden, too frantic, to allow him to brace himself against it. Even as she raced to the next peak, she felt the change in him.

He couldn't stop it. She wouldn't permit him to take without giving. His mind swam. Though he tried to clear it, fought to hold himself back, she seduced. Not his body, he'd have given that freely. She seduced his mind until it reeled with her. Emotion raged through him. Clean, hot, strong.

Tangled together, body and mind, they drove each other higher. They took each other over.

Chapter 8

They were both very careful. Neither Bryan nor Shade wanted to say anything the other could misunderstand. They'd made love, and for each of them it had been more intense, more vital, than anything they'd ever experienced. They'd set rules, and for each of them the need to abide by them was paramount.

What had happened between them had left them both more than a little stunned, and more wary than ever.

For a woman like Bryan, who was used to saying what she wanted, doing as she pleased, it wasn't easy to walk on eggshells twenty-four hours a day. But they'd made themselves clear before making love, she reminded herself. No complications, no commitments. No promises. They'd both failed once at the most im-

portant of relationships, marriage. Why should either
of them risk failure again?

They traveled in Oklahoma, giving an entire day to
a small-town rodeo. Bryan hadn't enjoyed anything as
much since the Fourth of July celebrations they'd seen
in Kansas. She enjoyed watching the heat of competition, the pitting of man against animal and man
against man and the clock. Every man who'd lowered
himself onto a bronc or a bull had been determined to
make it to the bell.

Some had been young, others had been seasoned,
but all had had one goal. To win, and then to go on
to the next round. She'd liked seeing that a game
could be turned into a way of life.

Unable to resist, she bought a pair of boots with
fancy stitching and a stubby heel. Since the van was
too small to permit indiscriminate souvenir buying,
she'd restrained herself this far. But there wasn't any
point in being a martyr about it. The boots made her
happy, but she resisted buying a leather belt with an
oversize silver buckle for Shade. It was just the sort
of gesture he might misunderstand. No, they wouldn't
give each other flowers or trinkets or pretty words.

She drove south toward Texas while Shade read the
paper in the seat beside her. On the radio was a raspy
Tina Turner number that was unapologetically sexy.

Summer had reached the point when the heat began
to simmer. Bryan didn't need the radio announcer to
tell her it was ninety-seven and climbing, but both she
and Shade had agreed to use the air-conditioning spar-
ingly on the long trips. On the open highway, the

breeze was almost enough. In defense, she was wearing a skimpy tank top and shorts while she drove in her bare feet. She thought of Dallas and an air-conditioned hotel room with cool sheets on a soft mattress.

"I've never been to Texas," she said idly. "I can't imagine any place that has cities fifty and sixty miles across. A cab ride across town could cost you a week's pay."

The paper crackled as he flipped the page. "You live in Dallas or Houston, you own a car."

It was like him to give a brief practical answer, and she'd come to accept it. "I'm glad we're taking a couple of days in Dallas to print. Ever spent any time there?"

"A little." He shrugged as he turned the next section of the paper. "Dallas, Houston—those cities are Texas. Big, sprawling, wealthy. Plenty of Tex-Mex restaurants, luxury hotels and a freeway system that leaves the out-of-towner reeling. That's why I routed in San Antonio as well. It's something apart from the rest of Texas. It's elegant, serene, more European."

She nodded, glancing out at the road signs. "Did you have an assignment in Texas?"

"I tried living in Dallas for a couple of years in between the overseas work."

It surprised her. She just couldn't picture him anywhere but L.A. "How'd you like it?"

"Not my style," he said simply. "My ex-wife stayed on and married oil."

It was the first time he'd made any sort of reference

to his marriage. Bryan wiped her damp hands on her shorts and wondered how to handle it. "You don't mind going back?"

"No."

"Does it..." She trailed off, wondering if she was getting in deeper than she should.

Shade tossed the paper aside. "What?"

"Well, does it bother you that she's remarried and settled? Don't you ever think back and try to figure out what messed things up?"

"I know what messed things up. There's no use dwelling on it. After you admit you've made a mistake, you've got to go on."

"I know." She pushed at her sunglasses. "I just sometimes wonder why some people can be so happy together, and others so miserable."

"Some people don't belong with each other."

"And yet it often seems like they do before they walk up the aisle."

"Marriage doesn't work for certain kinds of people."

Like us? Bryan wondered. After all, they'd both failed at it. Perhaps he was right, and it was as simple as that. "I made a mess out of mine," she commented.

"All by yourself?"

"Seems that way."

"Then you screwed up and married Mr. Perfect."

"Well, I..." She glanced over and saw him looking at her, one brow raised and a bland look of anticipation on his face. She'd forgotten he could make her laugh as well as ache. "Mr. Nearly Perfect, anyway."

She grinned. "I'd have been smarter to look for someone with flaws."

After lighting a cigarette, he rested his feet on the dash as Bryan was prone to do. "Why didn't you?"

"I was too young to realize flaws were easier to deal with. And I loved him." She hadn't realized it would be so painless to say it, to put it in the past tense. "I really did," she murmured. "In a naive, rose-tinted way. At the time I didn't realize I'd have to make a choice between his conception of marriage and my work."

He understood exactly. His wife hadn't been cruel, she hadn't been vindictive. She'd simply wanted things he couldn't give. "So you married Mr. Nearly Perfect and I married Ms. Socially Ambitious. I wanted to take important pictures, and she wanted to join the country club. Nothing wrong with either goal—they just don't mesh."

"But sometimes don't you regret that you couldn't make it fit?"

"Yeah." It came out unexpectedly, surprising him a great deal more than it surprised her. He hadn't realized he had regrets. He hadn't allowed himself to. "You're getting low on gas," he said abruptly. "We'll stop in the next town and fill up."

Bryan had heard of one-horse towns, but nothing fitted the phrase more perfectly than the huddle of houses just over the Oklahoma-Texas border. Everything seemed to be dusty and faded by the heat. Even the buildings looked tired. Perhaps the state was enriched by oil and growth, but this little corner had slept through it.

As a matter of habit, Bryan took her camera as she stepped from the van to stretch her legs. As she walked around the side of the van, the skinny young attendant goggled at her. Shade saw the boy gape and Bryan smile before he walked into the little fan-cooled store behind the pumps.

Bryan found a small, fenced yard just across the street. A woman in a cotton housedress and a faded apron watered the one colorful spot—a splash of pansies along the edge of the house. The grass was yellow, burned by the sun, but the flowers were lush and thriving. Perhaps they were all the woman needed to keep her content. The fence needed painting badly and the screen door to the house had several small holes, but the flowers were a bright, cheerful slash. The woman smiled as she watered them.

Grateful she'd picked up the camera she'd loaded with color film, Bryan tried several angles. She wanted to catch the tired, sun-faded wood of the house and the parched lawn, both a contrast to that bouquet of hope.

Dissatisfied, she shifted again. The light was good, the colors perfect, but the picture was wrong. Why? Stepping back, she took it all in again and asked herself the all-important question. What do I feel?

Then she had it. The woman wasn't necessary, just the illusion of her. Her hand holding the watering can, no more. She could be any woman, anywhere, who needed flowers to complete her home. It was the flowers and the hope they symbolized that were important, and that was what Bryan finally recorded.

Shade came out of the store with a paper bag. He saw Bryan across the street, experimenting with angles. Content to wait, he set the bag in the van, drawing out the first cold can before he turned to pay the attendant for the gas. The attendant, Shade noticed, who was so busy watching Bryan he could hardly screw on the gas cap.

"Nice van," he commented, but Shade didn't think he'd even looked at it.

"Thanks." He allowed his own gaze to follow the boy's until it rested on Bryan's. He had to smile. She was a very distracting sight in the swatch of material she called shorts. Those legs, he mused. They seemed to start at the waist and just kept going. Now he knew just how sensitive they could be—on the inside of the knee, just above the ankle, on the warm, smooth skin high on the thigh.

"You and your wife going far?"

"Hmm?" Shade lost track of the attendant as he became just as fascinated by Bryan.

"You and the missus," the boy repeated, sighing a little as he counted out Shade's change. "Going far?"

"Dallas," he murmured. "She's not..." He started to correct the boy's mistake about their relationship, then found himself stopping. The *missus*. It was a quaint word, and somehow appealing. It hardly mattered if a boy in a border town thought Bryan belonged to him. "Thanks," he said absently and, stuffing the change in his pocket, walked to her.

"Good timing," she told him as she crossed toward him. They met in the middle of the road.

"Find something?"

"Flowers." She smiled, forgetting the unmerciful sun. If she breathed deeply enough, she could just smell them over the dust. "Flowers where they didn't belong. I think it's..." She felt the rest of the words slide back down her throat as he reached out and touched her hair.

He never touched her, not in the most casual of ways. Unless they were making love, and then it was never casual. There was never any easy brush of hands, no gentle squeeze. Nothing. Until now, in the center of the road, between a parched yard and a grimy gas station.

"You're beautiful. Sometimes it stuns me."

What could she say? He never spoke soft words. Now they flowed over her as his fingers trailed to her cheek. His eyes were so dark. She had no idea what he saw when he looked at her, what he felt. She'd never have asked. Perhaps for the first time, he was giving her the opportunity, but she couldn't speak, only stare.

He might have told her that he saw honesty, kindness, strength. He might have told her he felt needs that were growing far beyond the borders he'd set up between him and the rest of the world. If she'd asked, he might have told her that she was making a difference in his life he hadn't foreseen but could no longer prevent.

For the first time, he bent toward her and kissed

her, with an uncharacteristic gentleness. The moment demanded it, though he wasn't sure why. The sun was hot and hard, the road dusty, and the smell of gasoline was strong. But the moment demanded tenderness from him. He gave it, surprised that it was in him to otter.

"I'll drive," he murmured as he slipped her hand into his. "It's a long way to Dallas."

His feelings had changed. Not for the city they drove into, but for the woman beside him. Dallas had changed since he'd lived there, but Shade knew from experience that it seemed to change constantly. Even though he'd only lived there briefly, it had seemed as though a new building would grow up overnight. Hotels, office buildings, popped up wherever they could find room, and there seemed to be an endless supply of room in Dallas. The architecture leaned toward the futuristic—glass, spirals, pinnacles. But you never had to look far to find that unique southwestern flavor. Men wore cowboy hats as easily as they wore three-piece suits.

They'd agreed on a midtown hotel because it was within walking distance of the darkroom they'd rented for two days. While one worked in the field, the other would have use of the equipment to develop and print. Then they'd switch.

Bryan looked up at the hotel with something like reverence as they pulled up in front of it. Hot running water, feather pillows. Room service. Stepping out, she began to unload her share of the luggage and gear.

"I can't wait," she said as she hauled out another case and felt sweat bead down her back. "I'm going to wallow in the bathtub. I might even sleep there."

Shade pulled out his tripod, then hers. "Do you want your own?"

"My own?" She swung the first camera bag strap over her shoulder.

"Tub."

She looked up and met his calm, questioning glance. He wouldn't assume, she realized, that they'd share a hotel room as they shared the van. They might be lovers, but the lack of strings was still very, very clear. Yes, they'd agreed there'd be no promises, but maybe it was time she took the first step. Tilting her head, she smiled.

"That depends."

"On?"

"Whether you agree to wash my back."

He gave her one of his rare spontaneous smiles as he lifted the rest of the luggage. "Sounds reasonable."

Fifteen minutes later, Bryan dropped her cases inside their hotel room. With equal negligence, she tossed down her shoes. She didn't bother to go to the window and check out the view. There'd be time for that later. There was one vital aspect of the room that demanded immediate attention. She flopped lengthwise on the bed.

"Heaven," she decided, and closed her eyes on a sigh. "Absolute heaven."

"Something wrong with your bunk in the van?"

Shade stacked his gear in a corner before pulling open the drapes.

"Not a thing. But there's a world of difference between bunk and bed." Rolling onto her back, she stretched across the spread diagonally. "See? It's just not possible to do this on a bunk."

He gave her a mild look as he opened his suitcase. "You won't be able to do that on a bed, either, when you're sharing it with me."

True enough, she thought as she watched him methodically unpack. She gave her own suitcase an absent glance. It could wait. With the same enthusiasm as she'd had when she'd plopped down, Bryan sprang up. "Hot bath," she said, and disappeared into the bathroom.

Shade dropped his shaving kit onto the dresser as he heard the water begin to run. He stopped for a moment, listening. Already, Bryan was beginning to hum. The combination of sounds was oddly intimate—a woman's low voice, the splash of water. Strange that something so simple could make him burn.

Perhaps it'd been a mistake to take only one room in the hotel. It wasn't quite like sharing the van in a campground. Here, they'd had a choice, a chance for privacy and distance. Before the day was over, he mused, her things would be spread around the room, tossed here, flung there. It wasn't like him to freely invite disorder. And yet he had.

Glancing up, he saw himself in the mirror, a dark man with a lean body and a lean face. Eyes a bit too hard, mouth a bit too sensitive. He was too used to his own reflection to wonder what Bryan saw when she looked at him. He saw a man who looked a bit weary and needed a shave. And he didn't want to wonder, though he stared at himself as an artist stares at his subject, if he saw a man who'd already taken one irrevocable step toward change.

Shade looked at his face, reflected against the hotel room behind him. Just inside the door were Bryan's cases and the shoes she'd carried into the room. Fleetingly, he wondered if he took his camera and set the shot to take in his reflection, and that of the room and cases behind, just what kind of picture he'd have. He wondered if he'd be able to understand it. Shaking off the mood, he crossed the room and walked into the bath.

Her head moved, but that was all. Though her breath caught when he strolled into the room, Bryan kept her body still and submerged. This kind of intimacy was new and left her vulnerable. Foolishly, she wished she'd poured in a layer of bubbles so that she'd have some mystique.

Shade leaned against the sink and watched her. If she had plans to wash, she was taking her time about it. The little cake of soap sat wrapped in its dish while she lay naked in the tub. It struck him that it was the first time he'd seen her, really seen her, in the light. Her body was one long, alluring line. The room was small and steamy. He wanted her. Shade wondered if a man could die from wanting.

"How's the water?" he asked her.

"Hot." Bryan told herself to relax, be natural. The water that had soothed her now began to arouse.

"Good." Calmly, he began to strip.

Bryan opened her mouth, but shut it again. She'd never seen him undress. Always they'd held to their own unspoken, strict code of ethics. When they camped, each of them changed in the showers. Since they'd become lovers, they'd fallen into a sense of urgency at the end of the day, undressing themselves and each other in the dark van while they made love. Now, for the first time, she could watch her lover casually reveal his body to her.

She knew how it looked. Her hands had shown her. But it was a far different experience to see the slopes, the contours. Athletic, she thought, in the way of a runner or a hurdler. She supposed it was apt enough. Shade would always expect the next hurdle and be prepared to leap over it.

He left his clothes on the sink but made no comment when he had to step over hers where she'd dropped them.

"You said something about washing your back," he commented as he eased in behind her. Then he swore lightly at the temperature of the water. "You like to take off a couple layers of skin when you bathe?"

She laughed, relaxed and shifted to accommodate him. When his body rubbed and slid against hers, she decided there was something to be said for small tubs. Content, she snuggled back against him, a move that at first surprised him, then pleased.

"We're both a little long," she said as she adjusted her legs. "But it helps that we're on the slim side."

"Keep eating." He gave in to the urge to kiss the top of her head. "It's bound to stick sooner or later."

"Never has." She ran her hand along his thigh, trailing from the knee. It was a light, casual stroke that made his insides churn. "I like to believe I burn up calories just thinking. But you…"

"Me?"

On a quiet sigh, Bryan closed her eyes. He was so complex, so…driven. How could she explain it? She knew so little of what he'd seen and been through. Just one isolated incident, she thought. Just one scar. She didn't have to be told there were others.

"You're very physical," she said at length. "Even your thought pattern has a kind of physical force to it. You don't relax. It's like—" She hesitated for another moment, then plunged. "It's like you're a boxer in the ring. Even between rounds you're tensed and waiting for the bell to ring."

"That's life, isn't it?" But he found himself tracing the line of her neck with his finger. "One long match. A quick breather, then you're up and dancing."

"I've never looked at it that way. It's an adventure," she said slowly. "Sometimes I don't have the energy for it, so I can sit back and watch everyone else go through the moves. Maybe that's why I wanted to be a photographer, so I could pull in little pieces of life and keep them. Think of it, Shade."

Shifting slightly, she turned her head so that she could look at him. "Think of the people we've met, the places we've been and seen. And we're only half-way done. Those rodeo cowboys,'' she began, eyes brightening. "All they wanted was a plug of tobacco, a bad-tempered horse and a handful of sky. The farmer in Kansas, riding his tractor in the heat of the day, sweating and aching and looking out over acres of his own land. Children playing hopscotch, old men weeding kitchen gardens or playing checkers in the park. That's what life is. It's women with babies on their hips, young girls sunning at the beach and kids splashing in little rubber swimming pools in the side yard.''

He touched her cheek. "Do you believe that?''

Did she? It sounded so simplistic.... Idealistic? She wondered. Frowning, she watched the steam rise from the water. "I believe that you have to take what good there is, what beauty there is, and go with it. The rest has to be dealt with, but not every minute of every day. That woman today...''

Bryan settled back again, not sure why it was so important for her to tell him. "The one in the house just across from where we stopped for gas. Her yard was burning up in the sun, the paint was peeling on the fence. I saw arthritis in her hands. But she was watering her pansies. Maybe she's lived in that tiny little house all her life. Maybe she'll never know what it's like to sit in a new car and smell the leather or fly first-class or shop at Saks. But she was watering her pansies. She'd planted, weeded and tended them because they gave her pleasure. Something of value, one bright foolish spot she can look at, smile at. Maybe it's enough.''

"Flowers can't grow everywhere."

"Yes, they can. You only have to want them to."

It sounded true when she said it. It sounded like something he'd like to believe. Unconsciously, he rested his cheek against her hair. It was damp from the steam, warm, soft. She made him relax. Just being with her, listening to her, uncurled something in him. But he remembered the rules, those they'd both agreed on. Keep it easy, he reminded himself. Keep it light.

"Do you always have philosophical discussions in the tub?"

Her lips curved. It was so rare and so rewarding to hear that touch of humor in his voice. "I figure if you're going to have one, you might as well be comfortable. Now, about my back..."

Shade picked up the soap and unwrapped it. "Do you want the first shift in the darkroom tomorrow?"

"Mmm." She leaned forward, stretching as he rubbed the dampened soap over her back. Tomorrow was too far away to worry about. "Okay."

"You can have it from eight to twelve."

She started to object to the early hour, then subsided. Some things didn't change. "What're you..." The question trailed off into a sigh as he skimmed the soap around her waist and up to her throat. "I like being pampered."

Her voice was sleepy, but he traced a soapy finger over her nipple and felt the quick shudder. He ran the soap over her in steady circles, lower, still lower, until all thought of relaxation was over. Abruptly, she twisted until he was trapped beneath her, her mouth fixed on his. Her hands raced over him, taking him to the edge before he had a chance to brace himself.

"Bryan—"

"I love to touch you." She slid down until her mouth could skim over his chest, tasting flesh and water. She nibbled, listening to the thunder of his heart, then rubbed her cheek against his damp flesh just to feel, just to experience. She felt him tremble and lie still a moment. When was the last time he'd let himself be made love to? she wondered. Perhaps this time she'd give him no choice.

"Shade." She let her hands roam where they pleased. "Come to bed with me." Before he could answer, she rose. While the water streamed from her, she smiled down at him and slowly pulled the pins from her hair. As it fell, she shook it back, then reached for a towel. It seemed they were through with words.

She waited until he stepped from the tub, then took another towel and rubbed it over him herself. He made no objection, but she could sense him building up the emotional defense. Not this time, she thought. This time it would be different.

As she dried him, she watched his eyes. She couldn't read his thoughts, she couldn't see beneath the desire. For now, it was enough. Taking his hand, she walked toward the bed.

She would love him this time. No matter how strong, how urgent, the need, she would show him what he made her feel. Slowly, her arms already around him, she lowered herself to the bed. As the mattress gave, her mouth found his.

The need was no less. It tore through him. But this time, Shade found himself unable to demand, unable to pull her to his pace. She was satiating him with the luxury of being enjoyed. Her lips took him deep, deeper, but lazily. He learned that with her, passion could be built, layer by finite layer, until there was nothing else. They smelled of the bath they'd shared, of the soap that had rubbed from his skin to hers. She seemed content to breathe it in, to breathe it out, while slowly driving him mad.

It was pleasure enough to see him in the late-afternoon sunlight. No darkness now, no shadows. To make love in the light, freely and without barriers, was something she hadn't even known she craved. His shoulders were still damp. She could see the sheen of water on them, taste it. When their mouths met, she could watch his eyes and see the desire there that echoed what pulsed inside her. In this they were the same, she told herself. In this, if nothing else, they understood each other.

And when he touched her, when she saw his gaze follow the trail of his hand, she trembled. Needs, his and hers, collided, shuddered, then merged together.

There was more here than they'd allowed themselves or each other before. At last this was intimacy, shared knowledge, shared pleasure. No one led, no one held back. For the first time, Shade dropped all pretenses of keeping that thin emotional barrier between them. She filled him, completed him. This time he wanted her—all of her—more than he'd ever wanted anything. He wanted the fun of her, the joy, the kindness. He wanted to believe it could make a difference.

The sun slanted in across the deep, vivid gray of her eyes, highlighting them as he'd once imagined. Her mouth was soft, yielding. Above him, her hair flowed down, wild, free. The lowering sun seemed trapped in her skin, making it gleam gold. She might have been something he'd only imagined—woman, lean, agile and primitive, woman without restraints, accepting her own passions. If he photographed her this way, would he recognize her? Would he be able to recapture the emotions she could push into him?

Then she tossed back her head and she was young, vibrant, reachable. This woman he'd know, this feeling he'd recognize, if he went away alone for decades. He'd need no photograph to remind him of that one astonishing instant of give and of take.

Shade drew her closer, needing her. You, he thought dizzily as their bodies merged and their thoughts twined. Only you. He watched her eyes slowly close as she gave herself to him.

Chapter 9

"I could get used to this."

With her camera settled comfortably in her lap, Bryan stretched back in the pirogue, the trim little dugout canoe they'd borrowed from a family who lived on the bayou. A few miles away was the bustling city of Lafayette, Louisiana, but here was a more slumberous view of summer.

Bees humming, shade spreading, birds trilling. Dragonflies. One whisked by, too fast for her camera, but slow enough to appreciate. Spanish moss hung overhead, shading and dipping toward the river as the water moved slowly. Why hurry? It was summer, fish were there for catching, flowers were there for picking. Cypress knees thrust their way out of the water, and an occasional frog stirred himself enough to plop from his pad and take a swim.

Why hurry, indeed? Life was there to be enjoyed.

As Shade had once pointed out, Bryan was adaptable. In the rush of Dallas, she'd worked long hours in the darkroom and on the street. All business. When the moment called for it, she could be efficient, quick and energetic. But here, where the air was heavy and the living slow, she was content to lie back, cross her ankles and wait for whatever came.

"We're supposed to be working," he pointed out.

She smiled. "Aren't we?" While she swung one foot in lazy circles, she wished they'd thought to borrow a fishing pole as well. What did it feel like to catch a catfish? "We took dozens of pictures before we got in the boat," she reminded him.

It'd been her idea to detour into the bayou, though she was all but certain Shade had topped her with his pictures of the family who'd welcomed them. She might've charmed them into the use of their boat, but Shade had won hands down with camera work.

"The one you took of Mrs. Bienville shelling beans has to be fabulous. Her hands." Bryan shook her head and relaxed. "I've never seen such hands on a woman. I imagine she could make the most elegant of soufflés right before she went out and cut down a tree."

"Cajuns have their own way of life, their own rules."

She tilted her head as she studied him. "You like that."

"Yeah." He rowed, not because they needed to get anywhere, but because it felt so good. It warmed his muscles and relaxed his mind. He nearly smiled, thinking that being with Bryan accomplished almost the same thing. "I like the independence and the fact that it works."

Bryan lay back, listening to the buzz and hum of insects, the sounds of the river. They'd walked along another river in San Antonio, but the sounds had been different there. Soft Spanish music from musicians, the clink of silver on china from the outdoor cafés. It had been fabulous at night, she remembered. The lights had glowed on the water, the water had rippled from the river taxis, the taxis had been full of people content with the Texas version of a gondola. She'd taken a picture of two young lovers, newlyweds perhaps, huddled together on one of the arched stone bridges above the water.

When they'd driven into Galveston, she'd seen yet another kind of Texas, one with white sand beaches, ferries and bicycle surreys. It'd been easier to talk Shade into renting one than she'd imagined. With a smile, she thought of just how far they'd come, and not only in miles. They were working together, and when he could be distracted, they played.

In Malibu, they'd gone their separate ways on the beach. In Galveston, after two hours of work, they'd walked hand in hand along the shore. A small thing for many people, Bryan mused, but not for either of them.

Each time they made love, there seemed to be something more. She didn't know what it was, but she didn't question it. It was Shade she wanted to be with, laugh with, talk with. Every day she discovered something new, something different, about the country and the people. She discovered it with Shade. Perhaps that was all the answer she needed.

What was it about him? Whether she chose to or not, there were times she wondered. What was it about Shade Colby that made her happy? He wasn't always patient. One moment he might be generous and something close to sweet, and the next he could be as cool and aloof as a stranger. Being with him wasn't without its frustrations for a woman accustomed to less fluctuating moods. But being with him was exactly what she wanted.

At the moment, he was relaxed. He wasn't often, she knew, but the mood of the river seemed to have seeped into him. Still, he was watching. Someone else might have floated down the river, glancing at the scenery, appreciating the overall effect. Shade dissected it.

This she understood, because it was her way as well. A tree might be studied for the texture of its leaves, the grain in the wood, the pattern of shade and light it allowed to fall on the ground. A layman might take a perfectly competent picture of the tree, but it would be only that. When Bryan took the picture, she wanted it to pull feelings out of the viewer.

She specialized in people, Bryan remembered as she watched Shade draw the oars through the water. Landscapes, still lifes, she considered a change of pace. It was the human element that fascinated her, and always would. If she wanted to understand her feelings about Shade, maybe it was time to treat him as she would any other subject.

Under half-lowered lashes, she studied and dissected. He had very dominating physical looks, she mused. Being dominated was definitely not her ambition in life. Perhaps that was why she was so often drawn to his mouth, because it was sensitive, vulnerable.

She knew his image—cool, distant, pragmatic. Part of it was true, she thought, but part of it was illusion. Once she'd thought to photograph him in shadows. Now she wondered what sort of study she'd get if she photographed him in quiet sunlight. Without giving herself a chance to think, she lifted her camera, framed him in and shot.

"Just testing," she said lightly when he arched a brow. "And after all, you've already taken a couple of me."

"So I have." He remembered the picture he'd taken of her brushing her hair on the rock in Arizona. He hadn't told her that he'd sent the print back to the magazine, even though he had no doubt it would be used in the final essay. Nor had he told her it was a print he intended to keep in his private collection.

"Hold it a minute." With brisk, professional movements, she changed her lens, adjusted for distance and depth and focused on a heron perched on top of a cypress knee. "A place like this," she murmured as she took two more insurance shots, "makes you think summer just goes on and on."

"Maybe we should take another three months traveling back and do autumn."

"It's tempting." She stretched back again. "Very tempting. A study on all seasons."

"Your clients might get testy."

"Unfortunately true. Still…" She let her fingers dip into the water. "We miss the seasons in L.A. I'd like to see spring in Virginia and winter in Montana." Tossing her braid back, she sat up. "Have you ever thought of chucking it, Shade? Just packing up and moving to, oh, say, Nebraska, and setting up a little studio. Wedding and graduation pictures, you know."

He gave her a long steady look. "No."

With a laugh, she flopped back. "Me either."

"You wouldn't find many megastars in Nebraska."

She narrowed her eyes but spoke mildly. "Is that another subtle shot at my work?"

"Your work," he began as he gently turned the boat back, "is uniformly excellent. Otherwise, we wouldn't be working together."

"Thank you very much. I think."

"And because of the quality of your work," he continued, "I wonder why you limit yourself to the pretty people."

"It's my specialty." She saw a clump of wildflowers on the mossy, muddy edge of the river. Carefully she adjusted her camera again. "And a great many of my subjects are far from pretty—physically or emotionally. They interest me," she said before he could comment. "I like to find out what's under the image and give a glimpse of it."

And she was well skilled at it, he decided. In truth, he'd discovered he admired her for it—not only for her skill, but for her perception. He simply couldn't rationalize her following the glitz trail. "Culture art?"

If he'd meant it as an insult, however mild, it missed its mark. "Yes. And if you asked, I'd say Shakespeare wrote culture art. Are you hungry?"

"No." Fascinating woman, he thought, as reluctant as ever to be fascinated. He craved her, it was true. Her body, her company. But he couldn't resolve the constant fascination she held for him, mind to mind. "You had a bowl of shrimp and rice big enough to feed a family of four before we started out."

"That was hours ago."

"Two, to be exact."

"Picky," she mumbled, and stared up at the sky. So peaceful, she mused. So simple. Moments like this were meant to be savored. Lowering her gaze, she smiled at him. "Ever made love in a pirogue?"

He had to grin. She made it impossible to do otherwise. "No, but I don't think we should ever refuse a new experience."

Bryan touched her tongue to her top lip. "Come here."

They left the lazy, insect-humming air of the bayou behind and landed in bustling, raucous New Orleans. Sweating trumpet players on Bourbon Street, merchants fanning themselves in the Farmers Market, artists and tourists around Jackson Square—it was a taste of the South, they both agreed, that was as far apart from the South as San Antonio had been apart from Texas.

From there, they traveled north to Mississippi for a touch of July in the Deep South. Heat and humidity. Tall, cool drinks and precious shade. Life was different here. In the cities, men sweated in white shirts and loosened ties. In the rural districts, farmers worked under the sweltering sun. But they moved more slowly than their counterparts to the north and west. Perhaps temperatures soaring to a hundred and more caused it, or perhaps it was just a way of life.

Children exercised the privilege of youth and wore next to nothing. Their bodies were browned and damp and dusty. In a city park, Bryan took a close-up of a grinning boy with mahogany skin cooling himself in a fountain.

The camera didn't intimidate him. As she homed in, he laughed at her, squealing as the water cascaded over him, white and cool, until he looked encased in glass.

In a small town just northwest of Jackson, they stumbled across a Little League game. It wasn't much of a field, and the bleachers looked as if they'd object to more than fifty people at a time, but they pulled off and parked between a pickup and a rusted-out sedan.

"This is great." Bryan grabbed her camera bag.

"You just smell hot dogs."

"That too," she agreed easily. "But this *is* summer. We might get to a Yankee game in New York, but we'll get better pictures here today." She hooked her arm through his before he could get too far away. "I'll reserve judgment on the hot dogs."

Shade took a long, sweeping view. The crowd was spread out, on the grass, in folding chairs, on the bleachers. They cheered, complained, gossiped and gulped iced drinks. He was all but certain everyone there knew one another by name or by sight. He watched an old man in a baseball cap casually spit out a plug of tobacco before he berated the umpire.

"I'm going to wander around a bit," he decided, considering a seat on the bleachers too limiting for the moment.

"Okay." Bryan had taken her own scan and considered the bleachers the focal point for what she wanted.

They separated, Shade moving toward the old man who'd already captured his attention. Bryan walked to the bleachers, where she and the onlookers would have a solid view of the game.

The players wore white pants, already grass-stained and dusty, with bright red or blue shirts emblazoned with team names. A good many of them were too small for the uniforms, and the mitts looked enormous on the ends of gangling arms. Some wore spikes, some wore sneakers. A few had batting gloves hung professionally from their back pocket.

It was the hats, she decided, that told of the individual's personality. One might wear it snug or tipped back, another tilted rakishly over the eyes. She wanted an action shot, something that would bring the color and the personalities together with the sport itself. Until something formed for her, Bryan contented herself with taking a shot of the second baseman, who passed the time until the batter stepped into the box by kicking his spikes against the bag and blowing bubbles with his wad of gum.

Scooting up another step, she tried her long lens. Better, she decided, and was pleased to see that her second baseman had a face full of freckles. Above her, someone snapped gum and whistled when the umpire called a strike.

Bryan lowered her camera and allowed herself to become involved in the game. If she wanted to portray the atmosphere, she had to let herself feel it. It was more than the game, she thought, it was the feeling of community. As the batters came up, people in the crowd called them by name, tossing out casual remarks that indicated a personal knowledge. But the sides were definitely drawn.

Parents had come to the game from work, grandparents had pushed away from an early dinner, and neighbors had chosen the game against an evening by the TV. They had their favorites, and they weren't shy about rooting for them.

The next batter interested Bryan mainly because she was a strikingly pretty girl of about twelve. At a glance, Bryan would've set her more easily at a ballet bar than home plate. But when she watched the way the girl gripped the bat and bent into her stance, Bryan lifted her camera. This was one to watch.

Bryan caught her in the first swing on a strike. Though the crowd moaned, Bryan was thrilled with the flow of movement. She might be shooting a Little League game in a half-forgotten town in Mississippi, but she thought of her studio work with the prima ballerina. The batter poised for the pitch, and Bryan poised for the next shot. She had to wait, growing impatient, through two balls.

"Low and outside," she heard someone mumble beside her. All she could think was, if the girl walked, she'd lose the picture she wanted.

Then it came over, too fast for Bryan to judge the placement of the ball, but the girl connected with a solid swing. The batter took off, and using the motor drive, Bryan followed her around the bases. When she rounded second, Bryan homed in on her face. Yes, Maria would understand that look, Bryan thought. Strain, determination and just plain guts. Bryan had her as she slid into third with a storm of dust and a swing of body.

"Wonderful!" She lowered the camera, so thrilled that she didn't even realize she'd spoken out loud. "Just wonderful!"

"That's our girl."

Distracted, Bryan glanced over to the couple beside her. The woman was her own age, perhaps a year or two older. She was beaming. The man beside her was grinning over a wad of gum.

Perhaps she hadn't heard properly. They were so young. "She's your daughter?"

"Our oldest." The woman slipped a hand into her husband's. Bryan saw the plain twin wedding bands. "We've got three others running around here, but they're more interested in the concession stand than the game."

"Not our Carey." The father looked out to where his daughter took a short lead on third. "She's all business."

"I hope you don't mind my taking her picture."

"No." The woman smiled again. "Do you live in town?"

It was a polite way to find out who she was. Bryan hadn't a doubt the woman knew everyone within ten miles. "No, I'm traveling." She paused as the next batter blooped to right field and brought Carey home. "Actually, I'm a freelance photographer on assignment for *Life-style*. Perhaps you've heard of it."

"Sure." The man jerked a head at his wife as he kept his eyes on the game. "She picks it up every month."

Pulling a release form out of her bag, she explained her interest in using Carey's picture. Though she kept it short and her voice low, word spread throughout the bleachers. Bryan found herself answering questions and dealing with curiosity. In order to handle it all in the simplest fashion, she climbed down from the bleachers, changed to a wide-angle lens and took a group shot. Not a bad study, she decided, but she didn't want to spend the next hour having people pose for her. To give the baseball fans time to shift their attention back to the game, she wandered to the concession stand.

"Any luck?"

She swiveled her head around to see Shade fall into step beside her. "Yeah. You?"

He nodded, then leaned on the counter of the stand. There was no relief from the heat, though the sun was lowering. It promised to be as sweltering a night as it had a day. He ordered two large drinks and two hot dogs.

"Know what I'd love?" she asked as she began to bury her hot dog under relish.

"A shovel?"

Ignoring him, she piled on mustard. "A long, cool dip in an enormous pool, followed closely by an iced margarita."

"For now you'll have to settle for the driver's seat of the van. It's your turn."

She shrugged. A job was a job. "Did you see the girl who hit the triple?" They walked over the uneven grass toward the van.

"Kid that ran like a bullet?"

"Yes. I sat next to her parents in the stands. They have four kids."

"So?"

"Four kids," she repeated. "And I'd swear she wasn't more than thirty. How do people do it?"

"Ask me later and I'll show you."

With a laugh, she jabbed him with her elbow. "That's not what I meant—though I like the idea. What I mean is, here's this couple—young, attractive. You could tell they even liked each other."

"Amazing."

"Don't be cynical," she ordered as she pulled open

the door to the van. "A great many couples don't, especially when they've got four kids, a mortgage and ten or twelve years of marriage under their belts."

"Now who's being cynical?"

She started to speak and frowned instead. "I guess I am," she mused as she turned on the engine. "Maybe I've picked a world that's tilted my outlook, but when I see a happily married couple with a track record, I'm impressed."

"It is impressive." Carefully, he stored his camera bag under the dash before he sat back. "When it really works."

"Yeah."

She fell silent, remembering the jolt of envy and longing she'd felt when she'd framed the Browns in her viewfinder. Now, weeks and miles later, it was another jolt for Bryan to realize she hadn't brushed off that peculiar feeling. She had managed to put it aside, somewhere to the back of her mind, but it popped out again now as she thought of the couple in the bleachers of a small-town park.

Family, cohesion. Bonding. Did some people just keep promises better than others? she wondered. Or were some people simply unable to blend their lives with someone else's, make those adjustments, the compromises?

When she looked back, she believed both she and Rob had tried, but in their own ways. There'd been no meeting of the minds, but two separate thought patterns making decisions that never melded with each other. Did that mean that a successful marriage de-

pended on the mating of two people who thought
along the same lines?

With a sigh, she turned onto the highway that would
lead them into Tennessee. If it was true, she decided,
she was much better off single. Though she'd met a
great many people she liked and could have fun with,
she'd never met anyone who thought the way she did.
Especially the man seated next to her with his nose
already buried in the newspaper. There alone they
were radically different.

He'd read that paper and every paper in every town
they stopped in from cover to cover, devouring the
words. She'd skim the headlines, glance over the style
or society pages and go straight for the comics. If she
wanted news, she'd rather have it in spurts on the
radio or blurbs on televisions. Reading was for relaxation, and relaxation was not an analysis of détente.

Relationships. She thought back on the discussion
she'd had with Lee just weeks before. No, she simply
wasn't cut out for relationships on a long-term basis.
Shade himself had pointed out that some people just
weren't capable of permanency. She'd agreed, hadn't
she? Why should the truth suddenly depress her?

Whatever her feelings were for Shade, and she'd
yet to define them satisfactorily, she wasn't going to
start smelling orange blossoms. Maybe she had a few
twinges when she saw couples together who seemed
to complete each other rather than compete, but that
was only natural. After all, she didn't want to start
making adjustments in her life-style to accommodate

someone else at this stage. She was perfectly content the way things were.

If she was in love... Bryan felt the twinge again and ignored it. *If* she was, it would complicate things. The fact was, she was very happy with a successful career, her freedom and an attractive, interesting lover. She'd be crazy if she wasn't happy. She'd be insane to change one single thing.

"And it doesn't have anything to do with being afraid," she said aloud.

"What?"

She turned to Shade and, to his astonishment and hers, blushed. "Nothing," she muttered. "Thinking out loud."

He gave her a long, quiet look. Her expression came very close to a baffled sort of pout. Giving in to the urge, he leaned over and touched a hand to her cheek. "You're not eating your hot dog."

She could have wept. For some absurd reason, she wanted to stop the van, drop her head on the steering wheel and drown herself in hot, violent tears. "Not hungry," she managed.

"Bryan." He watched her snatch her sunglasses from the dash and push them on, though the sun was riding low. "Are you all right?"

"Fine." She took a deep breath and kept her eyes straight ahead. "I'm fine."

No, she wasn't. Though strain in her voice was rare, he recognized it. Only a few weeks before, he'd have shrugged and turned back to his reading. Deliberately, he dropped the paper on the floor at his feet. "What is it?"

"Nothing." She cursed herself and turned up the radio. Shade simply switched it off.

"Pull over."

"What for?"

"Just pull over."

With more violence than necessary, Bryan swung the van toward the shoulder, slowed and stopped. "We won't make very good time if we stop ten minutes after we start."

"We won't be making any time at all until you tell me what's wrong."

"Nothing's wrong!" Then she gritted her teeth and sat back. It wasn't any use saying nothing was wrong if you snarled at the same time. "I don't know," she evaded. "I'm edgy, that's all."

"You?"

She turned on him with a vengeance. "I've a right to foul moods, Colby. You don't have a patent on them."

"You certainly have," he said mildly. "Since it's the first one I've witnessed, I'm interested."

"Don't be so damn patronizing."

"Wanna fight?"

She stared through the windshield. "Maybe."

"Okay." Willing to oblige, he made himself comfortable. "About anything in particular?"

She swung her head around, ready to pounce on anything. "Do you have to bury your face in a paper every time I get behind the wheel?"

He smiled maddeningly. "Yes, dear."

A low sound came from her throat as she stared through the windshield again. "Never mind."

"I could point out that you have a habit of falling asleep when you sit in this seat."

"I said never mind." She reached for the key. "Just never mind. You make me sound like a fool."

He put his hand over hers before she could turn the key. "You sound foolish skirting around whatever's bothering you." He wanted to reach her. Without being aware when, he'd passed the point where he could tell himself not to get involved and follow the advice. Whether he wanted it or not, whether she accepted it or not, he was involved. Slowly, he lifted her hand to his lips. "Bryan, I care."

She sat there stunned that a simple statement could spin through her with such force. *I care.* He'd used the same word when he'd spoken about the woman who'd caused his nightmare. Along with the pleasure his words brought her came an inescapable sense of responsibility. He wouldn't allow himself to care indiscriminately. Glancing up, she met his eyes, patient, puzzled, as they studied her face.

"I care too," she said quietly. She twined her fingers with his, only briefly, but it unsettled them both.

Shade took the next step carefully, not certain of her, or himself. "Is that what's bothering you?"

She let out a long breath, as wary as he now. "Some. I'm not used to it...not like this."

"Neither am I."

She nodded, watching the cars breeze by. "I guess we'd both better take it easy then."

"Sounds logical." And next to impossible, he thought. Right now he wanted to gather her close, forget where they were. Just hold her, he realized. It was all he wanted to do. With an effort, he drew back. "No complications?"

She managed to smile. Rule number one was the most important, after all. "No complications," she agreed. Again she reached for the key. "Read your paper, Colby," she said lightly. "I'll drive until dark."

Chapter 10

They took a slice out of Tennessee—Nashville, Chattanooga—caught the eastern corner of Arkansas—mountains and legends—and headed up through Twain's Missouri to Kentucky. There they found tobacco leaves, mountain laurel, Fort Knox and Mammoth Cave, but when Bryan thought of Kentucky, she thought of horses. Kentucky was sleek, glossy Thoroughbreds grazing on rich grass It made her think of long-legged foals running in wide pastures and wide-chested colts pounding the track at Churchill Downs.

As they crossed the state toward Louisville, she saw much more. Tidy suburban homes bordered the larger cities and smaller towns as they did in every state across the country. Farms spread acre after acre—tobacco, horses, grain. Cities rose with their busy office buildings and harried streets. So much was the same as it had been to the west and to the south, and yet so much was different.

"Daniel Boone and the Cherokees," Bryan murmured as they traveled down another long, monotonous highway.

"What?" Slade glanced up from the map he'd been checking. When Bryan was driving, it didn't hurt to keep an eye on the navigation.

"Daniel Boone and the Cherokees," Bryan repeated. She increased the speed to pass a camper loaded down with bikes on the back bumper and fishing poles on the front. And where were they going? she wondered. Where had they come from? "I was thinking maybe it's the history of a place that makes it different from another. Maybe it's the climate, the topography."

Shade glanced back down at the map, idly figuring the time and mileage. He didn't give the camper rolling along behind them more than a passing thought. "Yes."

Bryan shot him an exasperated smile. One and one always added up to two for Shade. "But people are basically the same, don't you think? I imagine if you took a cross section of the country and polled, you'd find out that most people want the same things. A roof over their heads, a good job, a couple weeks off a year to play."

"Flowers in the garden?"

"All right, yes." She gave a careless little shrug and refused to believe it sounded foolish. "I think most peoples' wants are fairly simple. Italian shoes and a trip to Barbados might add in, but it's the basic things that touch everyone. Healthy children, a nest egg, a steak on the grill.''

''You've a way of simplifying things, Bryan.''

''Maybe, but I don't see any reason to complicate them.''

Interested, he set down the map and turned to her. Perhaps he'd avoided digging too deeply into her, leery of what he might find. But now, behind his sunglasses, his eyes were direct. So was his question. ''What do you want?''

''I...'' She faltered a moment, frowning as she took the van around a long curve. ''I don't know what you mean.''

He thought she did, but they always seemed to end up fencing. ''A roof over your head, a good job? Are those the most important things to you?''

Two months before, she might've shrugged and agreed. Her job came first, and gave her whatever she needed. That was the way she'd planned it, the way she'd wanted it. She wasn't sure any longer. Since she'd left L.A., she'd seen too much, felt too much. ''I have those things,'' she said evasively. ''Of course I want them.''

''And?''

Uncomfortable, she shifted. She hadn't meant to have her idle speculation turned back on her. ''I wouldn't turn down a trip to Barbados.''

He didn't smile as she'd hoped he would, but continued to watch her from behind the protection of tinted glasses. ''You're still simplifying.''

"I'm a simple person."

Her hands were light and competent on the wheel, and her hair was scooped back in its habitual braid. She wore no makeup, a pair of faded cut-offs and a T-shirt two sizes too large for her. "No," he decided after a moment, "you're not. You only pretend to be."

Abruptly wary, she shook her head. Since her outburst in Mississippi, Bryan had managed to keep herself level, and to keep herself, she admitted, from thinking too deeply. "You're a complicated person, Shade, and you see complications where there aren't any."

She wished she could see his eyes. She wished she could see the thoughts behind them.

"I know what I see when I look at you, and it isn't simple."

She shrugged carelessly, but her body had begun to tense. "I'm easily read."

He corrected her with a short, concise word calmly spoken. Bryan blinked once, then gave her attention to the road. "Well, I'm certainly not full of mysteries."

Wasn't she? Shade watched the thin gold loops sway at her ears. "I wonder what you're thinking when you lie beside me after we've made love—in those minutes after passion and before sleep. I often wonder."

She wondered, too. "After we've made love," she said in a tolerably steady voice, "I have a hard time thinking at all."

This time he did smile. "You're always soft and

sleepy,'' he murmured, making her tremble. ''And I wonder what you might say, what I might hear if you spoke your thoughts aloud.''

That I might be falling in love with you. That every day we have together takes us a day closer to the end. That I can't imagine what my life will be like when I don't have you there to touch, to talk to. Those were her thoughts, but she said nothing.

She had her secrets, Shade thought. Just as he did. ''One day, before we're finished, you'll tell me.''

He was easing her into a corner; Bryan felt it, but she didn't know why. ''Haven't I told you enough already?''

''No.'' Giving in to the urge that came over him more and more often, he touched her cheek. ''Not nearly.''

She tried to smile, but she had to clear her throat to speak. ''This is a dangerous conversation to have when I'm driving on an interstate at sixty miles an hour.''

''It's a dangerous conversation in any case.'' Slowly, he drew his hand away. ''I want you, Bryan. I can't look at you and not want you.''

She fell silent, not because he was saying things she didn't want to hear, but because she no longer knew how to deal with them, and with him. If she spoke, she might say too much and break whatever bond had begun to form. She couldn't tell him so, but it was a bond she wanted.

He waited for her to speak, needing her to say something after he'd all but crossed over the line they'd drawn in the beginning. Risk. He'd taken one. Couldn't she see it? Needs. He needed her. Couldn't she feel it? But she remained silent, and the step forward became a step back.

"Your exit's coming up," he told her. Picking up the map, he folded it carefully. Bryan switched lanes, slowed down and left the highway.

Kentucky had made her think of horses; horses led them to Louisville, and Louisville to Churchill Downs. The Derby was long over, but there were races and there were crowds. If they were going to include in their glimpse of summer those who spent an afternoon watching races and betting, where else would they go?

The moment Bryan saw it, she thought of a dozen angles. There were cathedrallike domes and clean white buildings that gave a quiet elegance to the frenzy. The track was the focal point, a long oval of packed dirt. Stands rose around it. Bryan walked about, wondering just what kind of person would come there, or to any track, to plop down two dollars—or two hundred—on a race that would take only minutes. Again, she saw the variety.

There was the man with reddened arms and a sweaty T-shirt who pored over a racing form, and another in casually elegant slacks who sipped something long and cool. She saw women in quietly expensive dresses holding field glasses and families treating their children to the sport of kings. There was a man in a gray hat with tattoos snaking up both arms and a boy laughing on top of his father's shoulders.

They'd been to baseball games, tennis matches, drag races across the country. Always she saw faces in the crowd that seemed to have nothing in common except the game. The games had been invented, Bryan mused, and turned into industries. It was an interesting aspect of human nature. But people kept the games alive; they wanted to be amused, they wanted to compete.

She spotted one man leaning against the rail, watching a race as though his life depended on the outcome. His body was coiled, his face damp. She caught him in profile.

A quick scan showed her a woman in a pale rose dress and summer hat. She watched the race idly, distanced from it the way an empress might've been from a contest in a coliseum. Bryan framed her as the crowd roared the horses down the stretch.

Shade rested a hip on the rail and shot the horses in varying positions around the track, ending with the final lunge across the finish line. Before, he'd framed in the odds board, where numbers flashed and tempted. Now he waited until the results were posted and focused on it again.

Before the races were over, Shade saw Bryan standing at the two-dollar window. With her camera hanging around her neck and her ticket in her hand, she walked back toward the stands.

"Haven't you got any willpower?" he asked her.

"No." She'd found a vending machine, and she offered Shade a candy bar that was already softening in the heat. "Besides, there's a horse in the next race

called Made in the Shade." When his eyebrow lifted
up, she grinned. "How could I resist?"

He wanted to tell her she was foolish. He wanted
to tell her she was unbearably sweet. Instead, he drew
her sunglasses down her nose until he could see her
eyes. "What's his number?"

"Seven."

Shade glanced over at the odds board and shook his
head. "Thirty-five to one. How'd you bet?"

"To win, of course."

Taking her arm, he led her down to the rail again.
"You can kiss your two bucks goodbye, hotshot."

"Or I can win seventy." Bryan pushed her glasses
back in place. "Then I'll take you out to dinner. If I
lose," she continued as the horses were led to the
starting gate, "I've always got plastic. I can still take
you out to dinner."

"Deal," Shade told her as the bell rang.

Bryan watched the horses lunge forward. They were
nearly to the first turn before she managed to find
number 7, third from the back. She glanced up to see
Shade shake his head.

"Don't give up on him yet."

"When you bet on a long shot, love, you've got to
be ready to lose."

A bit flustered by his absent use of the endearment,
she turned back to the race. Shade rarely called her
by name, much less one of those sweetly intimate
terms. A long shot, she agreed silently. But she wasn't
altogether sure she was as prepared to lose as she
might've been.

"He's moving up," she said quickly as number 7 passed three horses with long, hard-driving strides. Forgetting herself, she leaned on the rail and laughed. "Look at him! He's moving up." Lifting her camera, she used the telephoto lens like a field glass. "God, he's beautiful," she murmured. "I didn't know he was so beautiful."

Watching the horse, she forgot the race, the competition. He was beautiful. She could see the jockey riding low in a blur of color that had a style of its own, but it was the horse, muscles bunching, legs pounding, that held her fascinated. He wanted to win; she could feel it. No matter how many races he'd lost, how many times he'd been led back to the stables sweating, he wanted to win.

Hope. She sensed it, but she no longer heard the call of the crowd around her. The horse straining to overtake the leaders hadn't lost hope. He believed he could win, and if you believed hard enough... With a last burst of speed, he nipped by the leader and crossed the wire like a champion.

"I'll be damned," Shade murmured. He found he had his arm around Bryan's shoulders as they watched the winner take his victory lap in long, steady strides.

"Beautiful." Her voice was low and thick.

"Hey." Shade tipped up her chin when he heard the tears. "It was only a two-dollar bet."

She shook her head. "He did it. He wanted to win, and he just didn't give up until he did."

Shade ran a finger down her nose. "Ever hear of luck?"

"Yeah." More composed, she took his hand in hers. "And this had nothing to do with it."

For a moment, he studied her. Then, with a shake of his head, he lowered his mouth to hers lightly, sweetly. "And this from a woman who claims to be simple."

And happy, she thought as her fingers laced with his. Ridiculously happy. "Let's go collect my winnings."

"There was a rumor," he began as they worked their way through the stands, "about you buying dinner."

"Yeah. I heard something about it myself."

She was a woman of her word. That evening, as the sky flashed with lightning and echoed with the thunder of a summer storm, they stepped into a quiet, low-lighted restaurant.

"Linen napkins," Bryan murmured to Shade as they were led to a table.

He laughed in her ear as he pulled out her chair. "You're easily impressed."

"True enough," she agreed, "but I haven't seen a linen napkin since June." Picking it off her plate, she ran it through her hands. It was smooth and rich. "There isn't a vinyl seat or a plastic light in this place. There won't be any little plastic containers of ketchup either." With a wink, she knocked a finger against a plate and let it ring. "Try that with paper and all you get is a thump."

Shade watched her experiment with the water glass next. "All this from the queen of fast food?"

"A steady diet of hamburgers is all right, but I like a change of pace. Let's have champagne," she decided as their waiter came over. She glanced at the list, made her choice and turned back to Shade again.

"You just blew your winnings on a bottle of wine."

"Easy come, easy go." Cupping her chin on her hands, she smiled at him. "Did I mention you look wonderful by candlelight?"

"No." Amused, he leaned forward as well. "Shouldn't that be my line?"

"Maybe, but you didn't seem in a rush to come out with it. Besides, I'm buying. However..." She sent him a slow, simmering look. "If you'd like to say something flattering, I wouldn't be offended."

Lazily, she ran a finger along the back of his hand, making him wonder why any man would object to the benefits of women's liberation. It wasn't a hardship to be wined and dined. Nor would it be a hardship to relax and be seduced. All the same, Shade decided as he lifted her hand to his lips, there was something to be said for partnership.

"I might say that you always look lovely, but tonight..." He let his gaze wander over her face. "Tonight, you take my breath away."

Momentarily flustered, she allowed her hand to stay in his. How was it he could say such things so calmly, so unexpectedly? And how could she, when she was used to casual, inconsequential compliments from men, deal with one that seemed so serious? Carefully, she warned herself. Very carefully.

"In that case I'll have to remember to use lipstick more often."

With a quick smile, he kissed her fingers again. "You forgot to put any on."

"Oh." Stuck, Bryan stared at him.

"Madame?" The wine steward held out the bottle of champagne, label up.

"Yes." She let out a quiet breath. "Yes, that's fine."

Still watching Shade, she heard the cork give in to pressure and the wine bubble into her glass. She sipped, closing her eyes to enjoy it. Then, with a nod, she waited until the steward filled both glasses. Steadier, Bryan lifted her glass and smiled at Shade.

"To?"

"One summer," he said, and touched his rim to hers. "One fascinating summer."

It made her lips curve again, so that her eyes reflected the smile as she sipped. "I expected you to be a terrible bore to work with."

"Really." Shade let the champagne rest on his tongue a moment. Like Bryan, it was smooth and quiet, with energy bubbling underneath. "I expected you to be a pain in the—"

"However," she interrupted dryly. "I've been pleased that my preconception didn't hold true." She waited a moment. "And yours?"

"Did," he said easily, then laughed when she narrowed her eyes at him. "But I wouldn't have enjoyed you nearly as much if it'd been otherwise."

"I liked your other compliment better," she mumbled, and picked up her menu. "But I suppose since you're stingy with them, I have to take what I get."

"I only say what I mean."

"I know." She pushed back her hair as she skimmed the menu. "But I— Oh look, they've got chocolate mousse."

"Most people start at the appetizers."

"I'd rather work backward, then I can gauge how much I want to eat and still have room for dessert."

"I can't imagine you turning down anything chocolate."

"Right you are."

"What I can't understand is how you can shovel it in the way you do and not be fat."

"Just lucky, I guess." With the menu open over her plate, she smiled at him. "Don't you have any weaknesses, Shade?"

"Yeah." He looked at her until she was baffled and flustered again. "A few." And one of them, he thought as he watched her eyes, was becoming more and more acute.

"Are you ready to order?"

Distracted, Bryan looked up at the well-mannered waiter. "What?"

"Are you ready to order?" he repeated. "Or would you like more time?"

"The lady'll have the chocolate mousse," Shade said smoothly.

"Yes, sir." Unflappable, the waiter marked it down. "Will that be all?"

"Not by a long shot," Shade told him, and picked up his wine again.

With a laugh, Bryan worked her way through the menu.

"Stuffed," Bryan decided over an hour later, as they drove through a hard, driving rain. "Absolutely stuffed."

Shade cruised through an amber light. "Watching you eat is an amazing way to pass the time."

"We're here to entertain," she said lightly. Snuggled back in her seat with champagne swimming in her head and thunder grumbling in a bad-tempered sky, she was content to ride along wherever he chose to go. "It was sweet of you to let me have a bite of your cheesecake."

"Half," Shade corrected her. Deliberately he turned away from the campground they'd decided on that afternoon. The wipers made quick swishing sounds against the windshield. "But you're welcome."

"It was lovely." She let out a sigh, quiet and sleepy. "I like being pampered. Tonight should get me through another month of fast-food chains and diners with stale doughnuts." Content, she glanced around at the dark, wet streets, the puddles at the curbs. She liked the rain, especially at night, when it made everything glisten. Watching it, she fell to dreaming, rousing herself only when he turned into the lot of a small motel.

"No campground tonight," he said before she could question. "Wait here while I get a room."

She didn't have time to comment before he was out of the van and dashing through the rain. No campground, she thought, looking over her shoulder at the narrow twin bunks on either side of the van. No skinny, makeshift beds and trickling showers.

With a grin, she jumped up and began to gather his equipment and hers. She never gave the suitcases a thought.

"Champagne, linen napkins and now a bed." She laughed as he climbed back into the van, soaking wet. "I'm going to get spoiled."

He wanted to spoil her. There was no logic to it, only fact. Tonight, if only for tonight, he wanted to spoil her. "Room's around the back." When Bryan dragged the equipment forward, he drove slowly around, checking numbers on the lines of doors. "Here." He strapped camera bags over his shoulder. "Wait a minute." She'd grabbed another bag and her purse by the time he'd pulled open her door from the outside. To her astonishment, she found herself lifted into his arms.

"Shade!" But the rain slapped into her face, making her gasp as he dashed across the lot to an outside door.

"Least I could do after you sprang for dinner," he told her as he maneuvered the oversize key into the lock. Bryan was laughing as he struggled to open the door holding her, the camera bags and tripods.

Kicking the door closed with his foot, he fastened his mouth on hers. Still laughing, Bryan clung to him.

"Now we're both wet," she murmured, running a hand through his hair.

"We'll dry off in bed." Before she knew his intention, Bryan was falling through the air and landing with two bounces full-length onto the mattress.

"So romantic," she said dryly, but her body stayed limp. She lay there, smiling, because he'd made a rare frivolous gesture and she intended to enjoy it.

Her dress clung to her, her hair fanned out. He'd seen her change for dinner and knew she wore a thin teddy cut high at the thigh, low over her breasts, and sheer, sheer stockings. He could love her now, love her for hours. It wouldn't be enough. He knew how relaxed, how pliant, her body could be. How full of fire, strength, vibrancy. He could want all of it, have all of it. It wouldn't be enough.

He was an expert at capturing the moment, the emotions, the message. Letting his own feelings hum, he reached for his camera bag.

"What're you doing?"

When she started to sit up, Shade turned back. "Stay there a minute."

Intrigued and wary, she watched him set his camera. "I don't—"

"Just lie back like you were," he interrupted. "Relaxed and rather pleased with yourself."

His intention was obvious enough now. Bryan lifted a brow. An obsession, she thought, amused. The camera was an obsession for both of them. "Shade, I'm a photographer, not a model."

"Humor me." Gently, he pushed her back on the bed.

"I've too much champagne in my system to argue with you." She smiled up at him as he held the camera over his face. "You can play if you like, or take serious pictures if you must. As long as I don't have to do anything."

She did nothing but smile, and he began to throb. So often he'd used the camera as a barrier between himself and his subject, other times as a conductor for his emotion, emotion he refused to let loose any other way. Now, it was neither. The emotion was already in him, and barriers weren't possible.

He framed her quickly and shot, but was unsatisfied.

"That's not what I want." He was so businesslike that Bryan didn't see it as a defense, only as his manner. But when he came over, pulled her into a sitting position and unzipped her dress, her mouth fell open.

"Shade!"

"It's that lazy sex," he murmured as he slipped the dress down over one shoulder. "Those incredible waves of sensuality that take no effort at all, but just are. It's the way your eyes look." But when his came back to hers, she forgot the joke she'd been about to make. "The way they look when I touch you—like this." Slowly, he ran a hand over her naked shoulder. "The way they look just after I kiss you—like this." He kissed her, lingering over it while her mind emptied of thought and her body filled with sensation.

"Like this," he whispered, more determined than

ever to capture that moment, make it tangible so that
he could hold it in his hands and see it. "Just like
this," he said again, backing off one step, then two.
"The way you look just before we make love. The
way you look just after."

Helplessly aroused, Bryan stared into the lens of the
camera as he lifted it. He caught her there, like a
quarry in the crosshairs of a scope, empty of thoughts,
jumbled with feeling. At the same time, he caught
himself.

For an instant her heart was in her eyes. The shutter
opened, closed and captured it. When he printed the
photograph, he thought as he carefully set down his
camera, would he see what she felt? Would he be
certain of his own feelings?

Now she sat on the bed, her dress disarrayed, her
hair tumbled, her eyes clouded. Secrets, Shade thought
again. They both had them. Was it possible he'd
locked a share of each of their secrets on film inside
his camera?

When he looked at her now, he saw a woman
aroused, a woman who aroused. He could see passion
and pliancy and acceptance. He could see a woman
whom he'd come to know better than anyone else. Yet
he saw a woman he'd yet to reach—one he'd avoided
reaching.

He went to her in silence. Her skin was damp but
warm, as he'd known it would be. Raindrops clung to
her hair. He touched one, then it was gone. Her arms
lifted.

While the storm raged outside, he took her and himself where there was no need for answers.

Chapter 11

If they had more time…

As August began to slip by, that was the thought that continued to run through Bryan's mind. With more time, they could have stayed longer at each stop. With more time, they might have passed through more states, more towns, more communities. There was so much to see, so much to record, but time was running out.

In less than a month, the school she'd photographed empty and waiting in the afternoon light would be filled again. Leaves that were full and green would take on those vibrant colors before they fell. She would be back in L.A., back in her studio, back to the routine she'd established. For the first time in years, the word *alone* had a hollow ring.

How had it happened? Shade Colby had become

her partner, her lover, her friend. He'd become, though it was frightening to admit, the most important person in her life. Somehow she'd become dependent on him, for his opinion, his company, for the nights they spent involved only with each other.

She could imagine how it would be when they returned to L.A. and went their separate ways. Separate parts of the city, she thought, separate lives, separate outlooks.

The closeness that had so slowly, almost painfully, developed between them would dissolve. Wasn't that what they'd both intended from the start? They'd made a bargain with each other, just as they'd made the bargain to work together. If her feelings had changed, she was responsible for them, for dealing with them. As the odometer turned over on the next mile, as the next state was left behind, she wondered how to begin.

Shade had his own thoughts to deal with. When they'd crossed into Maryland, they'd crossed into the East. The Atlantic was close, as close as the end of summer. It was the end that disturbed him. The word no longer seemed to mean finished, but over. He began to realize he was far from ready to draw that last line. There were ways to rationalize it. He tried them all.

They'd missed too much. If they took their time driving back, rather than sticking to their plan of going straight across the country, they could detour into so many places they'd eliminated on the way out. It made sense. They could stay in New England a week, two weeks after Labor Day. After long days in the van and the intense work they'd both put in, they deserved some time off. It was reasonable.

They should work their way back, rather than rush. If they weren't preoccupied with making time, making miles, how many pictures would come out of it? If one of them was special, it would be worth it. That was professional.

When they returned to L.A., perhaps Bryan could move in with him, share his apartment as they'd shared the van. It was impossible. Wasn't it?

She didn't want to complicate their relationship. Hadn't she said so? He didn't want the responsibility of committing himself to one person. Hadn't he made himself clear? Perhaps he'd come to need her companionship on some level. And it was true he'd learned to appreciate the way she could look at anything and see the fun and the beauty of it. That didn't equal promises, commitments or complications.

With a little time, a little distance, the need was bound to fade. The only thing he was sure of was that he wanted to put off that point for as long as possible.

Bryan spotted a convertible—red, flashy. Its driver had one arm thrown over the white leather seat while her short blond hair flew in the wind. Grabbing her camera, Bryan leaned out the open window. Half kneeling, half crouching, on the seat, she adjusted for depth.

She wanted to catch it from the rear, elongating the car into a blur of color. But she didn't want to lose the arrogant angle of the driver's arm, or the negligent way her hair streamed back. Already she knew she would dodge the plain gray highway and the other cars in the darkroom. Just the red convertible, she thought as she set her camera.

"Try to keep just this distance," she called to Shade. She took one shot and, dissatisfied, leaned out farther for the next. Though Shade swore at her, Bryan got her shot before she laughed and flopped back on her seat.

He was guilty of the same thing, he knew. Once the camera was in place, you tended to think of it as a shield. Nothing could happen to you—you simply weren't part of what was happening. Though he'd known better, it had happened to him often enough, even after his first stint overseas. Perhaps it was the understanding that made his voice mild, though he was annoyed.

"Don't you have more sense than to climb out the window of a moving car?"

"Couldn't resist. There's nothing like a convertible on an open highway in August. I'm always toying with the idea of getting one myself."

"Why don't you?"

"Buying a new car is hard work." She looked at the green-and-white road signs as she'd looked at so many others that summer. There were cities, roads and routes she'd never heard of. "I can hardly believe we're in Maryland. We've come so far and yet, I don't know, it doesn't seem like two months."

"Two years?"

She laughed. "Sometimes. Other times it seems like

days. Not enough time," she said, half to herself. "Never enough."

Shade didn't give himself the chance to think before he took the opening. "We've had to leave out a lot."

"I know."

"We went through Kansas, but not Nebraska, Mississippi, and not the Carolinas. We didn't go to Michigan or Wisconsin."

"Or Florida, Washington State, the Dakotas." She shrugged, trying not to think of what was left behind. Just today, Bryan told herself. Just take today.

"I've been thinking about tying them in on the way back."

"On the way back?" Bryan turned to him as he reached for a cigarette.

"We'd be on our own time." The van's lighter glowed red against the tip. "But I think we could both take a month or so and finish the job."

More time. Bryan felt the quick surge of hope, then ruthlessly toned it down. He wanted to finish the job his way. It was his way, she reminded herself, to do things thoroughly. But did the reason really matter? They'd have more time. Yes, she realized as she stared out the side window. The reason mattered a great deal too much.

"The job's finished in New England," she said lightly. "Summer's over, and it's back to business. My work at the studio will be backed up for a month. Still..." She felt herself weakening, though he said nothing, did nothing, to persuade her. "I wouldn't mind a few detours on the trip back."

Shade kept his hands easy on the wheel, his voice casual. "We'll think about it," he said, and let the subject they both wanted to pursue drop.

Weary of the highway, they took to the back roads. Bryan took her pictures of kids squirting each other with garden hoses, of laundry drying in the breeze, of an elderly couple sitting on a porch glider. Shade took his of sweating construction workers spreading tar on roofs, of laborers harvesting peaches and, surprisingly, of two ten-year-old businessmen hawking lemonade in their front yard.

Touched, Bryan accepted the paper cup Shade handed her. "That was sweet."

"You haven't tasted it yet," he commented, and climbed into the passenger's seat. "To keep down the overhead, they used a light hand on the sugar."

"I meant you." On impulse, she leaned over and kissed him, lightly, comfortably. "You can be a very sweet man."

As always, she moved him, and he couldn't stop it. "I can give you a list of people who'd disagree."

"What do they know?" With a smile, she touched her lips to his again. She drove down the neat, shady street appreciating the trim lawns, flower gardens and dogs barking in the yards. "I like the suburbs," she said idly. "To look at, anyway. I've never lived in one. They're so orderly." With a sigh, she turned right at the corner. "If I had a house here, I'd probably forget to fertilize the lawn and end up with crab grass and dandelions. My neighbors would take up a petition. I'd end up selling my house and moving into a condo."

"So ends Bryan Mitchell's career as a suburbanite."

She made a face at him. "Some people aren't cut out for picket fences."

"True enough."

She waited, but he said nothing that made her feel inadequate—nothing that made her feel as though she should be. She laughed delightedly, then grabbed his hand and squeezed. "You're good for me, Shade. You really are."

He didn't want to let her hand go, and released it reluctantly. Good for her. She said it so easily, laughing. Because she did, he knew she had no idea just what it meant to him to hear it. Maybe it was time he told her. "Bryan—"

"What's that?" she said abruptly, and swung toward the curb. Excited, she inched the car forward until she could read the colorful cardboard poster tacked to a telephone pole. "Nightingale's Traveling Carnival." Pulling on the brake, she nearly climbed over Shade to see it more clearly. "Voltara, the Electric Woman." With a half whoop, she nudged closer to Shade. "Terrific, just terrific. Sampson, the Dancing Elephant. Madame Zoltar, Mystic. Shade, look, it's their last night in town. We can't miss it. What's summer without a carny? Thrilling rides, games of skill and chance."

"And Dr. Wren, the Fire Eater."

It was easy to ignore the dry tone. "Fate." She

scrambled back to her own seat. "It has to be fate that we turned down this road. Otherwise, we might've missed it."

Shade glanced back at the sign as Bryan pulled away from the curb. "Think of it," he murmured. "We might've gotten all the way to the coast without seeing a dancing elephant."

A half hour later, Shade leaned back in his seat, calmly smoking, his feet on the dash. Frazzled, Bryan swung the van around the next turn.

"I'm not lost."

Shade blew out a lazy stream of smoke. "I didn't say a word."

"I know what you're thinking."

"That's Madame Zoltar's line."

"And you can stop looking so smug."

"Was I?"

"You always look smug when I get lost."

"You said you weren't."

Bryan gritted her teeth and sent him a killing look. "Why don't you just pick up that map and tell me where we are?"

"I started to pick it up ten minutes ago and you snarled at me."

Bryan let out a long breath. "It was the *way* you picked it up. You were smirking, and I could hear you thinking—"

"You're stepping into Madame Zoltar's territory again."

"Damn it, Shade." But she had to choke back a laugh as she drove down the long, unlit country road.

"I don't mind making a fool of myself, but I hate it when someone lifts an eyebrow over it."

"Did I?"

"You know you did. Now, if you'd just—"

Then she caught the first glimmer of red, blue, green lights flickering. A Ferris wheel, she thought. It had to be. The sound of tinny music came faintly through the summer dusk. A calliope. This time it was Bryan who looked smug. "I knew I'd find it."

"I never had a doubt."

She might've had something withering to say to that, but the lights glowing in the early-evening dusk, and the foolish piping music held her attention. "It's been years," she murmured. "Just years since I've seen anything like this. I've got to watch the fire eater."

"And your wallet."

She shook her head as she turned off the road onto the bumpy field where cars were parked. "Cynic."

"Realist." He waited until she maneuvered the van next to a late-model pickup. "Lock the van." Shade gathered his bag and waited outside the van until Bryan had hers. "Where first?"

She thought of pink cotton candy but restrained herself. "Why don't we just wander around a bit? We might want some shots now, but at night they'd have more punch."

Without the dark, without the bright glow of colored lights, the carnival looked too much like what it was—a little weary, more than a little tawdry. Its illusions were too easily unmasked now, and that wasn't why Bryan had come. Carnivals, like Santa Claus, had a right to their mystique. In another hour, when the sun had completely set behind those rolling, blue-tinted hills to the west, the carnival would come into its own. Peeling paint wouldn't be noticed.

"Look, there's Voltara." Bryan grabbed Shade's arm and swung him around to see a life-size poster that gave her lavish curves and scant cover as she was being strapped into what looked like a homemade electric chair.

Shade looked at the painted spangles over generous cleavage. "Might be worth watching after all."

With a quick snort, Bryan pulled him toward the Ferris wheel. "Let's take a ride. From the top we'll be able to see the whole layout."

Shade pulled a bill out of his wallet. "That's the only reason you want to ride."

"Don't be ridiculous." They walked over, waiting while the attendant let a couple off. "It's a good way of covering ground and sitting down at the same time," she began as she took the vacated seat. "It's sure to be an excellent angle for some aerial pictures, and…" She slipped a hand into his as they started the slow swing up. "It's the very best place to neck at a carnival."

When he laughed, she wrapped her arms around him and silenced his lips with hers. They reached the top where the evening breeze flowed clean and hung there one moment—two—aware only of each other. On the descent, the speed picked up and the drop had her stomach shivering, her mind swimming. It was no different from the sensation of being held by him, loved by him. They held tight and close through two revolutions.

Gathering her against his shoulder, Shade watched the carnival rush up toward them. It'd been years since he'd held someone soft and feminine on a Ferris wheel. High school? he wondered. He could hardly remember. Now he realized he'd let his youth slip by him because so many other things had seemed important at the time. He'd let it go freely, and though he wouldn't, couldn't, ask for the whole of it back, perhaps Bryan was showing him how to recapture pieces of it.

"I love the way this feels," she murmured. She could watch the sun go down in a last splashy explosion of arrogance, hear the music, the voices, ebb and fade as the wheel spun around. She could look down and be just removed enough from the scene to enjoy it, just separate enough to understand it. "A ride on a Ferris wheel should be required once a year, like a routine physical."

With her head against Shade's shoulder, she examined the scene below, the midway, the concessions, the booths set up for games of skill. She wanted to see it all, close up. She could smell popcorn, grilling meat, sweat, the heavy-handed after-shave of the attendant as their car swung by him. It gave her the overall view. This was life, a sidelong glance at it. This was the little corner of life where children could see wonders and adults could pretend for just a little while.

Taking her camera, she angled down through the cars and wires to focus in on the attendant. He looked a bit bored as he lifted the safety bar for one couple and lowered it for the next. A job for him, Bryan thought, a small thrill for the rest. She sat back, content to ride.

When it was dark, they went to work. There were people gathered around the wheel of fortune, plopping down a dollar for a chance at more. Teenagers showed off for their girls or their peers by hurling softballs at stacked bottles. Toddlers hung over the rope and tossed Ping-Pong balls at fishbowls, hoping to win a goldfish whose life expectancy was short at best. Young girls squealed on the fast-spinning Octopus, while young boys goggled at the posters along the midway.

Bryan took one telling shot of a woman carrying a baby on one hip while a three-year-old dragged her mercilessly along. Shade took another of a trio of boys in muscle shirts standing apart and doing their best to look tough and aloof.

They ate slices of pizza with rubber crusts as they watched with the rest of the crowd as Dr. Wren, Fire Eater, came out of his tent to give a quick, teasing demonstration of his art. Like the ten-year-old boy who watched beside her, Bryan was sold.

With an agreement to meet back at the entrance to the midway in thirty minutes, they separated. Caught up, Bryan wandered. She wasn't able to resist Voltara, and slipped into part of the show to see the somewhat weary, glossy-faced woman strapped into a chair that promised to zap her with two thousand volts.

She pulled it off well enough, Bryan thought, closing her eyes and giving a regal nod before the lever was pulled. The special effects weren't top-notch, but they worked. Blue light shimmered up the chair and around Voltara's head. It turned her skin to the color of summer lightning. At fifty cents a shot, Bryan decided as she stepped back out, the audience got their money's worth.

Intrigued, she wandered around in back of the midway to where the carnival workers parked their trailers. No colorful lights here, she mused as she glanced over the small caravan. No pretty illusions. Tonight, they'd pack up the equipment, take down the posters and drive on.

The moonlight hit the metal of a trailer and showed the scratches and dents. The shades were drawn at the little windows, but there was faded lettering on the side. Nightingale's.

Bryan found it touching and crouched to shoot.

"Lost, little lady?"

Surprised, Bryan sprang up and nearly collided with a short, husky man in T-shirt and work pants. If he worked for the carnival, Bryan thought quickly, he'd been taking a long break. If he'd come to watch, the lights and sideshows hadn't held his interest. The smell of beer, warm and stale, clung to him.

"No." She gave him a careful smile and kept a careful distance. Fear hadn't entered into it. The move had been automatic and mild. There were lights and people only a few yards away. And she thought he might give her another angle for his photographs. "Do you work here?"

"Woman shouldn't wander around in the dark alone. 'Less she's looking for something."

No, fear hadn't been her first reaction, nor did it come now. Annoyance did. It was that that showed in her eyes before she turned away. "Excuse me."

Then he had her arm, and it occurred to her that the lights were a great deal farther away than she'd have liked. Brazen it out, she told herself. "Look, I've people waiting for me."

"You're a tall one, ain't you?" His fingers were very firm, if his stance wasn't. He weaved slightly as he looked Bryan over. "Don't mind looking eye to eye with a woman. Let's have a drink."

"Some other time." Bryan put her hand on his arm to push it away and found it solid as a concrete block. That's when the fear began. "I came back here to take some pictures," she said as calmly as she could. "My partner's waiting for me." She pushed at his arm again. "You're hurting me."

"Got some more beer in my truck," he mumbled as he began to drag her farther away from the lights.

"No." Her voice rose on the first wave of panic. "I don't want any beer."

He stopped a moment, swaying. As Bryan took a good look in his eyes, she realized he was as drunk as a man could get and still stand. Fear bubbled hot in her throat. "Maybe you want something else." He skimmed down her thin summer top and brief shorts.

"Woman usually wants something when she wanders around half naked."

Her fear ebbed as cold fury rushed in. Bryan glared. He grinned.

"You ignorant ass," she hissed just before she brought her knee up, hard. His breath came out in a whoosh as he dropped his hand. Bryan didn't wait to see him crouch over. She ran.

She was still running when she rammed straight into Shade.

"You're ten minutes late," he began, "but I've never seen you move that fast."

"I was just— I had to..." She trailed off, breathless, and leaned against him. Solid, dependable, safe. She could have stayed just like that until the sun rose again.

"What is it?" He could feel the tension before he drew her away and saw it on her face. "What happened?"

"Nothing really." Disgusted with herself, Bryan dragged her hair back from her face. "I just ran into some jerk who wanted to buy me a drink whether I was thirsty or not."

His fingers tightened on her arms, and she winced as they covered the same area that was already tender. "Where?"

"It was nothing," she said again, furious with herself that she hadn't taken the time to regain her composure before she ran into him. "I went around back to get a look at the trailers."

"Alone?" He shook her once, quickly. "What kind

of idiot are you? Don't you know carnivals aren't just cotton candy and colored lights? Did he hurt you?"

It wasn't concern she heard in his voice, but anger. Her spine straightened. "No, but you are."

Ignoring her, Shade began to drag her through the crowds toward the parking section. "If you'd stop looking at everything through rose-colored glasses, you'd see a lot more clearly. Do you have any idea what might've happened?"

"I can take care of myself. I did take care of myself." When they reached the van, she swung away from him. "I'll look at life any way I like. I don't need you to lecture me, Shade."

"You need something." Grabbing the keys from her, he unlocked the van. "It's brainless to go wandering around alone in the dark in a place like this. Looking for trouble," he muttered as he climbed into the driver's seat.

"You sound remarkably like the idiot I left sprawled on the grass with his hands between his legs."

He shot her a look. Later, when he was calm, he might admire the way she'd dealt with an obnoxious drunk, but now he couldn't see beyond her carelessness. Independence aside, a woman was vulnerable. "I should've known better than to let you go off alone."

"Now just a minute." She whirled around in her seat. "You don't *let* me do anything, Colby. If you've got it in your head that you're my keeper or anything of the sort, then you'd better get it right out again. I answer to myself. Only myself.''

"For the next few weeks, you answer to me as well.''

She tried to control the temper that pushed at her, but it wasn't possible. "I may work with you," she said, pacing her words. "I may sleep with you. But I don't answer to you. Not now. Not ever.''

Shade punched in the van's lighter. "We'll see about that.''

"Just remember the contract." Shaking with fury, she turned away again. "We're partners on this job, fifty-fifty.''

He gave his opinion of what she could do with the contract. Bryan folded her arms, shut her eyes and willed herself to sleep.

He drove for hours. She might sleep, but there was too much churning inside him to allow him the same release. So he drove, east toward the Atlantic.

She'd been right when she'd said she didn't answer to him. That was one of the first rules they'd laid down. He was damned sick of rules. She was her own woman. His strings weren't on her any more than hers were on him. They were two intelligent, independent people who wanted it that way.

But he'd wanted to protect her. When everything else was stripped away, he'd wanted to protect her. Was she so dense that she couldn't see he'd been furious not with her but with himself for not being there when she'd needed him?

She'd tossed that back in his face, Shade thought grimly as he ran a hand over his gritty eyes. She'd put him very clearly, very concisely, in his place. And his place, he reminded himself, no matter how intimate they'd become, was still at arm's length. It was best for both of them.

With his window open, he could just smell the tang of the ocean. They'd crossed the country. They'd crossed more lines than he'd bargained for. But they were a long way from crossing the final one.

How did he feel about her? He'd asked himself that question time after time, but he'd always managed to block out the answer. Did he really want to hear it? But it was three o'clock in the morning, that hour he knew well. Defenses crumbled easily at three o'clock in the morning. Truth had a way of easing its way in.

He was in love with her. It was too late to take a step back and say no thanks. He was in love with her in a way that was completely foreign to him. Unselfishly. Unlimitedly.

Looking back, he could almost pinpoint the moment when it had happened to him, though he'd called it something else. When he'd stood on the rock island in the Arizona lake, he'd desired her, desired her more intensely than he'd desired anything or anyone. When he'd woken from the nightmare and had found her warm and solid beside him, he'd needed her, again more than anything or anyone.

But when he'd looked across the dusty road on the Oklahoma border and seen her standing in front of a sad little house with a plot of pansies, he'd fallen in love.

They were a long way from Oklahoma now, a long way from that moment. Love had grown, overwhelming him. He hadn't known how to deal with it then. He hadn't a clue what to do about it now.

He drove toward the ocean where the air was moist. When he pulled the van between two low-rising dunes, he could just see the water, a shadow with sound in the distance. Watching it, listening to it, he slept.

Bryan woke when she heard the gulls. Stiff, disoriented, she opened her eyes. She saw the ocean, blue and quiet in the early light that wasn't quite dawn. At the horizon, the sky was pink and serene. Misty. Waking slowly, she watched gulls swoop over the shoreline and soar to sea again.

Shade slept in the seat beside her, turned slightly in his seat, his head resting against the door. He'd driven for hours, she realized. But what had driven him?

She thought of their argument with a kind of weary tolerance. Quietly, she slipped from the van. She wanted the scent of the sea.

Had it only been two months since they'd stood on the shore of the Pacific? Was this really so different? she wondered as she stepped out of her shoes and felt the sand, cool and rough under her feet. He'd driven through the night to get here, she mused. To get here, one step closer to the end. They had only to drive up the coast now, winding their way through New England. A quick step in New York for pictures and darkroom work, then on to Cape Cod, where summer would end for both of them.

It might be best, she thought, if they broke there completely. Driving back together, touching on some of the places they'd discovered as a team, might be too much to handle. Perhaps when the time came, she'd make some excuse and fly back to L.A. It might be best, she reflected, to start back to those separate lives when summer ended.

They'd come full circle. Through the tension and annoyance of the beginning, into the cautious friendship, the frenzied passion, and right back to the tension again.

Bending, Bryan picked up a shell small enough to fit into the palm of her hand, but whole.

Tension broke things, didn't it? Cracked the whole until pressure crumbled it into pieces. Then whatever you'd had was lost. She didn't want that for Shade. With a sigh, she looked out over the ocean, where the water was green, then blue. The mist was rising.

No, she didn't want that for him. When they turned from each other, they should do so as they'd turned to each other. As whole, separate people, standing independently.

She kept the shell in her hand as she walked back toward the van. The weariness was gone. When she saw him standing beside the van watching her, with his hair ruffled by the wind, his face shadowed, eyes heavy, her heart turned over.

The break would come soon enough, she told herself. For now, there should be no pressure.

Smiling, she went to him. She took his hand and pressed the shell into it. ''You can hear the ocean if you listen for it.''

He said nothing, but put his arm around her and held her. Together they watched the sun rise over the east.

Chapter 12

On a street corner in Chelsea, five enterprising kids loosened the bolts on a fire hydrant and sent water swooshing. Bryan liked the way they dived through the stream, soaking their sneakers, plastering their hair. It wasn't necessary to think long about her feelings toward the scene. As she lifted her camera and focused, her one predominant emotion was envy, pure and simple.

Not only were they cool and delightfully wet while she was limp from the heat, but they hadn't a care in the world. They didn't have to worry if their lives were heading in the right direction, or any direction at all. It was their privilege in these last breathless weeks of summer to enjoy—their youth, their freedom and a cool splash in city water.

If she was envious, there were others who felt the

same way. As it happened, Bryan's best shot came from incorporating one passerby in the scene. The middle-aged deliveryman in the sweaty blue shirt and dusty work shoes looked over his shoulder as one of the children lifted his arms up to catch a stream. On one face was pleasure, pure and giddy. On the other was amusement, laced with regret for something that couldn't be recaptured.

Bryan walked on, down streets packed with bad-tempered traffic, over sidewalks that tossed up heat like insults. New York didn't always weather summer with a smile and a wave.

Shade was in the darkroom they'd rented, while she'd opted to take the field first. She was putting it off, she admitted, as she skirted around a sidewalk salesman and his array of bright-lensed plastic sunglasses. Putting off coping with the last darkroom session she'd have before they returned to California. After this brief stop in New York, they'd head north for the final weekend of summer in Cape Cod.

And she and Shade had gone back to being almost unbearably careful with each other. Since that morning when they'd woken at the beach, Bryan had taken a step back. Deliberately, she admitted. She'd discovered all too forcibly that he could hurt her. Perhaps it was true that she'd left herself wide open. Bryan wouldn't deny that somewhere along the way she'd lost her determination to maintain a certain distance. But it wasn't too late to pull back just enough to keep from getting battered. She had to accept that the season was nearly over, and when it was, her relationship with Shade ended with it.

With this in mind, she took a slow, meandering route back toward midtown and the rented darkroom.

Shade already had ten rows of proofs. Sliding a strip under the enlarger, he methodically began to select and eliminate. As always, he was more ruthless, more critical with his own work than he'd have been with anyone else's. He knew Bryan would be back shortly, so any printing he did would have to wait until the following day. Still, he wanted to see one now, for himself.

He remembered the little motel room they'd taken that rainy night just outside of Louisville. He remembered the way he'd felt then—involved, a little reckless. That night had been preying on his mind, more and more often, as he and Bryan seemed to put up fences again. There'd been no boundaries between them that night.

Finding the print he was looking for, he brought the magnifier closer. She was sitting on the bed, her dress falling off her shoulders, raindrops clinging to her hair. Soft, passionate, hesitant. All those things were there in the way she held herself, in the way she looked at the camera. But her eyes...

Frustrated, he narrowed his own. What was in her eyes? He wanted to enlarge the proof now, to blow it up so that he could see and study and understand.

She was holding back now. Every day he could feel it, sense it. Just a little bit more distance every day. But what had been in her eyes on that rainy night?

He had to know. Until he did, he couldn't take a step, either toward her or away.

When the knock came on the door, he cursed it. He wanted another hour. With another hour, he could have the print, and perhaps his answer. He found it a simple matter to ignore the knock.

"Shade, come on. Time for the next shift."

"Come back in an hour."

"An hour!" On the other side of the door, Bryan pounded again. "Look, I'm melting out there. Besides, I've already given you twenty minutes more than your share."

The moment he yanked open the door, Bryan felt the waves of impatience. Because she wasn't in the mood to wrestle with it, she merely lifted a brow and skirted around him. If he wanted to be in a foul mood, fine. As long as he took it outside with him. Casually she set down her camera and a paper cup filled with soft drink and ice.

"So how'd it go?"

"I'm not finished."

With a shrug, she began to set out the capsules of undeveloped film she'd stored in her bag. "You've tomorrow for that."

He didn't want to wait until tomorrow, not, he discovered, for another minute. "If you'd give me the rest of the time I want, I wouldn't need tomorrow."

Bryan began to run water in a shallow plastic tub. "Sorry, Shade. I've run out of steam outside. If I don't get started in here, the best I'll do is go back to the hotel and sleep the rest of the afternoon. Then I'll be behind. What's so important?''

He stuffed his hands in his pockets. ''Nothing. I just want to finish.''

''And I've got to start,'' she murmured absently as she checked the temperature of the water.

He watched her a moment, the competent way she set up, arranging bottles of chemicals to her preference. Little tendrils of her hair curled damply around her face from the humidity. Even as she set up to work, she slipped out of her shoes. He felt a wave of love, of need, of confusion, and reached out to touch her shoulder. ''Bryan—''

''Hmm?''

He started to move closer, then stopped himself. ''What time will you be finished?''

There were touches of amusement and annoyance in her voice. ''Shade, will you stop trying to push me out?''

''I want to come back for you.''

She stopped long enough to look over her shoulder. ''Why?''

''Because I don't want you walking around outside after it's dark.''

''For heaven's sake.'' Exasperated, she turned completely around. ''Do you have any idea how many times I've been to New York alone? Do I look stupid?''

''No.''

Something in the way he said it had her narrowing her eyes. ''Look—''

"I want to come back for you," he repeated, and this time touched her cheek. "Humor me."

She let out a long breath, tried to be annoyed and ended by lifting her hand to his. "Eight, eight-thirty."

"Okay. We can grab something to eat on the way back."

"There's something we can agree on." She smiled and lowered her hand before she could give in to the urge to move closer. "Now go take some pictures, will you? I've got to get to work."

He lifted his camera bag and started out. "Any longer than eight-thirty and you buy dinner."

Bryan locked the door behind him with a decisive click.

She didn't lose track of time while she worked. Time was too essential. In the dark she worked briskly. In the amber light, her movements flowed with the same rhythm. As one set of negatives was developed and hung to dry, she went on to the next, then the next. When at length she could switch on the overhead light, Bryan arched her back, stretched her shoulders and relaxed.

An idle glance around showed her that she'd forgotten the carryout drink she'd picked up on the way. Unconcerned, she took a long gulp of lukewarm, watered-down soda.

The work satisfied her—the precision it required. Now her thoughts were skipping ahead to the prints. Only then would the creativity be fully satisfied. She had time, she noticed as she took a quick glance at her watch, to fuss with the negatives a bit before he came back. But then she'd end up putting herself in the same position she'd put him in—leaving something half done. Instead, mildly curious, she walked over to study his proofs.

Impressive, she decided, but then she'd expected no less. She might just be inclined to beg for a blowup of the old man in the baseball cap. Not Shade's usual style, she mused as she bent over the strip. It was so rare that he focused in on one person and let the emotions flow. The man who'd taken it had once told her he had no compassion. Bryan shook her head as she skimmed over other proofs. Did Shade believe that, or did he simply want the rest of the world to?

Then she saw herself and stopped with a kind of dazed wonder. Of course she remembered Shade setting up that picture, amusing, then arousing her while he changed angles and f-stops. The way he'd touched her... It wasn't something she'd forget, so it shouldn't surprise her to see the proof. Yet it did more than surprise her.

Not quite steady, Bryan picked up a magnifying glass and held it over one tiny square. She looked...pliant. She heard her own nervous swallow as she looked deeper. She looked...soft. It could be her imagination or, more likely, the skill of the photographer. She looked...in love.

Slowly, Bryan set down the glass and straightened. The skill of the photographer, she repeated, fighting to believe it. A trick of the angle, of the light and shadows. What a photographer captured on film wasn't always the truth. It was often illusion, often that vague blur between truth and illusion.

A woman knew when she loved. That's what Bryan told herself. A woman knew when she'd given her heart. It wasn't something that could happen and not be felt.

She closed her eyes a moment and listened to the quiet. Was there anything she hadn't felt when it came to Shade? How much longer was she going to pretend that passion, needs, longings, stood on their own? Love had bound them together. Love had cemented them into something solid and strong and undeniable.

She turned to where her negatives hung. There was one she'd managed to ignore. There was one tiny slice of film she'd taken on impulse and then buried because she'd come to be afraid of the answer she'd find. Now, when she had the answer already, Bryan stared at it.

It was reversed, so that his hair was light, his face dark. The little sliver of river in the corner was white, like the oars in his hands. But she saw him clearly.

His eyes were too intense, though his body seemed relaxed. Would he ever allow his mind true rest? His face was hard, lean, with the only tangible sensitivity around his mouth. He was a man, Bryan knew, who'd have little patience with mistakes—his own or others'. He was a man with a rigid sense of what was important. And he was a man who was capable of harnessing his own emotions and denying them to another. What he gave, when he gave, would be on his terms.

She knew, and understood, and loved regardless.

She'd loved before, and love had made more sense then. At least it had seemed to. Still, in the end, love hadn't been enough. What did she know about making love work? Could she possibly believe that when she'd failed once, she could succeed with a man like Shade?

She loved now, and told herself she was wise enough, strong enough, to let him go.

Rule number one, Bryan reminded herself as she put the darkroom in order. No complications. It was a litany she had running through her head until Shade knocked on the door. When she opened it for him, she nearly believed it.

They'd reached the last stop, the last day. Summer was not, as some would wish it, endless. Perhaps the weather would stay balmy for weeks longer. Flowers might still bloom defiantly, but just as Bryan had considered the last day of school summer's conception, so did she consider the Labor Day weekend its demise.

Clambakes, beach parties, bonfires. Hot beaches and cool water. That was Cape Cod. There were volleyball games in the sand and blasting portable radios. Teenagers perfected the tans they'd show off during those first few weeks of school. Families took to the water in a last, frantic rush before autumn signaled the end. Backyard barbecues smoked. Baseball hung on gamely before football could push its way through. As if it knew its time was limited, summer poured on the heat.

Bryan didn't mind. She wanted this last weekend to be everything summer could be—hot, hazy, torrid. She wanted her last weekend with Shade to reflect it. Love could be disguised with passion. She could let herself flow with it. Long, steamy days led to long, steamy nights, and Bryan held on to them.

If her lovemaking was a little frantic, if her desires were a little desperate, she could blame it on the heat. While Bryan became more aggressive, Shade became more gentle.

He'd noticed the change. Though he'd said nothing, Shade had noticed it the night he'd come back to meet her at the darkroom. Perhaps because she rarely had nerves, Bryan thought she hid them well. Shade could almost see them jump every time he looked at her.

Bryan had made a decision in the darkroom—a decision she felt would be best for both herself and for Shade. Shade had made a decision in the darkroom as well, the day after, when he'd watched the print of Bryan slowly come to life.

On the ride west to east, they'd become lovers. Now he had to find a way on the ride west to court her, as a man does the woman he wants to spend his life with.

Gentleness came first, though he wasn't an expert at it. Pressure, if it came to that, could be applied later. He was more experienced there.

"What a day." After long hours walking, watching and shooting, Bryan dropped down on the back of the van where the doors were open wide to let in the breeze. "I can't believe how many half-naked people I've seen." Grinning at Shade, she arched her back.

She wore nothing but her sleek red bathing suit and a loose white cover-up that drooped over one shoulder.

"You seem to fit right in."

Lazily, she lifted one leg and examined it. "Well, it's nice to know that this assignment hasn't ruined my tan." Yawning, she stretched. "We've got a couple more hours of sun. Why don't you put on something indecent and walk down to the beach with me?" She rose, lifting her arms so they could wind easily around his neck. "We could cool off in the water." She touched her lips to his, teasing, taunting. "Then we could come back and heat up again."

"I like the second part." He turned the kiss into something staggering with an increase of pressure and change of angle. Beneath his hands, he felt her sigh. "Why don't you go ahead down, do the cooling-off? I've got some things to do."

With her head resting against his shoulder, Bryan struggled not to ask again. She wanted him to go with her, be with her every second they had left. Tomorrow she'd have to tell him that she'd made arrangements to fly back to the Coast. This was their last night, but only she knew it.

"All right." She managed to smile as she drew away. "I can't resist the beach when we're camped so close. I'll be back in a couple hours."

"Have fun." He gave her a quick, absent kiss and didn't watch as she walked away. If he had, he might've seen her hesitate and start back once, only to turn around again and walk on.

* * *

The air had cooled by the time Bryan started back to the van. It chilled her skin, a sure sign that summer was on its last legs. Bonfires were set and ready to light down on the beach. In the distance, Bryan heard a few hesitant, amateur guitar chords. It wouldn't be a quiet night, she decided as she passed two other campsites on the way to the van.

She paused a moment to look toward the water, tossing her hair back. It was loose from its braid and slightly damp from her dip in the Atlantic. Idly she considered grabbing her shampoo out of the van and taking a quick trip to the showers. She could do that before she threw together a cold sandwich. In an hour or two, when the bonfires were going steadily, and the music was at its peak, she and Shade would go back down and work.

For the last time, she thought as she reached for the door of the van.

At first, she stood blinking, confused by the low, flickering light. Candles, she saw, baffled. Candles and white linen. There on the little collapsible table they sometimes set between the bunks were a fresh, snowy cloth and two red tapers in glass holders. There were red linen napkins folded at angles. A rosebud stood in a narrow, clear glass vase. On the little radio in the back was low, soft music.

At the narrow makeshift counter was Shade, legs spread as he added a sprinkling of alfalfa to a salad.

"Have a nice swim?" he said casually, as if she'd climbed into the van every evening to just such a scene.

"Yeah, I... Shade, where did you get all this?"

"Took a quick trip into town. Hope you like your shrimp spicy. I made it to my taste."

She could smell it. Over the scent of candle wax, under the fragrance of the single rose, was the rich, ripe aroma of spiced shrimp. With a laugh, Bryan moved to the table and ran a finger down one of the tapers. "How did you manage all this?"

"I've been called adept occasionally." She looked up from the candle to him. Her face was lovely, clean-lined. In the soft light, her eyes were dark, mysterious. But above all he saw her lips curve hesitantly as she reached out for him.

"You did this for me."

He touched her, lightly, just a hand to her hair. Both of them felt something shimmer. "I intend to eat, too."

"I don't know what to say." She felt her eyes fill and didn't bother to blink the tears back. "I really don't."

He lifted her hand and, with a simplicity he'd never shown, kissed her fingers, one by one. "Try thanks."

She swallowed and whispered. "Thanks."

"Hungry?"

"Always. But..." In a gesture that always moved him, she lifted her hands to his face. "Some things are more important."

Bryan brought her lips to his. It was a taste he could drown in—a taste he could now admit he wanted to drown in. Moving slowly, gently, he brought her into his arms.

Their bodies fit. Bryan knew it was so, and ached from the knowledge. Even their breathing seemed to merge until she was certain their hearts beat at precisely the same rhythm. He ran his hands under her shirt, along her back, where the skin was still damp from the sea.

Touch me. She drew him closer, as if her body could shout the words to him.

Savor me. Her mouth was suddenly avid, hot and open, as if with lips alone she could draw what she needed from him.

Love me. Her hands moved over him as if she could touch the emotion she wanted. Touch it, hold it, keep it—if only for one night.

He could smell the sea on her, and the summer and the evening. He could feel the passion as her body pressed against his. Needs, demands, desires—they could be tasted as his mouth drew from hers. But tonight he found he needed to hear the words. Too soon, his mind warned as he began to lose himself. It was too soon to ask, too soon to tell. She'd need time, he thought, time and more finesse than he was accustomed to employing.

But even when he drew her away, he wasn't able to let go. Looking down at her, he saw his own beginning. Whatever he'd seen and done in the past, whatever memories he had, were unimportant. There was only one vital thing in his life, and he held it in his arms.

"I want to make love with you."

Her breath was already unsteady, her body trembling. "Yes."

His hands tightened on her as he tried to be logical. "Room's at a premium."

This time she smiled and drew him closer. "We have the floor." She pulled him down with her.

Later, when her mind was clearer and her blood cooler, Bryan would remember only the tumult of feeling, only the flood of sensation. She wouldn't be able to separate the dizzying feel of his mouth on her skin from the heady taste of his under hers.

She'd know that his passion had never been more intense, more relentless, but she wouldn't be able to say how she'd known. Had it been the frantic way he'd said her name? Had it been the desperate way he'd pulled the snug suit down her body, exploiting, ravishing, as he went?

She understood that her own feelings had reached an apex she could never express with words. Words were inadequate. She could only show him. Love, regrets, desires, wishes, had all culminated to whirl inside her until she'd clung to him. And when they'd given each other all they could, she clung still, holding the moment to her as she might a photograph faded after years of looking.

As she lay against him, her head on his chest, she smiled. They had given each other all they could. What more could anyone ask? With her eyes still closed, she pressed her lips against his chest. Nothing would spoil the night. Tonight they'd have candlelight and laughter. She'd never forget it.

''I hope you bought plenty of shrimp,'' she murmured. ''I'm starving.''

''I bought enough to feed an average person and a greedy one.''

Grinning, she sat up. ''Good.'' With a rare show of energy, she struggled back into the bulky cover-up and sprang up. Bending over the pot of shrimp, she breathed deep. ''Wonderful. I didn't know you were so talented.''

''I decided it was time I let you in on some of my more admirable qualities.''

With a half smile, she looked back to see him slipping on his shorts. ''Oh?''

''Yeah. After all, we've got to travel a long way together yet.'' He sent her a quiet, enigmatic look. ''A long way.''

''I don't—'' She stopped herself and turned to toy with the salad. ''This looks good,'' she began, too brightly.

''Bryan.'' He stopped her before she could reach in the cupboard above for bowls. ''What is it?''

''Nothing.'' Did he always have to see? she demanded. Couldn't she hide anything from him?

He stepped over, took her arms and held her face to face. ''What?''

''Let's talk about it tomorrow, all right?'' The brightness was still there, straining. ''I'm really hungry. The shrimp's cool by now, so—''

''Now.'' With a quick shake, he reminded both of them that his patience only stretched so far.

"I've decided to fly back," she blurted out. "I can get a flight out tomorrow afternoon."

He went very still, but she was too busy working out her explanation to notice just how dangerously still. "Why?"

"I've had to reschedule like crazy to fit in this assignment. The extra time I'd get would ease things." It sounded weak. It was weak.

"Why?"

She opened her mouth, prepared to give him a variation on the same theme. One look from him stopped her. "I just want to get back," she managed. "I know you'd like company on the drive, but the assignment's finished. Odds are you'll make better time without me."

He fought back the anger. Anger wasn't the way. If he'd given in to it, he'd have shouted, raged, threatened. That wasn't the way. "No," he said simply, and left it at that.

"No?"

"You're not flying back tomorrow." His voice was calm, but his eyes said a great deal more. "We go together, Bryan."

She braced herself. An argument, she decided, would be easy. "Now look—"

"Sit down."

Haughtiness came to her rarely, but when it did, it was exceptional. "I beg your pardon?"

For an answer, Shade gave her a quick shove onto the bench. Without speaking, he pulled open a drawer and took out the manila envelope that held his most recently developed prints. Tossing them onto the table, he pulled out the one of Bryan.

"What do you see?" he demanded.

"Myself." She cleared her throat. "I see myself, of course."

"Not good enough."

"That's what I see," she tossed back, but she didn't look down at the print again. "That's all there is."

Perhaps fear played a part in his actions. He didn't want to admit it. But it was fear, fear that he'd imagined something that wasn't there. "You see yourself, yes. A beautiful woman, a desirable woman. A woman," he continued slowly, "looking at the man she loves."

He'd stripped her. Bryan felt it as though he'd actually peeled off layer after layer of pretense, defense, disguise. She'd seen the same thing in the image he'd frozen on film. She'd seen it, but what gave him the right to strip her?

"You take too much," she said in a quiet voice. Rising, she turned away from him. "Too damned much."

Relief poured through him. He had to close his eyes on it for a moment. Not imagination, not illusion, but truth. Love was there, and with it, his beginning. "You've already given it."

"No." Bryan turned back, holding on to what she had left. "I haven't given it. What I feel is my responsibility. I haven't asked you for anything, and I won't." She took a deep breath. "We agreed, Shade. No complications."

"Then it looks like we both reneged, doesn't it?"
He grabbed her hand before she could move out of
reach. "Look at me." His face was close, candlelight
flickering over it. Somehow the soft light illuminated
what he'd seen, what he'd lived through, what he'd
overcome. "Don't you see anything when you look
at me? Can you see more in a stranger on the beach,
a woman in a crowd, a kid on a street corner, than
you do when you look at me?"

"Don't—" she began, only to be cut off.

"What do you see?"

"I see a man," she said, speaking quickly, passion-
ately. "A man who's had to see more than he should.
I see a man who's learned to keep his feelings carefully controlled because he isn't quite sure what would
happen if he let loose. I see a cynic who hasn't been
able to completely stamp out his own sensitivity, his
own empathy."

"True enough," he returned evenly, though it was
both more and less than he'd wanted to hear. "What
else?"

"Nothing," she told him, close to panic. "Nothing."

It wasn't enough. The frustration came through; she
could feel it in his hands. "Where's your perception
now? Where's the insight that takes you under the
glitter of some temperamental leading man to the
core? I want you to see into me, Bryan."

"I can't." The words came out on a shudder. "I'm
afraid to."

Afraid? He'd never considered it. She took emotions in stride, sought them, dug for them. He loosened his grip on her and said the words that were the most difficult for him to speak. "I love you."

She felt the words slam into her, knocking her breathless. If he said them, he meant them, of that she could be sure. Had she been so caught up in her own feelings that she hadn't seen his? It was tempting, it would be easy, to simply go into his arms and take the risk. But she remembered that they'd both risked before, and failed.

"Shade..." She tried to think calmly, but his words of love still rang in her head. "I don't—you can't—"

"I want to hear you say it." He held her close again. There was no place to go. "I want you to look at me, knowing everything you've said about me is true, and tell me."

"It couldn't work," she began quickly, because her knees were shaking. "It couldn't, don't you see? I'd want it all because I'm just idiot enough to think maybe this time—with you... Marriage, children, that's not what you want, and I understand. I didn't think I wanted them either, until everything got so out of control."

He was calmer now, as she became more frazzled. "You haven't told me yet."

"All right." She nearly shouted it. "All right then, I love you, but I—"

He closed his mouth over hers so there could be no excuses. For now, he could simply drink in the words and all they meant to him. Salvation. He could believe in it.

"You've a hell of a nerve," he said against her mouth, "telling me what I want."

"Shade, please." Giving in to the weakness, she dropped her head on his shoulder. "I didn't want to complicate things. I don't want to now. If I fly back, it'll give us both time to put things back in perspective. My work, your work—"

"Are important," he finished. "But not as important as this." He waited until her eyes slowly lifted to his. Now his voice was calm again. His grip eased, still holding her but without the desperation. "Nothing is, Bryan. You didn't want it, maybe I thought I didn't, but I know better now. Everything started with you. Everything important. You make me clean." He ran a hand through her hair. "God, you make me hope again, believe again. Do you think I'm going to let you take all that away from me?"

The doubts began to fade, quietly, slowly. Second chances? Hadn't she always believed in them? Long shots, she remembered. You only had to want to win badly enough.

"No," she murmured. "But I need a promise. I need the promise, Shade, and then I think we could do anything."

So did he. "I promise to love you, to respect you. To care for you whether you like it or not. And I promise that what I am is yours." Reaching up, he flipped open the cupboard door. Speechless, Bryan watched him draw out a tiny cardboard pot of pansies. Their scent was light and sweet and lasting.

"Plant them with me, Bryan."

Her hands closed over his. Hadn't she always believed life was as simple as you made it? "As soon as we're home."

Epilogue

"Cooperate, will you?"

"No." Amused, but not altogether pleased, Shade watched Bryan adjust the umbrellas beside and behind him. It seemed to him she'd been fiddling with the lighting a great deal longer than necessary.

"You said I could have anything I wanted for Christmas," she reminded him as she held the light meter up to his face. "I want this picture."

"It was a weak moment," he mumbled.

"Tough." Unsympathetic, Bryan stepped back to study the angles. There, the lighting was perfect, the shadows just where they should be. But... A long-suffering sigh came out. "Shade, stop glowering, will you?"

"I said you could take the picture. I didn't say it'd be pretty."

"No chance of that," she said under her breath.

Exasperated, she brushed at her hair, and the thin gold band on her left hand caught the light. Shade watched it glimmer with the same sort of odd pleasure he always felt when it hit him that they were a team, in every way. With a grin, he joined his left hand with hers, so that the twin rings they wore touched lightly.

"Sure you want this picture for Christmas? I'd thought of buying you ten pounds of French chocolate."

She narrowed her eyes, but her fingers laced with his. "A low blow, Colby. Dead low." Refusing to be distracted, she backed off. "I'll have my picture," she told him. "And if you want to be nasty, I'll buy my own chocolate. Some husbands," she continued as she walked back to the camera set on a tripod, "would cater to their wife's every whim when she's in my delicate condition."

He glanced down at the flat stomach under baggy overalls. It still dazed him that there was life growing there. Their life. When summer came again, they'd hold their first child. It wouldn't do to let her know he had to fight the urge to pamper her, to coddle her every moment. Instead, Shade shrugged and dipped his hands in his pockets.

"Not this one," he said lightly. "You knew what you were getting when you married me."

She looked at him through the viewfinder. His hands were in his pockets, but he wasn't relaxed. As always, his body was ready to move, his mind moving already. But in his eyes she saw the pleasure, the kindness and the love. Together they were making it work. He didn't smile, but Bryan did as she clicked the shutter.

"So I did," she murmured.

* * * * *

From No. 1 *New York Times* bestselling author Nora Roberts

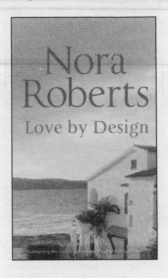

Two classic novels about the walls people build around their hearts and how to break them down...

Features

Loving Jack

and

Best Laid Plans

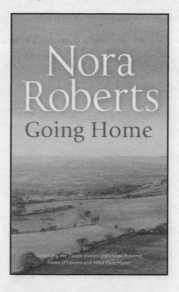

From No. 1 *New York Times* bestselling author Nora Roberts

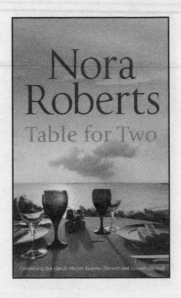

Two world class chefs discover an irresistible recipe for romance

Features

Summer Desserts

and

Lessons Learned

From No. 1 *New York Times* bestselling author Nora Roberts

The passionate heart of the city that never sleeps, in these two spell-binding novels…

Features

Local Hero

and

Dual Image

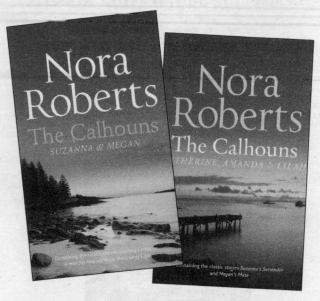